Her Highland Boss

MARION LENNOX
JESSICA GILMORE
ANNIE O'NEIL

First Published in Great Britain 2017
By Mills & Boon, an imprint of HarperCollins*Publishers*
1 London Bridge Street, London, SE1 9GF

HER HIGHLAND BOSS © 2017 Harlequin Books S. A.

The Earl's Convenient Wife, *In The Boss's Castle* and *Her Hot Highland Doc* were first published in Great Britain by Harlequin (UK) Limited.

The Earl's Convenient Wife © 2015 Marion Lennox
In The Boss's Castle © 2016 Jessica Gilmore
Her Hot Highland Doc © 2017 Annie O'Neil

ISBN: 978-0-263-92989-8

05-1117

THE EARL'S
CONVENIENT WIFE

BY
MARION LENNOX

Marion Lennox has written more than a hundred romances and is published in over a hundred countries and thirty languages. Her multiple awards include the prestigious US RITA® (twice), and the *RT Book Reviews* Career Achievement Award for 'a body of work which makes us laugh and teaches us about love'.

Marion adores her family, her kayak, her dog, and lying on the beach with a book someone else has written. Heaven!

With thanks to Rose M,
my new and wonderful neighbour and friend.
Gardening will never be the same again.

CHAPTER ONE

MARRY...

There was deathly silence in the magnificent library of the ancient castle of Duncairn. In specially built niches round the walls were the bottles of whisky Jeanie had scraped to afford. Weirdly, that was what she was focusing on. What a waste. How much whisky could she fit in a suitcase?

How many scores of fruitcakes would they make? There was no way she was leaving them behind. For him. For her prospective bridegroom?

What a joke.

She'd been clinging to the hope that she might keep her job. She knew the Lord of Duncairn didn't like her, but she'd worked hard to give Duncairn Castle the reputation for hospitality it now enjoyed.

It didn't matter. Her efforts were for nothing. This crazy will meant she was out on her ear.

'This must be a joke.' Alasdair McBride, the sixteenth Earl of Duncairn, sounded appalled. It was no wonder. She stood to lose her job. Alasdair stood to lose his...fiefdom?

'A last will and testament is never a joke.' Edward McCraig, of the prestigious law firm McCraig, McCraig & McFerry, had made the long journey from Edinburgh to be at today's funeral for Eileen McBride—Alasdair's grandmother and Jeanie's employer. He'd sat behind Jeanie in the Duncairn Kirk and listened to the eulogies with an air of supressed impatience. He wished to catch the last ferry back to the mainland. He was now seated in one of the library's opulent chairs, reading the old lady's wishes to her only surviving grandson—and to the live-in help.

He shuffled his papers and pushed his glasses further down his nose, looking at neither of them. Crazy or not, Eileen's will clearly made him uncomfortable.

Jeanie looked at Alasdair and then looked away. This might be a mess, but it had little to do with her, she decided. She went back to counting whisky bottles. Maybe three suitcases? She only had one, but there were crates in the castle cellars. If she was brave enough to face the dark and the spiders...

Could you sell whisky online?

She glanced back at Alasdair and found his gaze was following hers, along the line of whisky. With an oath—a mixture of fury and shock—he took three glasses from the sideboard and poured.

Soda-sized whiskies.

The lawyer shook his head but Jeanie took hers with gratitude. The will had been a nasty shock. It was excellent whisky and she couldn't take it all with her.

But it did need to be treated with respect. As the whisky hit home she choked and sank onto one of the magnificent down-filled sofas. A cloud of dog hair rose around her. She really had to do something about Eileen's dogs.

Or not. This will said they were no longer her problem. She'd have to leave the island. She couldn't take the dogs and she loved them. This castle might be over-the-top opulent, but she loved it, too. She felt...befuddled.

'So how do we get around this?' Clearly the whisky wasn't having the same effect on Alasdair that it was on her. His glass was almost empty. She looked at him in awe. Actually she'd been looking sideways at Alasdair all afternoon. Well, why not? He might be arrogant, he might have despised her from the first time he'd met her, but he'd always been worth looking at.

Alasdair McBride was thirty-seven years old, and he was what Jeanie's granny would have described as a man to be reckoned with. Although he didn't use it, his hereditary title fitted him magnificently, especially today. In honour of his grandmother's funeral he was wearing full highland regalia, and he looked awesome.

Jeanie always had had a weakness for a man in a kilt, and the Duncairn tartan was gorgeous. Okay, the Earl of Duncairn was gorgeous, she conceded. Six foot two in his stockinged feet, with jet-black hair and the striking bone structure and strength of the warrior race he'd so clearly descended from, Alasdair McBride was a man to make every eye in the room turn to him. The fact that he controlled the massive Duncairn financial empire only added to his aura of power, but he needed no such addition to look what he was—a man in control of his world.

Except...now he wasn't. His grandmother's will had just pulled the rug from under his feet.

And hers. *Marry?* So much for her quiet life as the Duncairn housekeeper.

'You can't get around it,' the lawyer was saying. 'The will is inviolate.'

'Do you think...?' She was testing her voice for the first time since the bombshell had landed. 'Do you think that Eileen might possibly have been...have been...?'

'Lady McBride was in full possession of her senses.' The lawyer cast her a cautious look as if he was expecting her to disintegrate into hysterics. 'My client understood her will was slightly...unusual...so she took steps to see that it couldn't be overturned. She arranged a certificate of medical competency, dated the same day she made the will.'

Alasdair drained the rest of his whisky and poured another, then spun to look out of the great bay window looking over the sea.

It was a magnificent window. A few highland cattle grazed peacefully in the late-summer sun, just beyond the ha-ha. Further on, past rock-strewn burns and craggy hills, were the remnants of a vast medieval fortress on the shoreline. Two eagles were soaring effortlessly in the thermals. If he used binoculars, he might even see otters in the burns running into the sea, Jeanie thought. Or deer. Or...

Or her mind was wandering. She put her glass down, glanced at Alasdair's broad back and felt a twist of real sympathy. Eileen had been good to her already, and in death she owed her nothing. Alasdair's loss, however, was appalling. She might not like the man, but he hadn't deserved this.

Oh, Eileen, what were you thinking? she demanded wordlessly of her deceased employer—but there was nothing Jeanie could do.

'I guess that's it, then,' she managed, addressing herself to the lawyer. 'How long do I have before you want me out?'

'There's no rush,' the lawyer told her. 'It'll take a while to get the place ready for sale.'

'Do you want me to keep trading? I have guests booked until the end of next month.'

'That would be excellent. We may arrange for you to stay even longer. It'd be best if we could sell it as a going concern.'

'No!' The explosion was so fierce it almost rocked the room. Alasdair turned from the window and slammed his glass onto the coffee table so hard it shattered. He didn't seem to notice.

'It can't happen.' Alasdair's voice lowered, no longer explosive but cold and hard and sure. 'My family's entire history, sold to fund...dogs' homes?'

'It's a worthy cause,' the lawyer ventured but Alasdair wasn't listening.

'This castle is the least of it,' he snapped. 'Duncairn is one of the largest financial empires in Europe. Do you know how much our organisation gives to charity each year? Sold, it could give every lost dog in Europe a personal attendant and gold-plated dog bowl for the rest of its life, but then it's gone. Maintained, we can do good—we *are* doing good. This will is crazy. I'll channel every penny of profit into dog care for the next ten years if I must, but to give it away…'

'I understand it would mean the end of your career—' the lawyer ventured but he was cut off.

'It's not the end of my career.'

If Lord Alasdair had had another glass, Jeanie was sure it'd have gone the way of the first.

'Do you know how many corporations would employ me? I have the qualifications and the skills to start again, but to haul apart my family inheritance on a stupid whim?'

'The thing is,' the lawyer said apologetically, 'I don't think it was a whim. Your grandmother felt your cousin treated his wife very badly and she wished to atone…'

'Here it is again. It all comes back to my wastrel cousin.' Alasdair spun around and stared at Jeanie with a look that was pretty much all contempt. 'You married him.'

'There's no need to bring Alan into this.'

'Isn't there? Eileen spent her life papering over his faults. She was blind to the fact that he was a liar and a thief, and that blind side's obviously extended to you. What was she on about? Marry Alan's widow? You? I'd rather walk on hot coals. You're the housekeeper here—nothing more. Marry anyone you like, but leave me alone.'

Her sympathy faded to nothing. 'Anyone I like?' she retorted. 'Wow. Thank you kindly, sir. As a proposal, that takes some beating.'

'It's the only proposal you're likely to get.'

'Then isn't it lucky I don't want one?'

He swore and turned again to the window. Jeanie's brief spurt of anger faded and she returned to shock.

Marriage…? To Alasdair? What *were* you thinking, Eileen? she demanded again of the departed Lady McBride.

Was she thinking the same as when she'd coerced Alan into marrying Jeanie? At least it was out in the open this time, she conceded. At least all the cards were on the table. The will spelt it out with startling clarity. It was an order to Alasdair. *Marry Jeanie, collect your inheritance, the only cost—one year of marriage. If not, inherit nothing.*

Oh, Eileen.

'I believe the time for angry words is not now.' The lawyer was clearing his papers into a neat pile, ready to depart, but his dry, lawyer's voice was sounding a warning. 'You need to be quite clear before you make rash decisions. I understand that emotions are…high…at the moment, but think about it. Neither of you are married. My Lord, if you marry Mrs McBride, then you keep almost the entire estate. Mrs McBride, if you marry His Lordship, in twelve months you get to keep the castle. That's a substantial amount to be throwing away because you can't get on.'

'The castle belongs to my family,' Alasdair snapped. 'It has nothing to do with this woman.'

'Your grandmother treated Jeanie as part of your family.'

'She's not. She's just as bad as—'

'My Lord, I'd implore you not to do—or say—anything in haste,' the lawyer interrupted. 'Including making statements that may inflame the situation. I suggest you take a couple of days and think about it.'

A couple of days? He had to be kidding, Jeanie thought. There was only one decision to be made in the face of this craziness, and she'd made it. She looked at Alasdair's broad back, at his highland kilt, at the size of him—he was practically blocking the window. She looked at the tense set of his shoulders. She could almost taste his rage and his frustration.

Get this over with, she told herself, and she gave herself a fraction of a second to feel sorry for him again. No more, though. Protect yourself, she scolded. Get out of here fast.

'Alasdair doesn't want to marry me and why should he?' she asked the lawyer. 'And I surely don't want to marry him. Eileen was a sweetheart but she was also a conniving matriarch. She liked pulling the strings but sometimes... sometimes she couldn't see that the cost was impossibly high. I've married one of her grandsons. I'm not marrying another and that's an end to it. Thank you for coming, sir. Should I ring for the taxi to collect you, in, say, fifteen minutes?'

'That would be excellent. Thank you. You've been an excellent housekeeper to Duncairn, Mrs McBride. Eileen was very fond of you.'

'I know she was, and I loved her, too,' Jeanie said. 'But sometimes...' She glanced again at Alasdair. 'Well, the family has always been known for its arrogance. The McBrides have been ordering the lives of Duncairn islanders for generations, but this time Eileen's taken it a step too far. I guess the Duncairn ascendancy is now in freefall but there's nothing I can do about it. Good afternoon, gentlemen.'

And she walked out and closed the door behind her.

She was gone. Thankfully. Alasdair was left with the lawyer.

Silence, silence and more silence. The lawyer was giving him space, Alasdair thought, and he should be grateful.

He wasn't.

His thoughts went back to his grandfather, an astute old

man whose trust in his wife had been absolute. He'd run the Duncairn financial empire with an iron fist. Deeply disappointed in his two sons—Alasdair's and Alan's respective fathers—the old man had left control of the entire estate in the hands of Eileen.

'By the time you die I hope our sons have learned financial sense,' he'd told her. 'You can decide who is best to take over.'

But neither of his sons had shown the least interest in the estate, apart from persuading Eileen to give them more money. They'd predeceased their mother, one in a skiing accident, one from a heart attack, probably caused by spending his life in Michelin-starred restaurants.

No matter. That was history. Eileen had come from a long line of thrifty Scots, and in Alasdair she'd found a family member who shared her business acumen and more.

As they'd turned the company into the massive empire it now was, Alasdair had tried to talk his grandmother into making it a public entity, making it safe if anything had happened to either of them. She'd refused. 'I trust you,' she'd told him but she'd maintained total ownership.

And now this…

'Surely it's illegal,' he said, feeling bone weary.

'What could be illegal?'

'Coercing us into marriage.'

'There's no coercion. The way your grandmother worded it…'

'You helped her word it.'

'Mr Duncan McGrath, the firm's most senior lawyer, helped her draft it, to make sure there were no legal loopholes.' The lawyer was suddenly stern. 'She was very clear what she wanted. The will states that the entire financial empire plus any other assets she owns are to be liquidated and left in equal parts to a large number of canine charities.

As an aside, she states that the only way the intentions of the will can be set aside is if you and Mrs McBride marry.'

'That woman is not a McBride.'

'She's Mrs McBride,' the lawyer repeated sternly. 'You know that she is. Your grandmother loved her and treated her as family, and your grandmother wanted to cement that relationship. The bequest to the canine charities can only be set aside if, within a month of her death, you and Mrs Jeanie McBride are legally married. To each other.'

'We both know that's crazy. Even…Mrs McBride… didn't consider it for a moment.' He ran his fingers through his hair, the feeling of exhaustion intensifying. 'It's blackmail.'

'It's not blackmail. The will is set up so that in the— admittedly unlikely—event that you marry, your grandmother provides for you as a family.'

'And if we're not?'

'Then she's done what any lonely old woman in her situation might do. She's left her fortune to dogs' homes.'

'So if we contest…'

'I've taken advice, sir. I was…astounded at the terms of the will myself, so I took the liberty to sound out a number of my colleagues. Legal advice is unanimous that the will stands.'

More silence. Alasdair reached for his whisky and discovered what he'd done. The table was covered with broken glass. He needed to call someone to clean it up.

Mrs McBride? Jeanie.

His cousin's wife had operated this place as a bed and breakfast for the past three years. As cook, housekeeper and hostess, she'd done a decent job, he'd had to concede. 'You should see how it is now,' his grandmother had told him, beaming. 'Jeanie's the best thing that's happened to this family.'

That wasn't true. Even though he conceded she'd looked

after this place well, it was by her first actions he'd judged her. As Alan's wife. She'd run wild with his cousin and she'd been beside him when he'd died. Together she and Alan had broken Eileen's heart, but Eileen had never been prepared to cut her loose.

Marrying Alan had branded her, he conceded, but that brand was justified. Any fool could have seen the crazy lifestyle his cousin had been living was ruinous. The money she and Alan had thrown round... That was why she was still looking after the castle, in the hope of inheriting something more. He was sure of it. For an impoverished island lass, the McBride fortune must seem seductive, to say the least.

Seduction... By money?

If she'd married for money once before...

His mind was suddenly off on a crazy tangent that made him feel ill.

Marriage... But what was the alternative?

'So what if we *did* marry?' he demanded at last, goaded into saying it.

'Then everything reverts to how it's been,' the lawyer told him. He was watching him cautiously now, as if he half expected Alasdair to lob whisky at him. 'If you and Mrs McBride marry and stay married for a period of no less than one year, you'll legally own the Duncairn empire with all it entails, with the exception of the castle itself. Mrs McBride will own that.'

'Just this castle?'

'And the small parcel of land on the same title. Yes. They're the terms of the will.'

'Does she have a clue how much this place costs to maintain? What she gets with the bed and breakfast guests couldn't begin to touch it. And without the surrounding land...'

'I'd imagine Mrs McBride could sell,' the lawyer said,

placing his papers back in his briefcase. 'Maybe to you, if you wish to continue the Duncairn lineage. But right now, that's immaterial. If you don't marry her, the castle will be part of the whole estate to be sold as one. Mrs McBride needs to consider her future with care, but maintenance of the castle is immaterial unless you marry.'

And there was the only glimmer of light in this whole impossible situation. If he didn't inherit, neither would she. It'd be great to be finally shot of her.

He didn't need this inheritance. He didn't. If he walked away from this mess, he could get a job tomorrow. There were any number of corporations that'd take his expertise.

But to walk away from Duncairn? His ancestral home…

And the company. So many people… He thought of the firm most likely to buy if he no longer had control and he felt ill. They'd merge. All his senior management… All his junior staff…Scotland was struggling after the global financial crisis anyway. How could they get new jobs?

They couldn't, and there was nothing he could do about it.

Unless…unless…

'She *has* been married before,' he said slowly, thinking aloud. He didn't like the woman one bit. He didn't trust her, but if he was careful… Initial revulsion was starting to give way to sense. 'She married my cousin so I'm assuming money's important to her. I guess—if it got me out of this mess, I might be prepared to marry. In name only,' he added hastily. 'As a business deal.'

Marriage… The idea made him feel ill. But Lords of Duncairn had married for convenience before, he reminded himself. They'd married heiresses to build the family fortunes. They'd done what had to be done to keep the estate safe.

And the lawyer was permitting himself a dry smile, as if his client was now talking like a sensible man. 'I've considered that option,' he told him. 'It would meet the requirements of the bequest—as long as you lived together.'

'Pardon?'

'Lady Eileen was very sure of what she wanted. She has…all eventualities covered.'

He exhaled and took a while to breathe again. Eventualities… 'Explain.'

'You and Mrs McBride would need to live in the same residence for a period of at least one year before the estate can be settled. However, Lady Eileen was not unreasonable. She acknowledges that in the course of your business you do need to travel, so she's made allowances. Those allowances are restrictive, however. In the twelve months from the time of your marriage there's an allowance for no more than thirty nights spent apart.'

Alasdair said nothing. He couldn't think what to say.

He'd loved his grandmother. None of what he was thinking right now had any bearing on that love. If he had her in front of him…

'She's also taken steps to ensure that this arrangement was kept.' The lawyer coughed apologetically. 'I'm sorry, but you would need to keep to…the intent of the will.'

'You mean she'd have us watched?'

'There are funds set aside to ensure the terms are being adhered to.'

He stared at the lawyer in horror. 'You're out of your mind. Next you'll be saying you'll be checking the sheets.'

'I believe,' the lawyer said and allowed himself another wintry smile, 'that your sleeping arrangements within the one residence would be entirely up to you and your…your wife. Mind…' he allowed the smile to widen '…she's an attractive wee thing.'

'Of all the…'

'Though it's not my business to say so, sir. I'm sorry.'

'No.' Though she was, Alasdair conceded, his thoughts

flying sideways again. He'd been astounded when his cousin had married her. Jeanie McBride was petite and freckled and rounded. Her soft brown shoulder-length curls, mostly tugged back into a ponytail, were nothing out of the ordinary. She didn't dress to kill. In fact, the first time he'd met her, he'd thought how extraordinary that the womanising Alan was attracted to such a woman.

But then she'd smiled at something his grandmother had said, and he'd seen what Alan had obviously seen. Her smile was like the sun coming out after rain. Her face lit and her freckles seemed almost luminescent. She had a dimple at the side of her mouth, and when she'd chuckled...

He hadn't heard that chuckle for a long time, he thought suddenly. He hadn't seen her smile, either.

In truth, he'd avoided her. His grandmother's distress over Alan's wasted life had been enough to make him avoid Jeanie and all she represented. He'd known she was caring for the castle and he acknowledged she'd seemed to be making a good job of it. She'd steered clear of him these past few months when he'd come to visit his grandmother. She'd treated him formally, as a castle guest, and he'd treated her like the housekeeper she was.

But she wasn't just a housekeeper. Right after Alan's death Eileen had said, 'She seems like a daughter to me,' and he'd thought, Uh-oh, she'll stick around until the old lady dies and hope to inherit, and now he was proved right.

She must be as shocked as he was about the will's contents. She'd get nothing unless they married...

That could be used to his advantage. His mind was racing. The only cost would be the castle.

And a year of his life...

The lawyer had risen, eager to depart. 'I'm sorry, sir. I understand I'm leaving you in a quandary but my task here was purely as messenger. I can see the taxi approaching. Mrs McBride has been efficient as always. Will you bid her farewell for me? Meanwhile, if there's anything else myself or my partners can do…'

'Tear up the will?'

'You and I both know that we can't do that. The will is watertight. From now on there's only a decision to be made, and I have no place here while you make it. Good luck, sir, and goodbye.'

CHAPTER TWO

THERE WAS TOO much to get his head around.

Alasdair paced the library, and when that wasn't big enough he took himself outdoors, through the great, grand castle entrance, across the manicured lawns, down the ha-ha and to the rough pastures beyond.

The shaggy highland cattle were still where they'd been while the lawyer had been making his pronouncements. The day had been warm and they were feeling the heat. If it got any hotter, they'd be wandering down to the sea and standing belly deep in the water, but for now they were lying on the rich summer grass, grazing where they could reach.

He loved the cattle. More, he loved this whole estate. His grandparents had made one small section of the castle liveable when his grandfather inherited, and they'd brought him here as a boy. He'd wandered the place at will, free from the demands his socialite parents put on him, free of the restrictions of being known as a rich kid. He'd fished, climbed, roamed, and when his grandmother had decided on restoration he'd been delighted.

Only that restoration had brought Jeanie into their lives.

If it hadn't been Jeanie, it would have been someone else, he thought grimly, striding down the line of battered fencing towards the bay. His grandmother's two dogs,

Abbot and Costello, elegant spaniels, beautiful, fast and dumb, had loped out to join him. The smell of rabbits would be everywhere, and the dogs were going nuts trying to find them.

Alan's wife…Jeanie…

His grandmother had said she'd loved her.

He'd thought his grandmother had loved him.

'So why treat us like this?' he demanded of his departed grandmother. 'If we don't marry, we'll have nothing.'

It was blackmail. Marry… The thing was nonsense.

But the knot of shock and anger was starting to untwist. Jeanie's assessment was right—his grandmother was a conniving, Machiavellian matriarch—so he might have expected something like this. Marriage to Alan's widow… Of all the dumb…

Eileen had loved reading romance novels. He should have confiscated every one and burned them before it was too late.

He reached the bay and set himself down on a great smooth rock, a foundation stone of an ancient fortress. He gazed out to sea but his mind was racing. Option one, no inheritance. Nothing. Walk away. The thought made him feel ill.

He turned and gazed back at the castle. He'd hardly been here these past years but it had always been in his mind. In his heart?

There'd been McBrides at Duncairn Castle since almost before the dinosaurs. Would he be the one to let it go?

The woodchip industry would move in, he thought. The pastures included with the castle title were mostly wild. The castle was heritage-listed, but not the land.

There were deer watching cautiously just above the horizon, but money was in woodchips, not deer. The land would go.

Which led—sickeningly—to option two.

Marriage. To a woman he couldn't stand, but who also stood to gain by the inheritance.

He gazed around again at the cattle, at the distant deer, at the water lapping the shores, the dogs barking in the distance, the eagles…

His land. Duncairn.

Was the thing impossible?

And the more he calmed down, the more he saw it wasn't. His apartment in Edinburgh was large, with separate living quarters for a housekeeper. He'd bought the place when he and Celia were planning marriage, and afterwards he'd never seen the point of moving. He worked fourteen-, fifteen-hour days, especially now. There were things happening within the company he didn't understand. Nebulous but worrying. He needed to focus.

He still could. He could use the Edinburgh house simply to sleep. That could continue and the terms of the will would be met.

'It could work,' he reasoned. 'The apartment's big enough for us to keep out of each other's way.'

But what will she do while you're away every day? The question came from nowhere, and he briefly considered it.

'She can shop, socialise, do what other wives do.'

Wives…

He'd have a wife. After Celia's betrayal he'd sworn…

Eileen had known that he'd sworn. That was why she'd done this.

He needed to suppress his anger. What he'd learned, hard and early, was that emotion got you nowhere. Reason was everything.

'It's only for a year,' he told himself. 'There's no choice. To walk away from everything is unthinkable.'

But walking away was still an option. He had money independent of Duncairn—of course he did. When he'd first started working in the firm, his grandmother had insisted on a salary commensurate with other executives of his standing. He was well-qualified, and even without this dubious inheritance he was wealthy. He could walk away.

But Duncairn…

He turned and looked back again at the castle, a great grey mass of imposing stone built by his ancestors to last for centuries. And the company… The financial empire had drawn him in since his teens. He'd worked to make it the best in the world, and to let it go…

'I'd be able to buy the castle from her when the year's up,' he told himself. 'You can't tell me she's not in for the main chance. If I'm the highest bidder, she'll take the money and run.'

Decision made. He rose and stretched and called the dogs.

'I'll do this,' he said out loud, addressing the ghost of his absent grandmother. 'Fine, Grandmother, you win. I'll talk to her and we'll organise a wedding. But that'll be it. It might be a wedding but it's not a marriage. If you think I'll ever be interested in Alan's leavings…'

Don't think of her like that.

But he couldn't help himself. Alan's betrayal, his gut-wrenching cruelty, was still raw after all these years and Jeanie was Alan's widow. He'd stayed away from this castle because he'd wanted nothing to do with her, but now…

'Now we'll have to share the same front door in Edinburgh,' he told himself. For a year. But a year's not so long when what's at stake is so important. *You can do it, man. Go take yourself a wife.*

She was in the kitchen. The kitchen was her solace, her joy. Cooks had been baking in this kitchen for hundreds of years. The great range took half the wall. The massive oak table, twenty feet long, was pocked and scratched from generations of chopping and rolling and kneading. The vast cobbled floor was worn from hundreds of servants, feeding thousands.

Eileen had restored the castle, making it truly sumptuous, but she'd had the sense to leave the kitchen free from modern grandeur. Jeanie had an electric oven tucked discreetly by the door. There was even a microwave and dishwasher in the vast, hall-like pantry, but the great stove was still lit as it seemed to have stayed lit forever. There was a sumptuous basket on each side for the dogs. The effect was old and warm and breathtaking.

Here was her place, Jeanie thought. She'd loved it the first time she'd seen it, and she'd found peace here.

She was having trouble finding peace now.

When in doubt, turn to scones, she told herself. After all these years she could cook them in her sleep. She didn't provide dinner for the castle guests but she baked treats for occasional snacks or for when they wandered in after dinner. She usually baked slices or a cake but right now she needed something that required no thought.

She wasn't thinking. She was *not* thinking.

Marriage...

She shouldn't care. She hadn't expected to inherit anything, but to tie the estate up as Eileen had... It didn't matter how much she disliked Alasdair; this was cruel. Had Eileen really been thinking it could happen?

And even though her thoughts should be on Alasdair, on the injustice done to him, there was also a part of her that hurt. No, she hadn't expected an inheritance, but she hadn't expected this, either. That Eileen could possibly think she could organise her down that road again... Try one grandson, if that doesn't work, try another?

'What were you thinking?' she demanded of the departed Eileen.

And then she thought: Eileen hadn't been thinking. She'd been hoping.

Those last few months of her life, Eileen had stayed at the castle a lot. Her normally feisty personality had turned inward. She'd wept for Alan, but she'd also wept for Alasdair.

'His parents and then that appalling woman he almost married…they killed something in him,' she'd told Jeanie. 'If only he could find a woman like you.'

This will was a fanciful dream, Jeanie thought, kneading her scone dough. The old lady might have been in full possession of her faculties, but her last will and testament was nothing more than a dream.

'She mustn't have thought it through,' she said to herself. 'She could never have thought we'd walk away from what she saw as irresistible temptation. She'd never believe we could resist.'

But Eileen hadn't had all the facts. Jeanie thought of those facts now, of an appalling marriage and its consequences, and she felt ill. If Eileen knew what she'd done, it'd break her heart.

But what could she do about it now? Nothing. Nothing, nothing and nothing. Finally she stared down and realised what she'd been doing. Kneading scone dough? Was she out of her mind?

'There's nothing worse than tough scones,' she told the world in general. 'Except marriage.'

Two disastrous marriages… Could she risk a third?

'Maybe I will,' she told herself, searching desperately for the light side, the optimistic bit of Jeanie McBride that had never entirely been quenched. 'Eventually. Maybe I might finally find myself a life. I could go to Paris—learn to cook French pastries. Could I find myself a sexy Parisian who enjoys a single malt?'

She almost smiled at that. All that whisky had to be useful for something. If she was honest, it wasn't even her drink of choice.

But since when had she ever had a choice? There was still the overwhelming issue of her debt, she thought, and the urge to smile died. Alan's debt. The bankruptcy hung over her like a massive, impenetrable cloud. How to be optimistic in the face of that?

She glanced out of the window, at the eagles who soared over the Duncairn castle as if they owned it.

'That's what I'd really like to do,' she whispered. 'Fly. But I'm dreaming. I'm stuck.'

And then a deep masculine response from the doorway made her almost jump out of her skin.

'That's what I'm thinking.'

Her head jerked from window to doorway and he was standing there. The Lord of Duncairn.

How long had he been watching? Listening? She didn't know. She didn't care, she told herself, fighting for composure as she tossed her dough into the waste and poured more flour into her bowl. McBrides...

But this man was not Alan. She told herself that, but as she did she felt a queer jump inside.

No, he wasn't Alan. He was nothing like him. They'd been cousins but where Alan had been out for a good time, this man was rock solid. Judgemental, yes. 'Harsh' and 'condemnatory' were two adjectives that described him well—and yet, gazing at the man in the doorway, she felt the weird inside flutter that she'd felt in the library.

Attraction? She had to be joking.

He was her feudal lord, she told herself harshly. She was a peasant. And when peasantry met gentry—run!

But for now she was the cook in this man's castle. She was forced to stay and she was forced to listen.

'Jeanie, my grandmother's treated us both badly,' he said and his tone was one of conciliation. 'I don't know what you wanted but you surely can't have expected this.'

She started at that. The anger she'd heard from him had

disappeared. What came through now was reason and caution, as if he wasn't sure how to proceed.

That made two of them.

'She hasn't treated me badly.' She made herself say it lightly but she knew it was true. Eileen had had no cause to offer her a job and a livelihood in this castle. There'd been no obligation. Eileen's action had been pure generosity.

'Your grandmother has been very, very good to me,' she added, chopping butter and starting to rub it into the new lot of flour. The action was soothing—an age-old task that calmed something deep within—and almost took her mind off the sex-on-legs image standing in the doorway. Almost. 'I've loved living and working here but jobs don't last forever. I don't have any right to be here.'

'You were married to Alan. You were… You *are* family.'

It was as if he was forcing himself to say it, she thought. He was forcing himself to be nice?

'The marriage was brief and it was a disaster,' she said curtly. 'I'm no longer your family—I'm your grandmother's ex-employee. I'm happy to keep running the castle until it's sold but then… Then I'm happy to go.' Liar, liar, pants on fire, she added silently to herself. It'd break her heart to leave; it'd break her heart to see the castle sold to the highest bidder. She had so little money to go anywhere, but there was no way she was baring her heart to this man.

Right now she was almost afraid of him. He was leaning against the doorjamb, watching her. He looked a warrior, as fierce and as ruthless as the reputation of the great lineage of Duncairn chieftains preceding him.

He was no such thing, she told herself fiercely. He was just a McBride, another one, and she needed to get away from here fast.

'But if we married, you could keep the castle.'

Jeanie's hands stilled. She stood motionless. In truth, she was counting breaths, or lack of them.

He'd said it as if it were the most reasonable thing in the world. *If you give me a penny, I'll give you an apple.* It was that sort of statement.

Ten, eleven, twelve… She'd have to breathe soon.

'Maybe it's reasonable,' Alasdair continued while she wondered if her breathing intended starting again. 'Maybe it's the only sensible course of action.' He'd taken his jacket off and rolled his sleeves. His arms were folded. They were great, brawny arms, arms that gave the lie to the fact that he was a city financier. His kilt made him seem even more a warrior.

He was watching her—as a panther watched its prey?

'It'd get us both what we want,' he said, still watchful. 'Alone, we walk away from everything we've worked for. Eileen's will is a nightmare but it doesn't have to be a total disaster. We need to work around it.'

'By…marrying?' Her voice came out a squeak but she was absurdly grateful it came out at all.

'It's the only way you can keep the castle.'

'I don't want the castle.'

That stopped him. His face stilled, as if he wasn't sure where to take it from there.

'No matter what Eileen's will says, the castle should never be my inheritance,' she managed. She was fighting to keep her voice as reasonable as his. 'The castle's my job, but that's all it is. You're the Earl of Duncairn. The castle's your ancestral home. Your grandmother's suggestion might be well-meant, but it's so crazy I don't believe we should even talk about it.'

'We need to talk about it.'

'We don't. I'm sorry your grandmother has left you in such a situation but that's for you to sort. Thank you, Lord Duncairn, for considering such a mad option, but I have scones to cook. I'm moving on. I'll work until the lawyer asks me to leave and then I'll be out of your life forever.'

* * *

Whatever he'd expected, it wasn't this. A straight-out refusal to even talk about it.

Okay, it was how he'd reacted, he decided, but he'd had
an hour's walk to clear his head. This woman clearly hadn't
had time to think it through.

To walk away from a castle… *This* castle.

What else was she angling for?

He watched her work for a bit while she ignored him,
but if she thought he'd calmly leave, she was mistaken.
This was serious.

Keep it as a business proposition, he told himself. After
all, business was what he was good at. Business was what
he was *all* about. Make it about money.

'I realise the upkeep would be far too much for you to
keep the castle long-term,' he told her, keeping his voice
low and measured. Reasoning as he talked. Maybe she
was still shocked at not receiving a monetary inheritance.
Maybe there was anger behind that calm façade of hers.

'The company has been funding long-term maintenance and restoration,' he continued, refusing to see the
look of revulsion on her face. Revulsion? Surely he must
be misreading. 'We can continue doing that,' he told her.
'If at the end of the year this inheritance goes through
and you don't wish to stay, the company can buy the castle from you.'

'You could afford that?' she demanded, incredulous?

'The company's huge. It can and it seems the most sensible option. You'll find I can be more than generous. Eileen
obviously wanted you looked after. Alan was my cousin.
I'll do that for him.'

But at that she flashed him a look that could have split
stone.

'I don't need looking after,' she snapped. 'I especially
don't need looking after by the McBride men.'

He got it then. Her anger wasn't just encompassing Eileen and her will. Her anger was directed at the McBride family as a whole.

She was holding residual anger towards Alan?

Why?

He and Alan had never got on and their mutual dislike had meant they never socialised. He'd met Jeanie a couple of times before she and Alan had married. Jeanie had worked as his grandmother's part-time assistant while she was on the island. On the odd times he'd met her she'd been quiet, he remembered, a shadow who'd seemed to know her place. He'd hardly talked to her, but she'd seemed... suitable. A suitable assistant for his grandmother.

And then Alan had married her. What a shock and what a disaster—and Jeanie had been into it up to her neck.

Until today he'd seen her as a money-grubbing mouse. The fire in her eyes now suggested the mouse image might possibly be wrong.

'Jeanie, this isn't about looking after—'

'Don't Jeanie me.' She glowered and went back to rubbing butter. 'I'm Mrs McBride. I'm Duncairn's housekeeper for the next few weeks and then I'm nothing to do with you.'

'Then we've both lost.'

'I told you, I've lost nothing. The castle's my place of employment, nothing more.'

'So you wouldn't mind moving to Edinburgh?'

Her hands didn't even pause. She just kept rubbing in the already rubbed-in butter, and her glower moved up a notch.

'Don't talk nonsense. I'm moving nowhere.'

'But you *are* moving out of the castle.'

'Which is none of your business.'

'I'm offering you a job.'

'I don't want a job.'

'If you don't have the castle, you need a job.'

'Don't mess with me, Alasdair McBride. By the way, the kitchen's out of bounds to guests. That's what you are now. A guest. The estate's in the hands of the executors, and I'm employed here. You have a bed booked for the night. The library, the dining room and your bedroom and sitting room are where you're welcome. Meanwhile I have work to do.'

'Jeanie…'

'What?' She pushed the bowl away from her with a vicious shove. 'Don't play games with me, Alasdair. Your cousin messed with my life and I should have moved away then. Right away.'

'I want to help.'

'No, you don't. You want your inheritance.'

'Yes,' he said and he lost it then, the cool exterior he carefully presented to the world. 'Yes, I do. The Duncairn financial empire is colossal and far-reaching. It's also my life. To break it up and use it to fund dogs' homes…'

'There are some very deserving dogs,' she snapped and then looked under the table to where Eileen's two dopey spaniels lay patiently waiting for crumbs. 'These two need a home. You can provide for them first.'

'Look!' He swore and hauled his phone from his sporran —these things were a sight more useful than pockets—and clicked the phone open. He flicked through a few screens and then turned it to face her. 'Look!'

'I have flour on my hands.' She glowered some more and she looked…sulky. Sulky but cute, he thought, and suddenly he found himself thinking…

Um…no. Not appropriate. All this situation needed was a bit of sensual tension and the thing was shot. He needed to stay calm, remember who she was and talk sense.

'Just look,' he said patiently and she sighed and rubbed her hands on her apron and peered at the screen.

'What am I looking at?'

'At a graph of Duncairn's listed charitable donations made in the last financial year,' he told her. 'The figure to the left represents millions. It scrolls off the screen but you can see the biggest beneficiaries. My grandfather and my grandmother after him refused to make Duncairn a listed company, so for years now the profits have either been siphoned back into the company to expand our power base, or used to fund worthwhile projects. AIDS, malaria, smallpox… Massive health projects have all been beneficiaries. Then there are smaller projects. Women's refuges, otter conservation, even dogs' homes.'

And Jeanie seemed caught. 'Those bars are…millions?' she whispered.

'Millions.'

'Then what was Eileen thinking, to leave the lot to just one cause?'

'You know what she was thinking,' Alasdair said wearily. 'We both do. She was blackmailing us into marriage, and as far as I can see, she's succeeded. I have no choice.' He sighed. 'The value of the castle ought to be enough for you, but if it's not, I'll pay you what you ask. I'll mortgage what I have to. Is that what you're after? You can name your terms but look at the alternative to us both. Use your head. I have no expectations of you, and I'll expect nothing from you as my wife. Eileen's will says we have to share a house for one full year before the inheritance is finalised, but I have a huge place in Edinburgh. I'll fund you well enough so you can be independent. Jeanie, do this, if not for the charities I represent, then for you. You'll earn even more than the castle this way. You've won. I concede. We'll marry and then we'll move on.'

And then he stopped. There was no more argument to present.

There was total silence and it lasted for a very long time.

* * *

Marriage...

Third-time lucky? The thought flashed through her mind and she put it away with a hollow, inward laugh. Lucky? With this man?

What he was proposing was purely business. Maybe that was the way to go.

This was a marriage for sensible, pragmatic reasons, she told herself, fighting desperately for logic. She could even feel noble, saving the Duncairn billions for the good of all the charities it assisted.

Noble? Ha. She'd feel sullied. Bought.

He thought she'd walk away with a fortune. If he only knew... But there was no point in telling him about the bankruptcy hanging over her head.

'Would you like to see through the place in Edinburgh?' he said at last. 'It's good, and big enough for us never to see each other. I'll have contracts drawn up that'll give you a generous income during the year, and of course we'll need a prenuptial agreement.'

'So I don't bleed you for anything else?'

'That wasn't what I was thinking.' But of course it was. It was an easy supposition—a woman who'd angled for the castle would no doubt think of marriage in terms of what she could get. 'But the castle will be worth—'

'Shut up and let me think.'

Whoa.

This woman was the hired help. She could see him thinking it. She was his cousin's leavings. The offer he'd made was extraordinary. That she would tell him to shut up...

He opened his mouth to reply, she glared—and he shut up.

More silence.

Could she? she thought. Dared she?

She thought suddenly of Maggie, her best friend on the island. Maggie was a fisherman's wife now, and the mother of two bright boys. Maggie was solid, sensible. She imagined Maggie's reaction when…if…she told her the news.

You're marrying another one? Are you out of your mind?

She almost grinned. It'd almost be worth it to hear the squeal down the phone.

But…

Act with your head. Do not be distracted, she told herself. You've done this in haste twice now. Get this right.

Marriage.

For a year. For only a year.

She'd have to live in Edinburgh, on Alasdair's terms.

No. Even the thought left her exposed, out of control, feeling as she'd vowed never to feel again. No and no and no.

She needed time to think, but that wasn't going to happen. Alasdair was leaning back, watching her, and she knew if she left this kitchen without making a decision the memory of this man would make her run. Physically, he was a stronger, darker version of Alan.

Alan had betrayed her, used her, conned her, but until that last appalling night he'd never frightened her. But this man… It almost as if he were looking straight through her.

So leave, she told herself. It'd be easy, to do what she'd first thought when the terms of the will were spelled out. She could stay with Maggie until she found a job.

A job, on Duncairn? There weren't any.

She glanced around her, at the great kitchen, at the big old range she'd grown to love, at the two dopey dogs at her feet. This place had been her refuge. She'd built it up with such care. Eileen had loved it and so had Jeanie.

It would have broken Eileen's heart if she'd known Alasdair was forced to let it go. Because of her? Because she lacked courage?

What if…? What if…?

'Think about it overnight,' Alasdair said, pushing himself away from the door. 'But I'm leaving in the morning. I need a decision by then.'

'I've made my decision.'

He stilled.

She'd poured the milk into the flour and turned it to dough without noticing. Now she thumped the dough out of the bowl and flattened it. She picked up her cutter and started cutting, as if perfectly rounded scones were the only thing that mattered in the world.

'Jeanie…'

She shook her head, trying to figure how to say it. She finished cutting her scones, she reformed and flattened the remaining dough, she cut the rest, she arranged them on the tray and then she paused.

She stared down at the scone tray. They were overworked, too. They wouldn't rise properly. She should give up now.

But she wouldn't give up. She'd loved Eileen. Okay, Eileen, you win, she told her silently and then she forced herself to look at the man before her.

'I'll do it if I can stay here,' she managed.

He didn't get it. He didn't understand where this was going, but business acumen told him not to rush in. To wait until she spelled out terms.

She was staring down at her scones. She put her hands on her waist and her head to one side, as if considering. She was considering the scones. Not him.

She had a tiny waist, he thought irrelevantly, for one so…curvy. She was wearing a tailored suit under her apron—for the funeral. Her suit had showed off her neat figure, but the tight ribbons of the apron accentuated it even more. She was curvy at the bottom and curvy at the top... Um, very curvy, he conceded. Her hair was tied up in a knot but wisps were escaping.

She had a smudge of flour on her cheek. He'd like to...

Um, he wouldn't like. Was he out of his mind? This was business. Stick to what was important.

He forced himself to relax, walking forward so he had his back to the fire. Moving closer.

He felt rather than saw her flush.

Inexplicably, he still had the urge to remove that smudge of flour, to trace the line of her cheekbone, but the stiffening of her spine, the bracing of her shoulders, told him he might well get a face covered in scone dough for his pains.

'We'd need to live in Edinburgh,' he said at last, cautiously.

'Then there's not even the smidgeon of a deal.'

'Why the hell...?'

And at that she whirled and met his gaze full on, her green eyes flashing defiance. She was so close...

She was so angry.

'Once upon a time I ached to get off this island,' she snapped. 'Once upon a time I was a fool. The islanders—with the exception of my father—support and care for me. In Edinburgh I have no one. I'd be married to a man I don't know and I can't trust. I've married in haste before, Alasdair McBride, and I'll not do so again. You have much more to gain from this arrangement than I have, so here are my terms. I'll marry you for a year as long as you agree to stay in this castle. Then, at the end of the year, I'll inherit what the will has decreed I inherit. Nothing more. But meanwhile, you live in this castle—in my home, Alasdair—and you live on my terms for the year. It's that or nothing.'

'That's ridiculous.' He could feel her anger, vibrating

in waves, like electric current, surging from her body to his and back again.

'Take it or leave it,' she said and she deliberately turned her back, deliberately broke the connection. She picked up her tray of unbaked scones and slid them into the trash. 'I'm trying again,' she told him, her back to him. 'Third-time lucky? It might work for scones.'

He didn't understand. 'I can't live here.'

'That's your decision,' she told him. 'But I have some very fine whisky I'm willing to share.'

'I'm not interested in whisky!' It was an explosion and Jeanie stilled again.

'Not?'

'This is business.'

'The whole year will be business,' she retorted, turning to the sink with her tray. 'I'm thinking it'll be shortbread for the guests tonight. What do you think?'

'I don't care what you give your guests.'

'But, you see, they'll be your guests, too, Lord Duncairn,' she told him. 'If you decide on marriage, then I'll expect you to play host. If you could keep wearing your kilt—a real Scottish lord playing host in his castle—I'll put you on the website. It'll pull the punters in in droves.'

'You're out of your mind.'

'And so was Eileen when she made that will,' Jeanie told him, still with her back to him. 'So all we can do is make the most of it. As I said, take it or leave it. We can be Lord and Lady of the castle together or we can be nothing at all. Your call, Lord Duncairn. I need to get on with my baking.'

CHAPTER THREE

FOUR WEEKS LATER Lord Alasdair Duncan Edward McBride, Sixteenth Earl of Duncairn, stood in the same kirk where his grandmother's funeral had taken place, waiting for his bride.

He'd wanted a register office. They both had. Jeanie was deeply uncomfortable about taking her vows in a church, but Eileen's will had been specific. Marriage in the kirk or nothing. Jeanie had felt ill when the lawyer had spelled it out, but then she'd looked again at the list of charities supported by the Duncairn foundation, she'd thought again of the old lady she'd loved, and she'd decided God would forgive her.

'It's not that I don't support dogs' homes,' she told Maggie Campbell, her best friend and her rock today. 'But I feel a bit of concern for AIDS and malaria and otters as well. I'm covering all bases. Though it does seem to the world like I'm buying myself a castle with marriage.' She hadn't told Maggie of the debt. She'd told no one. The whole island would think this deal would be her being a canny Scot.

'Well, no one's judging you if you are,' Maggie said soundly, hugging her friend and then adjusting the spray of bell heather in Jeanie's simple blue frock. 'Except me. I would have so loved you to be a bride.'

'I should have worn my suit. I'm not a bride. I'm half a

contract,' Jeanie retorted, glancing at her watch and thinking five minutes to go, five minutes left when she could walk out of here. Or run. Honestly, what was she doing? Marrying another McBride?

But Maggie's sister was a lawyer, and Maggie's sister had read the fine print and she'd got the partners in her firm to read the fine print and then she'd drawn up a prenuptial agreement for both Jeanie and Alasdair to sign and it still seemed…sensible.

'This is business only,' she said aloud now, and Maggie stood back and looked at her.

'You look far too pretty to be a business deal. Jeanie, tomorrow you'll be the Lady of Duncairn.'

'I… He doesn't use the title.' She'd tried joking about that to Alasdair. She'd even proposed using it in castle advertising but the black look on his face had had her backing right off. You didn't joke with Lord Alasdair.

Just Alasdair. Her soon-to-be husband.

Her…lord?

'It doesn't stop the title being there, My Ladyship.' Maggie bobbed a mock curtsy as she echoed Jeanie's thoughts. 'It's time to go to church now, m'lady. If m'lady's ready.'

Jeanie managed a laugh but even to her ears it sounded hollow. She glanced at her watch again. Two minutes. One.

'Ready, set, go,' Maggie said and propelled her to the door.

To marry.

Third-time lucky?

He was standing at the altar, waiting for his bride. He'd never thought he'd be here. Marriage was not for him.

He hadn't always believed that, he conceded. Once upon a time he'd been head over heels in love. He'd been twenty-two, just finishing a double degree in law and commerce, eager to take on the world. Celia had been a socialite, five years his senior. She was beautiful, intelligent, a woman who knew her way around Scottish society and who knew exactly what she wanted in a marriage.

He couldn't believe she'd wanted him. He'd been lanky, geeky, unsure, a product of cold parents and too many books, knowing little of how relationships worked. He'd been ripe for the plucking.

And Celia had plucked. When she'd agreed to marry him, he'd thought he was the luckiest man alive. What he hadn't realised was that when she was looking at him she was seeing only his title and his inheritance.

But she'd played her part superbly. She'd held him as he'd never been held. She'd listened as he'd told her of his childhood, things he'd never told anyone. He'd had fun with her. He'd felt light and free and totally in love. Totally trusting. He'd bared his soul, he'd left himself totally exposed—and in return he'd been gutted.

For a long time he'd blamed his cousin, Alan, with his charm and charisma. Alan had arrived in Edinburgh a week before he and Celia were due to marry, ostensibly to attend his cousin's wedding but probably to hit his grandmother for more money. He hadn't been involved with Jeanie then. He'd had some other bimbo on his arm, but that hadn't cramped his style. Loyalty hadn't been in Alan's vocabulary.

And it seemed it wasn't in Celia's, either.

Two days before his wedding, Alasdair had realised he'd left his briefcase at Celia's apartment. He'd had a key so he'd dropped by early, before work. He'd knocked, but of course no one had answered.

It was no wonder they hadn't answered. He'd walked in, and Celia had been with Alan. *With*, in every sense of the word.

So now he was about to marry...another of Alan's leavings?

Don't think of Alan now. Don't think of Celia. He said it savagely to himself but the memory was still sour and heavy. He'd never trusted since. His personal relationships were kept far apart from his business.

But here he was again—and he was doing what Celia had intended. Wedding for money?

This woman was different, he conceded. Very different. She was petite. Curvy. She wasn't the slightest bit elegant.

She was Alan's widow.

But right now she didn't look like a woman who'd attract Alan. She was wearing a simple blue frock, neat, nice. Her shoes were kitten-heeled, silver. Her soft brown curls were just brushing her shoulders. She usually wore her hair tied back or up, so maybe this was a concession to being a bride—as must be the spray of bell heather on her lapel—but they were sparse concessions.

Celia would have been the perfect bride, he thought tangentially. That morning, when he'd walked in on them both, Celia's bridal gown had been hanging for him to see. Even years later he still had a vision of how Celia would have looked in that dress.

She wouldn't have looked like this. Where Celia would have floated down the aisle, an ethereal vision, Jeanie was looking straight ahead, her gaze on the worn kirk floorboards rather than on him. Her friend gave her a slight push. She nodded as if confirming something in her mind—and then she stumped forward. There was no other word for it. She stumped.

A romantic bride? Not so much.

Though she was…cute, he conceded as he watched her come, and then he saw the flush of colour on her cheeks and he thought suddenly she looked…mortified?

Mortified? As if she'd been pushed into this?

It was his grandmother who'd done the forcing, he told himself. If this woman had been expecting the castle to fall into her lap with no effort, it was Eileen who'd messed with those plans, not him. This forced marriage was merely the solution to the problem.

And mortified or not, Jeanie had got what she wanted. She'd inherit her castle.

He'd had to move mountains to arrange things so he could stay on the island. He'd created a new level of management and arranged audits to ensure he hadn't missed anything; financial dealings would run smoothly without him. He'd arranged a satellite Internet connection so he could work here. He'd had a helipad built so he could organise the company chopper to get him here fast. So he could leave fast.

Not that he could leave for more than his designated number of nights, he thought grimly. He was stuck. With this woman.

She'd reached his side. She was still staring stolidly at the floor. Could he sense…fear? He must be mistaken.

But he couldn't help himself reacting. He touched her chin and tilted her face so she had no choice but to meet his gaze.

'I'm not an ogre.'

'No, but—'

'And I'm not Alan. Business only.'

She bit her lip and his suspicion of fear deepened.

Enough. There were few people to see this. Eileen's lawyer was here to see things were done properly. The minister and the organist were essential. Jeanie's friend Maggie completed the party. 'I need Maggie for support,' Jeanie had told him and it did look as if she needed the support right now. His bride was looking like a deer trapped in headlights.

He took her hands and they were shaking.

'Jeanie…'

'Let's…let's…'

'Not if you're not sure of me,' he told her, gentling now, knowing this was the truth. 'No money in the world is worth a forced marriage. If you're afraid, if you don't want it, then neither do I. If you don't trust me, then walk away now.'

What was he saying? He was out of his mind. But he'd had to say it. She was shaking. Acting or not, he had to react to what he saw.

But now her chin was tilting in a gesture he was starting to recognise. She tugged her hands away and she managed a nod of decision.

'Eileen trusted you,' she managed. 'And this is business. For castle, for keeps.' She took a deep breath and turned to the minister. 'Let's get this over with,' she told him. 'Let's get us married.'

The vows they spoke were the vows that were spoken the world over from time immemorial, between man and woman, between lovers becoming man and wife.

'I, Alasdair Duncan Edward McBride, take thee, Jeanie Margaret McBride... To have and to hold. For richer or for poorer. In sickness and in health, for as long as we both shall live.'

He wished—fiercely—that his grandmother hadn't insisted on a kirk. The minister was old and faded, wearing Wellingtons under his well-worn cassock. He was watching them with kindly eyes, encouraging them, treating them as fresh-faced lovers.

For as long as we both shall live...

In his head he corrected himself.

For twelve months and I'm out of here.

For as long as we both shall live...

The words were hard to say. She had to fight to get her tongue around them.

It should be getting easier to say the words she knew were just words.

The past two times, she'd meant them. She really had. They were nonsense.

Stupidly she felt tears pricking at the backs of her eyelids and she blinked them back with a fierceness born of an iron determination. She would not show this man weakness. She would not be weak. This was nothing more than a sensible proposition forced on her by a crazy will.

You understand why I'm doing it, she demanded silently of the absent Eileen. You thought you'd force us to become family. Instead we're doing what we must. You can't force people to love.

She'd tried, oh, she'd tried, but suddenly she was remembering that last appalling night with Alan.

'Do you think I'd have married you if my grandmother hadn't paid through the nose?'

Eileen was doing the same thing now, she thought bleakly. She was paying through the nose.

But I'm doing it for the right reasons. Surely? She looked firmly ahead. Alasdair's body was brushing hers. In his full highland regalia he looked…imposing. Magnificent. Frightening.

She would not be frightened of this man, she told herself. She would not. She'd marry, she'd get on with her life and then she'd walk away.

For as long as we both shall live…

Somehow she made herself say the words. How easy they'd been when she'd meant them but then they'd turned out to be meaningless. Now, when they were meaningless to start with, it felt as if something were dying within.

'You may kiss the bride,' the minister was saying and she felt like shaking her head, turning and running. But the old man was beaming, and Alasdair was taking her hands again. The new ring lay stark against her work-worn fingers.

Alasdair's strong, lean hands now sported a wedding band. Married.

'You may kiss the bride...'

He smiled down at her—for the sake of the kindly old minister marrying them? Surely that was it, but, even so, her heart did a back flip. What if this was real? her treacherous heart said. What if this man really loved...?

Get over it. It's business.

But people were watching. People were waiting. Alasdair was smiling, holding her hands, ready to do what was right.

Kiss the bride.

Right. She took a deep breath and raised her face to his.

'Think of it like going to the dentist,' Alasdair whispered, for her ears alone, and she stared up at him and his smile widened.

And she couldn't help herself. This was ridiculous. The whole thing was ridiculous. Jeanie Lochlan marrying the Earl of Duncairn. For a castle.

She found herself chuckling. It was so ridiculous she could do it. She returned the grip on his hands and she even stood on tiptoe so he could reach her.

His mouth lowered onto hers—and he kissed her.

If only she hadn't chuckled. Up until then it had been fine. Business only. He could do this. He could marry her, he could keep his distance, he could fulfil the letter of the deal and he could walk away at the end of twelve months feeling nothing. He intended to feel nothing.

But that meant he had to stay impervious to what she was; to who she was. He couldn't think of her as his wife at all.

But then she chuckled and something happened.

The old kirk. The beaming minister. The sense of history in this place.

This woman standing beside him.

She was in this for profit, he told himself. She was sure of what she wanted and how she was going to get it. She was Alan's ex-wife and he'd seen how much the pair of them had cost Eileen. He wanted nothing to do with her.

But she was standing before him and he'd felt her fear. He'd felt the effort it had cost her to turn to the minister and say those vows out loud.

And now she'd chuckled.

She was small and curvy and dressed in a simple yet very pretty frock, with white lace collar, tiny lace shoulder puffs and a wide, flouncy skirt cinched in at her tiny waist. She was wearing bell heather on her lapel.

She was chuckling.

And he thought, She's enchanting. And then the thought flooded from nowhere.

She's my wife.

It hit him just as his mouth touched hers. The knowledge was as if a floodgate had opened. This woman...

His wife...

He kissed her.

She'd been expecting...what? A cursory brushing of lips against lips? Or less. He could have done this without actually touching her. That would have been better, she thought. An air kiss. No one here expected any more.

She didn't get an air kiss. He'd released her hands. He put his hands on her waist and he lifted her so her mouth was level with his.

He kissed her.

It was a true wedding kiss, a lordly kiss, the kiss of the Lord of Duncairn claiming his bride. It was a kiss with strength and heat and passion. It was a kiss that blew her fragile defences to smithereens.

She shouldn't respond. She shouldn't! They were in a kirk, for heaven's sake. It wasn't seemly. This was a business arrangement, a marriage of convenience, and he had no right...

And then her mind shut down, just like that.

She'd never been kissed like this. She'd never felt like this.

Fire...

His mouth was plundering hers. She was raised right off her feet. She was totally out of control and there was nothing she could do but submit.

And respond? Maybe she had no choice. Maybe that was the only option because that was what her body was doing. It was responding and responding and responding.

How could it not? This was like an electric charge, a high-voltage jolt that had her locked to him and there was no escape. Not that she wanted to escape. The fire coursing through her body had her feeling...

Here was her home? Here was her heart?

This was nonsense. Crazy. Their tiny audience was laughing and cheering and she fought to bring them into focus. She fought desperately to gather herself, regain some decorum, and maybe Alasdair felt it because finally, finally he set her on her feet. But his dark eyes gleamed at her, and behind that smile was a promise.

This man was her husband. The knowledge was terrifying but suddenly it was also exhilarating. Where were smelling salts when a girl needed them? she thought wildly, and she took a deep, steadying breath and turned resolutely back to the minister. Get this over with, she pleaded silently, and let me get out of here.

But the Reverend Angus McConachie was not finished. He was beaming at her as a father might beam at a favourite daughter. In fact, the Reverend Angus had baptised her, had buried her mother, had caught her and her friends stealing strawberries from his vegetable patch, had been there for all her life. She'd tried to explain to him what this wedding was about but she doubted he'd listened. He saw what he wanted to see, the Reverend Angus, and his next words confirmed it.

'Before I let you go…' he was beaming as if he'd personally played matchmaker, and happy families was just beginning '… I wish to say a few words. I've known our Jeanie since the time she turned from a twinkle in her father's eye into a pretty wee bairn. I've watched her grow into the fine young woman she is today. I know the Lady Eileen felt the same pleasure and pride in her that I do, and I feel the Lady Eileen is looking down right now, giving these two her blessing.'

Okay, Jeanie thought. That'll do. Stop now. But this was the Reverend Angus and she knew he wouldn't.

'But it's been my sorrow to see the tragedies that have befallen our Jeanie,' the minister continued, his beam dipping for a moment. 'She was devoted to her Rory from the time she was a wee lass, she was a fine wife and when the marriage ended in tragedy we were all heartbroken for her. That she was brave enough to try again with her Alan was a testament to her courage—and, dare I say, it was also a testament to the Lady Eileen's encouragement? I dare say there's not an islander on Duncairn whose heart didn't break with her when she came home after such trouble.'

'Angus…' Jeanie hissed, appalled, but Angus's beam was back on high and there was no stopping him.

'And now it's three,' he said happily. 'Third-time lucky. I hear the Lady Eileen has her fingers in the pie this time, too, but she assured me before she died that this one would be a happy ever after.'

'She told you?' Alasdair asked, sounding incredulous.

'She was a conniving lass, your grandmother.' Angus beamed some more. 'And here it is, the results of that conniving, and the islanders couldn't be happier for you. Jeanie, lass, may third time be more than lucky. May your third time be forever.'

Somehow they made it outside, to the steps of the kirk. The church sat on the headland looking over Duncairn Bay. The sun was shining. The fishing fleet was out, but a few smaller boats were tied on swing moorings. Gulls were wheeling overhead, the church grounds were a mass of wild honeysuckle and roses, and the photographer for the island's monthly newsletter was asking them to look their way.

'Smile for the camera… You look so handsome, the pair of you.'

This would make the front cover of the *Duncairn Chronicle*, she knew—*Local Lass Weds Heir to Duncairn*.

Her father would be down in the pub now, she thought, already drinking in anticipation of profits he'd think he could wheedle from her.

'This is the third time?' Alasdair sounded incredulous.

'So?' Her smile was rigidly determined. Alasdair's arm was around her waist, as befitted the standard newlywed couple, but his arm felt like steel. There was not a trace of warmth in it.

'I assumed Alan was the only—'

'You didn't ask,' she snapped. 'Does it matter?'

'Hell, of course it matters. Did you make money from the first one, too?'

Enough. She put her hand behind her and hauled his arm away from her waist. She was still rigidly smiling but she was having trouble…it could so easily turn to rictus.

'Thanks, Susan,' she called to the photographer. 'We're

done. Thanks, everyone, for coming. We need to get back to the castle. We have guests arriving.'

'No honeymoon?' Susan, the photographer, demanded. 'Why don't you go somewhere beautiful?'

'Duncairn is beautiful.'

'She won't even close the castle to guests for a few days,' Maggie said and Jeanie gritted her teeth and pushed the smile a bit harder.

'It's business as usual,' she told them. 'After all, this is the third time I've married. I'm thinking the romance has worn off by now. It's time to get back to work.'

Alasdair drove them back to the castle. He'd bought an expensive SUV—brand-new. It had been delivered via the ferry, last week before Alasdair had arrived. Alasdair himself had arrived by helicopter this morning, a fact that made Jeanie feel as if things were happening far too fast—as if things were out of her control. She'd been circling the SUV all week, feeling more and more nervous.

She wasn't a 'luxury-car type'. She wasn't the type to marry a man who arrived by helicopter. But she had to get used to it, she told herself, and she'd driven the thing down to the kirk feeling…absurd.

'It's gorgeous,' Maggie had declared. 'And he's said you can drive it? Fabulous. You can share.'

'This marriage isn't about sharing, and my little banger is twenty years old. She's done me proud and she'll keep doing me proud.'

'Och, but I can see you sitting up beside your husband in this, looking every inch the lady.' Maggie had laughed and she'd almost got a swipe to the back of her head for her pains.

But now… She was doing exactly that, Jeanie thought. She was sitting primly in the front passenger seat with her hands folded on her lap. She was staring straight ahead and beside her was…her husband.

'Third time…'

It was the first time he'd spoken to her out of the hearing of their guests. As an opening to a marriage it was hardly encouraging.

'Um…' Jeanie wasn't too sure where to go.

'You've been married three times.' His mind was obviously in a repetitive loop, one that he didn't like a bit. His hands were clenched white on the steering wheel. He was going too fast for this road.

'Cattle and sheep have the right of way here,' she reminded him. 'And the cattle are tough wee beasties. You round a bend too fast and you'll have a horn through your windscreen.'

'We're not talking about cattle.'

'Right,' she said and subsided. His car. His problem.

'Three…' he said again and she risked a glance at his face. Grim as death. As if she'd conned him?

'Okay, as of today, I've been married three times.'

He was keeping his temper under control but she could feel the pressure building.

'Did my grandmother know?' His incredulity was like a flame held to a wick of an already ticking bomb.

But if he thought he had sole rights to anger, he had another thought coming. As if she'd deceive Eileen…

'Of course she knew. Eileen knew everything about me. I…loved her.'

And the look he threw her was so filled with scorn she flinched and clenched her hands in her lap and looked the other way.

Silence. Silence, silence and more silence. Maybe that's what this marriage will be all about, she thought bleakly. One roof, but strangers. Silence, with undercurrents of…

hatred? That was what it felt like. As if the man beside her hated her.

'Was he rich, too?' Alasdair asked and enough was enough.

'Stop.'

'What…?'

'Stop the car this instant.'

'Why should I?'

But they were rounding a tight bend, where even Alasdair had to slow. She unclipped her seat belt and pushed her door wide. 'Stop now because I'm getting out, whether you've stopped or not. Three, two…'

He jammed on the brakes and she was out of the door before they were completely still.

He climbed out after her. 'What the…?'

'I'm walking,' she told him. 'I don't do dinner for guests but seeing you live at the castle now you can have the run of the kitchen. Make yourself what you like. Have a happy marriage, Alasdair McBride. Your dislike of me means we need to be as far apart as we can, so we might as well start now.'

And she turned and started stomping down the road.

She could do this. It was only three miles, and if there was one thing Jeanie had learned to do over the years, it was walk. She loved this country. She loved the wildness of it, the sheer natural beauty. She knew every nook and cranny of the island. She knew the wild creatures. The sheep hardly startled at her coming and she knew each of the highland cattle by name.

But she was currently wearing a floaty dress and heels. Not stilettos, she conceded, thanking her lucky stars, but they were kitten heels and she wasn't accustomed to kitten heels.

Maybe when Alasdair was out of sight she'd slip them off and walk barefoot.

Ouch.

Nevertheless, a girl had some pride. She'd made her bed and she needed to lie on it. Or walk.

She walked. There was no sound of an engine behind her but she wasn't looking back.

And then a hand landed on her shoulder and she almost yelped. Almost. A girl had some pride.

'Don't,' she managed and pulled away to keep stomping. And then she asked, because she couldn't help herself, 'Where did you learn to walk like a cat?'

'Deerstalking. As a kid. My grandpa gave me a camera for my eighth birthday.'

'You mean you don't have fifty sets of antlers on your sitting-room walls back in Edinburgh?' She was still stomping.

'Nary an antler. Jeanie—'

'Mrs McBride to you.'

'Lady Jean,' he said and she stopped dead and closed her eyes. *Lady Jean...*

Her dad would be cock-a-hoop. He'd be drunk by now, she thought, boasting to all and sundry that his girl was now lady of the island.

His girl.

Rory... She'd never been her father's girl, but Rory used to call her that.

'My lass. My sweet island lassie, my good luck charm, the love of my life...'

That this man could possibly infer she'd married for money...

'Go away,' she breathed. 'Leave me be and take your title and your stupid, cruel misconceptions with you.'

And she started walking again.

To her fury he fell in beside her.

'Go away.'

'We need to talk.'

'Your car's on a blind bend.'

'This is my land.'

'*Your* land?'

There was a moment's loaded pause. She didn't stop walking.

'Okay, *your* land,' he conceded at last. 'The access road's on the castle title. As of marrying, as of today, it's yours.'

'You get the entire Duncairn company. Does that mean you're a bigger fortune hunter than me?'

'I guess it does,' he said. 'But at least my motive is pure. How much of Alan's money do you have left?'

And there was another statement to take her breath away. She was finding it hard to breathe. Really hard.

Time for some home truths? More than time. She didn't want sympathy, but this…

'You'd think,' she managed, slowly, because each word was costing an almost superhuman effort, 'that you'd have done some homework on your intended bride. This is a business deal. If you're buying, Alasdair McBride, surely you should have checked out the goods before purchase.'

'It seems I should.' He was striding beside her. What did he think he was doing? Abandoning the SUV and hiking all the way to the castle?

'I have guests booked in at four this afternoon,' she hissed. 'They'll be coming round that bend. Your car is blocking the way.'

'You mean it's blocking your profits?'

Profits. She stopped mid-stride and closed her eyes. She counted to ten and then another ten. She tried to do a bit of deep breathing. Her fingers clenched and re-clenched.

Nothing was working. She opened her eyes and he was

still looking at her as if she was tainted goods, a bad smell. He'd married someone he loathed.

Someone who married for profit... Of all the things she'd ever been accused of...

She smacked him.

She'd never smacked a man in her life. She'd never smacked anyone. She was a woman who used Kindly Mousers and carried the captured mice half a mile to release them. She swore they beat her back to the castle but still she kept trying. She caught spiders and put them outside. She put up with dogs under her bed because they looked so sad when she put them in the wet room.

But she had indeed smacked him.

She'd left a mark. *No!*

Her hands went to her own face. She wanted to sink into the ground. She wanted to run. Of all the stupid, senseless things she'd done in her life, this was the worst. She'd married a man who made her so mad she'd hit him.

She'd mopped up after Rory's fish for years. She'd watched his telly. She'd coped with the meagre amount he'd allowed her for housekeeping—and she'd never once complained.

And Alan... She thought of the way he'd treated her and still... She'd never once even considered hitting.

But now... What was she thinking? Of all the stupid, dumb mistakes, to put herself in a situation where she'd ended up violent...

Well, then...

Well, then what? A lesser woman might have burst into tears but not Jeanie. She wasn't about to show this man tears, no matter how desperate things were.

Move on, she told herself, forcing herself to think past the surge of white-hot anger. Get a grip, woman. Get yourself out of this mess, the fastest way you can. But first...

She'd smacked him and the action was indefensible. Do what comes next, she told herself. Apologise.

'I'm sorry.' Somehow she got it out. He was staring at her as if she'd grown two heads, and who could blame him? How many times had the Lord of Castle Duncairn been slapped?

Not often enough, a tiny voice whispered, but she wasn't going there. No violence, not ever. Had she learned nothing?

'I'm very sorry,' she made herself repeat. 'That was inexcusable. No matter what you said, I should never, ever have hit you. I hope... I hope it doesn't hurt.'

'Hurt?' He was still eyeing her with incredulity. 'You hit me and ask if it hurts? If I say no, will you do it again?' And it was almost as if he was goading her.

She stared at him, but her stare was blind.

'I won't...hit you.'

'What have I possibly said to deserve that?'

'You judged me.'

'I did. Tell me what's wrong about my judgement.'

'You want the truth?'

'Tell me something I don't know,' he said wearily and her hand itched again.

Enough. No more. Say it and get out.

He wanted the truth? He wanted something he didn't know? She took a deep breath and steadied.

Let him have it, then, she told herself. After all, the only casualty was her pride, and surely she ought to be over pride by now.

'Okay, then.' She was feeling ill, cold and empty. She hated what she was about to say. She hated everything that went with it.

But he was her husband, she thought bitterly. For now. For better or for worse she'd made the vows. The marriage would need to be annulled and fast, but meanwhile the truth was there for the telling. Pride had to take a back seat.

'I make no profit. I won't inherit the castle, no matter how married I am,' she told him. 'Believe it or not, I did this for you—or for your inheritance, for the Duncairn legacy Eileen cared so much about. But if I can't see you without wanting to hit out, then it's over. No lies are worth it, no false vows, no inheritance, nothing. I've tried my best but it's done.'

Done? The world stilled.

It was a perfect summer's day, a day for soaking in every ounce of pleasure in preparation for the bleak winter that lay ahead. But there was no pleasure here. There was only a man and a woman, and a chasm between them a mile deep.

Done.

'What do you mean?' he asked at last.

'I mean even if we managed to stay married for a year, I can't inherit,' she told him, in a dead, cold voice she scarcely recognised. 'I've checked with two lawyers and they both tell me the same thing. Alan left me with massive debts. For the year after his death I tried every way I could to figure some way to repay them but in the end there was only one thing to do. I had myself declared bankrupt.'

'Bankrupt?' He sounded incredulous. Did he still think she was lying? She didn't care, she decided. She was so tired she wanted to sink.

'That was almost three years ago,' she forced herself to continue. 'But bankruptcy lasts for three years and the lawyers' opinions are absolute. Because Eileen died within the three-year period, any inheritance I receive, no matter when I receive it, becomes part of my assets. It reverts to the bankruptcy trustees to be distributed between Alan's creditors. The fact that most of those creditors are any form of low-life you care to name is irrelevant. So that's it—the only one who stood to gain from this marriage was you. I agreed to marry you because I knew Eileen would hate the estate to be lost, but now… Alasdair, I should never have agreed in the first place. I'm sick of being judged. I'm tired to death of being a McBride, and if it's driving me to hitting, then I need to call it quits. I did this for Eileen but the price is too high. Enough.'

She took off her shoes, then wheeled and started walking.

Where was a spacecraft when she needed one? 'Beam me up, Scotty…' What she'd give to say those words.

Her feet wouldn't go fast enough.

'Jeanie…' he called at last but she didn't even slow.

'Take your car home,' she threw over her shoulder. 'The agreement's off. Everything's off. I'll see a lawyer and get the marriage annulled—I'll do whatever I need to do. I'd agreed to look after the castle for the next few weeks but that's off, too. So sue me. You can be part of my creditor list. I'll camp in Maggie's attic tonight and I'm on the first ferry out of here tomorrow.'

'You can't,' he threw after her, sounding stunned, but she still didn't turn. She didn't dare.

'Watch me. When I reach the stage where I hit out, I know enough is enough. I've been enough of a fool for one lifetime. Foolish stops now.'

CHAPTER FOUR

THERE WAS ONE advantage to living on an island—there were only two ferries a day. Actually it was usually a disadvantage, but right now it played into Alasdair's hands. Jeanie might be heading to Maggie's attic tonight but she'd still be here in the morning. He had time.

He needed time. He needed to play catch up. Jeanie was right: if she'd been a business proposition, he would have researched before he invested.

An undischarged bankrupt? How had he not known? The complications made his head spin.

The whole situation made his head spin.

He tried to get her to ride home with him but she refused. Short of hauling her into the SUV by force he had to let her be, but he couldn't let her walk all the way. He figured that was the way to fuel her fury and she was showing enough fury as it was. He therefore drove back to the castle, found her car keys hanging on a nail in the kitchen, drove her car back along the track until he reached her, soundlessly handed her the keys, then turned and walked back himself.

She must have spent a good hour trying to figure out how not to accept his help, or maybe she didn't want to pass him on the track. Either way, he was back at the castle when her car finally nosed its way onto the castle sweep.

Maybe he should have talked to her then, but he didn't have all the facts. He needed them.

Luckily he had help, a phone call away.

'Find anything there is to find out about Jeanie Lochlan, born on Duncairn twenty-nine years ago,' he told his secretary. Elspeth was his right-hand woman in Edinburgh. If anyone could unearth anything, it was her.

'Haven't you just married her?' Elspeth ventured.

'Don't ask. Just look,' he snapped and whatever Elspeth heard in his voice he didn't care.

Jeanie was back in her rooms downstairs. He was in his sitting room right over hers. He could hear her footsteps going back and forth, back and forth. Packing?

Finally he heard her trudge towards the front door.

He met her at the foot of the castle stairs and tried to take an enormous suitcase from her.

'I can manage.' Her voice dripped ice. 'I can cope by myself.'

And what was it about those few words that made him flinch?

She was shoving her case into the back of her battered car and he was feeling as if…feeling as if…

As if maybe he'd messed something up. Something really important.

Yes, he had. He'd messed up the entire Duncairn empire, but right now it felt much more personal.

She closed the lid of the boot on her car and returned. He stood and watched as she headed for the kitchen, grabbed crates and wads of newspaper and headed for the library.

He followed and stood at the door as she wrapped and stowed every whisky bottle that was more than a third full.

The B & B guests would come back tonight and be shattered, he thought. Half the appeal of this place on the web was the simple statement: *'Genuine Scottish Castle,*

*with every whisky of note that this grand country's ever
made free to taste.'*

He'd seen the website and had congratulated his grandmother on such a great selling idea.

'The whisky's Jeanie's idea,' Eileen had told him. 'I told
her I thought the guests would drink themselves silly, but
she went ahead and bought them anyway, out of her own
salary. She lets me replenish it now, but the original outlay
and idea were hers. So far no one's abused it. The guests
love it, and you're right, it's brilliant.'

And the guests were still here. They'd want their
whisky.

'And don't even think about claiming it,' she snapped
as she wrapped and stowed. 'I bought the first lot out of
my wages so it's mine. Be grateful I'm only taking what's
left. Alasdair, you can contact Maggie if you want my for-
warding address…for legalities. For marriage annulment.
For getting us out of this final foolishness. Meanwhile
that's it. I'm done and out of here. From this day forth I'm
Jeanie Lochlan, and if I never see a McBride again, it'll
be too soon.'

She picked up her first crate of whisky and headed to
the car. Silently he lifted the second and carried it after her.

She shoved both crates into the back seat and slammed
the door after them. Her little car shuddered. It really was
a banger, he thought.

Alan's wife. An undischarged bankrupt. Alan… He
thought of his cousin and he felt ill.

'Jeanie, can we talk?'

'We've talked. Goodbye.' She stuck out her hand and
waited until he took it, then shook it with a fierceness that
surprised him. Then she looked up at his face, gave one
decisive nod and headed for the driver's seat.

'I'm sorry about the castle,' she threw at him. She could
no longer see him. She was hauling on her seat belt, mov-

ing on. 'And I'm sorry about your company. On the upside, there are going to be some very happy dogs all over Europe.'

He stood and watched her as she headed out of the castle grounds, along the cliff road towards the village. When she disappeared from view he watched on.

His entire financial empire had just come crashing down. He should be gutted.

He was gutted but what was uppermost in his mind right now was that he'd hurt her. She'd hit him but the next moment she'd drawn back as if he'd been the one who'd hit her.

He had made assumptions, he thought, but those assumptions had been based on facts. He knew how much money Eileen had withdrawn from the company when Jeanie and Alan had married. 'It'll set them up for life,' Eileen had told him. 'I know Alan's not interested in the company but he is my grandson. He wants his inheritance now, and if it helps him settle, then he should have it.'

The amount she'd given the pair had been eye-watering. And yes, Alan's lifestyle had been ruinous but his death must have meant most of the capital was intact. Surely Alan couldn't have gambled that much?

Surely?

He'd always thought Jeanie's decision to come back here to the castle was an attempt to ingratiate herself with his grandmother. The contents of Eileen's will had proved him right.

The sight of her heading away in her ancient car gave him pause.

An undischarged bankruptcy...

If it was true, then the castle was forfeit no matter whether they married or not.

And with that thought came another. He'd loved the castle since he was a child, even when it was little more than a ruin. Eileen's restoration had made it fabulous. She'd been overwhelmingly proud of it—and so was he. He gazed up now at the turrets and towers, the age-old battlements, the great, grand home that had sheltered so many generations of his family. That had provided work for so many islanders...

He was the Lord of Duncairn. Even though he no longer used it, the title, but the castle and the island were still important to him. Desperately important. With her leaving, Jeanie had sealed the castle's fate. It would leave the family forever.

He was forcing his mind to think tangentially. If what she'd just told him was based on facts, then it wasn't Jeanie who'd sealed the castle's fate. It had been Alan.

He thought suddenly of the night Alan had been killed. He'd been driving a brand-new sports car, far too fast. A clear road. An inexplicable swerve to the left, a massive tree.

Jeanie had been thrown clear, suffering minor injuries. Alan had died instantly.

He'd thought until now it had been alcohol or drugs that had caused the crash, but now... Had it been suicide? Because of debt?

Had he tried to take Jeanie with him?

He'd been too caught up with Eileen's grief to ask questions. What sort of fool had he been?

A car was approaching, a low-slung, crimson sports car. The couple inside wore expensive clothes and designer sunglasses. The car spun onto the driveway, sending up a spray of gravel. The pair climbed out, looking at the castle in awe.

And they also looked at Alasdair. He was still in his wedding finery. Lord of his castle?

He'd lose the castle. Alan had gambled it away.

And he'd gambled more than the castle away. Jeanie…
He'd gambled with her life.

'Hi, there.' The young man was clearly American, and
he was impervious to the fact that Alasdair's gaze was
still following Jeanie's car. He flicked the boot open and
pointed to the baggage, then turned back to his partner.
'This looks cool,' he told her. 'And check out the doorman.
Great touch.' And he tossed the car keys to Alasdair, who
was so stunned that he actually caught them.

'This is just what we ordered—real Scotland,' he continued. 'Wow, look at those ruins down by the sea. You
can put them on the Internet, honey. And check out the
battlements. I've half a mind to put in an offer for the place,
doorman and all. But first, my love, let's check out this
whisky.' He glanced back at Alasdair. 'What are you waiting for, man? We need our bags straight away.'

'Carry your own bags,' Alasdair snapped. 'I don't work
in this place. I own it.'

Only he didn't.

'As far as short marriages go, this must be a record.'

Down in the village, Maggie had chosen a top-of-the-
range bottle from Jeanie's crates and had poured two
whiskies. They were sitting at Maggie's kitchen table, surrounded by the clutter of Maggie's kids, Maggie's fisherman husband and the detritus of a busy family. The ancient
stove was giving out gentle warmth but Jeanie couldn't
stop shaking. Maggie's hug had made her feel better, the
whisky should be helping, but she had a way to go before
shock lessened.

'So the marriage lasted less than an hour,' Maggie continued. 'I'm guessing…not consummated?'

'Maggie!'

'Just asking.' Maggie grinned and raised her glass.
'You might need to declare that to get an annulment—

or am I thinking of the bad old days when they checked the sheets?'

'I can hardly get a doctor to declare me a virgin,' Jeanie retorted, and Maggie's smile broadened. But behind her smile Jeanie could see concern. Real concern.

'So what happened? Did he come on too fast? Is he a brute? Tell me.'

If only, Jeanie thought, and suddenly, weirdly, she was thinking of her mother. Heather Lochlan had died when Jeanie was sixteen and Jeanie still missed her with an ache that would never fade.

'He's not a brute. He's just…a businessman.' She buried her face in her hands. 'Mam would never have let me get myself into this mess,' she whispered. 'Three husbands… Three disasters.'

'Your mam knew Rory,' Maggie retorted. 'Rory was no disaster. Your mam would have danced at your wedding.'

She well might have, Jeanie thought. Rory had been an islander, born and bred. He'd been older than Jeanie by ten years, and he'd followed his father and his grandfather's way to the sea. He'd been gentle, predictable, safe. All the things Jeanie's dad wasn't.

She'd been a mere sixteen when her dad had taken control of her life.

Her mam's death had been sudden and shocking, and Jeanie's dad had turned to drink to cope. He'd also pulled Jeanie out of school. 'Sixteen is well old enough to do the housework for me. I'm wasting no more of my money.'

She'd been gutted, but then Rory had stepped in, and amazingly he'd stood up to her father. 'We'll marry,' he'd told her. 'You can work in the fish shop rather than drudge for your father. You can live with my mam and dad.'

Safe… That was what Rory was. She'd thought she loved him, but…

But working in the fish shop, doing an online accountancy course because she ached to do something other than serve fish and clean, waiting for the times Rory came home from sea, fitting in with Rory's life…sometimes she'd dreamed…

It had never come to a point where she'd chafed against the bonds of loving, for Rory had drowned. She'd grieved for him, honestly and openly, but she knew she should never have married him. Safety wasn't grounds for a marriage. She'd found a part-time job with the island solicitor, and she'd begun to think she might see London. Maybe even save for a cruise…

But it had been so hard to save. She'd still been cleaning for her in-laws. She'd been earning practically nothing. Dreams had seemed just that—dreams. And then Eileen had come and offered her a job, acting as her assistant whenever she was on the island. And with Eileen… Alan.

Life had been grey and drab and dreary and he'd lit up everything around him. But…

There was that *but* again.

'Mam would have told me not to be a fool,' she told Maggie. 'Maybe even with Rory. Definitely with Alan and even more definitely with this one.'

'Maybe, but a girl has to follow her heart.'

'My heart doesn't make sense. I married Rory for safety. I married Alan for excitement. I married…this one…so he could keep his inheritance. None of them are the basis for any sort of marriage. It's time I grew up and accepted it.'

'So what will you do now?' Maggie was watching her friend with concern.

'I'm leaving the island. I never should have come back after Alan's death. I was just…so homesick and battered, and Eileen was kind.' She took a deep breath. 'No matter. I've enough money to tide me over for a few weeks and there are always bookkeeping jobs.' She raised her whisky to her friend. 'Here's to an unmarried future,' she said.

'Och,' Maggie exclaimed, startled. 'You can't expect me to drink to that.'

'Then here's to an unmarried Jeanie Lochlan,' Jeanie told her. 'Here's to just me and that's how it should be. I'm on my own and I'm not looking back.'

Alasdair was not on his own. He was surrounded by eight irate guests and two hungry dogs. Where did Jeanie keep the dog food? He had no idea.

He'd stayed in the castle off and on when his grandmother was ill, and after his grandmother's funeral. During that time the castle had been full of women and casseroles and offers of help. Since that time, though, he'd been back in Edinburgh, frantically trying to tie up loose ends so he could stay on the island for twelve months. He'd arrived this morning via helicopter, but the helicopter was long gone.

He was stuck here for the night, and the castle was full, not with offers of help, but with eight guests who all wanted attention.

'Where's the whisky, fella? We only came for the whisky.' That was the American, growing more and more irate.

'Jeanie has shortbread.' That was the shorter of two elderly women in hiking gear. 'I'm Ethel, and Hazel and I have been here a week now. We know she made it, a big tin. Hazel and I ate three pieces each last night, and we're looking forward to more. If you could just find it… Oh, and Hazel needs a hot-water bottle. Her bunion's playing up. I told her she should have seen the doctor before she came but would she listen? She's ready for a drop of whisky, too. When did you say Jeanie would be back?'

He'd assumed Jeanie had some help. Someone other than just her. These people were acting as if Jeanie were their personal servant. What the…?

'I'll ring the village and get whisky delivered,' he said and the American fixed him with a death stare.

'That's not good enough, man. It should be here now.'

'We've had a problem.'

'Is something the matter with Jeanie?' The lady called Ethel switched to concern, closely followed by visions of disaster. 'Where is she? And the whisky? You've lost it? Were you robbed? Is Jeanie hurt? Oh, she's such a sweetheart. If anything happened to her, we'd never forgive ourselves. Hazel, Jeanie's been hurt. Oh, but if it's robbery, should we stay here…?'

'It's not robbery.'

'It'll be that father of hers,' Hazel volunteered. 'He came when we were here last year, blustering his way in, demanding money. He took her whisky. Oh, she'll be mortified, poor lass.'

'But where's *our* whisky?' the American demanded and Hazel swung around and raised her purse.

'If you say one more word about whisky when our Jeanie's in trouble, this'll come down on your head,' she told him. 'My bunion's killing me and I could use something to hit. Meanwhile Mr… Mr…' She eyed Alasdair with curiosity.

'McBride,' Alasdair told her.

And with the word, the elderly lady's face sagged into relief. 'You're family? Oh, we're so glad. Ethel and I worry about her being here in this place all alone. We didn't know she had anyone. Is she really all right?'

'I… Yes. She just…needs to stay in the village tonight. For personal reasons.'

'Well, why shouldn't she?' the lady demanded. 'All the times we've stayed here, we've never known her to take a night off, and she works so hard. But we can help. The doggies need their dinner, don't you, doggies? And we can make our own hot-water bottles. If you light the fire in the sitting room, Ethel and I will feed the doggies and find the shortbread. Oh, and we'll take the breakfast orders, too, so you'll have them all ready.' Her face suddenly puckered. 'But if Jeanie's not back by the morning...Ethel and I come for Jeanie's porridge. We can cope without whisky but not without our porridge.'

The guests headed to the village for dinner, and by the time they returned Alasdair had whisky waiting. It wasn't enough to keep the Americans happy, but the couple had only booked for one night and for one night Alasdair could cope with bluster.

But one night meant one morning. Breakfast. Ethel and Hazel had handed him the menus, beaming confidence. He'd glanced through them and thought there was nothing wrong with toast.

He couldn't cope with breakfast—and why should he? This marriage farce was over. All he had to do was accept it. He could contact the chopper pilot, get him here first thing and be back in Edinburgh by mid-morning.

He'd be back in charge of his life—but Hazel and Ethel wouldn't get their porridge and the Duncairn empire was finished.

He glanced again at the menus. Porridge, gourmet omelettes, black pudding...Omelettes were easy, surely. Didn't you just break eggs into a pan and stir? But black pudding! He didn't know where to start.

Did Jeanie do it all? Didn't she have anyone to help?

The memory flooded back of Jeanie in the car. What had he said to her? That his car was...'*blocking your profits...*'

The moment he'd said it he'd seen the colour drain from her face. The slap had shocked her more than it had shocked him.

An undischarged bankruptcy?

He didn't know anything about her.

What had she said? *'This is a business deal. If you're buying, Alasdair McBride, surely you should have checked out the goods.'*

He'd set Elspeth onto a background check. Yes, he should have done it weeks ago but he'd assumed...

Okay, he'd assumed the worst—that Jeanie was as money-grubbing as her ex-husband. It had just seemed a fact.

He thought back to the one time—the only time—he'd seen Jeanie together with Alan. They'd just married. Alan had brought his new bride to the head offices of the Duncairn Corporation and introduced her with pride.

'Isn't she gorgeous?' he'd demanded of Alasdair and Alasdair had looked at Jeanie's short, short skirt and the leather jacket and boots and the diamond earrings and he'd felt nothing but disgust. The demure secretary he'd seen working with Eileen had been a front, he'd thought. The transformation made him wonder just how much his grandmother had been conned.

He was about to find out. 'You know what this means,' Alan had told him. 'I'm respectable now. The old lady thinks the sun shines out of Jeanie. She's already rethinking the money side of this business. Half this company should be mine and you know it. Now Eileen's thinking it, too.'

Eileen hadn't been thinking it, but she had settled an enormous amount on the pair of them. 'It's easier than to have the inheritance of the company split when I die, and Jeanie's excellent with money. She'll manage it.'

The next time he'd seen Jeanie, she'd been back here and his grandmother had been dying. There'd been no sign of the tight-fitting clothes or the jewels then. There'd been no sign of the brittle, would-be sophisticate—and there'd been no sign of the money.

On impulse he headed upstairs to the room his grand-mother had kept as her own. Eileen had spent little time here but when she'd known her time was close she'd wanted to come back. He had to clear it out—sometime. Not now. All he wanted to do now was look.

He entered, wincing a little at the mounds of soft pillows, at the billowing pink curtains, at the windows open wide to let in the warm evening air. Jeanie must still be caring for it. All signs of the old lady's illness had gone but the room was still Eileen's. Eileen's slippers were still beside the bed.

There were two photographs on the dresser. One was of him, aged about twelve, holding his first big salmon. He looked proud fit to burst. The other was of Alan and Jeanie on their wedding day.

Jeanie was holding a posy of pink roses. She was wearing a dress similar to the one she had on today. Alan was beaming at the camera, hugging Jeanie close, his smile almost…triumphant.

Jeanie just looked embarrassed.

So the tarty clothes had come after the wedding, he thought.

So the marriage to Alan had been almost identical to the one she'd gone through today?

Maybe it was. After all, he was just another McBride.

He swore and crossed to Eileen's desk, feeling more and more confused. The foundations he'd been so sure of were suddenly decidedly shaky.

What he was looking for was front and centre—a bound ledger, the type he knew Eileen kept for every transaction she had to deal with. This was the castle ledger, dealing with the day-to-day running of the estate. Jeanie would have another one, he knew, but, whatever she did, Eileen always kept a personal account.

He flicked through until he found the payroll.

Over the past couple of months there'd been a few on the castle staff. There'd been nurses, help from the village, the staff Alasdair had seen when he'd come to visit her. But before that... Leafing through, he could find only two entries. One was for Mac, the gillie. Mac had been gillie here for fifty years and must be close to eighty now. He was still on full wages, though he must be struggling.

The castle wasn't running as a farm. The cattle were here mostly to keep the grass down, but still... He thought of the great rhododendron drive. It had been clipped since the funeral. There was no way Mac could have done such a thing, and yet there was no mention of anyone else being paid to do it.

Except Jeanie? Jeanie, who was the only other name in the book? Jeanie, who was being paid less than Mac? Substantially less.

What was a good wage for a housekeeper? He had a housekeeper in Edinburgh and he paid her more than this—to keep house for one man.

His phone rang. Elspeth.

'That was fast,' he told her, but in truth he was starting to suspect that what she had to find was easy. He could have found it out himself, he thought. His dislike of Alan had stopped him enquiring, but now... Did he want to hear?

'I thought I'd catch you before you start enjoying your wedding night,' Elspeth said and he could hear her smiling. 'By the way, did you want more of those financial records sent down? I'm not sure what you're worried about. If you tell me, I can help look.'

'I'm not worried about the business right now,' he growled and heard Elspeth's shocked silence. What a statement!

But she regrouped fast. She was good, was Elspeth. 'I've been busy but this has been relatively simple,' she told him. 'From what I've found there's nothing to get in the way of having a very good time. No criminal record. Nothing. There's just one major hiccup in her past.'

And he already knew it. 'Bankruptcy?'

'You knew?'

'I… Yes.' But how long for? Some things weren't worth admitting, even to Elspeth. 'But not the details. Tell me what you have. As much as you have.'

'Potted history,' she said. Elspeth had worked for him for years and she knew he'd want facts fast. 'Jeanie Lochlan was born twenty-nine years ago, on Duncairn. Her father is supposedly a fisherman, but his boat's been a wreck for years. Her mother sounds like she was a bit of a doormat.'

'Where did you get this information?' he demanded, startled. This wasn't facts and figures.

'Where does one get all local information?' He could hear her smiling. 'The post office is closed today, so I had to use the publican, but he had time for a chat. Jeanie's mother died when she was sixteen. Her father proceeded to try to drink himself to death and he's still trying. The local view is that he'll be pickled and stuck on the bar stool forever.'

So far he knew…well, some of this. He knew she was local. 'So…' he said cautiously.

'When she was seventeen Jeanie got a special dispensation to marry another fisherman, an islander called Rory Craig,' Elspeth told him. 'I gather she went out with him from the time her mam died. By all reports it was a solid marriage but no kids. She worked in the family fish shop until Rory drowned when his trawler sank. She was twenty-three.'

And that was more of what he hadn't known about. The details of the first marriage. He'd suspected…

He'd suspected wrong.

'I guess she wouldn't be left all that well-off after that marriage,' he ventured and got a snort for his pains.

'Small family fishing business, getting smaller. The trawler sank with no insurance.'

'How did you get all this?' he demanded again.

'Easy,' Elspeth said blithely. 'I told the publican I was a reporter from Edinburgh and had heard Lord Alasdair of Duncairn was marrying an islander. He was happy to tell me everything—in fact, I gather the island's been talking of nothing else for weeks. Anyway, Rory died and then she met your cousin. You must know the rest.'

'Try me.'

'You mean you don't?'

'Eileen didn't always tell me…' In fact, she'd never told Alasdair anything about Alan. There'd been animosity between the boys since childhood and Eileen had walked a fine line in loving both. 'And Jeanie keeps herself to herself.'

'Okay. It seems your gorgeous cousin visited the island to visit his gran—probably to ask for money, if the company ledgers are anything to go by. He met Jeanie, he took her off the island and your grandmother paid him to marry her.'

'I…beg your pardon?'

'I'm good,' she said smugly. 'But this was easy, too. I asked Don.'

Don.

Alasdair had controlled the day-to-day running of the firm for years now, but Don had been his grandparents' right-hand man since well before Alasdair's time. The old man still had a massive office, with the privileges that went with it. Alasdair had never been overly fond of him, often wondering what he was paid for, but his place in his grandparents' affections guaranteed his place in the company, and gossip was what he lived for.

'So Don says…' Elspeth started, and Alasdair thought, This is just more gossip, I should stop her—but he didn't. 'Don says soon after Alan met Jeanie, he took her to Morocco. Eileen must have been worried because she went to visit—and Alan broke down and told her the mess he was in. He was way over his head, with gambling debts that'd make your eyes water. He'd gone to the castle to try to escape his creditors—that's when he met Jeanie—and then he'd decided to go back to Morocco and try to gamble his way out of trouble. You can imagine how that worked. But he hadn't told Jeanie. She still had stars in her eyes—so Eileen decided to sort it.'

'How did she sort it?' But he already knew the answer.

'I'd guess you know.' Elspeth's words echoed his thoughts. 'That was when she pulled that second lot of funds from the company, but she gave it to Alan on the understanding that no more was coming. She was sure Jeanie could save him from himself, and of course Alan made promise after promise he never intended to keep. I'm guessing Eileen felt desperate. You know how she loved your cousin, and she saw Jeanie as the solution. Anyway, after his death Eileen would have helped Jeanie again— Don says she felt so guilty she made herself ill—but Jeanie wouldn't have any of it. She had herself declared bankrupt. She accepted a minimal wage from Eileen to run the castle, and that's it. End of story as far as Don knows it.' She paused. 'But, Alasdair, is this important? And if it is, why didn't you ask Don before you married her? Why didn't you ask *her*?'

Because I'm stupid.

No, he thought grimly. It wasn't that. He'd known Alan gambled. He knew the type of people Alan mixed with. If he'd enquired… If he'd known for sure that Jeanie was exactly the same as Alan was, with morals somewhere between a sewer rat and pond scum, he'd never have been able to marry her.

Except he had believed that. He'd tried to suppress it, for the good of the company, for the future of the estate, but at the back of his mind he'd branded her the same as he'd branded Alan.

'She still married him,' he found himself muttering. How inappropriate was it to talk like this to his secretary about…his wife? But he was past worrying about appropriateness. He was feeling sick. 'She must have been a bit like him.'

'Don said Eileen said she was a sweet young thing who was feeling trapped after her husband died,' Elspeth said. 'She was working all hours, for Eileen when your grandmother was on the island but also for the local solicitor, and cleaning in her husband's family's fish shop as well. Being paid peanuts. Trying to pay off the debt left after her husband's trawler sank with no insurance. She was bleak and she was broke. Don thinks Alan simply seduced her off the island. You know how charming Alan was.'

He knew.

He sat at the chair in front of Eileen's dresser and stared at himself in the mirror. The face that looked back at him was gaunt.

What had he done?

'But it's lovely that you've married her,' Elspeth said brightly now. 'Doesn't she deserve a happy ending? Don said she made Eileen's last few months so happy.'

She had, he conceded. He'd been a frequent visitor to the castle as his grandmother neared the end, and every time he'd found Jeanie acting as nursemaid. Reading to her. Massaging her withered hands. Just sitting…

And he'd thought… He'd thought…

Yeah, when the will was read he'd expected Jeanie to be mentioned.

That was what Alan would have done—paid court to a dying woman.

'Is there anything else you need?' Elspeth asked.

Was there anything else he needed? He breathed out a few times and thought about it.

'Yes,' he said at last.

'I'm here to serve.' He almost smiled at that. Elspeth was fifty and bossy and if he pushed her one step too far she'd push back again.

'I need a recipe for black pudding,' he told her.

'Really?'

'Really.'

'I'll send it through. Anything else?'

'Maybe a recipe for humble pie as well,' he told her. 'And maybe I need that first.'

CHAPTER FIVE

MIDNIGHT. THE WITCHING HOUR. Normally Jeanie was so tired that the witches could do what they liked; she couldn't give a toss. Tonight the witches were all in her head, and they were giving her the hardest time of her life.

'You idiot. You king-size madwoman. To walk back into the McBride realm…'

Shut up, she told her witches, but they were ranting and she lay in the narrow cot in Maggie's tiny attic and held her hands to her ears and thought she was going mad.

Something hit the window.

That'll be more witches trying to get in, she told herself and buried her head under the pillow.

Something else hit the window. It sounded like a shower of gravel.

Rory used to do this, so many years ago, when he wanted to talk to her and her father was being…her father.

The ghost of Rory? That's all I need, she thought, but then another shower hit the window and downstairs Maggie's Labrador hit the front door and started barking, a bark that said terrorists and stun grenades were about to launch through the windows and a dog had to do its duty. Wake up and fight, the dog was saying to everyone in the house. No, make that everyone in the village.

There was an oath from Maggie's husband in the room

under Jeanie's, and, from the kids' room, a child began to cry.

And she thought…

No, she didn't want to think. This was nothing to do with her. She lay with her blanket pulled up to her nose as she heard Maggie's husband clump down the stairs and haul the door open.

'What do you think you're doing?' Dougal's shout was as loud as his dog's bark. 'McBride… It's McBride, isn't it? What the hell…? You might be laird of this island, but if you think you can skulk round our property… You've woken the bairns. Shut up!' The last words were a roar, directed at the dog, but it didn't work the way Dougal intended. From under her window came a chorus of frenzied barks in response.

Uh-oh. Jeanie knew those barks. Abbot and Costello! Alasdair was here and he'd brought Eileen's dogs for the ride.

And then it wasn't just Maggie's dog and Eileen's dogs. The neighbours' dog started up in response, and then the dogs from the next house along, and then the whole village was erupting in a mass of communal barking.

Lights were going on. Maggie's two kids were screaming. She could hear a child start up in the house next door.

Should I stay under the pillows? Jeanie thought. It had to be the wisest course.

'I need to speak to my wife.' It was Alasdair, struggling to make himself heard above the din.

His wife. She needed more pillows—the pillows she had didn't seem to be effective.

'Jeanie?' That was Maggie, roaring up the stairs. 'Jeanie!'

'I'm asleep!'

'Jeanie, you know how much I love you, but your man's

roaring in the street and he's woken the bairns. Either you face him or I will, and if it's me, it won't be pretty.'

Alasdair wasn't roaring in the street, Jeanie thought helplessly, but everyone else was. Everyone in Duncairn would know that the Earl of Duncairn was under Maggie's window—wanting his wife.

Everyone knew everything on this island, she thought bitterly as she hauled on jeans and a sweatshirt and headed downstairs. Why broadcast more? As if the whole mess wasn't bad enough... She didn't want to meet him. She did not. She'd had enough of the McBrides to last her a lifetime.

Dougal was still in the doorway, holding the dog back. He'd stopped shouting, but as she appeared he looked at her in concern. 'You sure you want to go out there, lass?'

She glowered. 'Maggie says I have to.'

There was a moment's pause while they both thought about it. 'Then better to do what Maggie says,' he said at last. Dougal was a man of few words and he'd used most of them on Alasdair. 'Tell him to quiet the dogs. I'll be here waiting. Any funny business and I'm a call away. And don't be going out there in bare feet.'

Her shoes were in the attic, two flights of stairs away. At home...at the castle...she always left a pair of wellies at the back door, but here it hadn't been worth her unpacking.

The only Wellingtons on the doorstep were Dougal's fishing boots.

But a girl had to do what a girl had to do. She shoved her feet into Dougal's vast fishing wellies and went to meet her...her husband.

He'd found out where Maggie lived. That had been easy— the island boasted one slim phone book with addresses included. He hadn't meant or wanted to wake the house but she'd told him she'd be sleeping in the attic. All he'd wanted was for her to put her head out to investigate the shower of stones, he'd signal her down and they could talk.

The plan hadn't quite worked. Now the whole village was waiting for them to talk, and the village wasn't happy. But as a collective, the village was interested.

'Have you run away already, love?' The old lady living over the road from Maggie's was hanging out of the window with avid interest. 'Well, it's what we all expected. Don't you go letting him sweet-talk you back to his castle. Just because he's the laird… There's generations of lairds had their way with the likes of us. Don't you be trusting him one inch.'

She might not be trusting him, he thought, but at least she was walking towards him. She was wearing jeans, an oversize windcheater and huge fishermen's boots. Her curls were tumbled around her face. By the light of the street lamp she looked young, vulnerable…and scared.

Heck, he wasn't an ogre. He wasn't even really a laird. 'Jeanie…'

'You'd better hush the dogs,' she told him. 'Why on earth did you bring them?'

'Because when I tried to leave they started barking exactly as they're barking now.' He needed to be calm, but he couldn't help the note of exasperation creeping in. 'And your guests have already had to make do with half a shelf of whisky instead of a full one, and bought biscuits instead of home-made. What did you do with the shortbread? If the dogs keep barking, we'll have the castle empty by morning.'

'Does that matter?' But she walked across to the SUV and yanked open the door. 'Shush,' she said. They shushed.

It was no wonder they shushed. Her tone said don't mess with me and the dogs didn't. She was small and cute and fierce—and the gaze she turned on him was lethal.

She glowered and then hesitated, glancing up at the lit

window over the road. 'It's all right, Mrs McConachie, I have him... I have things under control. Sorry for the disturbance, people. You can all go back to bed now. Close your windows, nothing to see.'

'You tell him, Jeanie,' someone shouted, and there was general laughter and the sound of assorted dogs faded to silence again.

But she was still glowering. She was looking at him as if he were five-day-old fish that had dared infiltrate the immaculate castle refrigerators.

Speaking of food... Why not start off on neutral territory?

'I don't know how to make black pudding,' he told her and her face stilled. The glare muted a little, as if something else was struggling to take its place. Okay. Keep it practical, he told himself, and he soldiered on. 'Two of your guests, Mr and Mrs Elliot from Battersea, insist they want black pudding for their breakfast. And Ethel and Hazel want porridge.'

'Hector and Margaret adore their black pudding,' she said neutrally, and he thought, Excellent, this was obviously the way to lead into the conversation they had to have.

'So how do you make it?'

'I don't. Mrs Stacy on the north of the island makes them for me and she gets her blood from the island butcher. I have puddings hanging in the back larder. You slice and fry at need. The shortbread's on top of the dresser—I put it where I can't reach it without the step stool because otherwise I'll be the size of a house. The porridge is more complicated—you need to be careful not to make it lumpy but there are directions on the Internet. I'm sure you can manage.'

'I can't.'

'Well, then...' She stood back, hands on her hips, looking as if he was a waste of space for admitting he couldn't make porridge. 'That's sad, but the guests need to find somewhere else as a base to do their hill climbing. They might as well get disgusted about their lack of black pudding and porridge tomorrow, and start looking elsewhere immediately.'

Uh-oh. This wasn't going the way he'd planned. She looked as if she was about to turn on her heels and retreat. 'Jeanie, there was a reason you agreed to marry me.' He needed to get things back on a sensible course now. 'Believe it or not, it's still the right thing to do. It was a good decision. You can't walk away.'

'The decision to marry? The right thing?'

'I believe it still is, even though…even though your reasons weren't what I thought they were. But long-term, it still seems sensible.'

'It did seem sensible.' She still sounded cordial, he thought, which had to be a good sign, or at least she still seemed neutral. But then she continued: 'But that was before I realised you think I'm a gold-digging harpy who's spent the last three years sucking up to Eileen so I can inherit the castle. Or maybe I did know that, but it got worse. It was before you inferred I'd married twice for money, three times if you count marrying you. You thought I was a tart the first time you saw me and—'

'I didn't.'

'Come off it. When Alan introduced us you looked like you'd seen lesser things crawl out of cheese. I concede the way I was dressed might have swayed you a little—'

'A little!' He still remembered how he'd felt as Alan had ushered her into his office. Appalled didn't begin to cut it.

'Alan said it was a joke,' she told him, a hint of defensiveness suddenly behind her anger. 'He said you were a judgemental prude, let's give you a heart attack. He said you were expecting him to marry a tart so let's show him one. I was embarrassed to death but Alan wanted to do it and I was naïve and I thought I was in love and I went along with it. It even seemed…funny. It wasn't funny, I admit. It was tacky. But Alan was right. You were judgemental. You still are. Eileen kept telling me you were nice underneath but then she loved Alan, too. So now I've been talked into doing something against my better judgement—again. It has to stop and it's stopping now. I'll get the marriage annulled. That's it. If you don't mind, my bed's waiting and you have oats to soak. Or not. Lumpy porridge or none at all, it's up to you. I don't care.'

And she turned and walked away.

Or she would have walked away if she hadn't been wearing men's size-thirteen Wellington boots. There was a rut in the pavement, her floppy toe caught and she lurched. She flailed wildly, fighting for balance, but she was heading for asphalt.

He caught her before she hit the ground. His arms went round her; he swung her high into his arms and steadied. For one moment he held her—he just held.

She gasped and wriggled. He set her on her feet again but for that moment…for that one long moment there'd been an almost irresistible urge to keep right on holding.

In the olden days a man could choose a mate according to his status in the tribe, he thought wryly. He could exert a bit of testosterone, show a little muscle and carry his woman back to his cave. Every single thing about that concept was wrong, but for that fleeting moment, as he held her, as he felt how warm, how slight, how yielding her body was, the urge was there, as old as time itself.

And as dumb.

But she'd felt it, too—that sudden jolt of primeval need. She steadied and backed, her hands held up as if to ward him off.

Behind them the door swung open. Dougal was obviously still watching through the window and he'd seen everything. 'You want me to come out, love?'

'It's okay, Dougal.' She sounded as if she was struggling for composure and that made two of them. 'I…just tripped in your stupid wellies.'

'They're great wellies.' That was Maggie, calling over Dougal's shoulder. 'They're special ones I bought for his birthday. They cost a fortune.'

'I think they're nice, too,' Alasdair added helpfully and she couldn't help but grin. She fought to turn it back into a glower.

'Don't you dare make me laugh.'

'I couldn't.'

'You could. Go away. I'm going to bed.'

Enough. He had to say it. 'Jeanie, please come back to the castle,' he said, pride disappearing as the gravity of the next few moments hit home. 'You're right, I've been a judgemental fool. I've spent the last few hours trawling through Eileen's financial statements. I can see exactly what she has and hasn't given you. I can see what a mess Alan left you in. I can see…what you've given Eileen.'

She stilled. 'I don't know what you mean.'

'For the last three years you've made this castle a home for her,' he told her. 'I know Eileen's official home was in Edinburgh, and she still spent too much time in the office, trying to keep her fingers on the company's financial affairs. But whenever she could, she's been here. When she became ill she was here practically full-time, only returning to Edinburgh long enough to reassure me there was no need for me to keep an eye on her. I thought she was staying here because she needed to keep an eye on you. I thought this was simply another financial enterprise. But tonight I spent a little time with your guests and some rather good whisky—'

'I didn't leave any good stuff behind.'

'I made an emergency dash. I spent a little time with them and they talked about why they've come back every year since you started running the B & B. They talked about how they and my grandmother talked about you and they talked about fun. How you and Eileen enjoyed each other's company, but that they'd always been welcome to join you. How Eileen sat in the library like a queen every night and presided over the whisky and talked about the estate as it's been, about my grandfather's ancestors and hers. It seems it didn't matter how often they heard it, they still loved it. And they talked about you, Jeanie, always in the background, always quietly careful that Eileen didn't do too much, that she didn't get cold, that she didn't trip on her stupid dogs. And then I looked at the wages and saw how little you've been paid. And Elspeth...'

'Who's Elspeth?' She sounded winded.

'My secretary. I asked her to do some long-overdue background checks. With the information you gave me this afternoon the rest was easy to find. She tells me that, as well as almost killing you that last night in his unpaid-for sports car, Alan died in debt up to his ears. He left you committed to paying them, even though most of them were to gambling houses and casinos. But somehow you seem to have become jointly responsible. I know Eileen would have paid them off, but they were vast debts, eye-watering debts, and you refused to let her help. You declared yourself bankrupt and then you accepted a minimal wage to stay on at the castle.'

'You have—'

'Been learning. Yes, I have. I've learned that this marriage arrangement gives you one more year in the castle but that's all it gives you. I'm still not sure why you agreed to marry me, but I'm pathetically grateful you did. Jeanie, I'm so sorry I misjudged you. Please come home.'

'It's not my home.'

'It is a home, though,' he said, gently now. 'That's what I didn't get. You made it Eileen's home and for that I can never thank you enough.'

'I don't want your thanks. Eileen let me stay. That was enough.'

'And I know I don't have the right, but I'm asking you to stay longer.'

'But not as your wife.'

'Legally as my wife. We both know that's sensible.'

'I don't do…sensible. I'm not very good at it. I have three dumb marriages to prove it.'

'Then do gut instinct,' he told her. 'Do what you think's right. Think back to the reasons you married me in the first place.'

'That's blackmail again.'

'It's not. I know I stand to gain a fortune by this transaction. You stand to gain nothing. That's what I hadn't understood. But we can work things out. If the company ends up in my name, I can buy the castle from the bankruptcy trustees. I intended to buy it from you anyway, but I can arrange for you to be paid more—'

'I don't want anything,' she snapped. 'Don't you get it? Don't you understand that there's nothing you can offer me that I want?'

'You do want another year in the castle. At the end of the year—'

'Don't even say it,' she told him. 'I will not be bought.'

Silence. What else could he say?

He could fix things if she let him. Duncairn Enterprises was extensive enough to soak up the purchase of the castle at market price. He could also settle a substantial amount on Jeanie when her bankruptcy was discharged, but he knew instinctively that saying that now would count for nothing. Right now, he had enough sense to know it would make things worse.

This woman—*his wife*—had married for a reason. She knew the good the company did. She knew how much the castle and the company meant to Eileen. He just had to hope those reasons were still strong enough.

'Jeanie, do you really want to get on that ferry tomorrow?' he asked. 'The dogs want you back at the castle. The guests want you. This does seem like cutting off your nose to spite your face. Please?'

'So…it's not just the porridge.'

'Not even the black pudding.'

'Alasdair…'

'There'll be no strings,' he said and held up his hands. 'I promise. Things will be as you imagined them when you agreed to this deal. You'll have a year's employment. You can use the year to sort what you want to do next and then you can walk away. There'll be no obligation on either of our parts.'

'No more insults?'

'I won't even comment on your footwear.'

She managed to smile again at that. It was faint but it was there.

And then there was silence. It was so deep and so long that Dougal opened the door again. He stood uncertainly on the doorstep. He made to say something but didn't. The silence lengthened. Finally he was dragged inside again by Maggie.

Maggie, at least, must understand the value of silence, Alasdair thought. The last light went off inside. Even if, as Alasdair suspected, Maggie was still lurking, she was giving them the pretence that they were alone.

The night was still and warm. The numbers of nights like this on Duncairn could be counted on less than a man's fingers. Everyone should be out tonight, he thought. The stars were hanging brilliant in the sky, as if they existed in a separate universe from the stars he struggled to see back in Edinburgh. The tide was high and he could hear the waves slapping against the harbour wall. Before dawn the harbour would be a hive of activity as the island's fishermen set to sea, but for now the village had settled back to sleep. There was no one here but this woman, standing still and watchful.

Trying to make her mind up whether to go or stay.

'Can I have the dogs?' she said at last, and he blinked.

'The dogs?'

'At the end of the year. That's been the thing that's hurt most. I haven't had time to find a job where I can keep them, and I can't see them living in an apartment in Edinburgh with you. If I stay, I'll have twelve months to source a job where they can come with me.'

'You'd agree to keeping on with the marriage,' he said, cautiously because it behoved a man to be cautious, 'for the dogs?'

'What other reason would there be?'

'For the company? So Duncairn Enterprises will survive?'

'That's your reason, not mine. Dogs or nothing, My Lord.'

'Don't call me that.'

She tilted her chin. 'I need something to hold on to,' she said. 'I need the dogs.'

He stared around at the two dogs with their heads hanging out of the window. Abbot was staring down at the road as if considering jumping. He wouldn't. Alasdair had been around this dog long enough to know a three-foot jump in Abbot's mind constituted suicide.

A moth was flying round Costello's nose. Costello's nose was therefore circling, too, as if he was thinking of snapping. He wouldn't do that, either. Risk wasn't in these two dogs' make-up and neither was intelligence.

'They're dumb,' he said, feeling dumbfounded himself.

'I like dumb. You know where you are with dumb. Dumb doesn't leave room for manipulation.'

'Jeanie…'

'Dumb or not, it's yes or no. A year at the castle, no insults, the dogs—and respect for my privacy. The only way this can work is if you keep out of my way and I keep out of yours.'

'We do still need to share the castle.'

'Yes, we do,' she agreed. 'But you'll be treated as a guest.'

'You mean you'll make the porridge?'

Her expression softened a little. 'I kind of like making it,' she admitted.

'So we have a deal?'

'No more insults?' she demanded.

'I can't think of a single insult to throw.'

'Then go home,' she told him. 'I'll be there before breakfast.'

'Won't you come back now?'

'Not with you,' she said flatly. 'I'll follow separately, when I'm ready. From now on, Alasdair McBride, this is the way we do things. Separately or not at all.'

How was a man to sleep after that? He lay in the great four-poster bed in the opulent rooms his grandmother had done up for him during the renovation and he kept thinking…of Jeanie.

Why hadn't his grandmother told him of her plight?

Because he'd never asked, he conceded. Eileen had known of the bad blood between the cousins. Revealing the mess Alan had left Jeanie in would have meant revealing even more appalling things of Alan than he already knew.

So she'd let him think Jeanie was a gold-digger?

No. Eileen wouldn't have dreamed he'd think Jeanie was

mercenary, he conceded, because anyone who met Jeanie would know that such a thing was impossible.

Except him. He'd met her, he'd judged her and he'd kept on judging her. He'd made the offer of marriage based on the assumption that she was out for what she could get, and he'd nearly destroyed his chances of success in doing it.

Worse, he'd hurt her. He'd hurt a woman who'd done the right thing by Eileen. A woman Eileen had loved. A woman who'd agreed to a marriage because…because he'd told her of the charities Duncairn supported? Because she could spend another year acting as a low-paid housekeeper? Because she loved two dopey dogs?

Or because she'd known Eileen would have wanted him to inherit. The realisation dawned as clear as if it were written in the stars.

She'd done it for Eileen.

Eileen had loved her and he could see why. She was a woman worthy of…

Loving?

The word was suddenly there, front and centre, and it shocked him.

Surely he was only thinking of it in relation to Eileen— but for the moment, lying back in bed in the great castle of his ancestors, he let the concept drift. Why had Eileen loved her?

Because she was kind and loyal and warm-hearted. Because she loved Eileen's dogs—why, for heaven's sake? Because she was small and cute and curvy and her chuckle was infectious.

There was nothing in that last thought that would have made Eileen love her, he decided, but it surely came to play in Alasdair's mind.

When she'd almost fallen, when he'd picked her up and held her, he'd felt…he'd felt…

As if she was his wife?

And so she was, he thought, and maybe it was the vows he'd made in the kirk so few hours ago that made him feel like this. He'd thought he could make them without meaning them, but now…

She was coming back here. His wife.

And if he made one move on her, she'd run a mile. He knew it. Alan had treated her like dirt and so had he. Today he'd insulted her so deeply that she'd run. This year could only work if it was business only.

He had to act on it.

There was a whine under the bed and Abbot slunk out and put his nose on the pillow. The dogs should be sleeping in the wet room. That was where their beds were but when he'd tried to lock them in they'd whined and scratched and finally he'd relented. Were they missing Jeanie?

He relented a bit more now and made the serious mistake of scratching Abbot's nose. Within two seconds he had two spaniels draped over his bed, squirming in ecstasy, then snuggling down and closing their eyes very firmly—*We're asleep now, don't disturb us.*

'Dumb dogs,' he told them but he didn't push them off. They'd definitely be missing Jeanie, he thought, and he was starting—very strongly—to understand why.

Why was she heading back to the castle? She was out of her mind.

But she'd packed her gear back into her car and now she was halfway across the island. Halfway home?

That was what the castle felt like. Home. Except it wasn't, she told herself. It had been her refuge after the Alan disaster. She'd allowed Eileen to talk her into staying on, but three years were three years too many. She'd fallen in love with the place. With Duncairn.

With the Duncairn estate and all it entailed?

That meant Alasdair, she reminded herself, and she

most certainly hadn't fallen in love with Alasdair. He was cold and judgemental. He'd married her for money, and he deserved nothing from her but disdain.

But he'd caught her when she'd fallen and he'd felt… he'd felt…

'Yeah, he'd felt like any over-testosteroned male in a kilt would make you feel,' she snapped out loud.

Her conversation with herself was nuts. She had the car windows open and she'd had to stop. Some of the scraggy, tough, highland sheep had chosen to snooze for the night in the middle of the road. They were moving but they were taking their time. Meanwhile they were looking at her curiously—listening in on her conversation? She needed someone to talk to, she decided, and the sheep would do.

'I'm doing this for your sakes,' she told them. 'If I go back to the castle, he can buy it from the bankruptcy trustees at the end of the year and it'll stay in the family.'

Maybe he'll let me stay on as caretaker even then?

That was a good thought, but did she want to stay as housekeeper/caretaker at Duncairn for the rest of her life?

'Yes,' she said out loud, so savagely that the sheep nearest her window leaped back with alarm.

'No,' she corrected herself, but maybe that was the wrong answer, too. That was the dangerous part of her talking. That was the part of her that had chafed against being part of Rory's family business, doing the books, cleaning the fish shop, aching to get off the island and do something exciting.

Well, she had done something exciting, she told herself bitterly. She'd met and married Alan and she'd had all the excitement a girl could want and more.

'So it's back in your box to you, Jeanie McBride,' she told herself and thought briefly about her name. Jeanie McBride. She was that. She was Alan's widow.

She was Alasdair's wife.

'At the end of the year I'm going back to being Jeanie Lochlan,' she told the last sheep as it finally ambled off the road. 'Meanwhile I'm going back to being house-keeper at Duncairn, chief cook and bottle washer for a year. I'm going back to taking no risks. The only thing that's changed for the next twelve months is that the house has one permanent guest. That guest is Alasdair McBride but any trouble from him and he's out on his ear.'

And you'll kick him out how?

'I won't need to,' she told the sheep. 'I hold all the cards.

'For a year,' she reminded herself, wishing the sheep could talk back. 'And for a year…well, Alasdair McBride might be the Earl of Duncairn but he's in no position to lord it over me. For the next year I know my place, and he'd better know his.'

CHAPTER SIX

ALASDAIR WOKE AT DAWN to find the dogs had deserted him. That had to be a good sign, he told himself, but he hadn't heard Jeanie return.

His room was on the ocean side of the castle. The massive stone walls would mean the sound of a car approaching from the land side wouldn't have woken him.

That didn't mean she was here, though.

He wanted—badly—to find out. The future of Duncairn rested on the outcome of the next few minutes but for some reason he couldn't bear to know.

He opened his laptop. He didn't even know if she'd returned but it paid a man to be prepared.

It paid a man to hope?

By eight o'clock he'd formed a plan of action. He'd made a couple of phone calls. He'd done some solid work, but the silence in the castle was starting to do his head in. He couldn't put it off any longer. He dressed and headed down the great staircase, listening for noise—listening for Jeanie?

He pushed open the door to the dining room and was met by...normal. Normal?

He'd been in this room often but this morning it was as if he were seeing it for the first time. Maybe it was because last night he'd almost lost it—or maybe it was because this morning it was the setting for Jeanie. Or he hoped it was.

Regardless, it was some setting. The castle after Eileen's amazing restoration was truly luxurious, but Eileen—and Jeanie, her right-hand assistant—had never lost sight of the heart of the place. That heart was displayed right here. The massive stone fireplace took half a wall. A fire blazed in the hearth, a small fire by castle standards but the weather was warm and the flame was there mostly to form a heart—and maybe to form a setting for the dogs, who lay sprawled in front of it. Huge wooden beams soared above. The vast rug on the floor was an ancient design, muted yet glorious, and matching the worn floorboards to perfection.

There were guests at four of the small tables, the guests he'd given whisky to last night. They gave him polite smiles and went back to their breakfast.

Porridge, he thought, checking the tables at a glance. Black pudding. Omelettes!

Jeanie *must* be home.

And almost as he thought it, there she was, bustling in from the kitchen, apron over her jeans, her curls tied into a bouncy ponytail, her face fixed into a hostess-like beam of welcome.

'Good morning, My Lord. Your table is the one by the window. It has a fine view but the morning papers are beside it if you prefer a broader outlook. Can I fetch you coffee while you decide what you'd like for your breakfast?'

So this was the way it would be. Guest and hostess. Even the dogs hadn't stirred in welcome. Jeanie was home. They had no need of him.

Things were back to normal?

'I just need toast.'

'Surely not. We have eggs and bacon, sausages, porridge, black pudding, omelettes, pancakes, griddle cakes… whatever you want, My Lord, I can supply it. Within reason, of course.' And she pressed a menu into his hands and retreated to the kitchen.

* * *

He ate porridge. No lumps. Excellent.

He felt…extraneous. Would he be served like this for the entire year? He'd go nuts.

But he sat and read his paper until all the guests had departed, off to tramp the moors or climb the crags or whatever it was that guests did during their stay. The American couple departed for good, for which he was thankful. The rest were staying at least another night. Jeanie was obviously supplying picnic baskets and seeing each guest off on their day's adventures. He waited a few moments after the last farewell to give her time to catch her breath, and then headed to the kitchen to find her.

She was elbow deep in suds in front of the sink. Washed pots and pans were stacked up to one side. He took a dishcloth and started to dry.

'There's no need to be doing that.' She must have heard him come in but she didn't turn to look at him. 'Put the dishcloth down. This is my territory.'

'This year's a mutual business deal. We work together.'

'You've got your company's work to be doing. There's a spare room beyond the ones you're using—your grandmother set it up as a small, private library for her own use. It has a fine view of the sea. We'll need to see if the Internet reaches there—if not you can get a router in town. Hamish McEwan runs the electrical store in Duncairn. He'll come out if I call him.'

Business. Her voice was clipped and efficient.

She still hadn't looked at him.

'We need to organise more than my office,' he told her. 'For a start, we need a cleaning lady.'

'We do not!' She sounded offended. 'What could be wrong with my cleaning?'

'How many days a year do you take guests?'

'Three-sixty-five.' She said it with pride and scrubbed the pan she was working on a bit harder.

'And you do all the welcoming, the cooking, the cleaning, the bed-making...'

'What else would I do?'

'Enjoy yourself?'

'I like cleaning.'

'Jeanie?'

'Yes.'

'That pan is so shiny you can see your face in it. It's time you stopped scrubbing.'

There were no more dishes. He could see her dilemma. She needed to stop scrubbing, but that would mean turning—to face him?

He lifted the pan from her hands, set it down and took her wet hands in his.

'Jeanie...'

'Don't,' she managed and tugged back but he didn't let her go.

'Jeanie, I've just been on the phone to Maggie.'

She stilled. 'Why?'

'To talk to her about you. You didn't tell her you were coming back here. She thought you'd gone to the ferry.'

He didn't tell her what a heart-sink moment that had been. She didn't need emotion getting in the way of what he had to say now.

'I thought I'd ring her this morning.' She sounded defensive. 'I thought... To be honest, when I left Maggie's I wasn't sure where I was going. I headed out near the ferry terminal and sat and looked over the cliffs for a while. I wasn't sure if I should change my mind.' She looked down at their linked hands. 'I'm still not sure if I should.'

'You promised me you'd come back.'

'I stood in the kirk and wed you, too,' she said sharply.

'Somewhere along my life I've learned that promises are made to be broken.'

'I won't break mine.'

'Till death do us part?'

'I'll rethink that in a year.'

'You have to be kidding.' She wrenched her hands back with a jerk. 'It's rethought now. Promises mean nothing. Now if you'll excuse me, I have beds to make, a castle to dust, dogs to walk, then the forecourt to mow. You go back to sorting your electrics.'

'Jeanie, it's the first day of our honeymoon.'

'Do you not realise I'm over honeymoons?' She grabbed the pan he'd just taken from her and slammed it down on the bottom shelf so hard it bounced. 'What were you thinking? A jaunt to a six-star hotel with a casino on the side? Been there, done that.'

'I thought I'd take you out to see the puffins.'

And that shocked her. She straightened. Stared at him. Stared at him some more. 'Sorry?'

'Have you seen the puffins this year?'

'I… No.'

'Neither have I. I haven't seen the puffins since my grandfather died, and I miss them. According to Dougal, they're still there, but only just. You know they take off midsummer? Their breeding season's almost done so they'll be leaving any minute. The sea's so calm today it's like a lake. You have all the ingredients for a picnic right here and Dougal says we can use his *Mary-Jane.*'

'*Dougal will lend you his boat?*'

'It's not his fishing boat. It's just a runabout.'

'I know that, but still…he won't even trust Maggie with his boat.'

'Maybe I come with better insurance than Maggie.'

'Do you even know how to handle a boat?'

'I know how to handle a boat.'

She stared at him, incredulous, and then shook her head. 'It's a crazy idea. As I said, I have beds—'

'Beds to make. And dusting and dog-walking and grass to mow.' He raised his fingers and started ticking things off. 'First, beds and general housework. Maggie's mam is already on her way here, bringing a friend for company. They'll clean and cook a storm. They're bringing Maggie's dog, too, who Maggie assures me keeps Abbot and Costello from fretting. They'll walk all the dogs. Maggie's uncle is bringing up the rear. He'll do the mowing, help Mac check the cattle, do anything on the list you leave him. He'll be here in an hour but we should be gone by then. Our boat's waiting. Now, can I help you pack lunch?'

'No! This is crazy.'

'It's the day after your wedding. It's not crazy at all.'

'The wedding was a formality. I told you, I don't do honeymoons.'

'Or six-star hotels, or casinos. I suspected not. I also thought that if I whisked you off the island you might never come back. But, Jeanie, you do need a holiday. Three years without a break. I don't know what Eileen was thinking.'

'She knew I wouldn't take one.'

'Because you're afraid?' he said gently. He didn't move to touch her. In truth, he badly wanted to but she was so close to running... 'Because you've ventured forth twice and been burned both times? I know you agreed to marry so I could inherit, but there's also a part of you that wants another year of safe. Jeanie, don't you want to see the puffins?'

'I...'

'Come with me, Jeanie,' he said and he couldn't help himself then, he did reach out to her. He touched her cheek, a feather-light touch, a trace of finger against skin, and why it had the power to make him feel...make him feel...

As if the next two minutes were important. Really important. Would she pull away and tell him to get lost, or would she finally cut herself some slack? Come play with him…

'I shouldn't,' she whispered, but she didn't pull back.

'When did you last see puffins?'

She didn't reply. He let his hand fall, though it took effort. He wanted to keep touching. He wanted to take that look of fear from her face.

What had they done to her? he wondered. Nice, safe Rory, and low-life Alan…

There was spirit in this woman and somehow it had been crushed.

And then he thought of the slap and he thought, No, it hadn't quite been crushed. Jeanie was still under there.

'Not since I was a little girl,' she admitted. 'With my mam. Rory's uncle took us out to see them.'

'Just the once?'

'I… Yes. He took tourists, you see. There were never places—or time—to take us.'

What about your own dad? he wanted to ask. Jeanie's father was a fisherman. He'd had his own boat. Yes, it was almost two hours out to the isolated isles, the massive crags where the puffins nested, but people came from all over the world to see them. To live here and not see…

His own grandparents had taken him out every summer. When he'd turned sixteen they'd given him a boat, made sure he had the best instruction, and then they'd trusted him. When his grandfather had died he'd taken Eileen out there to scatter his ashes.

'Come with me,' he said now, gently, and she looked up at him and he could see sense and desire warring behind her eyes.

'It's not a honeymoon.'

'It's a day trip. You need a holiday so I'm organising a series of day trips.'

'More than one!'

'You deserve a month off. More. I know you won't take that. You don't trust me and we're forced to stay together and you don't want that, but for now…you've given me an amazing gift, Jeanie Lochlan. Allow me to give you something in return.'

She compressed her lips and stared up at him, trying to read his face.

'Are you safe to operate a boat out there?' she demanded at last.

'You know Dougal. Do you think he'd lend me the *Mary-Jane* if I wasn't safe?'

Dougal's uncle had taught him how to handle himself at sea. Once upon a time this island had been his second home, his refuge when life with his parents got too bad, and sailing had become his passion.

'He wouldn't,' Jeanie conceded. 'So we're going alone?'

'Yes.' He would have asked Dougal to take them if it would have made Jeanie feel safer but this weather was so good every fisherman worth his salt was putting to sea today. 'You can trust me, Jeanie. We're interested in puffins, that's all.'

'But when you touch me, I feel…'

And there it was, out in the open. This *thing* between them.

'If we're to survive these twelve months, we need to avoid personal attraction,' he told her.

Her face stilled. 'You feel it, too.'

Of course I do. He wanted to shout it, but the wariness in her eyes was enough to give a man pause. That and reason. Hell, all they needed was a hot affair, a passionate few weeks, a massive split, and this whole arrangement would be blown out of the water. Even he had the sense to see hormones needed to take a back seat.

'Jeanie, this whole year is about being sensible. You're an attractive woman...'

She snorted.

'With a great smile and a big heart,' he continued. 'And if you put a single woman and a single man together for a year, then it's inevitable that sparks will fly. But we're both old enough and sensible enough to know how to douse those sparks.'

'So that's what we're doing for the next twelve months. Dousing sparks?' She ventured a smile. 'So do I pack the fire extinguisher today?'

'If we feel the smallest spark, we hit the water. The water temperature around here is barely above freezing. That should do it. Will you come?'

There was a moment's hesitation and then: 'Foolish or not, I never could resist a puffin,' she told him. 'My only stipulation is that you don't wear a kilt. Because sparks are all very well, Alasdair McBride, but you put a kilt on that body and sparks could well turn into a wildfire.'

He was free to make of that as he willed. She turned away, grabbed a picnic basket and started to pack.

He couldn't just manage a boat; he was one with the thing.

Jeanie had been in enough boats with enough men— she'd even worked as crew on Rory's fishing trawler—to recognise a seaman when she saw one.

Who could have guessed this smooth, suave business-man from Edinburgh, this kilted lord of all he surveyed at Duncairn, was a man who seemed almost as at home at sea as the fishermen who worked the island's waters.

The *Mary-Jane* was tied at the harbour wharf when they arrived, with a note from Dougal to Alasdair taped to the bollard.

Keep in radio contact and keep her safe. And I don't mean the boat.

Alasdair had grinned, leaped lightly onto the deck and turned to help Jeanie down. She'd ignored his hand and climbed down herself—a woman had some pride. And she was being very wary of sparks.

The *Mary-Jane* was a sturdy cabin cruiser, built to take emergency supplies out to a broken-down fishing trawler, or as a general harbour runabout. She was tough and serviceable—but so was the man at the helm. He was wearing faded trousers, heavy boots and an ancient sweater. He hadn't shaved this morning. He was looking…

Don't think about how he looks, she told herself fiercely, so instead she concentrated on watching him handle the boat. The Duncairn bar was tricky. You had to know your way, but Alasdair did, steering towards the right channel, then pausing, waiting, watching the sea on the far side, judging the perfect time to cross and then nailing it so they cruised across the bar as if they'd been crossing a lake.

And as they entered open water Jeanie found herself relaxing. How long since she'd done this? Taken a day just for her? Had someone think about her?

He wanted to see the puffins himself, she told herself, but a voice inside her head corrected her.

He didn't have to do this. He didn't have to bring me. He's doing it because I need a break.

It was a seductive thought all by itself.

And the day was seductive. The sun was warm on her face. Alasdair adjusted his course so they were facing into the waves, so she hardly felt the swell—but she did feel the power of the sea beneath them, and she watched Alasdair and she thought, There's power there, too.

He didn't talk. Maybe he thought she needed silence.

She did and she was grateful. She sat and let the day, the sea, the sun soak into her.

This was as if something momentous had happened. This was as if she'd walked through a long, long tunnel and emerged to the other side.

Was it just because she'd taken the day off? Or was it that she'd set her future for the next twelve months, and for the next year she was safe?

It should be both, but she knew it wasn't. It was strange but sitting here in the sun, watching Alasdair, she had an almost overwhelming sense that she could let down her guard, lose the rigid control she'd held herself under since the appalling tragedy of Alan, let herself be just…Jeanie.

She'd lost who she was. Somewhere along the way she'd been subsumed. Jeffrey's daughter, Rory's girlfriend and wife, then Alan's woman. Then bankrupt, with half the world seeming to be after her for money owed.

Then Eileen's housekeeper.

She loved being the housekeeper at Duncairn but the role had enveloped her. It was all she was.

But today she wasn't a housekeeper. She wasn't any of her former selves. Today she was out on the open sea, with a man at the helm who was…

Her husband?

There was nothing prescribed for her today except that she enjoy herself, and suddenly who could resist? She found herself smiling. Smiling and smiling.

'A joke?' Alasdair asked softly, and she turned her full beam onto him.

'No joke. I've just remembered why I love this place. I haven't been to sea for so long. And the puffins…I can't remember. How far out?'

'You mean, are we there yet?' He grinned back and it was a grin to make a girl open her eyes a little wider. It was a killer grin. 'Isn't that what every kid in the back seat asks?'

'That's what I feel like—a kid in the back seat.' And then she looked ahead to the granite rock needles that seemed to burst from the ocean floor, isolated in their grandeur. 'No, I don't,' she corrected herself. 'I feel like I'm a front-seat passenger. It's one of these rocks, isn't it, where the puffins are found?'

'The biggest one at the back. The smaller ones are simply rock but the back one has a landmass where they can burrow for nests. They won't nest anywhere humans can reach. It means we can't land.'

'We'd need a pretty long rope ladder,' Jeanie breathed, looking at the sheer rock face in awe. And then she forgot to breathe... 'Oh-h-h.'

It was a long note of discovery. It was a note of awe.

For Alasdair had manoeuvred the boat through a gap in the island rock face and emerged to a bay of calm water. The water was steel grey, fathoms deep, and it was a mass of...

Puffins. Puffins!

Alasdair cut the motor to just enough power to keep clear of the cliffs. The motor was muted to almost nothing.

The puffins were everywhere, dotted over the sea as if someone had sprinkled confetti—only this confetti was made up of birds, duck-sized but fatter, black and white with extraordinary bright orange bills; puffins that looked exactly like the ones Jeanie had seen in so many magazines, on so many posters, but only ever once in real life and that so long ago it seemed like a dream.

Comical, cute—beautiful.

'They have fish,' she breathed. 'That one has... It must be at least three fish. More. Oh, my...I'd forgotten. There's another. And another. Why don't they just swallow them all at once?'

'Savouring the pleasure?' Alasdair said, smiling just as

Aladdin's genie might have done in the ancient fairy tale. Granting what he knew was a wish…

'You look like a benevolent Santa,' Jeanie told him and he raised his brows.

'Is that an accusation?'

'I… No.' Because it wasn't. It was just a statement.

Though he didn't actually look like Santa, Jeanie conceded. This was no fat, jolly old man.

Though she didn't need to be told that. His skill at the wheel was self-evident.

Sex on legs…

The description hit her with a jolt, and with it came a shaft of pure fear. Because that had been how she'd once thought of Alan.

Life with Rory had been…safe. He'd lived and dreamed fishing and would never have left the island. He was content to do things as his father and grandfather had done before him. His mother cooked and cleaned and was seemingly content, so he didn't see that Jeanie could possibly want more.

He was a good man, solid and dependable, and his death had left Jeanie devastated. But two years later Alan had blasted himself into her life. She'd met him and she'd thought…

Yep, sex on legs.

More. She'd thought he was everything Rory hadn't been. He was exciting, adventurous, willing and wanting to try everything life had to offer. He'd taken her off the island and exposed her to a life that…

That she never wanted to go back to. A life that was shallow, mercenary, dangerous—even cruel.

Alan was a McBride, just as this man was.

Sex on legs? Get a grip, she told herself. Have you learned nothing? The only one who'll keep yourself safe is yourself.

But she didn't *want* to be safe, a little voice whispered, and she looked at Alasdair and she could see the little voice's reasoning but she wasn't going there. She wasn't.

'If you want to know the truth, I read about them last night,' Alasdair told her. He was watching the puffins—thankfully. How much emotion could he read in her face? 'They can carry up to ten small fish in their beaks at a time. It's a huge genetic advantage—they don't waste energy swallowing and regurgitating, and they can carry up to ten fish back to their burrows. Did you know their burrows can be up to two feet deep? And those beaks are only bright orange in the breeding season. They'll shed the colour soon and go back to being drab and ordinary.'

'They could never be ordinary,' she managed, turning to watch a puffin floating by the boat with…how many fish in its beak? Five. She got five.

She was concentrating fiercely on counting. Alasdair was still talking…and he usually didn't talk. He'd swotted up for today, she thought. Was finding out how many fish a puffin could hold a seduction technique?

The thought made her smile. No, she decided, and it settled her. He was taking her out today simply to be nice. He wasn't interested in her, or, if he was, it'd be a mere momentary fancy, as Alan's had been.

So get yourself back to basics, she told herself. Eileen had offered Alan money to marry her. She knew that now. The knowledge had made her feel sick, and here was another man who'd been paid to marry her.

Sex on legs? Not so much. He was a husband who was hers because of money.

Hold that thought.

'Will we eat lunch here?' she asked, suddenly brisk, unwinding herself from the back seat on the boat and heading for the picnic basket. 'Can you throw down anchor or should we eat on the way back?'

'We have time to eat here.' He was watching her, his brows a question. 'Jeanie, how badly did Alan hurt you?'

'I have sandwiches and quiche and salad and boiled eggs. I also have brownies and apples. There's beer, wine or soda. Take your pick.'

'You mean you're not going to tell me?'

'Past history. Moving on…'

'I won't hurt you.'

'I know you won't,' she said briskly. 'Because I won't let you. This is a business arrangement, Alasdair, nothing more.'

'And today?'

'Is my payment for past services.' She was finding it hard to keep her voice even but she was trying. 'You've offered and I've accepted. It's wonderful—no, it's magic— to be eating lunch among the puffins. It's a gift. I'm very, very grateful but I'm grateful as an employee's grateful to her boss for a day off. Nothing more.'

'It's not a day off. It's a week almost completely off and then I'm halving your duties for double the wages.'

Whoa? Double wages?

She should refuse, she thought, but then…why not just be a grateful employee? That was what she was, after all.

'Excellent,' she said and passed the sandwiches. 'Take a sandwich—sir.'

Employer/employee. That was a relationship that'd work, he thought, and it was fine with him—wasn't it?

He was grateful to Jeanie. She'd agreed to marry him, and in doing so she'd saved the estate. More, she'd made Eileen's last years happy. He was doing what he could to show he was grateful and she was accepting with pleasure.

It should be enough.

Their puffin expedition was magic. For Alasdair, who'd seen them so often in the past, they should feel almost commonplace, but in watching Jeanie watch them he was seeing them afresh. They were amazing creatures—and Jeanie's reaction was magic.

She tried hard to be prosaic, he thought. Her reactions to him were down-to-earth and practical, and she tried to tone down her reactions to the birds, but he watched her face, he watched the awe as she saw the birds dive and come up with beaks stuffed with rows of silver fish, he watched her turn her face to the sun and he thought, Here was a woman who'd missed out on the joy of life until now.

It was a joy to be able to share.

They returned to the castle late afternoon to find all the tasks done, the castle spotless, the grass mowed, the cattle tended. Jeanie entered the amazing great hall and looked up at the newly washed leadlight, the carpets beaten, the great oak balustrades polished, and he thought he detected the glimmer of tears.

But she said nothing, just gave a brisk nod and headed for her kitchen.

The baking was done. A Victoria sponge filled with strawberries and cream and a basket of chocolate brownies were sitting on the bench. Jeanie stared at them blankly.

'What am I going to do now?' she demanded.

'Eat them,' Alasdair said promptly. 'Where's a knife?'

'Don't you dare cut the sponge. The guests can have it for supper. You can have what's left.'

'Aren't I a guest?'

'Okay, you can have some for supper,' she conceded. 'But not first slice.'

'Because?'

'Because you're the man in the middle. Guest without privileges.'

'Guest with brownie,' he retorted and bit into a still-warm cookie. 'So tomorrow…otters?'

'What do you mean, otters?'

'I mean Maggie's mam and her friends are hired to come every weekday until I tell them not, and I haven't seen the Duncairn otters for years. They used to live in the burns running into the bay. I thought we could take a picnic down there and see if we can see them. Meanwhile I'm off to work now, Jeanie. You can go put your feet up, read a book, do whatever you want, whatever you haven't been able to do for the last few years. I'll see you at dinner.'

'Guests eat out,' she said blankly, but he shook his head.

'Sorry, Jeanie, but as you said, I'm the man in the middle. I'm a guest, but I'm also Lord of this castle. I'm also, for better or for worse, your husband.'

'There was nothing in the marriage contract about me feeding you.'

'That's why I'm feeding you,' he told her and at the look on her face he grinned. 'And no, I'm not about to whisk you off to a Michelin-ranked restaurant, even if such a thing existed on Duncairn, but Maggie's mam has brought me the ingredients for a very good risotto and risotto is one of the few things in the world I'm good at. So tonight I'm cooking.'

'I don't want—'

'There are lots of things we don't want,' he said, gentling now. 'This situation is absurd but there's nothing for it but for us both to make the most of it. Risotto or nothing, Jeanie.'

She stared at him for a long moment and then, finally, she gave a brisk nod. 'Fine,' she said. 'Good. I…I'll eat your risotto and thank you for it. And thank you for today. Now I'll…I'll…go do a stocktake of…of the whisky. There's all the new stuff you've bought. I keep a ledger. Call me when dinner's ready…sir…'

'Alasdair,' he snapped.

'Alasdair,' she conceded. 'Call me when dinner's ready. And thank you.'

She fled and he stood staring after her.

She was accepting his help. It should be enough.

Only it wasn't.

She felt weird. Discombobulated. Thoroughly disoriented. For the first time in over three years she had nothing to do.

Except think of the day that had just been.

Except think of Alasdair?

He was her husband. She should be used to having husbands by now. He was nothing different.

Except he was. He'd spent today working for nothing except her enjoyment.

He'd seen puffins many times before—the way he looked at them told her that. He also had work to do. She'd heard him at the computer almost all the time he'd been here. She'd heard the insistent ring of his telephone. Alasdair McBride was the head of a gigantic web of financial enterprises, and one look at the Internet had told her just how powerful that web was.

He'd spent the day making her happy.

'Because I agreed to keep our bargain,' she told herself. 'I'm saving his butt.

'The best way for him to keep his butt safe is for him to keep a low profile.' The dogs, well-fed and exercised, were sprawled in front of the kitchen range. They were fast asleep but she needed someone—anyone—to talk to. 'He must know that, and yet he risked it...

'To make me happy?' She thought of Rory doing such a thing. Rory was always too tired, she conceded. He had long spells at sea and when he was home he wanted his armchair and the telly. He'd taken time to spend with her before they were married but afterwards...it was as if he no longer had to bother.

And Alan? That was the same thing multiplied by a million. Pounds. He'd had well over a million reasons to marry her but when he had what he wanted, she was nothing.

And Alasdair? He, too, had more than a million reasons to marry her, she thought, way more, but she'd agreed to his deal. He'd had no reason to spend today with her.

'Maybe he thinks I'll back out,' she told the dogs but she knew it wasn't that.

Or maybe it was that she hoped it wasn't that.

'And that's just your stupid romantic streak,' she told herself crossly. 'And, Jeanie Lochlan, it's more than time you were over that nonsense.'

Her discussion with herself was interrupted by her phone. Maggie, she thought, and sure enough her friend was on the line, and Maggie was almost bursting with curiosity.

'How did it go? Oh, Jeanie, isn't he gorgeous? I watched you go out through the entrance with the field glasses—I imagine half the village did. Six hours you were out. Six hours by yourself with the man! And the amount he's given Dougal for the *Mary-Jane*, and what he's paying Mam and her friends… Jeanie, what are you doing not being in bed with your husband right now?'

She took a deep breath at that. 'He's not my real husband,' she managed but Maggie snorted.

'You could have fooled me. And Mam says he was just lovely on the phone and he's thanked her for the sponge cake and the brownies as though she wasn't even paid for them, and he's organised her to go back tomorrow and he says he's taking you to see otters. Otters! You know the old cottage down by the Craigie Burn? There's otters down there, I'm sure of it. You could light a fire and—'

'Maggie!'

'It's just a suggestion. Jeanie, you married the man and if you aren't in bed with him already you should be. Oh, Jeanie, I know he's not like Alan, I know it.'

'You've hardly met him.'

'The way he said his vows…'

'We were both lying and you know it.'

'I don't know it,' Maggie said stoutly. 'You went home last night, didn't you? One night married, three hundred and sixty-four to go—or should I multiply that by fifty years? Jeanie, do yourself a favour and go for it. Go for him.'

'Why would I?'

There was a moment's silence while Maggie collected her answer. One of the guest's cars was approaching. Jeanie could see it through the kitchen window. She took a plate and started arranging brownies. This was her job, she told herself. Her life.

'Because he can afford—' Maggie started but Jeanie cut her off before she could finish.

'He can afford anything he wants,' she conceded. 'But that's thanks to me. I told you how Eileen's will works. He gets to keep his fortune and I… I get to keep my independence. That's the way I want it, Maggie, and that's the way it's going to be.'

'But you will go to see the otters tomorrow?'

'Yes,' she said, sounding goaded. Which was how she felt, she conceded. She'd been backed into a corner, and she wasn't at all sure she could extricate herself.

By keeping busy, she told herself, taking the brownies off the plate and rearranging them more…artistically.

One day down, three hundred and sixty-four to go.

CHAPTER SEVEN

THEY DID GO to look for otters, and Alasdair decreed they would go to Craigie Burn. It was the best place to see otters, he told her, the furthest place on the estate from any road, a section of the burn where otters had hunted and fished for generations almost undisturbed. The tiny burnside cottage had been built by a long-ago McBride who'd fancied fishing and camping overnight in relative comfort. But at dusk and dawn the midges appeared in their hordes and the fishing McBride of yore had soon decided that the trek back to the comforts of the castle at nightfall was worth the effort. The cottage had therefore long fallen into disrepair. The roof was intact but the place was pretty much a stone shell.

Jeanie hadn't intended telling Alasdair about Craigie Burn—but of course he knew.

'I spent much of my childhood on the estate,' he told her as they stowed lunch into the day pack. 'I had the roaming of the place.'

'Alan, too?' she asked because she couldn't help herself. Alan had hardly talked of his childhood—he'd hardly talked of his family.

'My father and Alan's father were peas in a pod,' he said curtly. 'They were interested in having a good time and not much else. They weren't interested in their sons. Both our childhoods were therefore lonely but Alan thought he was lonelier here. The few times Eileen brought him here he hated it.'

He swung the pack onto his back and then appeared to check Jeanie out—as she checked the guests out before they went rambling, making sure boots were stout, clothing sensible, the wildness of the country taken into account when dressing. He gave a curt nod. 'Good.' The dogs were locked in the wet room. Maggie's mam would see them walked, for if the dogs were with them the possibility of seeing otters was about zero. 'Ready?'

'Ready,' she said, feeling anything but. What was she doing traipsing around the country with this man when she should be earning her keep?

But Alasdair was determined to give her a…honeymoon? Whatever it was called, it seemed she had no choice but to give in to him. She was still getting over sitting at the kitchen table the night before eating the risotto he'd prepared. It was excellent risotto, but…

But the man had her totally off balance.

They set off, down the cliff path to the rocky beach, then along the seafront, clambering over rocks, making their way to where Craigie Burn tumbled to the sea.

The going was tough, even for Jeanie, who was used to it. Alasdair, though, had no trouble. A few times he paused and turned to help her. She shook off his offer of assistance but in truth his concern made her feel…

As she had no right to feel, she told herself. She didn't need to feel like the 'little woman'. She'd had two marriages of being a doormat. No more.

'Tell me about your childhood here,' she encouraged as she struggled up one particularly rocky stretch. She asked more to take Alasdair's attention away from her heavy breathing than out of interest—she would not admit she was struggling.

But instead of talking as he climbed, Alasdair turned

and gazed out to sea. Did he sense how much she needed a breather? He'd better not, she thought. I will not admit I'm a lesser climber than he is.

But...without admitting anything...she turned and gazed out to sea with him.

'I loved it,' he said at last, and it had taken so long to answer she'd almost forgotten she'd asked. But his gaze was roving along the coastline, rugged, wild, amazing. 'My father and my uncle hardly spent any time here. They hated it. My grandparents sent them to boarding school in England and they hardly came back. They both married socialites, they lived in the fast lane on my grandparents' money and they weren't the least bit interested in their sons. But Alan loved their lifestyle—from the time he was small he wanted to be a part of it. He loved the fancy hotels, the servants, the parties. It was only me who hated it.'

'So you came back here.'

'We were dumped,' he told her. 'Both of us. Our parents dumped us with Eileen every school holidays and she thought the castle would be good for us. Alan chafed to be able to join his parents' lifestyle.' He gave a wry smile. 'Maybe I was just antisocial even then, but here...'

He paused and looked around him again. A pair of eagles was soaring in the thermals. She should be used to them by now, she told herself, but every time she saw them she felt her heart swell. They were magnificent and Alasdair paused long enough for her to know he felt it, too.

'Here was home,' Alasdair said at last. 'Here I could be myself. Eileen usually stayed when Alan and I were here. You saw the place before she renovated. She and my grandfather didn't appear to notice conditions were a bit...sparse. I don't think I noticed, either. I was too busy, exploring, fishing, trying not to think how many days I had left before I went back to school. Alan was counting off the days until he could leave. I wanted to stay for the rest of my life.'

'You didn't, though. You ended up based in Edinburgh. You hardly came here until…until Eileen got sick at the end.'

She was trying hard not to make her words an accusation but she didn't get it right. It sounded harsh.

There was a long silence. 'I didn't mean to be accusatory,' she ventured at last and he shook his head.

'I know you didn't. But I need to explain. At first I didn't come because I was immersed in business. I took to the world of finance like a duck to water, and maybe I lost perspective on other things I loved. But then… When Eileen started spending more time here, I didn't come because you were here.'

That was enough to give a girl pause. To make her forget to breathe for a moment. 'Did you dislike me so much?' she asked in a small voice and he gave an angry shrug.

'I didn't know you, but I knew Alan. I knew I hated him.'

'Because?'

'Because he was the sort of kid who pulled wings off flies. I won't sugar coat it. My father was older than his, so my father stood to inherit the title, with me coming after him. Alan's father resented mine and the resentment was passed on down the line. I don't know what sort of poison was instilled in Alan when he was small but he was taught to hate me and he knew how to hurt.'

Whoa. He hadn't talked of this before. She knew it instinctively and who knew how she knew it, but she did. What he was saying was being said to her alone—and it hurt to say it.

His eyes went to a point further along the coast, where the burn met the sea. 'It came to a head down here,' he told her, absently, almost as if speaking to the land rather than her. Apologising for not being back for so long? 'I loved the otters, and I used to come down here often. One day Alan followed me. I was lying on my stomach watching the otters through field glasses. He was up on the ridge, and he'd taken my grandfather's shotgun. He killed three otters before I reached him. He was eighteen months older than me, and much bigger, and I went for him and he hit me with the gun. I still carry the scar under my hairline. I was dazed and bleeding, and he laughed and walked back to the castle.'

'No...'

His mouth set in a grim line. 'Thinking back...that blow to my head... He nearly killed me. But I was twelve and he was fourteen, and I was afraid of him. I told Grandmother I'd fallen on the cliffs. Soon after that his parents decided he was old enough to join them in the resorts they stayed at, so I didn't have to put up with him any more. I never told Eileen what happened. In retrospect, maybe I should have.' And then he paused and looked at her. 'But you... You loved him?'

'No.'

'It doesn't matter. It's none of my business, but these last years... Just knowing you were here in the castle was enough to keep me away.'

'I'm so sorry.'

'You shouldn't have to apologise for your husband's faults.'

'But as you said, I married him.'

'I can't see you killing otters.'

'Is that why you took me to look at the puffins first?' she asked. 'To see how I reacted?'

'I was hardly expecting a gun.'

'I'd guess you weren't expecting a gun from Alan, either.' She sighed and took a deep breath—and it wasn't only because she needed a few deep breaths before tackling the rise in front of her. 'Okay, I understand. Alasdair, we don't need to go there any more. I'll stop judging you for not spending more time with your grandmother if you stop judging me for being married to Alan. I know I'm still… tainted…but we can work around that. Deal?'

He looked at her for a long moment, seeming to take in every inch of her. And then, slowly, his face creased into a smile.

It was an awesome smile, Jeanie thought. It was dark turning to light. It lit his whole face, made his dark eyes glint with laughter, made him seem softer, more vulnerable…

A warrior exposed?

That shouldn't be how she saw him, but suddenly it was. He was the Earl of Duncairn, and he wore armour, just as surely as his ancestors wore chain mail. His armour might be invisible but it was still there.

Telling her about the otters, telling her about Alan, had made a chink in that armour, she thought, and even though he was smiling she could see the hint of uncertainty. As if telling her had left him vulnerable and he didn't like it.

She had a sudden vision of him as a child, here in this castle. It was wild now; it would have been wilder then. Eileen had told her she'd brought both boys here during their school holidays. Jeanie had envisaged two boys with a whole estate to explore and love.

But later Eileen had said she'd often had to leave the boys with the housekeeper when she'd had to go back to Edinburgh, and Jeanie saw that clearly now, too. A twelve-year-old boy would have been subjected to the whims and cruelty of his older cousin. It wouldn't just have been the otters, she thought grimly. She knew Alan. There would have been countless cruelties during the years.

'This next bit's rough,' Alasdair was saying and he held his hand out. 'Let me help you.'

She looked down at his hand.

He was a McBride. He was yet another man who'd caught her at a weak moment and married her.

But the day was magic, the hill in front was tough and Alasdair was right beside her, smiling, holding out his hand.

'If I had one more brain cell, it'd be lonely,' she muttered out loud, to no one in particular, but Alasdair just raised his brows and kept on smiling and the sun was warm on her face and the otters were waiting, and a woman was only human after all.

She put her hand in his and she started forward again.

With Alasdair.

What followed was another magic day. Duncairn's weather was unpredictable to say the least, but today the gods had decided to be kind—more, they'd decided to put on Scotland at her most splendid. There was just enough wind to keep the midges at bay. The sky was dotted by clouds that might or might not turn to rain, but for now the sun shone, and the water in the burn was crystal clear.

Without hesitation Alasdair led them to a ledge near the cottage, a rocky outcrop covered with a thick layer of moss. It stretched out over the burn, but a mere ten feet above, so they could lie on their stomachs and peer over the edge to see what was happening in the water below.

And for a while nothing happened. Maybe it wouldn't, Alasdair conceded. Otters were notoriously shy. They could well have sensed their movement and darted back under cover, but for now they were content to wait.

Alasdair was more than content.

It was a strange feeling, lying on the moss-covered rock with Jeanie stretched out by his side.

His life was city-based now, mostly spent in Edinburgh but sometimes London, New York, Copenhagen, wherever the demands of his company took him. Under the terms of Eileen's will he'd need to delegate much of that travel for the next year. He'd thought he'd miss it, but lying next to Jeanie, waiting for otters to grace them with their presence, he thought suddenly, *Maybe I won't.*

What other woman had he ever met who'd lie on her stomach on a rock and not move, not say a word, and somehow exude a quality of complete restfulness? After half an hour the otters still hadn't shown themselves. He knew from past experience that half an hour wasn't long for these shy creatures to stay hidden, but did Jeanie know that? If she did, she didn't mind. She lay with her chin resting on her hands, watching the water below, but her eyes were half-closed, almost contemplative.

Her hair was tumbling down around her face. A curl was blocking his view. He wanted to lift it away.

She'd been Alan's wife.

Surely it didn't matter. He wanted to touch…

But if he moved he'd scare the otters, and he knew…he just knew that this woman would be furious with him— not just for touching her but for spoiling what she was waiting for.

She was waiting for otters, not for him.

Right. Watch on. He managed to turn his attention back to the water rippling beneath them.

'There…' It was hardly a whisper. Jeanie was looking left to where a lower overhang shaded the water, and there it was, a sleek, beautiful otter slipping from the shadows, with a younger one behind.

'Oh,' Jeanie breathed. 'Oh…'

She was completely unaware of him. All her attention was on the otters.

They were worth watching. They were right out from under the shadows now, slipping over the burn's rocky bed, nosing through the sea grasses and kelp, hunting for the tiny sea creatures that lived there.

'They eat the kelp, too,' Jeanie whispered but Alasdair thought she was talking to herself, not to him.

'They're stunning,' he whispered back. 'Did you know their coat's so thick not a single drop of water touches their skin?'

'That's why they're hunted,' she whispered back. 'You will…keep protecting them? After I've left?'

And there it was again—reality, rearing its ugly head. At the end of this year, this castle would go to Jeanie's creditors. He'd buy it and keep it—of course he would. He'd keep it safe. But he glanced at Jeanie and saw her expression and he thought, She's not sure.

He'd promised—but this woman must have been given empty promises in the past.

She was resting her chin on her hands and he could see the gold band he'd placed on her finger two days ago. For a year they were required to be officially married, and officially married people wore rings.

But now… What worth was a promise? Jeanie didn't trust him and why should she?

He glanced down at the otters, hunting now in earnest, despite the humans close by. They must sense their shadows, but they'd waited for almost an hour before resuming hunting. They'd be hungry. They'd be forced to trust.

As Jeanie had been forced to trust. She'd been put into an impossible situation. How to tell her…?

The ring…

One moment she was lying watching otters, worrying about their future, thinking would Alasdair really keep this estate? Would he keep caring for these wild creatures she'd come to love?

The next moment he'd rolled back a little and was tugging at his hand. Not his left hand, though, where she'd placed the wedding ring that meant so little. Instead he was tugging at his right hand.

At the Duncairn ring.

She'd seen this ring. It was in every one of the portraits of the McBride earls, going back in time until the names blurred and Eileen's history lesson had started seeming little more than a roll call.

Each of those long-dead earls had worn this ring, and now it lay on Alasdair's hand. It was a heavy gold signet, an intricate weaving, the head of an eagle embossed on a shield, with the first letters of the family crest, worn but still decipherable, under the eagle's beak: LHV.

Loyalty, honour, valour.

Alan had mentioned this ring, not once, but often. 'He's a prig,' he'd said of Alasdair. 'And he's younger than me. He thinks he can lord it over me just because he wears the damned ring…'

The 'damned ring' was being held out to her. No, not held out. Alasdair was taking her hand in his and sliding the ring onto the middle finger of her right hand. It fitted—as if it was meant to be there.

She stared down at it, stunned. So much history in one piece of jewellery… So many McBride men who'd worn this ring…

'Wh-what do you think you're doing?' she stammered at last, because this didn't make sense.

'Pledging my troth.'

'Huh?' Dumb, she thought, but that was how she was feeling. Dumb. And then she thought: she shouldn't be here. Her fragile control felt like crumbling. This man seemed as large and fierce and dangerous as the warriors he'd descended from.

Loyalty, honour, valour…

This was the McBride chieftain. He was placing a ring on her finger, and the ring took her breath away.

'Jeanie, I have nothing else to show you I'm serious.' In the kirk, Alasdair's vows had been businesslike, serious, but almost…clinical. Here, now, his words sounded as if they came from the heart. 'I'm promising you that at the end of this year of marriage I will make your life secure. As well, I will buy this castle for what it's worth and Alan's creditors will be paid. I'll treat it as the last of Alan's share of the estate. He was, after all, just as much Eileen's grandson as I was.'

'You don't have to make me secure,' she managed, still staring at the ring. 'And Alan wasn't worth—'

'I'm not judging,' he told her. 'And I refuse to think of Alan after this. To be honest, it took courage to come here. I haven't been back to this place since that day he hurt the otters. But I have come, to find life has moved on. But it needs faith to face it. So here's my faith in you, and I'm hoping you can find that faith in me. At the end of the year I'll take on this estate and I'll care for it as Eileen would have wanted it cared for. And as I suspect you want it cared for. And I will ensure your future…'

'I don't want anything.'

'I know you don't. You don't seem to put yourself into the equation at all, but I'm putting you there. It seems you canna keep the castle, Jeanie lass, no matter what Eileen's will says, but you can keep the heart of it. As long as you wear this ring, this estate will be safe, our Jeanie. I promise you. Hand on this ring, I swear.'

He'd lapsed into broad Scottish, the voice of his ancestors, the voice of his people. He was lying full-length on a bed of moss over a rippling burn, he was looking at her as no man had ever looked at her, and the way he spoke… It was as if he were kneeling before a throne, head bowed, swearing fealty to his king.

Swearing fealty to…her?

'Alasdair…' It was hard to breathe, much less speak.

She had to fight for the words. 'There's no need,' she managed. 'You don't have to do this. Besides...' She stared at the intricate weaving of gold on her finger and her heart failed her. 'I'll probably lose it in a pudding mix.'

He smiled then, but his smile was perfunctory, the gravity of the moment unchanged. 'I know you won't. I trust you with it, Jeanie, as you trust me with the castle.' His hand closed over hers, folding her fingers, the ring enclosed between them. 'I'm asking that you trust me back.'

'I can... I can trust you without the ring.'

'Why would you?'

'Because...' How to say it? There were no words.

And the truth was that until now, until this moment, she hadn't trusted. Yes, he was Lord of Duncairn but he was just another man, like her father, like Rory, like Alan. A man to be wary of. A man who sought to control.

Was this ring another form of control? She searched for the control angle, and couldn't find it.

She had no doubt as to the significance of this ring. She could hear it in his voice—that it meant as much to him as it had to every other earl who'd ever worn it.

Trust... He was offering it in spades.

'I'll give it back,' she managed. 'At the end of the year.'

'You'll give it to me when you've seen what I intend doing with this place,' he told her. 'When you see me hand the wilderness areas over to a trust to keep it safe in perpetuity. When you have total faith, Jeanie McBride, then you can give it back.'

'I have faith now.'

'You don't,' he said softly and his hold on her hand tightened. 'You can't. But you will.'

And then it rained.

She'd been so caught up, first with the otters and then with...well, with what she'd been caught up with, that she hadn't noticed the clouds scudding in from the west. Now, suddenly, the sun disappeared and the first fat droplets splashed down.

And Alasdair was tugging her to her feet, smiling, as if something had been settled between them that made going forward easy.

Maybe it had.

And maybe, Jeanie thought as she scrambled with Alasdair to reach the shelter of the cottage, as she didn't quibble about the feel of his hand still holding hers, as she fought to regain her breath and composure, maybe something had settled inside her as well.

Trust? She'd never trusted. She'd walked into this marriage blind, knowing only that circumstances once again had thrust her into making vows. But now… For some reason it was as if a weight was lifting from her shoulders, a weight she hadn't known she was carrying.

This year could work. This year could almost be…fun? Such a word was almost nonexistent in her vocabulary. As a child of a dour, grim fisherman and then as Rory's wife, a man under the thumb of his family, a man with limited horizons and no ambition to change, life had been hard and pretty much joyless. Life with Alan, so tantalising at first, had ended up filled with nothing but terror, and since that time she'd been subsumed with guilt, with debt, with responsibilities.

Today, though…today she'd lain in the sun and watched otters and this man had given her his ancestral ring. He'd given her trust…

And then he pushed open the cottage door and all thoughts of trust went out of the window.

She'd been in this cottage before. She'd walked this way with the dogs—it was a fair trek from the castle but at times during the past three years she'd needed the effort it required. Sometimes trekking the estate was the only way to get rid of the demons in her head, but even when she was fighting demons she still liked staying dry. On the west coast of Scotland rain came sudden and fierce. She'd walked and watched the sky—as they hadn't today—and she'd used this cottage for shelter.

She knew it. Any furniture had long gone, the windows were open to the elements and the place seemed little more than a cave.

But today... Someone had been in here before them. The room they walked into was a combination of kitchen/living, with a hearth at one end. The hearth had always been blackened and empty, but now... It contained a massive heap of glowing coals. Firewood was stacked beside it. The stone floor in front of it had been swept of debris and a rug laid in front. With the fire at its heart, the room looked almost cosy.

She hadn't noticed smoke from the chimney. Why?

She'd been too aware of Alasdair, that was why. Of all the stupid...

'How on earth...?' she managed, staring at the fire in disbelief, and Alasdair looked smug.

'Insurance,' he told her. 'There's never a day on this island when you're guaranteed of staying dry, and I'm a cautious man. I never take risks without insurance.' But he was frowning at the rug. 'I didn't ask for the rug, though. That's a bit over the top.'

'You think?' Her voice was practically a squeak. 'Who did this? Not you. Surely...'

'You don't think I could have loped up here before breakfast?'

'No!' And her tone was so adamant that he grinned.

'That's not a very complimentary way to talk to your liege lord.'

She told him where he could put his liege lord and his grin widened. 'I talked to Mac about getting the fire lit,' he confessed. 'Mac can't walk up here himself any more—I need to do something about gillie succession planning—but he does know a lad, who came up here and lit it for him.'

'A lad?' Jeanie breathed. And then she closed her eyes. 'No.' It was practically a groan. 'It won't be one lad. It'll be two. He'll have asked Lachlan and Hamish McDonald, two of the biggest wastrels this island's ever known. They're twins, they're forty, their mother still irons their socks and they do odd jobs when they feel like it. And they gossip. Mac's their uncle. Do you realise what you've done? This'll be all over the island before we get back to the castle that you and I have lain by the fire here and…and…'

'And what, Jeanie?' His smile was still there but his eyes had become…watchful?

'And nothing,' she snapped and walked forward and grabbed the backpack from his shoulders and started to unpack. 'We'll eat the sandwiches I made and then we'll go home. And why did you pack wine? If you think I could climb these crags after a drink…'

'I could carry you.' He sounded almost hopeful.

'You and whose bulldozer? Get real.' She was totally flustered, trying to haul the lunch box from the backpack, trying not to look at him. She tugged it free with a wrench and shoved it down onto the hearth.

Alasdair stooped. His hand came over hers before she could rise again and his laughter died.

'I'm not into seduction,' he told her. His words echoed into the stillness. 'You're safe, Jeanie. This fire's here to keep us warm and dry, nothing more. I won't touch you.'

There was a long pause. 'I never said you'd try,' she said at last.

'You look like you expect it.'

She was struggling, trying to get it right, trying to explain this…panic. 'It's this ring,' she said at last. She stared

down at the magnificent Duncairn signet and she felt…
small. Frightened? At the edge of a precipice?

But still Alasdair's hand was over hers, warm, steady,
strong. They were crouched before the fire. His face in the
firelight was strong and sure.

'The ring is simply a promise,' he told her. 'It's a promise to keep the faith, to keep your faith. You needn't fear.
I'm not into taking women against their will.'

'Not even…' Her voice was scarcely a whisper. 'Not
even the woman you've taken as your wife?'

'You're not my wife,' he said, evenly now. 'We both
know that this is a business relationship, despite what
Hamish and Lachie may well have told the islanders. So
let's have our sandwiches, and I intend to drink at least
one glass of this truly excellent wine—my grandmother
kept a superb cellar. You can join me or not, but whatever
you do, my Jeanie, know that seduction is off the agenda.'

Which was all very well, she thought crossly as she did
what was sensible. She ate her sandwiches and she drank
one glass—only one—of wine, and she thought she should
have settled, but why did he have to have called her *my
Jeanie*? And *Jeanie lass*?

It was merely familiar, she told herself as she cleared
their debris into the backpack. Any number of the older
folk on the island called her Jeanie lass. Any number of
islanders referred to her as our Jeanie.

But Alasdair McBride was not a member of the island's
older folk. Nor was he really an islander.

It shouldn't matter. It didn't matter.

It did. It made her feel…

Scared.

'It does seem a shame to waste the rug. Do you want a
nap before we head back?' Alasdair was watching her—
and the low-life was laughing again. But not laughing out

loud. It was more a glint behind his eyes, a telltale quiver of the corners of his mouth, the way his eyes met hers...

Laughter never seemed too far away. What did this man have to laugh about? she demanded of herself. Didn't he know life was hard?

But it wasn't hard for him. This man was the Earl of Duncairn. He could laugh at what he wanted.

He could laugh at her if he wanted. She couldn't afford to respond.

'It's stopped raining and we're getting out of here fast,' she said with acerbity. 'I wouldn't be surprised if there are field glasses trained on this doorway right now. There's no way I'm having the islanders conjecturing about my supposed love life.'

'They're conjecturing already,' he told her. 'And there's hardly shame attached. We are married.'

'We're not married,' she snapped again. 'Do you want to see the otters again before we head back?'

'Yes.' The sun was shining again. 'Why not?'

'Then let's go,' she told him. 'But keep twenty paces distant, Alasdair McBride, and no closer or this ring gets tossed in the burn.'

'You wouldn't.' She'd touched him on the raw then; his face had even paled. She relented. Some things were too precious to even joke about.

'No. I wouldn't. Are you sure you don't want it back?'

'I don't want it back,' he told her. 'I trust you. And you can trust me, Jeanie, whether it's at twenty paces or a whole lot closer.'

A whole lot closer? There was the crux of the matter, she decided. He was too gorgeous for his own good.

Her problem was, she thought as she lay in bed that night and stared up into the darkness...her major problem was that she wouldn't mind getting a whole lot closer to Alasdair.

Or just a bit?

No. At three in the morning her mind was crystal clear and there was no way she could escape honesty. A whole lot closer was what she wanted.

She was out of her mind. A whole lot closer was exactly what sensible Jeanie would never allow herself to think about.

Except she was thinking about it. She was lying sleepless in the small hours. Alasdair's wedding band lay on one finger, his ancestral signet lay on another and she felt…she felt…

'Like a stupid serving maid having ideas above my station,' she told herself crossly and threw back the covers and went to stare out of the window.

She could see the sea from her bedroom. The moon was almost full, sending streams of silver across the water, almost into her room. It felt as if she could walk out of the bedroom and keep on walking…

'As maybe you should if you feel like this,' she told herself. 'Use some brains.

'I don't want to.'

Above her, in the vast, imposing bedroom that had been the bedroom of Earls of Duncairn for centuries past, lay the current Earl of Duncairn. The four-poster bed was enormous. His bedroom was enormous. Eileen had giggled when she'd been making decisions about restoring the castle and she'd told Jeanie she wanted a bedroom fit for a lord. Together they'd chosen rich velvet drapes, tapestries, rugs, furnishings…

To say it was lavish was an understatement. Apart from the servants' rooms she used and had—with some difficulty—kept free from Eileen's sumptuous plans, this castle was truly astonishing.

'It's enough to make its lord feel he can snap his fingers and any servant girl will come running,' she said out loud and then she caught her breath with where her thoughts were taking her.

This servant girl wouldn't mind running—but this servant girl should turn and run as far from this castle as possible.

'I was good today,' she told herself. 'I was sensible.

'Excellent,' she told herself. 'That's two days down, three hundred and sixty-three to go.'

But… There was a voice whispering in the back of her head and it wasn't a small voice, either. You're married to him. It wouldn't hurt.

'Are you out of your mind? Of course it'll hurt.' She ran her fingers through her tangled curls and the signet ring caught and hurt. 'Excellent,' she told herself. 'Just keep doing that. Pull your hair whenever you think of being an idiot.

'And he doesn't want you, anyway.'

She let her mind drift back to her mind-set when she'd married Rory. She'd still been a kid when she'd married him. He'd been safe, he'd been kind, and when she'd taken her vows she'd felt…as if a new net had been closing over her? He'd protected her from her father, and she'd been grateful, but that hadn't stopped her lying in bed at night after a wild night watching the telly feeling…was this all there was?

Which was why, two years after Rory's death, she'd been ripe for the picking. She had no doubt now that the only reason Alan had been attracted to her was to persuade his grandmother to give him money, but the means he'd used to attract… Excitement, adventure, travel had seemed a wild elixir, a drug impossible to resist, and by the time she'd woken to reality she'd been in so far it had been impossible to extricate herself.

And now here she was, wanting to…wanting to…

'I want nothing,' she told herself. 'For heaven's sake, Jeanie, grow a little sense. Put your head in a bucket of cold water if you must, but do not walk headlong into another emotional mess.'

'Get some sense.' On the floor above, in a bedroom so vast it made him feel ridiculous, Alasdair was staring at the slivers of moonlight lighting the dark and he was feeling pretty much the same.

'If you sleep with her, how the hell are you going to extricate yourself? You'll be properly married.

'There's no thought of sleeping with her.'

But there was. No matter how much his head told him it was crazy, his body was telling him something else entirely.

'It's just this stupid honeymoon idea,' he told himself. 'I never should have instigated it. Leave her to get back to her work and you get back to yours.'

Except…how long since she'd had a holiday? Yesterday and today she'd lit up. Clambering up the scree today, lying on the moss-covered rocks, watching the otters, she'd seemed younger, happier…free.

What had two husbands done to her? What had they done *for* her?

Saddled her with debt and regrets, that was what. Hell, she deserved a break.

'But not with me.' He said it out loud.

He should call off this honeymoon idea. But no, he couldn't do that. He'd told her they'd have a week.

She could have a week, he thought. She could do whatever she wanted, just not with him.

That's not a honeymoon.

'Right.' He was talking into the dark. 'It's not and it's not supposed to be.

'You'll tell her how?

'Straight out. She'll be relieved.

And what was there in that that made his gut twist?

Honesty. He could at least give her that. She deserved no less.

She deserved…

That he think seriously about what he was letting himself in for.

CHAPTER EIGHT

SHOULD ONE MAKE a special dinner to celebrate a one-month anniversary?

The weather had closed in, the sleet was driving from the north and she had no guests booked for the night. Jeanie was staring into the refrigerator, vacillating between sausages or something fancy. She had beef in the freezer. She had mushrooms for guests' breakfasts. She had excellent red wine, bought by Eileen and stocked in the castle larder.

Beef Bourguignon was hardly Scottish, but she could serve the rest of the red wine alongside, and make a lovely mash, and maybe make a good apple pie as well. She had clotted cream…

'And he'll eat it at his desk as he's eaten his dinner at his desk every night for the last month.' She slumped down at the table. The two dogs put their noses on her knee and whined.

'Yeah, the weather's getting to you, too,' she told them, but she knew it wasn't that. She'd grown up with Duncairn weather. She usually enjoyed the gales that blasted the island, donning wellies and mac and walking her legs off, the dogs at her side.

She'd walked her legs off this afternoon but it hadn't stopped the feeling of…desolation?

'Which is dumb,' she told the dogs and gave herself a mental shake. 'As is making any kind of anniversary dinner when all it means is that we've put up with each other for a month.

'And it's working okay,' she added after a moment, as if she was reassuring herself.

It was. Sort of. After the dumb idea of the honeymoon, which had lasted two days before he'd pulled out and she'd agreed with relief, Alasdair had decreed she have one day a week completely off. But not with him.

Their lives had settled into a pattern. She cared for the castle and the guests. Alasdair worked in his rooms or he headed to Edinburgh for the day. When that happened his chopper would arrive at dawn and bring him back before dusk, so one of his precious nights of freedom wouldn't be used up.

He walked but he walked alone. He kept himself to himself and she did the same.

He'd spent three nights in Hong Kong and it shouldn't have made any difference, but it did. The castle was empty for his going.

And now he was back. Today he was spending the entire day here. The weather was too rough for the chopper.

He was trapped—and that was how she felt, too. She worked on but she was so aware of him overhead. It was as if the entire month had been building. Every sense was tuned...

'And I'm getting stupid in my old age,' she told the dogs. 'I'm not a needy woman. I'm not.' She stared around the kitchen in frustration. She needed more to do. Anything. Fast.

Then the kitchen door swung open. Alasdair was standing there, in his casual trousers and sweater, his hair ruffled as if he'd raked it and raked it again.

'Jeanie?'

'Mmm?' Somehow she made herself sound non-committal. Somehow.

'This weather's driving me nuts.'

'You *are* on Duncairn.'

'I am,' he told her. 'And I'm thinking at the end of eleven months I'll be back in Edinburgh full-time and what will I have to show for these months? So I'm thinking… Jeanie, would you teach me to cook something other than spaghetti or risotto?'

If Duncairn had split in two and drifted in different directions in the sea, she couldn't have been more astonished.

'Cook,' she said blankly and he gave her a lopsided smile.

'If you would.'

'Why?'

Why? The question hung in the air between them. It needed an answer and Alasdair was searching for one.

The fact that Jeanie was in the kitchen wasn't enough—though it was certainly a factor.

For the past month he'd put his head down and worked. Duncairn Enterprises took all his time and more. There seemed to be some sort of financial leak at head office. It was worrying, but over the past few weeks he'd almost welcomed it, sorting painstakingly through the remaining financial web his grandmother had controlled, rejecting the inclination to do anything else.

This afternoon he'd thought, Why? He could call in outside auditors to do what he'd been doing. He wasn't happy about letting outsiders look at possible financial problems of his grandmother's making, but then his grandmother was past caring, and Jeanie was downstairs.

So why not go downstairs and join her? It had been an insistent niggle and this afternoon it had become a roar. Because he didn't want to get emotionally involved? He'd spent a month telling himself to form any sort of relationship would be courting catastrophe. If it didn't work out and she walked, it would be a disaster. He knew the way forward was to move with caution.

But for the past month he'd lived in the same house with Jeanie. He'd watched the dogs fly to meet her every time she left the house. He'd watched from his windows whenever she took them out, striding out across the pasture, stopping to speak to the cattle, the dogs wild with excitement at her side.

He'd listened to her sing as she did the housework. He'd heard her laugh with the guests, or empathise with them about bad roads or lost suitcases or general travel fatigue.

He'd eaten while he worked, separate from the other guests, working through a pile of papers a foot high, and he'd been aware of the aromas coming from the kitchen. He'd watched the dogs fly back and forth...

And this afternoon he'd cracked. He stood at the kitchen door and felt mildly foolish but hell, he was here, he'd said it and he was seeing this through.

And she'd asked why.

'I'm fed up with playing Lord of the castle,' he told her and she looked up at him and smiled.

'You can hardly knock back the title. It's what you are.'

'While you play servant.'

'That's what I am.'

'No.' It was an explosion that had the dogs starting out from under the table. Abbot even ventured a feeble bark.

'Your grandmother employed me to housekeep for the castle,' Jeanie said mildly. 'That's what I've been doing for the last three years. I have one more year to go.'

'You were Alan's wife. You deserve—'

'I deserve nothing for marrying Alan.'

'My grandmother thought you did.' Why was he getting into this conversation? He surely hadn't intended to.

'Your grandmother was kind and sentimental and bossy.

She felt sorry for me, end of story. Now if you'll excuse me, I need to get on…'

'Cooking. What do you intend to cook?'

'You're the only guest in the house tonight. What would you like me to cook?'

'I'm not a guest.'

'No, but in my mind that's how I'm seeing you. It keeps me sane. Now…requests? Sausages? Beef Bourguignon? Anything else that strikes your fancy?'

She was wearing a pink, frilly apron over her jeans and windcheater. It was tied with a big bow at the back, almost defiantly, as if she knew the bow was corny but she liked it anyway. She really was impossibly cute, he thought. Jeanie Lochlan, Domestic Goddess. Jeanie McBride…

His wife.

'Singing hinnies,' he told her. 'And I want to make them.'

'You're serious?'

'Do you know how to make them?' he asked.

'You're asking me, an islander born and bred, if I know how to make singing hinnies?'

'I'm sorry. Of course you do.'

'My granny's singing hinnies were famous.'

'Is the recipe a family secret?'

'Possibly.' She eyed him thoughtfully. 'Though some might say you're family now.'

And what was there in that to give him hope? He almost took the apron Jeanie took from the pantry and offered him. But it was pink, too. Did she expect him to wear a bow as well?

'You'll get batter on your lovely sweater.'

'I have more.'

'Of course you do,' she retorted and he looked at her— just looked.

'Oops,' she said and out peeped one of her gorgeous

smiles. 'Servant giving master lip. Servant needs to learn to shut up.'

'Jeanie?'

'Yes…sir?'

'Teach me to cook,' he demanded and she saluted and her smile widened. 'What do I do?'

'What you're told, My Lord,' she retorted. 'Nothing else.'

He made singing hinnies and 'awesome' was too small a word for it. There was no explaining it. Either he was a natural-born cook or…

Or Jeanie was the world's best teacher. She certainly was good. She stood and instructed as he rubbed the butter into flour, as he made the perfect batter, as he heated the griddle on the stove, greased it with lard and finally popped his hinnie on to cook. It hissed and spluttered and rose. He flipped it over and it was done. Perfection! He placed it on a plate in the range's warming drawer and went on to make another, feeling about ten feet tall.

Closing a million-dollar deal against a business rival had never felt this good.

And then, when the last hinnie was on the plate, Jeanie put a teapot, mugs and butter and jam on a plate.

'My sitting room or yours?' she asked and that was a statement to give a man hope as well. He'd never been in Jeanie's tiny apartment. He'd seen it on the plans, a bedroom with a small living space specifically designed for a housekeeper. To be invited… Boundaries were certainly being shifted.

The castle was magnificent, lavish, amazing. Jeanie's apartment…wasn't. He stepped through the door and blinked. Gone were the opulent colours, drapes, rugs, furnishings of the ancient and historical treasure that was Duncairn Castle. This was just…home.

The dogs bounded in before him and nosedived to the

hearth. The fire was crackling, emitting a gentle heat. The room was faded, homey, full of books and magazines and odds and sods: seashells in chipped bowls, photos in un-matched frames, ceramic dogs and the odd shepherdess—what was it with ceramic shepherdesses?—an old cuckoo clock, squashy furniture… All discards, he thought, from the rest of the castle, removed as Eileen had spent a for-tune on redecorating.

He thought of his magnificent living quarters upstairs and suddenly it had lost its appeal.

'Get your cooking into you before it's cold,' Jeanie told him, still smiling, so he sat in one of her squashy armchairs and he ate four singing hinnies and drank two cups of tea, and Jeanie sat on the mat with the dogs and ate two singing hinnies and drank one cup of tea and then they were done.

Done? Jeanie cleared the cups and lifted the tray to one side. To safety? The world steadied—waiting to see what would happen?

The way he was feeling… She was so… Jeanie. There was no other word to describe her. Jeanie.

He slid down onto the mat beside her. The action was deliberate. One more boundary crossed?

He shouldn't be pushing boundaries. He, of all people, knew how important boundaries were, but maybe this one could be…stretched?

'Jeanie,' he said softly and he reached out and took her hand, not the hand wearing the wedding ring because for some reason the wedding ring was not where promises were to be made, but her right hand where lay the heavy signet of the Duncairn line.

'Jeanie,' he said again, and then, because he couldn't help himself, 'I'd really like to kiss you. No pressure. If you say no, then I won't ask you again.'

'Then I'd best say yes,' she said, softly, amazingly, wonderfully. 'Because I can't stand it one moment longer. I'd really, really like it if you kissed me.'

She was out of her mind. She should not be doing this—she should not!

She was and she had no intention of stopping.

They were on the rug before the fire. His hands cupped her face, he looked into her eyes for a long, long moment, the world held its breath—and then he drew her mouth to his and kissed her.

And she'd never been kissed like this. Never. It was as if she'd found her home. Her centre. Her heart.

There was all the tenderness in the world in his kiss, and yet she could feel the strength of him, the heat, the need. The sheer arrant masculinity of him.

How could a kiss be a life changer? How could a kiss make her feel she'd never been alive until this moment?

How could a kiss make her feel as if her world were melting, the outside fading to nothing, that everything were disappearing except this man, this moment, this kiss?

The heat…the strength…the surety… For that was what it was, she thought in the tiny part of her mind that was still available for rational thought. Surety?

Home.

She was twenty-nine years old. She'd spent twenty-nine years failing at this relationship business. She'd had a weak mother, a bully for a father, a husband who was no more than a mirror of his family's business, then another who was vain and selfish and greedy.

This man might be all those things underneath, she thought, but there was no hint of it in his kiss. Her head should override what her body was telling her, what his kiss was telling her, but this kiss couldn't be ignored. This kiss was making her body feel as if it were no longer hers.

Rightly or wrongly, all that mattered was that, for this

moment, Alasdair McBride wanted her and she wanted him, as simple as that. One man, one woman and a desire so great that neither could pull back. Sense had no place here. This desire was as primeval as life itself and she'd gone too far to pull back.

Too far to pull back? That was crazy. It was only a kiss. She could break it in a moment.

But she had no intention of breaking it. This kiss was taking her places she'd never been, places she hadn't known existed. Her hands had somehow found their way to his hair, her fingers sliding through the thick thatch of jet black, her hands drawing him closer so she could deepen…deepen…

She heard a tiny sound from far away and she thought, That's me. Moaning with desire? What sort of dumb thought was that?

Dumb maybe, but the time for asking questions was over. If this moment was all she had of this man, her body knew she'd take it.

Weak perhaps? Stupid? Was it Jeanie being passive? Was this the Jeanie of old?

No. She felt her world shift and shift again and she knew this was no passive submission. Her hands held him even tighter and then tugged until his arms came around her and he drew her up to him, so his dark eyes could gleam into hers.

'Jeanie McBride, can I take my wife to bed?'

If the dogs hadn't been there, they might have made love right where they were—he certainly wanted to—but the dogs were gazing on with interest and, even though they were only dogs, it was enough to make a man take action.

Or maybe it was because he wanted to take this woman to bed with all the honour he could show her? Maybe this moment was too important to rush?

He wasn't sure what the reason was. Hell, his brain was mush, yet he knew enough to gather her into his arms and sweep her against his chest and carry her up the great, grand staircase to his rooms, to his bedroom, to the massive four-poster bed that was the place the Earls of Duncairn had taken their brides for generations past.

His bride?

She'd married him a month ago and yet a month ago she hadn't felt like this. He hadn't felt like this. As if this was his woman and he'd claim her and honour her and protect her from this day forth.

What had changed?

Nothing...and everything.

He'd spent the past month watching her. He'd come to her with preconceptions, prejudiced beyond belief by her marriage to his cousin. Those prejudices had been smashed by Jeanie, by her laughter, her courage, by everything about her. Every little thing.

He'd spent a month waiting for this new image to crack. Waiting for the true Jeanie to emerge.

It hadn't happened, or maybe...maybe it had. For the image he'd built up was a woman with a brave heart and an indomitable spirit.

What he held in his arms now was a woman of fire. A woman who, as he laid her down on his bed, as he hauled off his sweater and drew her to him, took the front of his shirt in her two hands and ripped...

'If you knew how long I've wanted to do this,' she murmured. And then she stopped because his chest was bare and she was gazing at him in awe...and then shifting just slightly so she could kiss...

She was adorable, he thought. She was stunning, beautiful, wild. She still had a smear of flour on her face from cooking. He'd never seen anything so beautiful in his life.

'If you've wanted to see me naked,' he said and he couldn't get his voice steady for the life of him, 'how do you think I've wanted to see you?'

And then she smiled, a smile of sheer transparent happiness, a smile that shafted straight to his heart.

Jeanie woke as the first rays of light crept over the sea through the window.

She woke and she was lying in the arms of the man she loved.

The knowledge almost blindsided her. She couldn't move. She could hardly breathe. She was lying tucked under his arm. He was cradling her—even in sleep? Her skin was against his skin. She could feel his heartbeat.

Her man. It was a feeling so massive it threatened to overwhelm her.

When she was young she'd loved Rory, large, dependable Rory, who'd wanted to please and protect her—as long as it hadn't interfered with his routine. She had loved him, she thought, but never like this. Never with this overwhelming sense of belonging.

For a short time she'd also thought she'd loved Alan. How long had it taken her to find the true Alan under the sham of the charming exterior? Too long.

But now… With Alasdair…

True waters run deep?

Where had that saying come from? She didn't know. She didn't even know if she had it right, but the words came to her now and she felt almost overwhelmed by their rightness.

This man was deep, private, a loner. She knew the story of his parents. She knew from Eileen about his solitary childhood and she'd learned more from him.

And now… She'd learned more in the past hours than she could even begin to understand. He'd wanted her but this was more than that. The words he'd murmured to her through the night, the way he'd held her, the way he'd looked at her…

He'd shed his armour, she thought. Her great warrior had come home.

'Penny for them.' His voice startled her. It was still sleepy, but there was passion behind the huskiness. There was tenderness, too, and she thought last night wasn't just…last night. The armour was still discarded.

He was still hers.

'I was feeling like we should advertise singing hinnies as the world's new aphrodisiac,' she managed. 'Known only to us.'

'Let's keep it that way,' he said and gathered her closer. 'Just between us. It feels…excellent. Jeanie…'

'Mmm?' She lifted her face so she was pillowed on his chest. She liked his chest. As chests went, his was truly magnificent. The best?

'I don't know if I'm going to be any good at this.'

'At…'

'At marriage.'

She thought about that for a moment, assembling ideas and discarding them until she found the right one.

'Just lucky we're not, then.'

'We are.'

'No.' She pushed herself up so she was looking down at him, into his beautiful dark eyes, so she could see him clearly, all of him. He was her husband, her body was screaming at her—but she knew he wasn't.

'Alasdair, I've been down that path,' she said, slowly but surely, knowing that, no matter what her body was telling her, what she said was right. 'Twice now I've taken wedding vows and meant them. This time we spoke them but we didn't mean them. They were lies from the start so maybe that's the way it's meant to be. We've made the vows but now we need to prove them. We shouldn't even think of marriage before…unless…we fall in love.'

'Jeanie, the way I feel—'

'Hush,' she told him and put a finger to his lips. 'We both feel,' she told him. 'And maybe for you it's the first time, but for me… Alasdair, if this is for real, then it has to feel real. I won't have you held to me by vows we made when we were under duress. Let's leave this for a year.'

'A year…' He shook his head, his eyes darkening. He lifted one of her curls and twisted it and the sensation of the moving curl was enough to drive her wild all by itself. 'I have news for you. I don't think I can wait a minute.'

She was struggling to keep her voice even, to say what needed to be said. 'That's the way I feel, too, and I think… I think that's okay.'

'It has to be okay—wife.'

'No.' She drew back, still troubled. She had to make him see. 'I'm not your wife, Alasdair. For now I'm your lover, and I'd like… I'd like to stay your lover. Last night was…'

'Mind-shattering,' he said and she wanted to melt but she mustn't. She mustn't.

'We didn't go into last night with vows, though,' she managed. 'Alasdair…'

'Jeanie?'

He was driving her wild with wanting, but she had to say it. 'If at the end of the year we still want to marry, then…then we can think about it, but no pressure. We're not married until then.'

'So we're merely lovers?'

'I don't think merely comes into it.'

'Neither do I,' he said and he smiled and tugged her back to him. 'Maybe you're right,' he told her. 'A year of self-enforced courtship. A year where I'm locked in Duncairn Castle with my Jeanie, and at the end—'

'I'm not your Jeanie, and we'll worry about the end at the end.'

'But for the next few moments?'

And finally she managed to smile. Finally she let herself relax and savour being where she most wanted to be in the world. 'Let's just take each few moments as they come.'

'Starting now?'

And he smiled back at her, a dark, dangerous smile that had her heart doing back flips. He tugged her closer and he didn't need to wait for a response.

'Yes,' she breathed and then she could scarcely breathe at all.

CHAPTER NINE

LIFE HAD TO RESTART, a new norm had to be established, the world had to realign on its axis.

Lovers but not husband and wife?

It was working, Jeanie conceded as week followed week, as summer faded to autumn, as the castle settled to its new routine. Duncairn guests were now welcomed by a host as well as a hostess. Alasdair drew back on his visits to Edinburgh. He still worked during the day, sometimes from dawn, but at five every afternoon he kitted himself out in full highland regalia and came down the massive stairway to greet their guests.

Their guests. That was what it felt like. It was even fun, Jeanie conceded, sitting in the great library watching guests sipping their whisky, listening to Alasdair draw them out, listening to them tell of their travels, watching them fall under his spell.

It was also excellent for business. Although she nobly didn't advertise it, it was soon all over the web that the Earl of Duncairn Castle greeted his guests in person, and bookings went up accordingly.

'By the time you get your castle back it might be paying for itself,' she teased him that night.

For the nights were theirs. Their lives had fallen into a pattern. They walked the dogs at midday or when there was a break in the weather. They greeted the guests together. They had a brief dinner together. They came together at night.

Every night he was hers.

'We'll get the castle valued and add to your wages accordingly,' he told her. 'You needn't worry about the effort you're putting in not being appreciated.'

'I'm not worried about value.'

'You should be.'

But how to explain to him she didn't give a toss? How to say that she was living for the moment, and if, at the end of the year, this wasn't a marriage, then she'd not want anything to remind her of what could have been?

For she'd fallen in love, she conceded, as the weeks wore on. Alasdair might be able to hold himself apart, segment his life into times he could spend with her and times he couldn't, but there was no way she could.

He'd thought this could be a marriage, but Jeanie knew what bad marriages were, and she wanted more.

Did he think of her at all when he was elbow deep in his endless paperwork, phone calls, negotiations, flying trips to Edinburgh, fast international flights for imperative meetings? she wondered.

Did he fly back to her thinking, I want to get back to Jeanie? Or did he fly back thinking he had to get back to fulfil the stipulations of his grandmother's will?

At night, held in his arms, cocooned in the mutual passion, he felt all hers. But at dawn he was gone again.

She rose each day and got on with her work but she couldn't help listening for when the dogs' pressure got too much and she'd hear his study door open.

'Walk?'

How could she ever say no? It'd be like cutting her heart from her body. She donned her mac and her walking boots, they set off in whatever direction the dogs led them and she thought as she walked that she'd never been happier.

Except…

Except this was still compartmentalised. While they walked they talked of the castle, of the guests they'd had the night before, of the eagles, the otters, the wild things that crossed their path.

She tried, a few times, to ask about his work. Each time he answered politely, telling her what she wanted to know but no more.

The message was clear. His work was one compartment. She was another.

In those times she knew he wasn't hers completely. She could see it in his eyes—this was a midday walk between business sessions. His mind was on deals, plans, business she had no part in.

And she was part of his plans for the castle. As the weeks wore on she realised that. His decision to dress and come down to greet their guests was a business decision and a good one. She was part of that section of his business dealings but not the rest.

'I should be happy,' she told the dogs, because there was no one else to talk to. 'How many wives know their husband's business?'

She'd known Rory's—he'd bored her to snores with details of every last fish.

She'd been forced to know Alan's. He'd involved her in it to the point where she'd thought she was drowning.

Alasdair kept his business separate. She thought…she guessed…there was something worrying him about the business but she wasn't permitted to know what.

'It's his right to keep to himself,' she told the dogs. 'We could still… We might still be married, even if…'

Even if…

'He has less than a year to let me in,' she whispered. She was sitting by her hearth, supposedly reading, but she'd given the book up to hug the dogs. She needed hugging.

It was late at night, she was tired and soon she'd go to bed but she could hear the distant murmur of Alasdair on the phone. Who was he talking to? Who knew?

Should she go to bed and wait?

'Of course I will,' she told the dogs. She had to be up early in the morning to get the guests' breakfasts, but, no matter how early she rose, Alasdair would rise earlier.

Ten more months to make a marriage?

'It's not going to work,' she said bleakly.

'So tell him,' she told herself.

'How can I?' She hugged the dogs tighter. 'How can I?' she asked them again. 'He's given me so much…how can I ask for more?'

It was working better than he'd thought possible. Somehow he seemed to have succeeded at this marriage business. Somehow he'd got it right.

For it was working. He spent his days immersed in doing what he'd been doing ever since his grandfather had taken him into the company's headquarters. That had always been his way of blocking out…life? He'd hated his parents' life, the life he'd been born to. His engagement to Celia had been an unmitigated disaster. When he'd realised how much she'd taken from him and how stupid he'd been, he'd backed into his world of business and he loved it. The cut and thrust of the financial world, where he knew the odds, where he held the cards, where he knew when to play and when to walk away… It was where he wanted to be.

The financial leaks he was dealing with now were troubling but intriguing. They were taking most of his attention, but gloriously, unexpectedly, Jeanie was fitting into the edges. She didn't intrude. She kept to herself but when he wanted her she was there. His perfect woman…

And then Elspeth dropped her bombshell.

* * *

If Jeanie Lochlan was Alasdair's perfect wife, Elspeth was his perfect secretary. She was the one person in his business world he trusted absolutely, and when she rang one afternoon and asked could she see him, the answer had to be 'of course'. The chopper was in Edinburgh. 'It'll be quicker if I come to you,' she told him. 'I need to talk face-to-face.'

The vague worries he'd been confronting for the past few weeks coalesced into a knot of trouble.

'I'll talk when I get there. There are too many ears in this place.' She disconnected and he stared at nothing.

The dogs were waiting for their walk and Jeanie was waiting with them. He joined her and he walked but his mind was all over the place.

'Is something wrong?' Jeanie asked as they reached the clifftops and he realised he hadn't spoken since they'd left the castle.

'I… No. My secretary's flying in at two. If needs be, can we put her up for the night?'

'Of course.'

'Thank you.'

'It's your castle,' she said gently, but he was no longer listening. He was playing scenarios out in his mind. Something was badly wrong. He knew it.

'Can I help?' she asked and he shook his head again and managed a smile.

'That'd be like me offering to fix your burned scones.'

'You can share my burned scones,' she told him, but she said it so lightly he hardly heard and his mind was off on tangents again.

She said little more. They returned to the house. She headed for the kitchen and closed the door behind her. He hesitated and then followed her.

'Jeanie, I might not be down to play host this evening.'

'We can cope without you,' she said, giving him a bright

smile. 'The dogs and I put on a glorious welcome all by ourselves.'

'You lack the kilt.'

'We lack the title, too,' she said and her smile became a little more relaxed. 'The punters want to see the Earl of Duncairn, but they'll have to cope with portraits today. Isn't that the chopper landing?'

It was. He nodded and headed out to see it land.

He'd been right to be worried. Elspeth was distressed. As soon as he met her he could see the rigidity in her face, the fact that this was bad. He led her inside.

'Can I get you some tea? Jeanie could make us—'

'I don't want your wife bothered. Does she know about the business?'

'No.'

'Then let's leave it like that. The less people who know about this, the better. Alasdair, it's Don.'

'Don?' His grandmother's friend? 'What on earth…?'

'You know your grandparents gave him total trust? Last month you asked for the accounts to be audited, for everything your grandmother oversaw to be checked to make sure there weren't any gaps that hadn't been filled. The accounts that went through your grandmother's office were the only ones not subject to company scrutiny. Now it seems…' She took a deep breath. 'It seems you were right in your suspicions. You've been wondering for years how the Antica Corporation seem to be second-guessing us. They haven't been guessing. There's been an income stream from them flowing straight to Don's bank account.'

'Straight…'

'Well, not straight.' Elspeth handed over a folder. 'He couldn't do that, because the tax people would have caught him, so he's been streaming cash through the company accounts. Until Eileen's death the order's always been to leave Don's affairs to Don—maybe it was a measure of your grandparents' trust in him. So Don's financial dealings with the company have been audited for the first time ever. He's hidden it incredibly carefully. They've had to probe and probe, but finally it's exposed, and it's a hornet's nest. There's talk of insider trading—Don's been buying shares of companies we've dealings with and he's been buying them with money coming from Eileen's charity funds. There's so much… This has ramifications as far as the eye can see. The auditors want to call in the police. They need to talk to you but I thought it best I talk to you first.'

She watched them leave.

'I'll be back in a couple of days,' Alasdair said curtly, his face blank.

'What's wrong?'

'It's nothing to concern you. Apologise to the guests.'

Fine, she told herself. Life went on. She didn't need him.

She greeted the guests. She took the dogs for another walk. She made dinner for herself and had to force herself to eat, but the look on his face stayed with her. And with it came other doubts.

It's nothing to concern you.

She'd thought she had a marriage.

No, she conceded as the night wore on to the small hours and sleep wouldn't come. Until this afternoon she'd tried to pretend she had a marriage but as he'd left, with his face still impassive, revealing nothing of the turmoil she guessed was underneath, she'd felt…

Ill.

'Unless he comes back and tells me about it…' she whispered to the dogs, but she knew he wouldn't.

Because reality was finally sinking in.

They didn't have a marriage at all.

What followed was messy, nasty, heartbreaking. At least Eileen wasn't alive to see it, Alasdair thought. He wouldn't press charges—how could he? It'd make the company seem lax, and as well as that…it'd show the world he'd trusted.

Do not trust.

'Thank God I have Jeanie,' he told himself as the auditors unravelled the web of financial deceit and he saw the full extent of the betrayal of his grandparents' trust. 'Thank God I can go back to Jeanie. I can trust her. Separation of worlds is the only way to go. If I keep our lives separate, it'll work. It's the only way it can.'

He was away for two days. He returned late in the afternoon, the chopper flying in low from the east, setting him down and taking off almost as soon as he'd cleared the blades.

Jeanie was working in the kitchen. She saw the chopper land through the window. She let the dogs out and watched them race hysterically towards him. She watched him set down his bulging briefcase so he could greet them—and she thought maybe she should be doing the same.

The little wife, welcoming her husband home after his foray into the big, bad world.

He'd gone away looking as if he'd been slugged with a shock that was almost unbearable. He hadn't phoned. He'd told her nothing.

She wiped her hands slowly on the dishcloth and went to the door to greet him.

He looked exhausted. He looked…bleak. She wanted to put her arms around him and hug—but he was still in his business suit. His face said he still belonged to that other world.

And then he saw her waiting, and his face changed.

She saw it. He'd left here shocked and disoriented. Something bad had happened—she didn't have to be Einstein to figure that out. He'd been immersed in whatever it was for two days, and now he was home.

Now she watched him slough off whatever had made him look as if he'd come back from a war and turn into Alasdair. Into the man who took her to his bed.

His face creased into the smile she knew and loved. He reached her in three long strides, he had her in his arms and he swung her round and round as if she were a featherweight rather than a slightly too-curvy housekeeper who liked her own cooking.

His face radiated pleasure, and when finally he stopped swinging he set her down, cupped her face and kissed her.

A girl could drown in that kiss.

Not. She would not. For somewhere in the back of her head there was a place where passion couldn't reach. And it was ringing alarm bells that she'd heard before.

Once upon a time she'd fancied she was in love with Rory. He'd been the answer to her prayers, she'd been joyous when he'd asked her to marry him, but a tiny part of her had voiced doubts.

Do you want to spend the rest of your life cleaning his fish and watching football on the telly?

She'd ignored the voice. And then with Alan… That same little voice as she'd left the island with him, as she'd headed off to the world she'd dreamed of, the same voice had been whispering…

What does a man like this want with a girl like me? This doesn't make sense. Why is Eileen looking like she's worried?

And now that same dratted voice was no longer whispering. It was shouting.

He's in trouble and he's not telling me. I'm just the little wife, not to be worrying her head about such things. I'm just the cook and bottle washer, and a warm body in his bed.

'Alasdair,' she managed. 'What's happened?'

'Nothing that need concern you. Give me thirty minutes. I need to make a couple of calls and I'll be with you.'

'I'll be in the kitchen.'

He must have heard the strain in her voice. 'Is something wrong?'

'Nothing that need concern you.'

'Jeanie—'

'Go and get changed,' she told him, feeling suddenly weary beyond belief. 'I'll see you when you're ready.'

The calls stretched to an hour. He hadn't meant them to, but if Don's fraud wasn't to hit the front pages of the financial papers, there were people he had to placate. He'd used an outside auditor and outside audit firms had their own leaks. Rumours were swirling and they had to be settled.

The legal problems were another matter. They were still a minefield to be faced.

When finally he reached the kitchen he was beyond exhaustion. Jeanie was waiting. He smiled at seeing her, hoping like hell she wouldn't ask what was wrong again, immeasurably thankful for her presence.

She was making shortbread, pressing dough into wooden moulds with thistles carved into them, then tapping the shaped dough out onto trays. He sank into a chair and watched. She let him be for a while. Three moulds. Four.

'Do you enjoy making them?' It was a bit of an inane question but he was feeling inane right now.

'I'm good at it.' She looked down at the perfect circles. 'It's supposed to be what a good Scottish housewife does.'

That was a jarring note. 'You'd rather be doing something else?'

'Learning to fly,' she said, unexpectedly. She gestured to the window where, in the distance, he could see the eagles soaring in the thermals. 'Like those guys. But each to his own. They fly. I make shortbread. Alasdair, I need to ask you again. What's wrong?'

'Just a problem at headquarters.'

'A big problem.' It wasn't a question.

'Maybe.' His tone said no more questions.

She looked at him for a long moment and then filled a couple more moulds. The shortbread shapes looked beautiful, perfect circles with a thistle etched on top. He hardly noticed.

It was enough that she was here. That was all he wanted, Jeanie, a safe haven where he could bury the outside world.

He glanced outside at the eagles and thought he was very glad she wasn't out there flying. He wanted her here.

A good Scottish housewife?

'Alasdair, let me in,' she said and his thoughts focused. The almost animal instinct to relax, to let himself be... just disappeared.

'How do you mean?'

'You know what I mean.' She took a deep breath and steadied. 'Something's happened, something bad. I could read Elspeth's face. I could see your shock. You left looking like death. I've heard nothing from you for two days and you return looking like you've been through the wringer. You say it's nothing to concern me. You have me worried.'

'Don't worry.'

'You lie in my arms every night and I shouldn't worry for you?'

He didn't want this conversation. He was too tired. 'Jeanie, you're separate. You're here, you're part of this place and that's all that matters. I can't believe what we've managed to forge. If you knew how much I've been aching to come back to you...'

'You're back and you're hurting.' Her tone was neutral. 'But you don't want to tell me why?'

'You're not part of that world.'

'And you don't want me to know about it?'

'I don't want to have to trust…'

And as soon as he said it, he knew he'd killed something. He saw it in her face. He might just as well have slapped her.

If he hadn't been so tired, he would have phrased it better, thought of some way round it, thought of how he could deflect it. But the words had been said, and they seemed to hang over his head, like a sword, about to come crashing down.

'You don't trust,' she said, softly now, as if she, too, feared the sword.

'I do. I can.'

'You mean you can trust me with the parts of your world you allow me to share. The part that likes hinnies and shortbread and walking the dogs and holding me at night. But there are parts you won't entrust to me.'

'No. I…'

'Are they state secrets? Stuff that'd bring down countries, stuff worth so much secret agents might torture me to make me confess?'

He managed a smile. 'Hardly. Jeanie—'

'Then what?' She ran a hand through her curls, leaving a wash of flour she didn't notice. 'What's so important?'

'It's just that our worlds are different.' He was too tired to explain. He couldn't get it right. 'I don't interfere with your life—'

'As I see it, you've interfered a lot.' Her voice was calm, but the shuttered look was down. 'You married me to save your inheritance. You're walking in and out of my world as you like, but it's all one-way.'

'You don't want to be part of my world.'

'Part of your business world?'

'Right. It has nothing to do with you.'

'And if it did…I'd likely betray something? Do you really think that?'

'No.' It was he who was raking his hair now. He was so tired he couldn't get this right, but he had to. What to say?

And in desperation he said it. 'Jeanie, I've fallen in love with you.' The words were out and they didn't sound so bad. In fact, they sounded okay. Good, even. This house, this woman, this home… 'This is everything I want,' he told her. 'And I don't want to mess with that.'

He'd just told a woman he loved her. It was big. It was momentous—but Jeanie was staring at him as if he'd offered poison. 'So…sharing might mess with it?'

'I don't know,' he said honestly. 'Maybe. All I know is that I love what we have here. Can you not just accept that?'

'I already have accepted it.' But her voice was dead. Whatever response he'd been hoping for, he knew it wasn't this.

'You mean you love me?'

'No. Or maybe. But it doesn't matter. It can't matter.' She was looking stricken. She took two steps back from the table as if she needed to put distance between them. 'I mean I've been married before, Alasdair. Married, but not *married*. Married on just the terms you're offering.'

And that got him. 'How can you compare me to Alan?'

'Or Rory?' she added. 'I'm not comparing men. I'm comparing marriages. They've been three very different… disasters but the same each time. They say some people go on repeating the same mistake for the rest of their lives. It's time I stopped.'

'Jeanie…'

'Rory was older than me,' she said, still in that cold, dead voice. He wanted to go to her but the look on her face was a shield all by itself. 'He was like my big brother. When my mam died, I was gutted but Rory stood up for me. He stood up to my bully of a father. He made me feel safe and when he married me I thought I was the luckiest woman on the island. The problem was, that's who I was. The little woman, to be protected. I never shared Rory's world. I was a tiny part of it. I was the woman who kept the home fires burning, who cleaned and cooked and worked for his parents, but when he wanted to talk he went out with the boys. I never knew anything that troubled him. I was his wife and I knew my place.'

'I don't—'

'Think you're like that? No? And then there was Alan.' She was talking fast now, her hands up as if to prevent him interrupting. Or taking her in his arms? Her hands said do neither. 'Alan blew me away with his fun, his exuberance, the way he embraced…everything. I was still young and I was stupid and I'd been bogged down by grief at Rory's death for so long that I fell for him like a ton of bricks. And when he asked me to marry him I was dazzled. But Alan, too, had his secrets. The biggest one was that he was up to his neck in debt. He was desperate for his grandmother to bail him out and he thought by marrying someone she was fond of he'd get her to agree. She did, but at what cost? I was trapped again, a tiny part of a life I couldn't share.'

'This is nothing like that.' He was on his feet now, angry. That she would compare him to his cousin…

'I know you're not.' Her voice softened. 'I know you're nothing like Alan. But you have your demons, too. You've let me close enough to see them, but, Alasdair, whether I see them or not is irrelevant. You won't share.'

'I want to be married. This can work.'

'You don't want to be married.' She shook her head, as if trying to work it out for herself. 'The thing is that I have a different definition of marriage from you. Marriage is supposed to be the joining together of two people—isn't it? That's what I want, Alasdair. That's what I dream of. But you…you see marriage as the joining together of the little bits you want to share.'

'You don't want to know about my business.'

'Maybe I don't,' she said slowly. 'But that's not what I'm talking about. You don't want to trust. You don't want to share because it'll make you somehow more exposed. And I don't want that sort of semi-commitment. More, I'll run a mile before I risk it. I'm sorry, Alasdair, but it has to end. The vows we took were only mock. You say you love me. It's a wonderful compliment but that's all it is—a compliment. We need to work out a way forward but the little loving we've been sharing isn't the way to go. It has to end and it will. Right now.'

He looked ill but she wouldn't allow herself to care. She mustn't. Something inside was dying but she couldn't let herself examine it. Like a wounded creature of the wild, she needed to be left alone. She wanted to find a place where she could hide.

To recover? How did she recover? She felt dead inside. Hopeless.

'Alasdair, you're too tired to take this in.' She forced herself to sound gentle—to play the concerned wife? No. She was a concerned friend now, she told herself. Nothing more. 'How long since you slept?'

'I can't—'

'Remember? Go up and sleep. We'll talk later.'

'We'll talk now.' It was a possessive growl and instinctively she backed away.

'Not now. There's nothing to say until you've thought it through.'

'You won't leave while I sleep?'

'No.'

'And after that?'

'We'll talk tomorrow. Go to bed.'

'Jeanie…'

'Alasdair, I have guests arriving in half an hour and I have work to do. Please…leave me be.' She turned to put trays of her shortbread into the oven.

If he came up behind her, she thought, if he touched her, how could she keep control? She was so close to the edge…

But he didn't come. She waited, every nerve in her body, every sense tuned to the man behind her. If he touched her…

She'd break. She'd said what she had to say. She'd meant it but her body didn't mean it. Her body wanted him.

She wanted him, but the cost was too high. The cycle had to be broken, right here, right now.

Please… It was a silent prayer and in the end she didn't know whether it was for him to leave or for him to stay. Please…

And in the end who knew whether the prayer was answered?

He left.

He was too tired to think straight. He was too tired to fight for what he wanted.

The mess in Edinburgh had needed a week to sort, but, with only twenty-eight nights away from the castle permissible under the terms of the will, he'd had to get home. So he'd worked through, forty-eight hours straight.

His head was doing weird things. It was as if Jeanie's words had been a battering ram, and he'd been left concussed.

It must be exhaustion, he told himself. He should have stayed another night in Edinburgh—he could have managed it in his schedule—but he'd wanted to get home.

To Jeanie.

She was downstairs and she wasn't coming up. She intended to sleep in her own apartment. He'd be going to bed alone.

Maybe it was just as well. He needed time to think. He had to get it sorted.

Maybe she was talking sense. Maybe the type of relationship she was demanding wasn't something he could give?

His head hurt.

He showered and his head didn't clear. The night was closing in. All he saw was fog.

He headed for his bedroom and there was a bowl of soup and toast and tea by his bed.

'Try to eat,' the note beside it said. 'Things will look better in the morning.'

How could they look better?

Was she talking about Don? About the betrayal?

He hadn't told her about Don. He hadn't let her close.

He stared down at the simple meal, thinking he wanted her to be here while he ate it.

He wanted her as an accessory to his life?

It was too hard. He couldn't make his mind work any more. He managed half the meal. He put his head on the pillow and slept.

She shouldn't have cooked for him. The little wife preparing supper for her businessman husband, home after a frantic two days at the office? Ha.

But this much was okay, she told herself. She'd waited until she heard the sound of his shower and then slipped his meal in unseen, as she'd done a hundred times for guests who'd arrived late, who hadn't been able to find a meal in town or who were ill or in trouble.

He was a guest, she told herself. That was the way it was now. He was a guest in the bed and breakfast she worked in. Nothing more.

CHAPTER TEN

HE WAS TROUBLED by dreams but still he slept, his body demanding the rest it so badly needed. He hadn't set his alarm and when he woke it was nine o'clock and he could hear the sound of guests departing downstairs.

He lay and let the events of the past two days seep back into his consciousness. He allowed them in piece by piece, assessing, figuring out what had gone wrong, how he could have handled things better.

The financial and legal mess Don had left would have ramifications into the future. He should let his mind dwell on that as a priority. Instead his brain skipped right over and moved on...

To Jeanie.

There was a scratch at the door. The dogs. He rose to let them in and found an envelope had been slipped under the door. Like a checkout slip from a hotel? *Thank you for your patronage—here's the cost?*

He snagged the envelope, let the dogs in and went back to bed. Abbot and Costello hit the covers with joy. He patted them but his pat was perfunctory.

'Nice to see you, too, guys. Settle.'

And they did settle, as if they, too, knew the contents of the envelope were important.

He lay back on the bed, reluctant to open it but it had

to be done. It contained two pages of what looked like…
a contract?

Note first.

Dear Alasdair,

You'll be worried by now that I'm going to leave. If
I do, then of course things revert to their former disaster. I won't do that to you. Just because my emotional needs don't match yours, there's no need to
bring down the Duncairn Empire.

Alasdair, your grandmother's will was fanciful
—an old lady's wish born out of fondness for me.
But she's already done so much for me—more than
enough—so this is how it will be.

I'll stay until the end of the twelve months, as your
housekeeper. I'll accept a decent wage, but that's all.
At the end of the year I'll walk away and I'll take
nothing. The following contract, signed by me and
witnessed by the guy who delivered this morning's
groceries, grants you every right to the castle.

I know Alan's creditors will still claim it, but you
can then pay them out if you wish. Or not. It's nothing to do with me. All I want—and I do want this—
is the dogs. Oh, and what's left of my whisky. I've
given up the idea of selling it online so I'll be making awesome Christmas cakes for generations. That's
my own little Duncairn Legacy.

Meanwhile, if you sign the contract, that's what
it says and that's where we'll leave it. It's as professional as I can make it.

It's been lovely, Alasdair, but we should never
have mixed business with pleasure. You're right—
our lives are separate.

Oh, and your ring is in the safe in your grand-

mother's room. I have no right to it, and it's too precious to lose.

Yours back to being formal.

Jeanie

He lay and stared at the ceiling while the dogs settled,
draped themselves over him, slept.

Our lives are separate.

Downstairs he heard Jeanie start to hoover. In a while
she started to hum and then to sing.

If he didn't know better, he'd think she was happy. She
wasn't. He'd lived in the same castle as this woman for
almost two months. He could hear the note of determined
cheerfulness. The courage.

She had a great voice, he thought inconsequentially.
With the hoover in the background it was the best…

Jeanie…

Too precious to lose?

Hell.

The dogs were letting him go nowhere—or maybe it
was his mind letting him go nowhere. What he'd learned
in a crisis was to get all the facts before he made a move
and he didn't have all the facts before him yet. Or he did,
but they weren't in the proper order. He needed to marshal
them, set them in a line, examine them.

But they wouldn't stay in line. They were jumping at
him from every which way, and overriding all of them was
the sound of Jeanie singing.

The contract fell off the coverlet, onto the floor. He
let it lie.

Done. Dusted. Sorted. Jeanie had told him the end of
this particular story. Move on.

It'd been all right when he'd thought he'd been buying
her out, he thought savagely. Why wasn't it okay now?

His phone interrupted. It was his chief lawyer, calling

to talk about Don. Listening to what the man was telling him, he felt some relief—but suddenly the lawyer was talking about something else. Jeanie's bankruptcy?

What he told him made Alasdair pay more attention than all the details of Don's betrayal.

Why tell him this now? he demanded, but it had only been after a long examination of all the contracts that the lawyers had felt sure.

He disconnected feeling…discombobulated. Talk about complications! What was he going to do with this?

He needed to walk. He needed to get his mind clear before he talked to her.

'Come on, guys,' he told the dogs, tossing back the covers. 'Let's go discuss this with the otters.'

She hoovered every inch of the castle and then some. Halfway through the hoovering she heard Alasdair come down the stairs, the dogs clattering after him. She held her breath but she heard them head straight for the wet room. The back door slammed and then she heard silence.

He'd taken the dogs for a walk? Good.

'But I'm taking the dogs when I go,' she muttered and she tried to make herself sound angry but in the end all she felt like was crying.

But she would not cry. Not again. Not over a man— even if he was Alasdair. She had to keep it together and get the next ten months over with. For ten months she had to live in the castle so their mock marriage could stay intact. She had to stay sane.

She would.

She sniffed and sniffed again, and then walked determinedly to the back door. Alasdair and the dogs were over the brow of the first hill. Out of earshot? Excellent. She took a deep breath, stood on the top step and let fly.

'Don't you dare get attached to those dogs,' she yelled,

to the departing Alasdair, to the world in general. 'They're mine. I don't have a right to your castle, but your grandma's dopey dogs are mine, and I'll fight for them.'

And the whisky?

'And the whisky, too,' she yelled but he was long gone and nobody heard.

She wouldn't cry. *She would not.*

Instead she went back inside and returned to her hoovering. 'Back to being the char,' she told herself and then she forced a mocking smile. 'But back to being your own woman as well. It's about time you learned how.'

He headed along the cliffs, to Craigie Burn, to the place where he and Jeanie had watched the otters. The dogs were wild with excitement, but then they were always wild with excitement. They raced deliriously around him but finally settled to his gentle amble, keeping him in sight but leaving him to himself. When he paused at the point where the burn cut him off from wild woods beyond, the dogs found a rabbit warren and started digging. Next stop China, he thought, as he watched the dirt flying. Any Duncairn rabbit was safe from this pair. They were closer to burying each other than catching anything.

He left them be. He headed for the cottage, sat on the rock above the water and stared at nothing in particular. He had things to be thinking, things to be working out, but his mind seemed to have gone into shutdown.

Jeanie had given him what he wanted—hadn't she? It was selfish to want more.

The dogs were yapping in the distance and he found himself smiling. Stupid dogs.

At the end of the year he wouldn't have them.

He could buy others. He could find dogs with a bit more intelligence.

He could find...another woman?

And there his thoughts stopped.

Another woman?

A wife?

He didn't want a wife. He wanted Jeanie.

Two different things.

But he'd treated her as…just a wife, he conceded, thinking of the past few weeks. *A housewife.* He'd played the businessman, and Jeanie was his appendage. Each had their clear delineation of responsibility. Each only interacted on a need-to-know basis.

Except Jeanie hadn't treated their marriage like that, he thought. She hadn't compartmentalised as he had. She'd welcomed him into her kitchen, into her bed, into her life.

She'd told him everything he wanted to know about this business, this island, her life. She'd opened herself to him, whereas he…

He'd done what would work. He'd resisted the temptation to trust because trust only led to trouble.

A movement by the water's edge caught his eye. Welcoming the diversion from thoughts that were taking him nowhere, he let himself be distracted. The pocket of his hiking jacket always held a pair of field glasses. He hauled them out and focused.

A pair of sea otters were at the water's edge beneath him, devouring the end of what looked like the remains of a rather large fish. He watched, caught by their beauty and their activity, welcoming the diversion.

What was a group of sea otters called? A raft? He found himself wondering why.

And then he found out. The fish finished, the otters slipped back into the water and drifted lazily out midstream. They stayed hard up against each other and he focused his glasses to see more clearly.

They were linked. Hand in hand? Paw in paw? They floated on the surface, their faces soaking up the rays of the weak autumn sun, replete, relaxed, ready for sleep? Together they made a raft of two otters. Their eyes were closed. They were only two, but their raft was complete.

Jeanie would like to see this.

And then he thought: I can show her—but at the end of the year she'll walk away.

Because he couldn't trust? No, because he didn't want to trust. He didn't want to risk…

Risk what? Losing his business? She'd saved that for him. This estate? It'd survive as well.

What, then?

Did trust have to mean betrayal?

In his world, it did. His parents had shown him no loyalty whatsoever. They'd dumped him whenever they could. He'd had one disastrous engagement, which had ended in betrayal. He'd been humiliated to the core. And now Don… An old family friend. A man his grandparents had trusted completely.

He'd lost through betrayal. His parents. His fiancée. Don. The hurt from his parents was ongoing. His father had died without ever showing him affection. His mother… she was with someone in the US. Someone fabulous, someone rich, someone who didn't want anything to do with her past.

And now… If his grandmother had known about Don, it would have broken her heart, he thought. Oh, Eileen, you should have learned. Counter betrayal by not trusting. Don't leave yourself open to that devastation.

Eileen had loved Jeanie. She'd trusted her completely.

Was that why she'd engineered this marriage—because she'd trusted Jeanie to love her grandson? What an ask.

The otters were drifting further downstream, seemingly asleep, seemingly oblivious to their surroundings. Were they pups? he wondered. A mother and her offspring? A mating pair?

Did otters mate and stay mated? He needed to find out.

He watched them float and found himself thinking that what he was seeing was perfect trust. They were together and that seemed all that mattered.

But...they were floating towards the point where the burn met the incoming sea.

The burn was running gently, but the sea was not so gentle. There must have been a storm out in the Atlantic not long since, because the sea was wild. The breakers were huge and the point where the waves washed into the mouth of the burn was a mass of white water.

The otters were almost there.

Were they pups? Didn't they know? Dumb or not, he found himself on his feet, staring helplessly at them, wanting to yell...

His glasses were still trained on their heads. Just as they reached the point where the wash of surf could have sucked them in, he saw one stir and open its eyes...

What followed was a swift movement—a nudge? They were both awake then, diving together straight into the wash, surfacing on a wave, cruising on its face across the surf—then back into the safety and relative calm of the burn.

He watched them glide sleekly back up the burn, past him, then drift together again, once more forming a raft—then close their eyes and proceed to do it all over again.

Trust...

And suddenly it was as if invisible cords were breaking from around him. He felt light, strange—free.

Thoughts came after the sensation. It was as if his body already knew what his mind would think. He had to watch the otters for a while as his mind caught up.

But catch up it did.

The otters trusted.

Rafted together, two lots of senses looked onto the outside world. Who knew if otters hunted together, but, if they did, two must be able to work more effectively than one. Two had devoured a truly excellent salmon that might well have been too much for one. Rafted together, they seemed a larger animal, a bigger presence to possibly deter predators.

Rafted together, they could have fun?

Fun.

Trust. Dependence.

Love.

The thoughts were almost blindsiding him. He wasn't sure what to do with them but when he finally rose there was only one thing he knew for certain.

He had to share.

CHAPTER ELEVEN

'COME AND SEE.'

Three words. He said them but he hardly knew whether she'd accept or not.

He'd brought the dogs home, settled them, given them a bone apiece. He'd fetched another pair of field glasses and then put a rug into a backpack and a bottle of wine. Hopeful, that. Then he'd searched for Jeanie. She was in the library, wiping her whisky bottles clean. She was polishing...for the sake of polishing?

'Come where?' She didn't turn to face him. There must be a smear on the bottle she had in her hand. It was taking all her concentration.

'To Craigie Burn. I need you to come, Jeanie. Please.'

She shouldn't come. She shouldn't go anywhere near this man. He...did things to her. He touched her without touching her.

He made her feel exposed and raw, and open to a pain that seemed to have been with her all her life.

'Please,' he said again and she set down the whisky bottle with a steadying clink.

'The guests arrive at four. I'll be back by then?'

'You will.' It was a promise and it steadied her.

'Give me five minutes to change.'

What did he want? Why was she going? She was an

idiot, she told herself as she went to fetch a sweater and coat. A blind idiot.

Come and see, he'd said, so she went.

'I was born a fool,' she told herself as she headed for the back door where he stood waiting. 'Have you no idea how to defend yourself?'

Come and see, he'd said and she had no weapons at all.

The otters were gone. Of course they were; they were wild creatures who went where they willed. They'd hunted and eaten and moved on. Who knew where they were now? Alasdair stood on the cliff and surveyed the water below.

No otters.

It didn't matter.

'Come and see…what?' Jeanie asked beside him. They'd walked here in almost total silence. Who knew what she was thinking? It was enough that she trusted him to take her here, he thought. He wouldn't ask more.

'I want you to see the otters,' he told her. 'They were here this morning. They're not here now but I still want you to see them.'

She looked at him in silence for a long moment. 'Right,' she said. 'You know they might not appear again for a week?'

'They'll appear if you close your eyes and let yourself see.'

There was another silence, longer this time. And then she closed her eyes.

'I'm watching.'

Trust…

It took his breath away. It was a small thing, doing what he'd asked, coming with him, closing her eyes on demand, but that she would put her trust in him…

He wanted to take her into his arms, tell her he loved her, sweep her into the moment.

Instead he made himself take his time. He spread his blanket on the ground, took her arms and pressed her gently to sit.

'What can you hear?'

'The burn,' she said, promptly. 'The water rippling down over the rocks. The waves in the distance. There's a bird somewhere...a plover? If it's thinking about swooping while I have my eyes closed...'

'It's not thinking about swooping. You're safe.'

'I trust you. Thousands wouldn't. What do you want me to see, Alasdair?'

And there was a note of restraint in her voice that told him this was hard for her. Trust was hard?

She had no reason to trust him. No reason at all.

'I want you to see the otters,' he told her, gently now. He sank down beside her and took her hand. He felt her stiffen, he felt the sharp intake of her breath and then he felt her consciously force herself to relax.

'Word picture?' she said and she had it. He had to smile. He might have guessed this woman would know what he was about.

'I watched them this morning,' he told her. 'Imagine them just below this overhang, on the great rock covered with weed. Two otters. I don't know if they were young or old, male or female, mother and cub, but I'm imagining... something in them was like us. Two creatures blessed with having all Duncairn as our domain.'

'I won't—'

'Stay with your eyes closed, Jeanie. Keep seeing the otters, but while you do I need you to listen to what I want to tell you. I need to say this first because I can't talk of the future without clearing the past. Jeanie, I would never marry you for the castle. I'm asking you to accept that. I've been thinking of this all night. Thinking it makes it impossible to ask...but today, looking at the otters, I thought, maybe I *can* ask you to trust. But before I ask… Jeanie, the castle is yours.'

Her forehead wrinkled. 'I don't understand.'

He put his finger to her lips. 'Hush, then. Hear me out. This has nothing to do with you or me. It's a legal opinion. I've had Duncairn's best legal minds look at the mess that Alan left you with. He assigned you his debt, he died and you were somehow lumbered with it. You'd signed contracts…'

'I know. I was stupid.'

'He was your husband. You weren't stupid, you were trusting and you were intimidated. But you were also conned. But the lawyers have demanded copies and it's taken time. The contracts contain pages of small print, but on all of them your name appears only on the first page. Did you read all those contracts?'

'I didn't even see the rest,' she confessed. 'Alan only ever gave me one page. There was no hint of more. He said it was so he could use the house Eileen had given us as security for business dealings. I thought…it was Alan's right—Eileen's gift had been to Alan.'

'Eileen wanted to keep you safe, but that's beside the point. The lawyers say there was no financial advantage to you included in the contracts Alan had you sign. If you'd initialled each page, if there was proof you'd read them in full, then the contracts could have held water, but as it is… Jeanie, those debts aren't binding. There was no need for you to be declared bankrupt. If Eileen had given you a decent lawyer instead of offering you a place here as housekeeper, she would have been doing you a much bigger service.'

'But I love it here.' She still had her eyes closed. She was feeling the salt in the autumn air, listening to the ocean, to the water rippling over the rocks. What he was saying seemed almost dreamlike. She didn't want to think of Alan and contracts and debt. Or even the castle. They all seemed a very long way away. 'What are our otters doing now?'

'They've just caught fish,' he told her. 'A fish apiece. They're eating them slowly, savouring them. They must be sated—the fishing must have been good this morning. Jeanie, we can discharge your bankruptcy right now. The lawyers are already instigating proceedings. As of now you're free of debt, and if we can manage to stay together for the next ten months, then Eileen's wishes are granted. You get the castle. I get the remainder.'

She had to force herself to focus. 'I don't want the castle. You're the Earl of Duncairn. It's your right.'

'I don't have rights. The otters are finishing their fish, right now. They're doing a little grooming.'

'I love watching otters groom. Are they sleek? Are they beautiful?'

'The sun's shining on their coats. The one on the left has fish caught in his whiskers. He's using his paws to get himself clean, then grooming his paws as well. How can we train the dogs to do that?'

'That's…my problem.'

'I'd like it to be ours.' He said it almost nonchalantly, as if it didn't matter at all. 'They've finished grooming now. They're slipping back into the water. They're slipping under, doing a few lazy circles, maybe getting rid of the last trace of fish. Jeanie, I had to tell you about the castle. I don't mean I'm reluctant to tell you. It's just that you need to know before…before I ask you something else.'

'Why?'

It was a tiny word, half whispered.

'Because what I'm about to say demands trust,' he told her. 'Because if I ask you to marry me properly, then you might think that I'm doing it now because of the castle. For castle, for keeps. I wouldn't do that, Jeanie.'

'I don't—'

'The otters have come together now,' he told her and he took her hands in his. She was shaking. Hell, *he* was shaking. She tugged away but when he went to release her she seemed to change her mind. Her hands held his as if he were an anchor in a drifting world.

'They're floating,' he told her. 'But the burn is running down to the sea. They'll end up on the rocks where the surf breaks.'

'They'll turn.'

'I know they will.' His grip on her hands tightened. What happened in the next few moments was so important—all his life seemed to be hanging in the balance. 'But look what they're doing now. They're catching paws. Catching hands.'

'I've seen them do that,' she whispered, unsure where he was going but willing to still see his otters. 'It's called rafting. A raft of otters.'

'So have I but I didn't get it until this morning,' he told her. 'I'm watching them float almost into the surf. They have their eyes closed, as yours are closed now, but one's aware. Just as the rocks grow sharp and jagged, just before they're in peril, his eyes fly open, and he moves and his partner's nudged and they dive away to safety. And then watch them, Jeanie. They disappear under the water, they glide unseen…and then they're upstream and they're rafting again and they're floating down, loving the water, loving the sun on their faces, but this time it's the other otter who stays aware, who does the nudging. Who keeps them both safe.'

'Why are you telling me this?' She seemed breathless. Her face was turned to the sun. Her eyes were still closed as if she didn't want to let go the vision.

'Because they've learned to trust, Jeanie,' he said softly. 'And because they trust, they can have fun. Because they trust, they can eat together, hunt together, float together. And as I lay on this rock this morning and I watched them, I thought of the way I've compartmentalised my life. I thought of how you've been hurt in the past by just such compartments and here I was doing it all over again. I've hurt you, Jeanie, and I'm sorry.'

He was finding it hard to keep talking. So much depended on this moment. So much…

'Jeanie, now, with the castle, you must know that it's yours,' he told her. 'You know the only way I can have any claim on it is to marry you properly so I need to say it upfront. For you need to know that I want to marry you no matter what you do. If you want to sell the castle to care for all the dogs of Europe, then it has to be okay with me. As long as you let me share your life. As long as you let me take your hand and let me float beside you.'

Her eyes were still closed. He was watching her face and he saw a tiny tic move at the corner of her mouth. Revulsion? Anger?

'You want me to float?' she demanded at last.

'With me.'

'In the burn? You'd be out of your mind. It's freezing.'

And the tic was laughter. Laughter! 'Metaphorically,' he said, with all the dignity he could muster.

'You don't really want to float with me?'

'If you want to float, then I'll float,' he said heroically and the tic quivered again.

'In your kilt?'

'If you ask it of me.'

'For castle, for keeps,' she mused and he couldn't bear it.

'Jeanie, open your eyes.'

'I'm still watching otters. They're having fun.'

'We could have fun.'

'You'd want to share my whisky.'

'Guilty as charged. And your dogs. I'd want to share your dogs.'

'I might want more.'

'Okay.' He was ready to agree to anything. Anything at all. 'But…can we get smart ones?' he suggested, cautiously, and then even more cautiously… 'And maybe eventually a bairn or two?'

The tic quivered. 'Bairns! With you spending thirty days a year away from the castle?'

'I've been thinking about that. Jeanie, I do need to travel to keep the company viable. I'd like the castle to stay as our home—if you're happy to share—but if I need to leave… would you fancy travelling with me?'

'Floating, you mean?'

'It would be my very great honour to keep you safe from rocks and rapids, but I'm looking forward now, Jeanie, and I can't see rapids. If you agreed to marry me, if we can both find it in ourselves to trust, then I can't see a rock in sight. But right now I'm thinking about flying.'

'Flying…'

'If you'd truly like to learn to fly—and you can't make shortbread forever—then flying's an option. Jeanie, what I've been doing for the last few days is complicated. I'll explain it all to you later, in all the detail you want, but, in a nutshell, Eileen's best friend in the company has betrayed her trust, a thousand-fold, leaving a legal and financial nightmare. That's why I had to leave in such a hurry. For a while I thought the foundations of the company might give, but we've done some massive shoring up, and this morning's legal advice is that we'll survive. The insider trading Don was involved in will fall on his head, not the company's. We might well need to adopt economies, however, so combining roles might be just what Duncairn Enterprises needs.'

'How…how do you mean?'

'Your role, for instance.' He wanted to tug her into his arms. It took an almost superhuman effort not to, but he had to keep control. So much hung on what he had to say right now.

'If you would like to reach for the sky,' he managed, 'how about a new role? Not Jeanie McBride, Alasdair's wife. How about Jeanie McBride, pilot and partner? You'd need lessons—lots of lessons—and that could be...fun?'

'Lessons?'

'Flying lessons. If that's your dream, Jeanie, I don't see why you shouldn't have it.'

'You'd teach me to fly?' Her eyes flew wide.

'Not me,' he said hurriedly. 'I'd sit in the passenger seat with my eyes closed. It's not a good look for a teacher. But we could find someone to teach you, and if you were flying, I'd be right with you. Trusting you like anything.'

She shook her head in wordless astonishment and he had to force himself to keep going. All he wanted to do was to kiss her, but he had this one chance. Don't blow it, he told himself. Say it like it is.

'It's not for castle, for keeps, Jeanie love,' he said, gently but urgently. 'If you agree...it's for *us*, for keeps. It's for us, for fun. For us, forever. Jeanie McBride, I love you. Whatever you do or say now, that's unchanged—I love you whatever you decide to do. But I do need to ask. Jeanie, I'd like to say our vows again, but this time for real. This time I'd like to say those vows aloud, and, if you let me, I'd like to mean them for the rest of our lives.'

There was a long, long silence. She blinked in the sunlight. Her gaze was a long, in-depth interrogation where he couldn't begin to guess the outcome.

'You'd trust me,' she said at last. 'With the bad things as well as the good?'

'I might try to protect—'

'No protection. Just trust.'

'Okay,' he said humbly. 'Trust first.'

'Really with the flying?'

'Really with the flying.' And then he added honestly, 'Unless you end up stunt flying, in which case no love in the land is big enough.'

'Coward.'

'I'd rather be a chicken than a dead hen.'

She grinned at that. 'I can't see the Lord of Duncairn as a dead hen.'

'And you can't expect the Lord of Duncairn to be a complete doormat,' he agreed. 'I might try to protect, but I'll do my best to let you fly free, stunt flying not included. Any other exclusions you want, just say the word. Meanwhile, if there's any company details you might like to know, just ask. Jeanie, I've been thinking, watching our otters...'

'Are you sure there were otters?'

'There were otters. Jeanie, I really would like to share. I'm not sure how to yet, but I need to try. If you trust me, that is. If you'd trust me to share, to love you, to hold you in honour...'

'And make me watch invisible otters? And help me fly?'

'Yes. Yes and yes and yes.'

There was another silence then, longer than the last. The whole world seemed to be holding its breath. Alasdair had almost forgotten how to breathe. This slip of a woman, this sprite, his amazing Jeanie, she held his heart in the palm of her hand.

'I don't suppose,' she said, diffidently now, gesturing to the dilapidated cottage behind them, 'that you thought to lay the fire?'

'No,' he said, reluctantly. 'This morning got a bit busy.'

'You so need a partner.' And amazingly her eyes twinkled with laughter and he felt his heart lurch with the beginnings of joy. 'I guess...we could make do without. It's not raining. The pasture up here is nice and soft, and if we wander around the next headland, the curve of the cove makes it private.'

'Are you suggesting what I think you might be suggesting?'

'I might be,' she said demurely. 'Though we'll need to ring Maggie's mam to deal with the guests.'

'I already did,' he said and he smiled at her and she smiled right back. Shared laughter...the best part of loving bar none.

But then she turned and looked towards the faraway castle, high on the headland in the distance, and her face twisted with something he didn't understand.

'Lady of Duncairn Castle,' she said softly, at last. 'I don't think I'll be very good at it.'

'No castle ever had a lady more worthy. Jeanie, I love you.'

'I love you, too,' she said softly. 'Otters or not. Wealth or not. Castle or not. Eileen would be pleased.'

'I'll bet she knows,' he told her and, enough, it was time. A man had to do what a man had to do. He was the Lord of Duncairn and this was his lady. His wife. He swept her up and held her in his arms and stood for a long, long moment on the crag over the burn, looking out over the sea.

And something settled in his heart, something so deep and so pure that he felt almost as if he were being reborn.

'If I was Tarzan right now, I suspect I'd beat my chest and yodel,' he told his love, and she chuckled and looped her arms around his neck and held.

'Don't you dare drop me.'

'I wouldn't,' he told her and he kissed her then, long and deep and hard, with all the love in his heart, with all the tenderness he could summon, with all the joy of the future in the link between them.

And then he turned and carried his lady to the waiting wild grasses of Duncairn Island.

The two eagles soared on the thermals, and two otters drifted lazily downstream again, at one with their world, at peace.

It didn't matter. The world continued apace. The Lord and Lady of Duncairn might know in their hearts that all was well on their estate, but for now they weren't watching. They were otherwise engaged.

And they were otherwise engaged for a very long time.

* * * * *

IN THE
BOSS'S CASTLE

BY
JESSICA GILMORE

A former au pair, bookseller, marketing manager and seafront trader, **Jessica Gilmore** now works for an environmental charity in York. Married with one daughter, one fluffy dog and two dog-loathing cats, she spends her time avoiding housework and can usually be found with her nose in a book. Jessica writes emotional romance with a hint of humour, a splash of sunshine and a great deal of delicious food—and equally delicious heroes!

For Audrey, Rob, Josh, Michaela and Lily.
With much love always. x

PROLOGUE

Hi, Hope,
Truthfully I was a little shocked when they asked
me to job swap with you for six months. I thought
I was way too far down the food chain, especially
since I changed careers and found myself back at
the bottom of the ladder again. But I've never left
the US—so my bags are packed, I actually have a
passport and I'm on my way to London before they
change their minds!

I guess you want to know a little about the
stranger coming to take over your life? There's no
big scandals you'll be glad to know, so no need to
warn the neighbours or hide the family silver. I'm
Maddison and I've been working for DL Media for
just over three years, I started out in the PR and
events team before Brenda, my boss (soon to be
yours) poached me for Editorial. It's a step down
in some ways—back to making coffees and book-
ing taxis and a lot less managing my own time,
but somehow she convinced me that it'll be worth
it. It's nice to be wanted for my brains and not my
contact list, at least that's what I tell myself when I
pick up her dry cleaning. Because, in between the

taxis and the coffee pick-ups, she is teaching me a lot—you're lucky to be working with her.

She's very focused, doesn't see the point of any life outside work and is absolutely obsessed with glass ceilings and reaching full potential, blah-blah-blah. It's not that I don't want all that, I'm as ambitious as they come in some ways, but I do want more. I want it all. I want to meet the right guy and settle down, picket fence, big dog, rugrats and all. Don't tell Brenda that!

I thought I'd found the right guy. Bart. AKA Bartholomew J Van De Grierson III. But turns out he's not The One or rather I'm not The One for him. At least not right now. He wants a break. Thinks we should 'explore other options'. So this opportunity has come at the right time for me. I'm exploring other options on the other side of the Atlantic and putting my career first for a change. Maybe working with Brenda has influenced me more than I knew!

I do hope he misses me at least a little, though...

So—New York! It's the greatest city on earth, I promise. My biggest advice? Pack light! The good news is you'll be living in the Upper East Side and it is fabulous! The bad news? No one expects to swing a cat in a New York studio, but mine...? You couldn't swing a mouse. But, hey, location is everything, right? And when you sit on the fire escape with your morning coffee and watch the sun rise over Manhattan you won't want to be anywhere else.

Welcome to New York. City of reinvention, city of dreams...

Maddison.

* * *

Hi, Maddison...

Welcome to London and London's greatest borough. I've compiled a 'Welcome' file which tells you absolutely everything you need to know, in alphabetical order, from where the boiler is—and the number of a good plumber—to the best place to buy coffee locally. There's a guide to buses and Oyster cards (no Tube here in Stokey) under T for Transport, and a comprehensive section on work (W for Work) to help you find your feet right away.

I hope you feel at home here. Stoke Newington is pretty sought-after now, but when my parents moved here it was still a scruffy, community-minded part of the East End—and even with all the swanky bars and yoga studios I miss the place I grew up in. Not so community-minded when you are more likely to bump into nannies and cleaners than neighbours, and everyone is obsessed with extending and rainforest wetrooms. But it's still home and I can't imagine living anywhere else. Except maybe New York, of course...

I am so excited about moving to New York for a whole six months. I've always wanted to travel but never had the opportunity. Faith, my younger sister, is on a gap year and seeing the world, lucky thing—but living in a new city and progressing my career? That's an amazing opportunity.

I've also been at DL Media for around three years. Before that I was working at a local solicitors' firm which fitted in with Faith's school hours. But as soon as she was old enough for me to commute to work I came to DL, at first as a general

PA, before getting the opportunity to work with Kit Buchanan as an editorial assistant.

Brenda sounds like just what I need—a real mentor. Kit, your boss-to-be, is... Well, he's brilliant. Everyone agrees with that. It's just I'm not sure he ever sees me. Sometimes I feel like I'm just a piece of efficient office furniture.

In fact it's been a really long time since anyone has seen me as anyone worth knowing. It gets a little lonely, to be honest, especially now that Faith is making it very clear that now she's grown up she doesn't need me to fuss over her.

Maybe she's right. Maybe it's time to put me first.

Starting with New York!

Enjoy London.

Love, Hope x

CHAPTER ONE

MADDISON CARTER OPENED the opaque glass door, leaned against the door frame and held up her perfectly manicured hand, a piece of paper dangling from her fingertips. 'Messages,' she announced.

Kit Buchanan pushed his chair away from his desk and blinked at her. His expression might seem sleepy and unconcerned to the casual observer but after just four weeks Maddison knew better. 'You could email them to me,' he suggested, a teasing gleam in his blue eyes. This conversation was getting as predictable as the sunrise. So she used paper and a pen and preferred her lists on thick white paper, not on an electronic device? It didn't make her a Luddite, it made her efficient.

'And have you ignore them? I think not.'

Kit sighed. The soft *here she goes again* sigh he used about this time every day. 'But, Maddison, maybe I like ignoring messages.' His eyes laughed up at her but she refused to smile back, even a little. She wasn't colluding with him.

'Then get an answering service. Or a machine or just answer your cell phone every once in a while and then I...' she brandished the list '...I wouldn't have to tell your girlfriends that you're in a meeting twenty times a day.'

His eyebrows rose. 'Twenty times? How very keen.'

Okay, she might have exaggerated slightly but just one conversation with the terribly polite and terribly condescending Camilla was enough and three definitely enough to drive the most precise person to hyperbole. Maddison ignored the interruption and, in a deliberately slow voice, began to read from the paper. 'Right, your mother called and said please call her back, today, and confirm you are going to the wedding, it's a three-line whip and if you don't RSVP soon she will do it for you. Your sister called and said, and I quote, "Tell him if I have to go to this damn wedding on my own I will make him suffer in ways he can't even imagine and don't think I won't do it…"'

Maddison paused as she reread the words. She liked the sound of Kit's sister, Bridget, with her soft, lilting voice and steely words.

'And Camilla called three times, can you please answer your cell, how can she expect to get ready for a wedding in just a couple of weeks if you won't even confirm that you're taking her, you inconsiderate bas…' She looked up and allowed herself one brief smile. 'I didn't catch the rest of that sentence.'

'The hell you didn't,' he said softly. The smile still curved his mouth and he was still leaning back in the vast, black leather chair but the glint had disappeared from his eyes. 'Everyone seems *very* keen to make sure I attend this wedding.'

'If you would just RSVP they'd stop calling.' Maddison didn't care whether he went to the darn wedding or not. She just wanted to stop fielding calls about it.

'I will, as soon as I've decided.'

'Decided?'

'Whether I'm going or not.'

Maddison heaved a theatrical sigh. 'Great. Can I beg

you to do just one thing? Put Camilla out of her misery.'
Sure, the woman spoke to Maddison as if she were some
sort of servant, and sure, she sounded like a snooty character in a Hugh Grant movie, all clipped vowels and lots
of long *r*'s, but she was getting a little more desperate
with every call. Maddison would never allow herself to
beg for a man's attention but she knew all too well what
it felt like to see the spark die even as she did her best
to keep it going. Knew what it felt like to see the emails
and texts diminish, hear the call go straight to voicemail.

Kit stared at her, his eyes narrowed. 'I didn't know that
advising on my personal life was in your job description.'

Maddison took a deep breath, willing herself to stay
calm. 'Nor did I and yet here I am, taking calls from your
girlfriend eight hours a day.'

'Ex-girlfriend.'

'She…what?'

His eyes caught hers, the blue turned steely. 'Ex-girlfriend. She just wants to come to the wedding. Thinks
if I take her to meet the parents then things might start
again between us. So you see, I'm not a total git.'

Whatever *that* might be. Maddison stared down at
the list, her righteous indignation draining away. 'Okay.
I apologize—although in my defence it seems that
Camilla doesn't understand the *ex* part of your relationship. Maybe she needs reminding. And you *really* should
call your mother.'

He didn't respond for a long moment and Maddison
kept her eyes on the list, knowing she had gone too far.
She was normally so good at keeping her cool but Kit
Buchanan was just so…so *provoking*.

She started at his unexpected laugh. 'There are times
when you remind me of my school matron. I will, I promise. How are things looking for tonight?'

The abrupt turn of subject was a relief. She had spent far too long today on Kit Buchanan's social life; work was a much safer subject. Maddison looked at her list again, composing herself as she did so. 'The caterers are already there and setting up, so are the bar staff. The warehouse confirmed that they have sent two hundred books across ready for the signing. I got late acceptances from five people, their names have been added to the entrance list and the door staff are primed; three people sent in late apologies, I replied on your behalf and arranged for books and goody bags to be sent to their offices. Oh, and I popped into the venue last night after work and took a last look around. Everything is in order.'

'Very efficient, as always, thank you, Maddison.' The words were perfect but the amusement in his tone took the edge off his praise and despite herself she could feel her cheeks flush. Kit always seemed to be laughing at her and it was…unsettling. She wanted respect, not this knowing humour. But so far, no matter what she did, respect seemed to be eluding her. And, dammit, it rankled. She was usually so much better at impressing the right people in the right ways.

She certainly wasn't used to feeling discombobulated several times a day.

She eyed her boss. He was still lounging back in his chair, an unrepentant gleam in his eye as he waited for her response. Hoping that she would lose her cool, no doubt. Well, she wasn't going to give him the satisfaction but, oh, her fingers curled; it was tempting.

It didn't help that Kit was young—ish. Handsome if you liked brown tousled hair that needed a good cut, dark stubble and blue eyes, if you found scruffy chic, like some hipster cross between a college professor and an outdoorsman, attractive. Maddison didn't. She liked her men clean-cut, clean-shaven and well turned out.

But, even if he wore head-to-toe *couture*, Kit Buchanan still wouldn't be her type. *Bart* was her type: tall, athletic, with a good job in banking, a trust fund and a bloodline that ran back to Edith Wharton's innocent age and beyond. Not to mention the brownstone. Breaking up with the brownstone was almost harder than saying goodbye to the man. She'd invested eighteen months in that relationship, spent eighteen months moulding herself into the perfect consort. All for nothing. She was back at square one.

Although, he *had* said a break. Maddison clung on to those words, hope soothing the worry and doubt clawing her insides. Everyone knew that taking a break wasn't the same thing as breaking up. And if Bart saw that she was having an amazing time in London without him then surely he would realize he had made a very big mistake? Maybe this distance, this time apart was a good thing, the push he needed to take things to the next level.

She just needed to start *having* the amazing time. So far Maddison's London experiences had been confined to work, takeaways and working her way through Hope McKenzie's formidable box-set collection. Watching *Sex and the City* instead of living it. Surely she at least deserved to be *flirting* in the city?

Kit's voice brought her back to her present surroundings—thousands of miles away from her unexpected failure. 'Anything else on that list of yours or is it all neatly ticked and crossed out?'

Okay. This was it. She'd spent the last four weeks regrouping, licking her wounds, grateful for the opportunity to recover and plan far away from the all-too-knowing eyes of her New York social group. She'd been so *sure* of Bart, shown her hand too early and lost spectacularly. But it was time to reassert herself, professionally at least. Then maybe she would get her confidence—and her man—back. Maddison willed herself to sound composed, her voice not to tremble. 'I think you should rewrite your speech for tonight.'

Kit went very still, like a predator watching his prey. 'Oh? Why?'

'It's very clinical.' She kept her eyes focused on him even as her knees trembled and every instinct screamed at her to stop talking and to back out of the door before she got her ass fired. 'You've spent the whole four weeks I've been here absolutely absorbed in your work. You barely noticed that Hope had gone. You've been in before me every morning, not stopped for lunch unless you had a meeting and who knows what time you leave? But the speech? It has no passion in it at all.'

Kit didn't take his eyes off her, his face utterly expressionless. 'Have you read it? The book?'

Had she what? 'I...of course.'

'Could you do a better job?'

She flinched at the cold words, then tossed her head up and glared at him. 'Could I write an introductory speech that sounds like I value the author, think the book is worth reading and convince the room that they need to read it too? Yes. Yes, I could.'

'Great.' He pulled his chair back to his desk and refocused his eyes on his screen. 'You have an hour. Let's see what you come up with.'

'Great speech.'

Kit suppressed a sigh as yet another guest complimented him. It *had* been a great speech and he'd delivered it well, a nice mingling of humour and sincerity. Only he hadn't written it. Embellished it, ad-libbed a little but he hadn't written it. Maddison had been annoyingly right: his own effort had lacked passion.

Kit knew all too well why that was. Three years ago he'd lost any passion, any zest for life, any hope—and now it seemed as though he'd lost the ability to fake it as well.

Which was ridiculous. He was the king of faking it—at work, with the ever so elegant Camilla and her potential replacements, with his friends. The only place he couldn't convincingly pretend that he was the same old Kit was with his family. Especially not with his family and with the wedding looming on the horizon like a constant reminder of all that he had lost. He needed to sort that out and fast. He knew he had to RSVP. He knew he had to attend. He just couldn't bring himself to commit to it because once he did it would become real. Thank goodness for his new project. At least that helped him forget, for a little while at least.

Forgetting was a luxury.

He caught sight of Maddison, gliding through the crowds as untouchably serene as ever. Kit's eyes narrowed as she stopped to murmur something in a waitress's ear, sending the girl scurrying off with her tray. As usual Maddison had it all under control. Just look at the way she glided around the office in her monochrome uniform of black trousers and perfectly ironed white blouse like some sort of robot: efficient, calm and, until today, he could have sworn completely free of any emotion.

It was a shame. No one whose green eyes tilted upwards with such feline wickedness, no one with hair like the first hint of a shepherd's sunset, no one with a wide, sweet mouth should be so *bland*.

But she hadn't been so bland earlier today. Instead she

had been bursting with opinions and, much as she had tried to stay calm, not let him see the exasperation in those thickly lashed eyes, she had let her mask slip a little.

And then she had written that speech. In an hour. Yes, she definitely had hidden depths. Not, Kit reminded himself, that he was planning to explore them. He was just intrigued, that was all. Turned out Maddison Carter was a bit of an enigma and he did so like to figure out a puzzle.

Kit excused himself from the group of guests, brushing another compliment about his speech aside with a smile and a handshake as he slowly weaved his way through the throng, checking to make sure everyone was entertained, that the buzz was sufficient to ensure the launch would be a success. The venue was inspired, an old art deco cinema perfectly complementing the novel's historical Jazz Age setting. The seats had been removed to create a party space and a jazz band set up on the old stage entertained the crowd with a series of jaunty tunes. Neon cocktails circulated on etched silver trays as light shone down from spotlights overhead, emphasizing the huge, jewel-coloured rectangular windows; at the far end of the room the gratified author sat at a vintage desk, signing books and holding court. The right people were here having the right sort of time. Kit had done all he could—the book would stand or fall on its own merits now.

He paused as Maddison passed by again, that damn list still tucked in one hand, a couple of empty glasses clasped in the other. He leaned against the wall for a moment, enjoying watching her dispose of the glasses, ensure three guests had fresh drinks, introduce two lost-looking souls to each other, all the while directing the wait staff and ensuring the queue for signed books progressed. A one-woman event machine.

How did she do it? She looked utterly calm, still in her favourite monochrome uniform although she had changed her usual well-tailored trousers for a short skirt, which swished most pleasingly around what were, Kit had to admit, a fine pair of legs, and there was no way the silky, clingy white blouse, which dipped to a low vee just this side of respectable, was the same as the crisp shirt she had worn in the office. Her hair was no longer looped in a loose knot but allowed to curl loosely around her shoulders. She looked softer, more approachable—even though she was brandishing the dreaded list.

She was doing a great job organizing this party. He really should go and tell her so while he remembered.

By the time Kit had manoeuvred his way over to Maddison's corner of the room she was deep in conversation with an earnest-looking man. Kit rocked back on his heels and studied her. Good gracious, was that a smile on her face? In fact, that dip of her head and the long demure look from under her eyebrows was positively flirtatious. Kit neatly collected two cocktails from a passing tray and watched as the earnest man slipped her a card. Did he know him? He knew almost every person there. Kit ran through his memory banks—yes, a reviewer for one of the broadsheets. Not a bad conquest, especially if she could talk him into positive reviews.

'Flirting on the job?' he said quietly into her ear as the earnest man walked away, and had the satisfaction of seeing her jump and the colour rush to her cheeks, emphasizing the curve in her heart-shaped face.

'No. I was just…'

'Relax, Maddison, I was teasing. It's past eight o'clock. I think you're on your own time now. This lot will melt away as soon as they realize that these are no longer being served.' He handed her the pink cocktail before tasting his own blue confection and grimaced as the sweet yet medicinal taste hit his tongue. 'Or maybe not. Is this supposed to taste like cough syrup? Anyway, cheers. Great job on the party.'

'Thank you.' It was as if a light had been switched on in her green eyes, turning them from pretty glass to a darker, more dangerous emerald. 'Hope started it all. I just followed her instructions.'

'The party favours were your idea, and the band, I believe.'

Her eyes lit up even more. 'I didn't know you'd noticed. It just seemed perfect, nineteen twenties and a murder mystery.' The guests' goody bags contained chocolate murder weapons straight out of a golden-age crime novel: hatpins and candlesticks, pearl-handled revolvers and a jar-shaped chocolate labelled Cyanide. The cute chocolates had caused quite a stir and several guests were trying to make sure they went home with a full set. Turned out even this jaded crowd could be excited by something novel and fun.

'Excuse me.'

Kit looked around, an enquiring eyebrow raised, only for the young man hovering behind him to ignore him entirely while he thrust a card in Maddison's direction. 'It was lovely to meet you earlier. Do give me a call. I would love to show you around London. Oh, and happy birthday.'

'Thank you.' She accepted the card with a half-smile, sliding it neatly into her bag. Kit tried to sneak a look as the card disappeared into the depths. How many other cards did she have in there? And what had the young man said?

'It's your birthday?'

Maddison nodded. 'Today.'

'I didn't realize.' Kit felt strangely wrong-footed. How hadn't he known? He'd always remembered Hope's birthday although, come to think of it, that was because she made sure it was in his work calendar and lost no opportunity to remind him that flowers were always acceptable, chocolates even more so and vouchers for the local spa most acceptable of all. 'I'm so sorry you had to work. I hope you have exciting plans for the rest of your evening and weekend?'

Maddison paused, her eyes lowered. 'Sure.' But her tone lacked conviction.

'Like?' Kit cursed himself as he pushed. She'd said she had plans so he should take her word at face value and leave her in peace. He didn't need to know the details; she was a grown woman.

A grown woman in a new city where she knew hardly anyone.

Maddison took a visible deep breath before looking directly at him, a smile pasted on to her face. 'A film and a takeaway. I'm going to explore the city a little more tomorrow. Low-key, you know? I don't know many people here yet.'

'You're staying in alone, on your birthday?'

'I have a cocktail.' She waved the glass of pink liquid at him. 'It's okay.'

He'd heard the lady. She said she was okay—and, judging by the cards she was collecting, the room was full of men who would gladly help her celebrate any way she wished to.

Only she was new to the country… Kit had thought his conscience had died three years ago but some ghost of it was struggling back to life. 'What about the other girls at work? None of them free?'

'It's a little awkward, you know? Technically I'm at the

same level as all the other assistants but they all sit in the same office and I'm on the executive floor so we don't see each other day-to-day.' She hesitated. 'I think Hope didn't really socialize so there's this assumption I'm the same.' She shrugged. 'It's fine. I just haven't prioritized making friends since I got here. There's plenty of time.' She attempted another full smile; this one nearly reached her eyes. 'I'm actually quite good at it when I try.'

His conscience gave another gasp. He should have thought to check that she was settling in, but she had been so efficient from day one. *Besides*, the annoying ghost of conscience past whispered, *if you had noticed, what would you have done about it*? But she *had* put a lot of work in tonight and it *was* her birthday… Even Kit couldn't be so callous as to abandon her to a lonely night of pizza and a romcom. 'I can't possibly let you go home alone to watch a film on your birthday, especially after all the hard work you put in today. The least I can do is buy you a drink.' He looked at his blue drink and shuddered. 'A real drink. What do you say?'

CHAPTER TWO

SHE SHOULD HAVE said no.

The last thing Maddison needed was a pity date. Even worse, a pity date with her *boss*. But Kit had caught her at a vulnerable moment. Nice as it was to be flirted with by not just one, or two, but several men at the party, all of whom had their own teeth, hair and impressive-sounding job titles, she couldn't help but remember this time last year and the adorable little inn in Connecticut Bart had whisked her off to. Three months ago she was reasonably confident that this birthday he'd propose—not break up with her two months before.

Which meant she wouldn't be married at twenty-seven and a mother by twenty-eight. Her whole, carefully planned timetable redundant. Somehow she was going to have to start again. Only she had no idea how or who or where…

Happy birthday to me. Maddison sighed, the age-long loneliness forcing its way out of the box she had buried it in, creeping back around her heart, her soul. It wasn't that she minded the lack of cards and presents. She'd got used to that a long time ago. But she couldn't help feeling that at twenty-six her birthday should matter to someone. Especially to her. Instead she'd been in denial all day. She wasn't sure why she'd mentioned it to the young sales guy, maybe some pathetic need to have some kind of acknowledgement, no matter how small.

That's enough. She wasn't a wallower, she was a fighter and she never, ever looked back. Maddison pushed herself off the plush velvet sofa and paced the length of the room. If she did have to wait in Kit Buchanan's house while he changed then she might as well take advantage and find out as much as she could about him. From the little she had gathered he was a constant source of speculation at work, but although the gossips were full of theories they had very few solid facts. A few juicy titbits could give her a way in with the social groups at work. She couldn't just bury herself and her sore pride away for the whole six months like some Roman exile marooned on a cold and damp island.

After all, the weather in London was much nicer than she had expected.

At least it was just her pride that hurt. She'd never be foolish enough to give away her heart without some kind of security.

Stop thinking about it, Maddison scolded herself, looking up at the high ceiling as if in supplication. She had five months left in London; she needed to start living again so she could return to New York full of European polish and fizzing with adventure. If that didn't bring Bart back on his knees, diamond ring in one hand, nothing would. After all, didn't they say absence made the heart grow fonder? Think how fond he could grow if word got back to him of just how good a time she was having in London...

A piece of elaborate-looking plaster work caught her eye. Original, she'd bet, just like the tiles on the hallway floor and the ceiling roses holding the anachronistically modern lights. The huge semi-detached house overlooking a lushly green square was the last place she'd expected Kit to live; she would have laid money on some kind of trendy apartment, all glass and chrome, not the white-painted Georgian house. It was even more impressive than Bart's brownstone.

She hadn't seen much in the way of personal touches so far. A tiled hallway with no clutter at all, just a hat stand, a mirror and an antique sideboard with a small bowl for his keys. There was nothing left lying around in the living room either except a newspaper on the coffee table, neatly folded at the nearly completed crossword, and just one small photo on the impressive marble mantle—a black-and-white picture of two teenage boys, grinning identical smiles, hanging over the rail on a boat. She had no trouble identifying the younger one as Kit, although there was something about the smile that struck her as different from the smile she knew. Maybe it was how wide, how unadulterated, how wholehearted it was, so different from the cynically amused expression she saw every day.

The sound of footsteps on the stairs sent her scuttling back to her seat, where she grabbed the newspaper and scanned it, carefully giving the impression she had been comfortably occupied for the last ten minutes.

'Sorry to keep you. I spilled some of that green stuff on my shirt and didn't fancy going out smelling like the ghost of absinthe past.' Kit walked into the room and raised an eyebrow. Maddison had kicked off her shoes and was curled up in a corner of the sofa, the newspaper on her knee, looking as studiously un-detective-like as possible. 'Comfy?'

'Hmm? No, I was fine. Just finishing off your crossword. I think it's Medusa.'

'I beg your pardon?'

'Six down. *Petrifying snakes.* Medusa.'

'Here, give me that.' He took the paper off her and stared at the clue. 'Of course. I should have thought...' He looked back up and over at her, his eyes impossibly blue as they took her in.

'Do you like puzzles, Maddison?'

'I'm sorry?' It took all her resolution to stay still under such scrutiny. It was as if he were looking at her for the first time, as if he were weighing her up.

'Puzzles, quizzes? Do you like them?'

'Well, sure. Doesn't everyone?' He didn't reply, just stared at her in that disconcertingly intense way. 'I mean, when I was a kid I wanted to be Nancy Drew.' When she hadn't dreamed of being Rory Gilmore, that was. She swung her legs to the floor. 'I believe you mentioned a drink.'

He didn't move for a long second, his eyes still focused on her, and then smiled, the familiar amused expression sliding back on to his face like a mask. 'Of course. It's not far. I hope you don't mind the walk.'

Maddison hadn't known what to expect on a night out with Kit Buchanan: a glitzy wine bar or maybe some kind of private members' bar, all leather seats and braying, privileged laughter. She definitely hadn't expected the comfortable pub Kit guided her into. The walls were hung with prints by local artists, the tables solid square wood surrounded by leather sofas and chairs. It was nearly full but it didn't feel crowded or loud; it felt homely, like a pub from a book. The man behind the bar nodded at Kit and gave Maddison a speculative look as Kit guided her to a nook by the unlit fire before heading off to order their drinks.

'I got a sharing platter as well,' he said as he set the bottle of Prosecco on the table and placed a glass in front of her. 'I don't know about you but I'm starving. I never get a chance to eat at those work parties. It's hard to schmooze with a half-eaten filo prawn in my mouth.'

'When I started out in events sometimes canapés were all I did eat,' Maddison confessed, watching as he filled her glass up. 'New York is pricey for a girl out of college and free food is free food. Some days I would long for a good old-fashioned sub or a real-sized burger rather than an assortment of finger food! Turns out a girl can have too much caviar.'

'Happy birthday.' Kit handed her a glass before taking the seat opposite her, raising his glass to her. 'You worked in events?'

She nodded. 'After I graduated I joined a friend's PR and events company.' It had been the perfect job, working in the heart of Manhattan with the heart of society—until her friend had decided she preferred attending parties to planning them, being in the headlines rather than creating them. 'After that I landed a junior management role at DL Media and then Brenda poached me. I've only worked in editorial for the last six months,' she added. She still wasn't sure how Brenda had persuaded her to leave the safe world of PR for the unknown waters of editorial. It was the first unplanned move Maddison had made in a decade. It still terrified her, both the spontaneity and the starting again.

'Six months? I did wonder why you were still at an assistant level when you are obviously so capable.' The words were casually said but Maddison sat up a little straighter, pride swelling her chest.

She looked around the room, not wanting Kit to see just how the offhand praise had affected her. 'It's nice here. Is this where you bring all the girls?'

'You're the first.'

She turned and looked at him, laughter ready on her lips but there was no answering smile. He was serious. 'Consider me honoured. Why not? It's pretty convenient.'

Kit shrugged. 'I don't like to bring anyone home. It gives them ideas. One moment a cosy dinner, the next a sleepover and before you know it they're rearranging the furniture and suggesting a drawer. Besides, Camilla and her ilk only like to go to places where they can see and be seen. This place isn't anywhere near trendy enough for them.'

It sounded pretty lonely. Maddison knew all about that. 'So if you don't want to share your home or local with these girls, why date them?'

His eyes darkened for a stormy moment. 'Because I am in absolutely no danger of falling in love with any of them.'

He had said too much. This was supposed to be a casual 'thank you and by the way happy birthday' drink, not a full-on confessional. He didn't need or deserve absolution. Maddison stared at him, her eyes wide and mouth half-open as if he were some kind of crossword clue she could solve, and for once he couldn't think of the right kind of quip to turn her attention aside. He breathed a sigh of relief as the waitress came over, their Mediterranean platter balanced high on one hand, and broke the mounting tension.

'If I'd known you had overdosed on canapés I'd have ordered something more substantial,' he said, gesturing at the bowls of olives and sundried tomatoes, hummus and aioli. 'The bread's reasonably sized though.'

'No, this is good, thanks.' But she sounded thoughtful and her eyes were still fixed disturbingly on him. Kit searched for a change of subject.

'Have you heard from Hope?' That was safe enough.

Maddison speared a falafel and placed it delicately onto her plate, every movement precise, just as she was in the office. 'A couple of emails. I think she's settled in.' She smiled then, a completely unguarded, full-on smile, and Kit's chest twisted at the openness of it. 'She intimidates me a little. I thought I was organized, but Hope? She beats me every time. Did you know she left me a printed-out file, all alphabetized, with instructions on what to do if the boiler breaks and when the trash goes out? Half of it is about what I need to do if her sister, Faith, comes home early from her travels or phones or something. I mean, the girl's nineteen. Cut her some slack!' But although the words were mocking there was a wistfulness in Maddison's face that belied them.

She took a deep breath and her features recomposed until she was back to her usual calm and efficient self. 'Anyway, some of her neighbours have dropped round and been welcoming, which is very kind but they're older and have kids. They're nice but a night spent in talking about the cost of childcare isn't exactly something I can contribute to.'

Kit grimaced. 'No, I can empathize with that. It seems that every time I go out now someone is talking about nannies or the importance of organic baby food.' Each time it was a reminder that his friendship group was moving on without him, the teasing about his bachelor status beginning to grate.

She raised her eyes to his. 'Don't you want kids? One day?'

He laughed shortly. 'Why does it all come back to kids and marriage? I thought society had evolved beyond that. Why not just enjoy some company for a while and then move on?'

Maddison was frozen, her fork in her hand. 'That's really what you think? Poor Camilla.'

Kit frowned. 'She knew the score. I don't pretend to be anything different, to want anything different, Maddison. If she wants to change the rules without checking to see if I'm still playing along then that's not my problem.'

'People change. No one goes into a relationship expecting it to stay static. Relationships evolve. They grow or they end. It's the way it has to be.'

'I don't agree. It's perfectly possible for two people to enjoy themselves with no expectations of anything more. Look, Camilla said she was happy enough with a casual thing but it didn't take long before she started pushing for more. If she'd been more honest with herself, with me, at the beginning, then she wouldn't have got hurt.'

'Wow. You've actually made me feel a little sorry for her.' The colour was high on her cheeks and he opened his mouth to do what? Defend himself? No, to put her straight, but anything he might have said was drowned out as the pub's PA system crackled into life with an announcement of that night's quiz.

Maddison straightened and looked around, her eyes bright like a child promised a treat. 'Oh, I haven't done a quiz since college. Do you want to...? I mean, we've barely started on the wine and there's all that bread to eat.'

Interesting. Kit sat back and looked at her; she was practically fizzing with anticipation. His mind flashed back to the completed crossword, to the way she had meticulously sorted every single problem that had come his way for the last four weeks. *I wanted to be Nancy Drew*, she had said.

Could he trust her? It wasn't just that he didn't want any of his commercial rivals getting any hint of what he was up to; he didn't want it known internally either. He didn't want project-management groups and focus studies and sales input. That would come, but not yet. Not while he was enjoying the thrill of the new.

'Maddison,' he said slowly. 'How would you like to be my guinea pig?'

'Your *what*?' She couldn't have looked more outraged if he'd asked her if she wanted to eat a guinea pig.

'Guinea pig. Testing out my new product.'

Her eyes narrowed. 'How very marketing friendly of you. I was under the impression that we produced books.'

'Oh, we do. I do.' He considered her for a moment longer. She didn't really know anyone to tell and didn't strike him as the gossiping type anyway. He should trust her. He hadn't come this far without taking some risks.

Kit had started his publishing career while still at Cambridge, republishing forgotten golden-age crime books for a nostalgic audience. Two years later he'd diversified into digital genre publishing before selling his company to DL Media for a tidy sum and an executive position. The sale had paid for his house and furnished him with a nice disposable income and a nest egg, but lately he'd been wondering if he'd sold his soul, not just his company.

He had had no idea just how different things would be. The sole guy in charge of a small but growing company was a million miles away from a cog in a huge international corporation—even an executive cog. And although the perks and salary were nice—more than nice—he missed the adrenaline rush of ownership. This project was making his blood pump in almost the same way as building up his imprint had. While he was working on it he almost forgot everything else that had changed in the last few years.

Maddison's eyes were fixed on his face. 'So what is this product?'

Kit watched her every reaction. 'Okay, so we produce entertainment and information. I am planning to marry the two together.'

Maddison frowned. 'And you want me to bless the happy couple?'

'I want you to road-test them.' He took a deep breath. He was going in. 'I'm planning a series of new interactive guidebooks.'

'Okay…' Scepticism was written all over her face. 'That's interesting but does anyone even use guidebooks any more?'

Kit had been expecting that. 'Guidebooks available in every format from eBook to app to good old-fashioned paper copies.'

'I still don't see…'

He took pity on her. 'The difference is that they don't tell you what to see, they give you clues. Each guidebook is a treasure hunt.'

She leaned forward, a spark of interest lighting up her face, transforming her from merely pretty to glowingly beautiful. Not that Kit was interested in her looks. It was her brains he was after; he was certainly not focusing on how her eyes lit up when she was engaged or the way her blouse dipped a little lower as she shifted forward. 'A treasure hunt? As in X marks the spot?'

He tore his eyes away from her mouth. *Focus, Buchanan.* 'In a way. Tourists can pick from one of five or so themed routes—historical, romantic, wild, fictional or a mixture of all the themes and follow a series of clues to their mystery destination, taking in places of interest on the way. Each theme will have routes of varying length ranging from an afternoon to three days, allowing people to adapt the treasure hunt to their length of stay, although I very much hope even cynical Londoners will want to have a go.'

'Yes.' She nodded slowly, her still-half-full plate pushed to one side as she took in every word. 'I see, each hunt would have a unique theme depending on the place like, I don't know, say a revolution theme in Boston? It wouldn't just be tourists, though, would it? I mean, something like this would work for team building, bachelor and bachelorette parties, family days out...' Satisfaction punched through him. She'd got it. 'And what's the prize—or is taking part enough?'

'Hopefully the satisfaction of a job well done, but successful treasure hunters will also be able to pick up some discounts for local restaurants and attractions. I'm looking into building some partnerships. To launch it, however, I am planning real treasure—or a prize at least.'

Maddison leaned back and picked up her wine glass. 'And you want me to what? Source the prize for you?'

Kit shook his head. 'No, I want you to test the first few routes. The plan is to launch next year, simultaneously in five cities around the world. Each launch will open up on the same day and teams will compete against each other. But for now, in order to present a full proposal to marketing, we've been concentrating on drawing up the London routes—and I want to know how hard it is, especially to non-Brits, if the timings work and, crucially, if it's fun.'

'So, this will be part of my job?'

Kit picked up his own glass; he was about to ask a lot from her. 'We're still very much in concept stage at the moment. This would be in your own time at weekends. But...' he smiled directly at her, turning up the charm '...you said yourself you needed to get out and about...'

'I didn't say that at all. For all you know I am completely happy with takeaways and box sets. Maybe that's the whole reason I took this job,' she protested.

He watched her carefully, looking for an advantage. 'But you're spending your weekends alone. I know the routes but not the clues so I want to see how it works in practice. I was going to go around on my own but here you are, new to London. A non-Brit. It's perfect. You can follow the clues and I'll accompany you and see how it works.'

'I…'

'I don't expect you to do it for nothing,' he broke in before she talked herself out of it or pointed out that spending every weekend with her boss was not her idea of fun. 'Each route we complete has a prize. An experience of your choice, fully paid. Gigs, concerts, theme parks, restaurants—you name it.'

'Anything I want?'

'Anything.' Now where had that come from? He would be spending all week and most of the next few weekends with her, did he really want to add in leisure time as well? But before he could backtrack Maddison held out her hand.

'In that case you have a deal,' she said.

In for a penny… He took her soft, cool hand in his. 'Deal. I'm looking forward to getting to know you better.'

Why had he said that? That wasn't part of the deal. So she was proving to be a bit of an enigma, a girl who liked a challenge? They were reasons to stay away, not get closer. But this was purely business and business Kit could handle. It was all he had left, after all.

CHAPTER THREE

ALTHOUGH CLISSOLD PARK couldn't hold a candle to her own beloved Central Park, the small London park had a quirky charm all its own. There might not be a fairy-tale castle or boats for hire on the little duck-covered lakes, but it was always buzzing with people and a circuit made for a pretty run.

Maddison increased her pace, smiling as she overtook a man pushing a baby in a jogger. Not so much difference between Clissold and Central Parks after all—and yes, right on cue, there it was: a t'ai chi ch'uan class. City parks were city parks no matter their location and size.

The biggest difference was that dogs roamed unleashed and free through the London park; in Central Park they would be allowed to walk untethered only in the doggy-exercise areas. Maddison nervously eyed a large, barrel-chested brown dog hurtling towards her, the sweat springing onto her palms nothing to do with the exercise. Could it smell her fear? She wavered, torn between increasing her pace and stopping to back away from it when it jumped, running directly…past her to retrieve a ball, slobber flying from its huge jowls. Maddison's heart hammered and she gulped in some much-needed air. She hated dogs; they were unpredictable. She'd found that out the hard way—and had the scar on her thigh to prove it.

At least her mom had dumped that particular boyfriend after his dog had attacked Maddison, but whether it was the dog bite that had precipitated the move or some other misdemeanour Maddison had never known.

Maddison increased the pace again, the pain in her chest and the ache in her thighs a welcome distraction from thoughts of the past—and the immediate future. In one hour Kit Buchanan would be knocking on her door and she would be spending the whole day with him. Whatever had possessed her to agree?

On the other hand she didn't have anything better to do. And despite her reservations she had had fun last night. For the first time in a long time she had been able to relax, to be herself. She only needed to impress Kit professionally; what he made of her socially wasn't at all important.

It was a long time since she hadn't had to worry about that.

Maddison turned out of the park and began to run along the pavement, dodging the myriad small tables cluttering up the narrow pavements outside the many cafes and coffee shops that made up the main street, until she reached the small road where she was staying. Her stomach twisted as she opened the front door and stepped over the threshold, the heaviness in her chest nothing to do with the exercise.

Try as she might to ignore it, staying in Hope's old family home was opening up old wounds, allowing the loneliness to seep through. It wasn't the actual living alone—apart from the semesters sleeping in her college dorm Maddison had lived by herself since she was sixteen. No, she thought that this unshakeable melancholy was because Hope's home was, well, a home. A much-loved family home with the family photos clustered on the dresser downstairs, the battered kitchen table, the scuff marks in the hallway where a generation of shoes had been kicked off to prove it.

And sure, Maddison wouldn't have picked the violet-covered wallpaper and matching purple curtains and bedspread in her room, just as she would have stripped the whole downstairs back for a fresh white and wood open-plan finish, but she appreciated why Hope had preserved the house just the way it must have been when her parents died. There was love in every in-need-of-a-refresh corner.

Losing her parents so young must have been hard but at least Hope had grown up with them, in a house full of light and happiness.

Maddison's childhood bedroom had no natural light and pretty near little happiness. The thin bunks and thinner walls, the sound of the TV blaring in if she was lucky, silence if she wasn't. If she was alone. It was only temporary, her mother reassured her, just somewhere to stay until their luck changed.

Only it never did. That was when Maddison stopped believing in luck. That was when she knew it was down to her, only her.

Maddison found herself, as she often did, looking at the photos displayed on the hallway sideboard. Both girls were slim with dark hair and dark eyes but whereas Hope looked perpetually worried and careworn, Faith sparkled with vitality. Reading between the lines of Hope's comprehensive file, Maddison got the impression that the older sister was the adult in this house, the younger protected and indulged. But Faith was nineteen! At that age Maddison had been on her own for three years and was putting herself through college, the luxury of a year spent travelling as remote as her chances of discovering a secret trust fund.

Maddison picked up her favourite photo. It was taken when their parents were still alive; the whole family were grouped on a beach at sunset, dressed in smart summery clothes. Faith must have been around six, a small, merry-faced imp with laughing eyes and a naughty smile, holding hands with her mother. Hope, a teenager all in black, was standing in front of her father, casual in his arms. She was probably at the age where she was so secure in her parents' love and affection she took it for granted, embarrassed by any public show. It used to make Maddison mad to see how casually her schoolmates treated their parents, how dismissive they could be of their love.

One day Maddison wanted a photo like this. She and her own reliable, affectionate husband and their secure, happy children. A family of her own. It wasn't too much to ask, was it? She'd thought she was so close with Bart and now here she was. As far away as ever. The heaviness in her chest increased until she wanted to sink to her knees under the burden.

Stop it, she told herself fiercely. Kit would be here soon and she still had to shower and change. Besides, what good had feeling sorry for herself ever done? Planning worked. Timetables worked. Things didn't just happen because you wished for them or were good. You had to make your own destiny.

It didn't take Maddison long to get ready or to post a few pictures of her evening's adventures onto her various social-media accounts, captioning them 'Birthday in London'—and if they were carefully edited to give the impression that she was a guest at the party, not working, and that there was a whole group at the pub, well, wasn't social media all about perception?

Her phone flashed with notifications and Maddison quickly scrolled through them. It was funny to see life carrying on in New York as if she hadn't left: the same parties, the same hook-ups and break-ups. She chewed her lip as she scrolled through another Friday night of cocktails, exclusive clubs and VIP bars. At least her bank balance was healthier during her London exile. Keeping up with the Trustafarians without a trust fund was a constant balancing act. One she was never in full control of. Thank goodness she had landed a rent-controlled apartment.

Still, she had to speculate to accumulate and if Maddison wanted the security of an Upper East Side scion with the houses, bank balance and guaranteed happy life to match, then she needed to make some sacrifices. And she didn't just want that security, she needed it. She knew too well what the alternatives were and she had no intention of ever being that cold, that hungry, that despised ever again.

The sound of the doorbell snapped her back to reality. She stood, breathing in, trying to squash the old fears, the old feelings of inadequacy, the knowledge that she would never be good enough, back into the little box she hid them in. She should have learned from Pandora; some things were better left locked away.

The doorbell sounded again before she made it downstairs and she wrenched the front door open to find Kit leaning against the door frame, looking disturbingly casual in faded jeans and a faded red T-shirt. Morning. Recovered from your victory yet?'

Maddison felt the heat steal over her cheeks. Maybe it hadn't been the most dignified thing in the world to fling her arms up in the air and whoop when she and Kit were declared pub-quiz champions but it *had* been her birthday. And they had won pretty darn convincingly. 'Are you kidding? I want a certificate framed for my wall so I can show it to my grandkids in forty years' time.'

She grabbed her bag and stepped out, pulling the door shut behind her.

Kit waited while she double-and then triple-locked the door as per Hope's comprehensive instructions. 'Right. As I mentioned yesterday we need to keep things as simple as possible. The idea is to give people a fun and unique way of seeing London, not to bamboozle them completely. Plus our target market is going to be tourists, the vast majority of whom aren't English, so we need to make this culturally accessible to everyone whether it's a girl from New York…' he smiled at Maddison '…or a family from China or a couple from France.'

'More of a scavenger hunt than a treasure hunt?'

'A mix of the two. Every destination is accessible by Tube or bus to make it easier, at least to start with, and we're putting the nearest stop with each clue with directions from that stop. On the app and on the online version you won't get the next clue until you put in an answer for the current quest but that would be impossible on paper. The discounts you get will be linked to how many correct answers you have in the end.'

'And what's to stop people going online and cheating?'

'Eventually? Nothing. But hopefully the fun of the quest will stop them wanting to find shortcuts. And the discounts will be the kind you get with most standard tourist passes so nice to have but not worth cheating for.'

'Have you thought about randomizing it? You know, every fifth hundred correct—or completed—quest gets something extra? Just to add that bit more spice into it.'

'No.' He stared at her. 'But that's a great idea. I'll plan that in. Good thinking, Maddison.'

'Just doing my job.' But that same swell of pride flared up again. 'So, what's the plan? Where are we starting off? Literary? History?'

Kit held up a map and grinned. 'Neither. How do you feel about seeing the wild side of London?'

'When you said wild...' Maddison stood still on the path and stared '...I thought you meant the zoo!'

'Nope.' Kit shook his head solemnly but his eyes were shining with suppressed laughter. He seemed more relaxed, more boyish out and about. It was almost relaxing. But last night's words beat a warning tattoo through her head. There was a darkness at the heart of him and she needed to make sure she wasn't blinded by the veneer.

Not that she was attracted to Kit. Obviously not. A handsome face and a keen brain might be enough to turn some girls' heads but she was made of stronger stuff. No being led astray by blue eyes and snug-fitting jeans for Maddison, no allowing the odd spark of attraction to flare into anything hotter. Think first, feel after, that was her motto.

Speaking of which, she was here to think. Maddison looked around. She was used to city parks—Central Park was her gym, garden, playground and sanctuary—but the sheer number of green spaces on the map Kit held loosely in one hand had taken her aback. London was surprisingly awash in nature reserves, parks, heaths, woods and cemeteries. Yes, cemeteries. Like the one lying before her, for instance. Winding paths, crumbling mausoleums and trees, branches entwining over the paths as they bent to meet each other like lovers refusing to be separated even by death. Maddison put one hand onto the wrought-iron gate and raised a speculative eyebrow. 'Seriously? You're sending people to graveyards? For fun?'

'This is one of London's most famous spots,' Kit said as he led the way through the gates and into the ancient resting place. Maddison hesitated for a moment before following him in. It was like entering another world. She had to admit it was surprisingly peaceful in a gloomy, gothic kind of way. Birds sang in the trees overhead and the early-summer sun did its valiant best to peep through the branches and cast some light onto the grey stone fashioned into simple headstones, huge mausoleums and twisted, crumbling statues. 'There's a fabulous Victorian cemetery near you in Stoke Newington too but there's no Tube link so I didn't include it in the tour.'

'You can save it for the future, a grave tour of London.'

'I could.' She couldn't tell whether he was ignoring her sarcasm or taking her seriously. 'There are seven great Victorian cemeteries, all fantastic in different ways. But I love disused ones best, watching nature reclaim them, real dust-to-dust, ashes-to-ashes stuff.'

'Don't tell me.' She stopped still and put her hands on her hips. 'You wore all black as a teenager and had a picture of Jim Morrison on your wall? Wrote bitter poetry about how nobody understood you and went vegetarian for six months.'

'Naturally. Doesn't every wannabe creative? You forgot learning two chords on a guitar and refusing to smile. Does that sum up your teen years too?'

It certainly hadn't. She hadn't had the luxury. People didn't like their waitresses, babysitters, baristas and cleaners to be anything but perky and wholesome. Especially when their hired help had a background like Maddison's. She'd had to be squeaky clean in every single way. The quintessential all-American girl, happy to help no matter how demanding her customer, demeaning the job and low the pay.

'Not my bag,' she said airily. 'I like colour, light and optimism.'

Kit grinned and began to pick his way along the path.

On either side mausoleums, gravestones and crumbling statues, some decorated with fading flowers, formed a curious honour guard. 'What was your bag? Let me guess: cheerleader?'

Maddison tossed her hair back. 'Possibly.'

'Mall rat?'

'I would say Mall Queen,' she corrected him.

'Daddy's credit card, a cute convertible and Homecoming Queen?'

'Were you spying on me?' she countered. Actually it had been a rusty bike she had saved up for herself and then repaired. Not a thing of beauty but she had been grateful at the time.

He fell into step beside her, an easy lope to his stride. Her brightly patterned skirt, her neat little cashmere cardigan and elegant brogues were too bright, too alive for this hushed, grey and green world and yet Kit fitted right in, despite his casual jeans. He belonged. 'So where did you spend your cheerleading years?'

'You wouldn't have heard of it. It's just a typical New England small town.' Maddison was always careful not to get too drawn into details; that was how a girl got caught out. She didn't want anyone to know the sordid truth. She much preferred the fiction. The life she wished she had led. So she kept the generalities the same and the details vague. 'How about you? Have you always lived in London?'

He looked surprised at her question. 'No, I'm from Kilcanon. It's by the sea, on the coast south of Glasgow on a peninsula between the mainland and the islands. Scotland,' he clarified as she frowned.

'You're Scottish?' How had she not known that?

'You can't tell?'

'You don't sound Scottish, you sound British!'

He laughed. 'We don't all sound like Groundskeeper Willie, well, not all the time.'

'Do you miss it?' She only had the haziest idea about Scotland, mostly bare-chested men in kilts and romantic countryside. It sounded pretty good; maybe she should pay it a visit.

'Every day,' he said so softly she almost couldn't hear the words. 'But this is where I live now.'

'I love living in New York but I wouldn't want to raise my children there.'

'Children?' He raised his eyebrows. 'How many are you planning?'

'Four,' she said promptly. 'Two girls, two boys.'

His mouth quirked into a half-smile. 'Naturally. Do they have names?'

'Anne, Gilbert, Diana and Matthew. This week anyway. It depends on what I've been reading.' Actually it was always those names. They gave her hope. After all, didn't Anne Shirley start off with nothing and yet end up surrounded by laughter and love?

'Let's hope you're not on a sci-fi kick when you're actually pregnant then, or your kids could end up with some interesting names. Why so many?'

'Sorry?'

'Four children. That's a lot of kids to transport around. You'll need a big car, a big house—a huge washing machine.'

'I'm an only child,' she said quietly. That, for once, wasn't a prevarication, not a stretch of the truth. And she had vowed that when she got her family, when she had kids, then everything would be different. They would be wanted, loved, praised, supported—and they would have each other. There would be no lonely nights shivering under a thin comforter and wishing that there were just one person to share it with her. One person who understood. 'It gets kind of lonely. I want my children to have the most perfect childhood ever.'

The childhood she was meant to have had. The one she had been robbed of when her mother refused to name her father. All she had said was that he was a summer visitor. One of the golden tribe who breezed into town in expensive cars with boats and designer shades and lavish tips. Maddison could have been one of them, but instead she had been the trailer-trash daughter of an alcoholic mother. No gold, just tarnish so thick hardly anyone saw through it to the girl within. Even when she had got out, the tarnish had still clung—until she left the Cape altogether and reinvented herself.

Kit looked directly at her as she spoke, as if he could see through to the heart of her. But he couldn't; no one could. She had made sure of that. And yet her pulse sped up under his gaze, hammering so loudly she could almost hear the beat reverberate through the cemetery. She cast about for a change of subject.

'How about you? Do you have any brothers and sisters besides Bridget?'

Kit wandered over to a statue of a lichen-covered dog waiting patiently for eternity. Maddison shivered a little, relieved of the warmth of his gaze, pulling her cardigan a little tighter around her. 'There were three of us.'

Were?

Her unspoken question hung in the air. 'My sister's a lot younger, she's still at university, but my brother...he died. Three years ago.'

'I'm sorry,' she said softly. 'You must miss him.'

He turned, his smile not reaching his eyes. 'Every day. Okay, where are we headed?'

Maddison swallowed. It was a clear change of subject.

He was not going to discuss his loss with her. There was no reason why he should; they barely knew each other. And yet there had been a connection last night, and now as they wandered through the gravestones. Maybe she'd imagined it. After all, didn't she know how powerful imagination was? How important.

She held up the piece of paper and read out the first clue once again. "'Take the Northern line to Archway. Walk up Highgate Hill and through Waterlow Park to the final resting place of the city. Unite at the grave where you have nothing to lose but your chains. The last words on the fourth line are…?'" She paused and looked up at Kit. 'Unite at the grave? What does that mean? We have to split up?'

'See, this is where in the actual trail you'll read the information about Highgate Cemetery in the guidebook and hopefully work the clue out from there. Here.' He passed her his phone. 'Read that.'

She took it carefully and squinted down at the screen, angling it away from the sun so that she could make out the words. "'Famous people buried here include Douglas Adams, George Eliot and Christina Rossetti, although many people bypass even these luminaries and head straight to the grave of Karl Marx…" Oh! Of course.' She read through the rest of the list. 'Lizzie Siddal's buried here too? I'd love to see her grave. I did a paper on the Pre-Raphaelites at college.'

'Take your time. The whole point of this is that it's fun and a way to explore London, not to tear around like some kind of city-wide scavenger hunt.'

'True, but I'm testing it, not doing it for real,' she pointed out. 'I can come back. I might even explore the one in Stoke Newington. Maybe you've converted me to gothic tourism.'

'That's the aim. I'll get you on to a Ripper tour yet. Look, there's a tour guide. Why don't you ask him the way?'

'Only if you take my photo when we get there.' Maddison examined the picture of the grave in fascination. 'I've seen a lot of hipster beards since I got to London but Karl Marx has them all beat. I want to capture that for posterity.' It wasn't quite the type of picture she had intended to fill her social-media sites with but hey. Let Bart see she had hidden depths.

And more importantly that she was out, about and having fun.

Only, Maddison reflected as she walked towards the guide to ask for directions, it wasn't all for show. She probably wouldn't have chosen to spend her weekend in this way but she *was* having fun. And even more oddly, until the last minute she hadn't thought about Bart once all morning.

She'd been banking on absence making the heart grow fonder but in her case it seemed that out of sight really was out of mind. Well, good. Maddison Carter didn't hang around weeping about any guy, no matter how perfect he was. And the more she made that clear, the more likely he would be banging on her door the second she got back to New York, begging for a second chance.

That was the plan, wasn't it? But the image didn't have its usual uplifting effect and for the first time Maddison couldn't help wondering that if she had to go to such extraordinary efforts to persuade Bart that she was the girl for him then maybe, just maybe, he wasn't the guy for her.

And if he wasn't, then she had no idea what to do next.

CHAPTER FOUR

'WHAT HAVE YOU got planned for me today?' Maddison looked up at the threatening-looking sky and wrinkled her nose. 'And what did you do with the sunshine?'

'I forgot to order it.' Kit gestured towards the end of the street. 'Shall we?'

'Okay, but there better be more transport today because, I am warning you, my feet are planning on going on strike after two miles.'

He wasn't surprised by her declaration. They had covered a huge amount of distance the day before, walking to Hampstead Heath from Highgate where, after deciphering the clue, Maddison had found out the opening times of the famous all-season open-air pool. From there they had travelled to first Regent's and then Hyde Park before searching for Peter Pan's statue in Kensington Gardens. Less a leisurely treasure hunt, more a route march through London's parks.

And Maddison hadn't complained once.

She had turned all his preconceptions on their head this weekend. She had surprised him, shamed him a little, with the speech she had produced, with her sharp criticism of his own effort. Charmed him with her unabashed competitiveness in the pub quiz; and yesterday she had unflaggingly followed the clues, suggesting improvements and possible new additions. Not once had she moaned about sore feet or tried to steer him into a shop. He tried to imagine Camilla under similar circumstances and suppressed a smile. Unless her treasure hunt took her down Bond Street she was likely to give up at the first clue.

What was he doing with women like Camilla? He'd thought he was choosing wisely, safely, but maybe he would be better off on his own. It was what he deserved, after all. Although sometimes his dating habits seemed like some eternal punishment, his own personal Hades.

Maddison stopped. 'The bus stop is just here. I was a bit horrified when I realized I was going to have to bus in to work but actually I love that I spend every day on a real red double-decker. It's like an adventure. I never quite know where it might take me.'

Kit's mouth curled into a reluctant smile, his bitter thoughts banished by her enthusiasm. Turned out Maddison Carter had quite the imagination. 'Doesn't it stop at the bus stop outside work?'

'Well, yeah, that's where I choose to get off. But sometimes I wonder if it might turn an unexpected corner and poof. There I am, in Victorian London, or Tudor London. Even in New York I don't feel that. Oh, we have some wonderful old houses back home but they're babies compared to some of the buildings I see here.'

'We'll have to do the history tour next. That will blow your mind.' The bus pulled in at that moment and they got on, tapping their cards on the machine by the driver before ascending the narrow, twisting staircase to the top deck. Yesterday was the first time Kit had been on a bus in a really long time, and personally he was struggling to see any hint of adventure travelling in the slow, crowded vehicle, but to test the routes properly he needed to travel the way his intended market would. However long it took.

He would taxi home though; that wouldn't be cheating.

The bus lurched forward as he slid into a narrow seat beside Maddison. She was wearing the same brightly patterned skirt as yesterday teamed with another neat cashmere cardigan, this one in a bright blue that emphasized the red tones in her hair. She looked like a bird of paradise, far too elegant for the top deck of a bus—or a hike through a park. She had turned away to stare out the window, no doubt daydreaming of time-travelling adventures as the bus progressed slowly down a narrow street, stopping every few hundred yards to allow passengers on and off.

It was a good thing they had all day.

Kit shifted in his seat, trying to arrange his legs comfortably. 'Did you have a nice evening? A date with one of your conquests from the party?' Whatever she had done it had to have been better than his evening, an engagement party for an old friend. Camilla had been there, all quivering emotion and hurt eyes, his attempt to speak rationally to her thwarted by tears. It was funny, he thought grimly, how he had stuck to his word and yet somehow ended up the villain of the piece. At least she finally seemed to have accepted that they were over, had been over for some weeks and, no, he wasn't going to change his mind.

'A date?' Maddison turned and stared at him. 'I only met those men on Friday. It would be a bit early for me to accept a date off any of them even if they did ask me.'

Kit grinned at the indignation in her voice. 'Oh, I'm sorry. Do you need references and to meet the parents first?'

She didn't smile back, her face serious. 'No, but you

never accept an invitation to a same-weekend date. Especially not for a first date.'

'You don't? How very unspontaneous.'

'Of course not.' She was sounding confused now. 'A girl needs to make sure any potential guy understands that she's a busy person, that she won't just drop everything for them.'

Kit frowned. 'But what if you don't have plans? What if you're turning down a night out for a box set and a takeaway?'

'It doesn't matter. If he doesn't respect you enough to try and book you in advance then he never will. You'll be relegated to a last-minute hook-up and once you're there you never move on.' Maddison turned to him, her eyes alight with curiosity. 'Isn't it like this in London?'

'I don't think so. Not that I've ever noticed. I say, "Want to grab a drink?" They say yes. Simple.' Simple at first, anyway.

'Or no. Surely sometimes they say no.'

Kit paused. 'Maybe.' But the truth was they usually said yes.

'Wow.' Maddison looked around as if answers were to be found somewhere on the bus. 'There's more than just an ocean between us, huh? Guess I'll never get a date in London. Or I'll end up civilizing your whole dating scene. Grateful women will build statues to me.'

The women Kit knew played enough mind games without adding some more to their repertoires. 'Remind me never to talk to a woman of dating age in New York again; I shudder to think of all the rules I must have inadvertently broken.' Although it must make life a little clearer, all these rules. It never failed to catch him unawares how quickly it could escalate—a coffee here, a drink there and suddenly there were expectations.

He suppressed a grin at Maddison's appalled face and couldn't resist shocking her a little more. 'If you want to meet someone in London then you need to be a lot less rigid. Over here we meet someone, usually in the pub, fancy them, don't know what to say to them, drink too much, kiss them, send some mildly flirty texts and panic that they'll be misconstrued and repeat until you're officially a couple.'

Maddison stared at him suspiciously. 'That's romantic.'

'You've seen *Four Weddings and a Funeral*, right? Think about it. If Andie MacDowell had understood the British Way of Dating she would never have married the other man, she would have just made sure she turned up at Hugh Grant's local pub a couple of times and that would be that.'

'Four Weddings, Three Nights Out and a Funeral?'

'That's it. Now you're ready to go. If you're looking, that is—or is there someone with the perfect dating etiquette waiting for you back in New York?'

'We're on a break.' The words were airily said but, glancing at her, Kit was surprised to see a melancholy tint to her expression. Sadness mixed with something that looked a lot like fear.

'Because you came here?'

'Not really.' She shook her head, a small embarrassed laugh escaping her. 'I can't believe I'm telling you this.'

'I don't mind.'

Maddison paused, as if she were weighing up whether to carry on. 'Rule number two of dating,' she said eventually. 'Don't talk about your other relationships. Always seem mysterious and desirable at all times. Remember, rejected goods are never as attractive. Rules are rules, even when you're talking to your boss!'

'Your way sounds like a lot of hard work.' Kit stole a glance at her. Her face was pale, all the vibrant colour bleached out of it. He had been subjected to tears, tempers and sulks by his exes, often all three at once, and remained totally unmoved, but Maddison's stillness tugged at him. He wanted to see the warmth return to her expression; after all, he knew all about pain and regret, what a burden it was, how it infected everything. 'Look, if you want to talk about it forget I'm your boss. I've got a sister, remember? Sometimes I think she uses me as her very own Dear Diary.'

Maddison slid a long look up at him and Kit tried to look as confide-worthy as possible. It wasn't curiosity, not exactly. He just got the impression that she didn't let things out very often. Didn't allow her vulnerabilities to show. 'Rule number three, never assume you're exclusive, not until it's been formalized.' She sighed. 'I didn't assume but I let myself believe it was imminent. That he was in it for the long-term.'

'And you were? In it for the long-term?'

She nodded. 'When I first met him, right then, before we even spoke, before we had coffee or went for a walk or kissed. When I first met him I looked at him and I knew. Knew that I could grow old with him.'

Kit blinked. 'Like love at first sight?' He couldn't keep the scepticism out of his voice.

'No.' She shook her head, strawberry-blonde tendrils shaking with the motion. 'Not love. But compatibility, you know? That would grow into love? Two old people rocking on their porch at the end of a long day.'

'You got all that before hello?'

'The way he was standing, his hair, the cut of his suit. It said he was…' She paused, looking up at the bus roof as if for inspiration. 'He just looked like the way I always imagined my future to look. Does that make any sense at all? Have you never thought that way? That you could grow old with someone?'

Kit hesitated. 'Once,' he admitted reluctantly. 'But not straight away.' But the words didn't quite ring true. The reality was that right from the start he had been so dazzled by the image Eleanor portrayed that he had failed to look beneath the carefully applied gloss to the woman underneath.

'What happened?'

Kit tried to smile, as if it were nothing, but he knew all too well that it looked like a grimace. 'She married my brother.'

Maddison opened her mouth then shut it again. He understood that. What was there to say, after all? Kit pulled his phone out of his pocket and busied himself looking at emails. The subject was closed—it should never have been open at all.

Half an hour and a Tube train later they alighted at Notting Hill. He had been careful not to catch her eye, to start another conversation, knowing one more careless confession would shatter everything he worked so hard to contain. But they were here now and the game was back on. And so must he be. He switched on his usual smile, the one that was barely skin-deep.

'Ready?' Kit handed Maddison the first clue and, with one sweeping, comprehensive look at him, she took it. His message had been received and understood.

'"Turn left out of the station until you reach Holland Walk. What is Henry's man doing outside the place where East meets West and the Dutch play?"' she read aloud. 'How international. Are we still doing wild London?'

'Just for today.' After this he was planning south to the Chelsea Physic Garden and then east to Greenwich

Park. Next weekend he was hoping that they could do the historical tour and literary the week after that—and then he would have enough data to put together a full proposal and Maddison could have her weekends back again.

As could he. The usual long, lonely weekends unless he buried himself with work or left London for two days of something outdoors, strenuous and a little dangerous.

Maddison repeated the clue to herself as they walked up the tree-lined splendour of Holland Park Avenue, past the white-painted, ornately decorated houses of this most exclusive of areas, breathing in a deep satisfied sigh as they turned into the park. 'I do love the countryside.'

Kit grinned. 'This isn't countryside, city girl. Two minutes that way and you're back in the heart of the city.' He stared unseeingly at the nearest tree. 'Back home there's nothing *but* trees and grass, water and mountains. The nearest supermarket's an hour's drive away on single-track roads, nothing remotely urban for miles around.'

'Sounds remote.'

'Yes.' He closed his eyes and pictured Kilcanon on a perfect day, the evening drawing in over the water, the vibrant greens fading to grey. Like Odysseus sitting on Circe's island, he felt a sudden piercing longing for his home. But unlike Odysseus there would be no happy homecoming at the end of his journey. His exile was self-imposed, necessary—and permanent. 'It's like no place on earth. But this is my home now, there's no going back. Not for me.'

And just like that he closed down, just as he had on the bus, and Maddison had no idea how to reach him— or even whether she should try. After all, they weren't friends, were they? They worked together, that was all.

But she didn't like to see anyone in pain and the darkness had returned, his eyes more navy than blue, his lips compressed as if he were holding all the emotions in the world tightly within.

'Because of your ex? And your brother?' The conversation from the graveyard yesterday returned to her and she stopped still, shock reverberating through her as she put the clues together. 'Wait, she married your brother, who died?' She regretted the words the second they snapped out of her mouth; there must have been a more sensitive way to have put it.

'Yes.'

'I'm sorry. For both.'

'Thank you.' They began to wander along the path, following the signs to the Japanese garden, Maddison mentally ticking off part of the clue as she went.

'It can't have been easy for you.' And that, she thought with a grimace, was the understatement of the century.

His mouth twisted. 'I accepted long ago that the Eleanor I thought I was in love with doesn't exist. I just wish I had really been able to forgive Euan while I still could. I said I had, of course, but I never did. Not because she chose him over me. But because *he* chose *her* over me.' His mouth snapped shut and he marched along the path as if, like the White Rabbit, they were late.

Maddison walked slowly behind, giving Kit the space he needed. She didn't know a lot about families but she understood betrayal, knew that the worst wounds were inflicted by those who should put you first. No wonder he wasted his time with women who were safe, women he would never allow in too deep.

But his wounds were festering. When had he said his brother had died? Three years ago? And he still hadn't dealt. If she didn't push now, maybe he never would.

But there were dangers in confidences. That was how bonds were formed, friendships forged. She should know; she'd honed her listening skills a long time ago—the right questions, a sympathetic face. She knew the drill. Used it to navigate her way into the right groups, the right cliques, the right life.

But this time she could use her skills for good. To help.

Darn altruism. She didn't have the time or space for it.

She stood, teetering on her decision. Flip the conversation back to clues and parks and grisly tours or probe deeper. She knew which was sensible…

Kit was standing by the entrance to the Japanese garden, a scruffy silhouette, hands in pockets. Maddison picked up her pace and closed the distance between them, mind made up. Light, frivolous words prepared. Only: 'Were you close?' fell from her lips instead.

He turned his head to look at her, his eyes distant, granite-like in their bleakness. Maddison stepped back, the shock almost physical. Gone was the annoying, teasing boss, gone her focused if entertaining weekend companion, in his place a hard-faced stranger reeking of grief.

'Once.'

'Until Eleanor?'

'Until Eleanor.' He walked into the garden, Maddison following, taking a moment to admire the deep oranges and reds in the expertly arranged planting perfectly setting off the delicate waterfalls and sculptures. She joined Kit on the wide stone bridge and stood by him, looking at the koi as they swam in the pond.

'She was everything I didn't know I wanted.'

Maddison's heart twisted at the words. Wasn't that what she aimed to be? Hadn't she tried to learn Bart? To be everything he didn't know he wanted? But her intentions were more honourable; if he wanted her, offered her the security she craved, she would look after his heart as if it were her own, do her very best to give him hers. Not break him into pieces.

'We were close, Euan and I. There's barely a year and a half between us and he was the oldest—he never let me forget that. But he had asthma and it held him back sometimes and I, I didn't let him forget that.'

He paused, still staring into the pond as if the koi carp could give him the answers she couldn't. But like her they just listened.

'I was in my last year at Cambridge when I brought Eleanor home. I'd never brought a girl back before. I couldn't wait for my family to meet her. But he couldn't help himself, couldn't help making even her into a competition and this time he won. How was I supposed to forgive him for that?'

Without thinking Maddison reached across the carefully maintained space between them and laid a hand on Kit's arm. It was firm, as she'd known it would be, warm. She wanted to leave her hand there, flesh on flesh, to allow her fingers to slip down the muscled forearm, to link around his wrist. Her heart began to hammer, every millimetre of her uncomfortably aware of his proximity, of the feel of him under her suddenly unsteady hand.

She had never experienced a visceral reaction like this over a mere touch before.

She had never had a reaction like this before. Period.

Slowly, as if her hand were an unarmed grenade and not a part of her own body, Maddison lowered her hand back to her side. Kit was continuing as if nothing had happened, as if he hadn't even felt the pressure of her hand, let alone the almost explosive chemical reaction when skin touched skin.

Which was good, right? No, it was great. No awkwardness, no apologies. She'd just done what any normal person would do at a moment like this. Offered some comfort. Awkward comfort, sure. But all completely appropriate and above board.

'In that moment I was exiled from my home. Came home for holidays and Christmases, pretended I was fine, that there was no problem on my side. But I couldn't stay for long, not while they lived in Kilcanon. It's got worse since he died. I feel it more than ever. Going back gets harder every time. His absence seems larger every time.'

Maddison took a deep breath, steadying her voice as best she could. 'Did she love him?' She badly wanted the answer to be yes. After all, she'd been ready to love Bart, hadn't she? Ready to give him her body and soul in return for the security he guaranteed. She wasn't one of those gold-digging fakes ready to barter themselves away for a lifestyle. She was just cautious, that was all. Not ready to commit her heart too soon. Not till she knew it was safe.

'I'd like to think so, I really do. At least, I hope he believed she did. I hope he died thinking she adored him just as he adored her. Of course, her forthcoming nuptials to an older, richer and more influential man might point the other way but, hey, what do I know about grief?'

'A fair bit from the sound of it,' she said softly and he grimaced.

'It's been three years. It's time I moved on and accepted my responsibilities to the family. That's what my parents think. Not that *they've* really moved on. I'm not sure they'll ever accept the fact that Euan has gone and I am all that's left. Poor seconds.'

'I'm sure they don't think that.'

He laughed, a short bitter sound. 'You've spoken to my mother. You must have worked out what a disappointment I am.'

'I know she wants to hear from you, that messages through me aren't enough.' What would it be like to have a mother who cared? Who tried and tried to get through to you even when you were too grief-stricken and hurt to respond. 'Wait, Eleanor's wedding. Is that the wedding I keep getting calls about?'

'The very same. She's marrying a neighbour of ours and my parents are very insistent that we all go along and bless her new marriage. It's the right thing to do. And they're right, and yet I just can't bring myself to accept the damn invite. It's like if I do, that's it. Euan has gone and it was all for nothing.'

CHAPTER FIVE

IT HAD BEEN a long day and by the time Maddison had noted down the maker of the clock situated just outside the Royal Observatory in Greenwich Park she was beat. She flopped onto a bench with an exaggerated sigh. 'That's half of London off my sightseeing list.'

'See, virtue is its own reward.' Kit had his trademark amused smile back in place as if the heartfelt conversation in Holland Park had never taken place. Maddison couldn't help thinking that it was for the best. She'd mentioned her hopes for Bart, he'd opened up about his brother. They were even. No more depth required. And next weekend she would be armed with an entire list of small talk and safe topics to make sure they went no further.

'Actually…' she smiled sweetly at him '…reward is its own reward. Event of my choosing, remember?' Even as she said the words she wondered if she was playing with fire, spending more time alone with Kit Buchanan. But an event was different; if she chose wisely they wouldn't have to communicate at all. And it all made good copy for her social-media sites. She had a ton of pictures to add over the week: the Japanese garden at Holland Park, another gorgeous garden in the equally gorgeous Chelsea and the slightly disappointing visit to Vauxhall. It was a perfectly adequate park but she had secretly been hoping that the old pleasure gardens were still intact with winding, tree-lined paths full of lurking rakes, and a ballroom brimming with waltzing, masked partygoers. Now that would have got a lot of 'likes'. A few pictures of her dallying with breeches-clad rakes and surely Bart would have been over on the next plane.

Although given the choice she'd have been tempted to stick with the rakes… Maddison pushed the disloyal thought aside. Her plans with Bart were—had been—about forever. She wouldn't throw that away for a rake, no matter how tight his breeches.

Nor for a pair of blue eyes and an easy smile. Not that the owner was offering.

'Of course. Your prize. What's tempting you? Dinner at Nobu, drinks at the Garrick, Shakespeare at The Globe?' Kit leaned against the railings and looked out at the view and, despite herself, Maddison couldn't stop her gaze skimming over his denim-clad rear. The worn jeans fitted him just right; even breeches couldn't improve that posterior. 'Or some sort of concert? Your wish is my command.'

'Seriously, anything?'

'That was the deal. Why?' He turned, his eyes creased, a wicked gleam warning her that she wasn't going to be impressed with his next suggestion. She folded her arms and glared at him. It had as much effect as bombarding him with kittens. 'Do you fancy something more risqué? I'm unshockable, you know, quite happy to take you to a burlesque club or into Soho for something a little edgier if that's what you fancy.'

Maddison had an irrepressible urge to play along, just to see how far he'd go. 'Burlesque is very two years ago. Once you've spent a year learning how to unfold yourself from a giant martini glass in little more than a feather boa it quite takes the mystique away. It was great exercise, though, really worked the abs and the glutes—especially hanging upside down on a rope.'

'I'd pay good money to see that,' he said softly and Maddison barely repressed a shiver as the gleam in his eye intensified, darkened. Maybe she didn't want to find out how far he would go. Maybe she was the one who was happy staying right here.

'I'm out of practice.'

'Isn't that a shame?'

Okay, it was definitely time to change the subject. 'Opera. I'd really like to go to the opera, in Covent Garden.'

The gleam was wiped away as if it had never been. 'Opera?'

'You did say anything,' Maddison pointed out sweetly, enjoying the look of horror on his face.

'True. I am a man of my word. But are you sure? Huge ladies in nighties collapsing and dying over twenty minutes of yowling? Because I'm sure there's a complete extended *Lord of the Rings* trilogy showing somewhere. You, me, twelve hours of orcs?'

'You have a very outdated view of opera. Not the twenty-minute-dying thing,' she added truthfully. 'That's pretty standard, but the casting and staging is equal to the singing now. But if you really hate the idea I'll go by myself.'

'No, no, I promised. Any preference?'

The temptation to demand a full repertoire of Wagner almost overwhelmed her but she resisted. 'You choose, whatever's on. The experience will be enough.'

He shook his head. 'Opera,' he muttered. 'Okay, caterwauling and extensive death scenes it is, but you have one more task before you fully earn it. I want to walk under the Thames, see if it's worth including in a tour, and as we're so close you can come with me. Tell me if it should be on every tourist's wish list.'

'Walk under the Thames?' Maddison stared up at him. 'I hate to break it to you but I left my scuba-diving stuff at home.'

'Luckily for you there's a staircase and a fully tiled tunnel. No masks or tanks required. I believe it's perfectly safe. About one hundred and twenty years old though so there may be a few cracks…'

Maddison's pulse had already sped up at the words *walk* and *under* but *cracks* sent it hammering into overdrive. 'Why walk when there are perfectly good bridges and cable cars?'

'History. It was put in to help dock workers get to work on time from the other side of the river. I'm joking, Maddison, it's perfectly safe, not a crack to be seen. The damage from World War II was repaired, well around then I think. It's a great addition to the history tour but I just want to see how long it takes and look for things I can use for a clue. If you really hate the idea then…'

'No. It's fine.' It wasn't but no way was she playing the weak, pathetic female. 'I just think you exceeded the walking quota for today and now here you are adding a whole river's worth of extra steps. I'm just calculating how much it's worth. Interval drinks at the opera for a start.'

It wasn't that she was claustrophobic, not at all. She was fine in her tiny studio, wasn't she? And sure, she didn't like flying, but nobody really liked being cheek by jowl with a bunch of strangers in a tin can in the sky. It was just she didn't like feeling that she had no escape. It was too much like the tiny, airless room in the trailer, the door shut and not being allowed to come out, not even to use the toilet or to get a drink. It was being help-less that got to her. And walking under a river seemed a pretty darn vulnerable thing to do.

'Drinks as well? That might make the actual opera part a little more palatable.' He extended a hand. 'Come along, Miss Carter, we can't be lounging around here all day. We have waters to conquer.'

Why had she agreed when it was obvious how much she didn't want to go into the tunnel? Daniel had probably been much more eager to go into the lions' den—but, unlike Daniel, Maddison had no need to martyr herself. Kit had suggested more than once that she could wait for him by the domed entrance but she brushed his sugges-tion aside with a curt, 'I'm fine, honestly.'

Which was the least honest thing he had heard this week. Fine didn't usually mean pale, big-eyed and mute.

The entrance to the tunnel was by the Cutty Sark, the permanently moored Victorian clipper, and Kit made a note to try and work the boat into the history quiz—with the Royal Observatory so close it would give treasure hunters a good reason to come this far east. But he didn't stop as he steered Maddison past the tourists queuing up for a tour; if she was going to insist on doing something that so obviously freaked her out, then they should get it over with as soon as possible.

They bypassed the glass door lifts at the tunnel en-trance, choosing to access the tunnel through the spiral staircase instead, and began the descent still in silence. There must have been one hundred or so steps and Kit breathed a sigh of relief when they reached the bottom, Maddison still safely by his side.

'Okay, keep your eyes out for clues,' he said as cheer-fully as he could, as if a mute, white-faced Maddison were a completely normal companion. 'Interpretation, some carving or plaque we could use. I was wondering about the number of steps but lost count halfway down.'

'So did I.'

'She speaks! So, what do you think?'

Maddison swivelled, taking in the tunnel. It was, Kit had to admit, less than spectacular, the floor a grubby gravel path, the circular walls curving low overhead, completely covered with white rectangular tiles. A line of lights ran ahead, murkily lighting the way. If he was planning to write a crime novel, then this would make a perfect location. If it weren't for the CCTV and other pedestrians, that was. He stepped aside as a family came by, the children yelling excitedly as their voices echoed off the walls.

'It's a little like being in the Tube. If I didn't know I wouldn't have guessed we were under the river.'

'Those Victorians missed a trick. They should have put in glass walls so we could gaze in delight on the murky depths of the Thames, looking out for shopping trolleys and the occasional body.'

'Charming. I so wish they had.'

'Ready? I'm going to warn you now that we're not getting out the other end; there's not a huge amount to see there and I want to take a closer look at the Cutty Sark.'

'There and back again? That's going to cost ices *and* drinks at the opera.' But her voice wasn't so stilted and her posture more natural. Whatever Maddison had been afraid of obviously hadn't materialized—and she was right: it was very much like walking through a connection tunnel at a Tube station. A long connection tunnel. One the width of the Thames, in fact.

And the Thames was wider than he'd realized. 'Seen anything?' They had walked maybe around five hundred yards and he had yet to see a single identifying item that would make the tunnel suitable as a treasure-hunt destination.

'Not a thing. Maybe there will be something at the other end we can direct them to.' She sounded completely normal now, if a little weary.

The lights flickered and she froze, her eyes wide. Not so normal after all, just putting on a good front. Maybe they would have to exit at the far end after all. Kit wasn't sure he wanted to bring her back through the tunnel if she was going to be so jumpy.

'Maybe, otherwise...' But before he could finish his suggestion the lights flickered again and then a third time, before with no further ceremony simply blinking out. Kit blinked and blinked again, the darkness so very complete he didn't know where the tips of his fingers were, which way he was facing.

'What the...?' he swore softly. 'Maddison, where are you? Are you okay?' She didn't reply but he could hear her breathing, fast, shallow, panicked breaths getting hoarser and hoarser as her breathing sped up.

'Maddison.' He put out a hand, feeling for her, conscious of a mild panic, a little like playing blind man's bluff, that moment when you reach out into the unknown, patting the air gingerly, hoping to touch hair or a sleeve. But there were no answering giggles, just increasingly hoarse breaths. He felt again but his hands brushed nothing more substantial than air. Damn.

'Maddison, it's okay. I'm going to get my phone. It has a light on it. Okay? Just slow down, lass.' The affectionate word slipped from his tongue before he was aware. A word that belonged at home, to a past life, a past time. 'Breathe. Breathe.' He kept speaking in a low, measured voice while he fumbled for his phone, breathing a sigh of relief when he located it. It took him three expletive-ridden tries to press his fingerprint onto the lock screen but eventually the phone was on and he could press the torch icon. Immediately a beam of light sprung out from the back, casting a pale glow over the wall in front of him. He moved it to the side and finally located Maddison.

She was utterly rigid, her eyes wide in shock, the blood completely drained from her face as if she were looking into Hades. Kit reached out and took a hand, wincing at the iciness of her flesh. All thoughts of boundaries and assistants and company policies when it came to line managers and their staff disappeared as he shrugged off his jacket, wrapping it around her and pulling her in tight so that he could rub her arms, her back, her hands, trying desperately to transfer some warmth from him to her. She was shaking now, her teeth chattering, but her breathing slowed as he held her. She still didn't utter a single word.

It could only have been a minute at the most but it felt like an eternity. The silence as absolute as the dark, punctuated only by her panicked breath and his murmured comfort. It was almost a shock when the lights came on with no ceremony, just with a dull flicker. Maddison started, stared at the light—and then burst into tears. Convulsive, silent sobs that racked her body as if they would tear her apart.

'Hey, hey, it's okay.' Kit continued to rub her back, his hands moving in slow, comforting circles, but now the lights were back on, now she was responding to his comfort, albeit in a damp, sobbing way. It was hard for him not to notice just how perfectly his hand fit the contours of her back. How her hair was lightly fragranced, a subtle floral scent that made him think of spring. Of how perfectly she fitted into him, her head under his chin and her breasts—oh, dear God, her breasts—nestled enticingly against his chest.

No, not enticingly. She was in pain and shock. What kind of monster found that enticing?

Her waist was supple and her legs gloriously long. The kind of legs a man wanted wrapped round him...

Kit swallowed, his hands stilling as he tried to push the unwanted, forbidden thoughts away. She was in love with someone else, remember? She wanted a porch swing with that someone, which wasn't a sign of commitment he was familiar with, it must be some American thing, but it sounded serious. And even if she weren't...

She was bright and quick and ridiculously attractive, not to mention the perfect breasts and the long legs and the hair. Girls like Maddison deserved to be put up on pedestals and worshipped. Even if she were free she wasn't for him. He didn't deserve her, would never deserve a woman like her. He deserved shallow and superficial and downright annoying at best. Really he would be better off on his own. He deserved a lifetime of loneliness.

After a few minutes during which Kit studiously counted the tiles over her shoulders, anything to take his mind off just how closely they were pressed together, Maddison's breathing slowed down to the odd gulp, her sobs transmuted to small shudders, her tears finally stemmed. 'I'm so sorry.' She stepped back and he was instantly cold, instantly empty. He wanted to drag her back against him, allow his hands to explore every inch of her body in a way that had nothing to do with comfort, everything to do with lust. Kit's eyes dropped to the lush tilt of her mouth, swollen from tears, and wanted to crush it under his until her sobs were a distant memory.

He took a step back of his own. 'That's okay. Come on, let's get out of here.'

'I…I…I'm not good in the dark.'

'You don't have to explain anything.' His voice was gruff as he forced the words out. 'Are you okay to walk? I think we both need a stiff drink.'

Maddison cradled the brandy Kit had insisted on buying for her. 'I am really…'

'Sorry,' he supplied. 'I know. But you don't need to be. There is absolutely nothing to apologize for.'

'A twenty-six-year-old woman so afraid of the dark she has a meltdown? That's beyond an apology.' She buried her head in her hands. 'I am completely pathetic. Do you know I sleep with a night light? Like a little kid?'

She had slept with a night light since she was eight, since the night she had woken to hear a noise snuffling outside her trailer. There were coyotes on the Cape but her mind had immediately jumped to bears—or something worse. Maddison had blinked against the total darkness, heart hammering, mind buzzing with a fear completely alien to her eight-year-old mind.

'Mommy.' But her voice was hoarse with fear, the word barely more than a whisper. 'Mommy?'

At some level she'd known, known even if she could call out it would be no use, that her mother had gone out once she was asleep, that she often went out when Maddison was asleep, known that she was all alone in an old trailer in the middle of the woods. That anyone or anything could come and break into the trailer and nobody was there to save her.

Maddison looked up at Kit, her hands gripping the brandy, and took in a deep, shuddering breath, trying to get the panic back under control, where it belonged. 'You know what I love about living in New York? It's never dark. The light shines in through my window all night long.'

Kit reached over and laid his hand over hers, a warm, comforting clasp. She wanted to lace her fingers through his and hold on tight, let him anchor her to the daylight and the sunshine and the busy city street, pull her out of the darkness of the past.

But only she could do that. She needed security, she needed a family of her own to make up for her long, lonely childhood. She wanted the kind of money that meant walls were always thick, lights were always on and that she never, ever had to spend a night on her own.

'We all have our Achilles' heel,' he said, his fingers a comfortable caress on hers. 'No one has to be strong all the time, Maddison.'

She shook her head. He really didn't get it. 'I do,' she told him as she eased her hand out from under his, ignoring the chill on her now-empty hand in the space where he had touched her, the need for his warmth. 'I do. Weakness makes you vulnerable. Strength, security, that's what counts, Kit.'

He was looking at her as if he wanted to see into the heart of her but her barriers were well crafted and she wasn't letting him in. 'What happened, Maddison?'

She picked up the brandy and took a hefty swig, coughing a little as the strong liquor hit the back of her throat. 'Nothing happened, Kit. It's just life is like this treasure hunt of yours. There are winners and there are losers and you should know by now, I really like to win.'

CHAPTER SIX

'IS THIS WHAT you were hoping for? Because we can always duck out and do something else. Something that doesn't take quite so long.' Kit stared down at the programme, dismay written all over his face. 'Three acts? *Three*.'

'It's less than three hours in total,' Maddison looked around at the glittering sea of people and suppressed an excited shiver. 'And it could be a lot worse. Just think, it could have been Wagner.'

Kit shuddered dramatically. 'I'm definitely not putting this in the guidebook.'

His voice was a little loud and several heads turned disapprovingly. She elbowed him meaningfully. 'It's culture, you have to include it. You can't assume everyone is going to be a philistine just because you are. Besides, you must have known what to expect. This can't be your first opera.'

'Oh, it can. It will also be my last,' he said darkly. 'I didn't realize your cooperation would have quite so high a price. And I'm not just talking about the tickets—or these gin and tonics.'

Maddison repressed a smile. He might be acting all grumpy, but Kit had gone well above and beyond their agreement. 'Thank you.' She squeezed his arm. 'I didn't expect a gala night. This is really incredible.' She managed to stop the next words tumbling out before her sophisticated girl-about-town image was well and truly blown, but she couldn't keep her eyes from shining her gratitude. *No one has ever done anything like this for me before...*

Maddison looked around for the umpteenth time, trying to keep her excitement locked down deep inside. *Play it cool, Maddison Carter, you belong here.* And tonight she really did. Kit hadn't just brought her to the Royal Opera House, he'd gone all out and hired a box at a first-night gala performance of *Madame Butterfly.*

The cause was fashionable, the tickets sought after and London's great and good were out in force, the women's jewels competing with the huge, dazzling chandeliers, the men in exquisitely cut tuxedos. It was like stepping back in time to Edwardian England—and she, Maddison Carter, was right in the middle of it. A real Buccaneer. She might not own any heirloom jewels, but the man on her arm was one of the most striking in the room and she had intercepted more than one envious glance in their direction.

And everything was fine. She'd been worried on Monday that he would be careful with her, that her breakdown would change his attitude. It had been a relief when he had been his usual, slightly annoying self. In fact it was as if the weekend, the confidences, had never happened. Which was as it should be, because there had been moments when she had felt far too close to him, far too at ease.

Far too attracted.

Maddison sipped her drink, the sharp notes of the gin and tonic a relief. Where had that thought come from? Tunnels aside, she was having a good time with her extracurricular work, but treasure hunts and a heart to heart weren't going to get her the happy-ever-after, all-American dream, were they? She needed to remember her goals: a good marriage, a family of her own, security—emotionally and financially.

She took another sip. Tomorrow. She'd remember it tomorrow. It would be rude not to give her total concentration to the night ahead.

'Do you actually like opera?' Kit murmured in her ear, his breath warm, intimate, on her bare shoulder.

She turned to face him, pushing the disquieting thoughts away. 'I love it.' He arched a disbelieving eyebrow and she laughed. 'Honestly. I grew up with it. How could I not?'

For the first time, discomfort twisted in her as she stretched the truth. She *had* grown up with opera, but not in the way she was implying.

Every summer, Maddison would pick out the men she hoped were her long-lost father and watch them, waiting for recognition to spark in their eyes. Only it never did. They didn't even notice her. The year she turned ten she'd spent the summer hanging out on the beach all day, pretending as usual that she belonged to one of the laughing, happy families enjoying their vacation by the sea. Pretend that any moment they would look up, see her and call her, pull her sand-covered body in close, wrap her in a towel, hand her an ice-cold drink while alternating between kisses and scolding her for straying so far away.

It was so much better than the reality—an empty trailer and cold leftovers. If she was lucky.

Her favourite families owned or rented houses right on the beach. As evening fell and the beach emptied she would sit in the dunes and watch them. And that was when she had first noticed him, the tall, broad man who lifted his daughter up with one hand, who spent hours constructing the perfect sandcastle, who sang opera as he grilled dinner for his family on the beach-house patio.

She watched him every summer until the year she turned fourteen and realized that daydreams were never going to change anything.

But she couldn't shed the knowledge that if she'd lived with him, with somebody like him, with her real father, then maybe she would have had the childhood she wanted, the one she invented for herself as soon as she left Bayside: a childhood filled with singing arias, with ballet matinees and Saturday trips to the museum. The moment she hit New York she tried to re-create that childhood and fill in the gaps in her knowledge, spending her wages on cheap matinee seats up in the gods, museum tours, absorbing a childhood's worth of culture.

And it had brought her here, to the most glamorous place she had ever been in her entire life.

Her little black-and-white dress might be on the demure side but it held its own, every perfect seam screaming its quality. She smoothed out the heavy material with a quiet prayer of gratitude to the woman who had hired Maddison as a maid, giving her a room when Maddison left home at sixteen. Thanks to Mrs Stanmeyer, Maddison had had the space and time to study her last two years at school—and her benefactress's influence had secured Maddison a scholarship and bursary at a private liberal arts college in New Hampshire. In its ivy-covered buildings she'd both got her degree and reinvented herself.

And she never forgot Mrs Stanmeyer's advice: Maddison only bought the very best of everything. It meant her wardrobe was limited but it was timelessly classy and made to last. It allowed her to fit in anywhere.

The past faded away as the music swelled and surrounded her. Every note exquisite, every aria a dream.

She squeezed her eyes shut and let the music take over, offering wordless thanks to the man in the beach house. He wasn't Maddison's real father, she knew that now—truthfully she'd known it then—but he'd given her a gift nonetheless. She might have had to train herself to appreciate this music, but her training wheels were long since discarded and she was all-in. Every atom of her.

Finally the last lingering note died away and the audience was frozen in that delicious moment between performance and applause. Still tingling, Maddison turned to Kit. Had he hated it? Was he bored? She really hoped he got it.

That he understood a part of her.

His eyes were open and alert, which was a definite bonus; Bart liked to see and be seen doing culturally highbrow activities, but Maddison suspected if he could have got away with earplugs he would have—as it was she wasn't convinced he didn't snooze the best part of any performance away. Kit, however, was leaning forward, his arm on the balustrade and his eyes fixed onto the stage below.

She couldn't wait any longer. 'So? Did you hate it? You hated it. If you're bored we should go. Honestly…'

Kit reached out and covered her gesturing hand with his, sparks igniting up and down her arm as his fingers clasped hers. 'I wasn't bored. I…I don't know if I'm enjoying it exactly. I mean, offer me a trade for a sticky, beer-covered floor, some drums and guitars and a mosh pit and I'd take it, but I have to admit I'm…' he paused, raking a hand through his hair '…moved.'

'That's a start.' The glow inside was gladness. She'd introduced him to something new, something life enhancing. It had nothing to do with the hand still holding hers, nothing at all. 'Would you come again?'

There was no pause this time. 'Yes. Yes, I would.' Surprise lit up his face as he spoke. 'Wow, that was unexpected. I didn't know I was going to say that.' His fingers tightened, a cool clasp blazing a heated trail straight up her arm. 'Thank you.'

Maddison tried not to look at their entwined hands, not to behave as if this was in any way odd. 'For what?'

'For making me try something new.' The words were simply said but his gaze held a barely concealed smoulder, one that ignited every nerve right down to her bare toes.

'You're very welcome.' She tried to sound non-committal but couldn't stop the soft smile curving her lips, couldn't stop her eyelashes fluttering down in an unexpectedly shy gesture. What was going on? This wasn't how she operated. She hadn't tried to learn him by heart, hadn't tried to mould herself into what she thought he wanted. She was being herself, as much as she ever could be, thinking of nothing but work and yet unexpectedly finding herself having fun.

It had been a long time since fun had figured in her plans.

By some unspoken mutual accord their hands unclasped as Kit ushered her from the box to collect their interval drinks.

The corridors were buzzing with people, the bar even more so. Luckily there was no queuing; instead, here in the rarefied environs of the dress circle on a gala night, trays of champagne and canapés were circling amongst the chattering crowds. Kit neatly snagged two glasses off a passing waitress and passed one to Maddison, raising his own glass to her as he did so.

'To trying new things.' His eyes gleamed a bright blue in the glittering lights, a devilish glint flickering in the depths. Maddison's mind whirled with confusion, with an unexpected, unwanted desire to press a little closer. For those eyes to look at her with even more heat, more devilry. Her dizziness increased as his eyes held hers, the rest of the room falling away.

This was it, a dim, distant part of her analysed as she stood there, staring up at him. This was what attracted Camilla and her ilk to him, even though he warned them away, warned them that he wasn't in it for the medium-term, let alone forever. But when he focused, really focused, he could make a girl feel as if she were the only person worth knowing in the room. The only person *in* the room.

And yet she was pretty sure he didn't do it on purpose; this was no practised trick, no calculated seductive move.

That was what made it so dangerous, made him so very dangerous.

Even she, mistress of her own heart and destiny, might get swept away. For a very little while.

Or not… She was too seasoned a player to fold her hand at the first eye contact and warm, intimate glance. Maddison took a deep breath, stepping back, out of the seductive circle of his spell. 'To new things,' she agreed. 'It's the ballet next.'

Kit smiled appreciatively. 'Oh, no, it's my turn to choose next and I quite fancy seeing the demure and always put-together Maddison Carter in a mosh pit. Up for it?'

A what? Maddison opened her mouth to deliver what was definitely going to be a stinging retort as soon as she could think of one, when a languid hand draped itself on Kit's shoulder, a statuesque middle-aged brunette spinning him around as she pressed a kiss onto his suddenly rigid cheek. Only a muscle beating in his jawline showed any emotion.

Maddison shivered, suddenly chilled. Had they turned the air conditioning up? Hard to imagine how very warm she'd been just a few seconds before.

'Kit, dearest. I thought it was you but Charles said I must be mistaken. Kit at the opera! And yet here you are…'

Kit was still supremely still, only that pulsing muscle and the flash of anger in his eyes betraying any sign of life. 'Not mistaken, Laura. Hello, Charles.' He nodded over Laura's shoulder at the tall, balding man behind her.

'Gracious, Kit, last place I would have expected to see you. Not your usual style of thing.'

'No,' he agreed, his voice smooth. 'It's not. It is, however, very much Maddison's style and so here you find me.' He smoothly stepped out of Laura's possessive clasp and took Maddison's arm, ushering her forward, his hand holding her tight as if he feared she might run—or that he might. 'Laura, Charles, this is Maddison Carter. Maddison, this is Charles and Laura Forsyth.' He paused then before continuing, his voice still as urbanely smooth as the richest cream. 'Eleanor's parents.'

'Lovely to meet you.' Her words were as mechanical as her smile, Maddison's mind sprinting ahead as she watched Laura Forsyth's unsubtle summing up. Maddison held her chin up, as unconcerned as if she hadn't noticed the slow appraisal; she had nothing to hide, clothes-wise at least. Her outfit might be demure but the quality was unmistakable.

'American? How long are you over for? So nice of Kit to take you around.'

Maddison's eyes narrowed at the thinly hidden derisive note in the older woman's voice. Did Laura Forsyth think she could be put down so easily? It had been a long time since Maddison had allowed herself to be dismissed in a couple of sentences.

She would wipe that smile right off Mrs Forsyth's suspiciously wrinkle-free face.

Maddison plastered a bright smile on to her own naturally wrinkle-free thank you very much face and moved even closer to Kit, slipping under his arm, her own snaking round his waist as she turned to him. 'Isn't it? Kit's being very hospitable.' Maddison laid an extra-slow drawl onto the last two words, filling them with an unmistakable innuendo, and felt him quiver but whether it was with humour or anger she had no idea.

What the heck was she doing? Had she taken leave of her senses? She picked *now* to lose her temper, to behave spontaneously? It was going to look great on her résumé when Kit fired her. Reason for dismissal? Inappropriate temptress at the opera.

The older woman's eyes narrowed. 'He always was good-hearted, weren't you, Kit? Eleanor always said you put yourself out for others. We will be seeing you next week, won't we? It would mean a lot to Eleanor. After all, you're still family. I *had* hoped that, well, never mind that now. But for Euan's sake, Kit, you should come to her wedding.' Her eyes flickered towards Maddison. 'You are welcome to bring a guest, of course.'

'That's very kind of you, Laura. I am very busy and we weren't sure we could spare the time, were we, Maddison? But it would be a shame not to show you Scotland while you're here. So, thank you, Laura. We'd love to accept. Please do pass my apologies on to Eleanor for taking so long to respond.'

We? Hang on a second. Maddison worked to keep her smile in place. He was calling Laura Forsyth's bluff, surely. He didn't actually expect Maddison to attend a wedding in Scotland. With him. With his whole family. His ex-girlfriend and dead brother's widow's wedding. Did he?

There weren't enough opera tickets in the world.

The smile faltered on Laura Forsyth's face. 'How lovely. Eleanor will be delighted. We'd better get on. Charles has clients here. I'll see you—both—next weekend.' She kissed Kit again before disappearing into the crowd.

Maddison freed herself and rounded on Kit. He looked completely unruffled.

She folded her arms and glared at him. 'What did you just do?'

'Accepted the wedding invitation.' How could he look so calm and so darn amused? Did he think this was funny? 'After all, you've been reminding me to for weeks. I thought you'd be pleased.'

Thought she'd be *what*? 'I don't care whether you go or not, I just wanted you to decide either way and for the many, many phone calls to stop. I wanted you to make a decision for you. Not for me! Why did you do that? Now she'll think that I… That we…'

'She thought that the second you cosied into me. It wouldn't have been gentlemanly of me to push you away and explain that, sorry, you were my over-familiar assistant, and once she had included you in the invitation it seemed rude to accept for just me.'

Okay, she *had* been the one pressing in close in a proprietary fashion. 'I shouldn't have…' how had he put it? '…cosied into you like that. It was silly. It was just the way she looked at me. I got mad.' This was why she kept her temper, her feelings, under close control—usually, at least. Look what trouble acting impulsively could do.

'Apology accepted.' Maddison nearly choked at his smooth words. 'And now you've accepted responsibility for the whole situation you can see it's too late to backtrack now.' His mouth curved wickedly and she didn't know whether she wanted to wipe the smile off his face—or kiss it off.

Wipe, definitely wipe.

'Too late? I could have had plans. I might have plans.' Kit shot her a knowing look and Maddison scowled. 'Okay, I don't have plans but she doesn't know that. Just tell her I mixed up my dates. Or I'm ill. Or I had to leave the country.'

'Or you could just come with me.'

Maddison stilled. 'Why?'

Kit shrugged. 'Why not? Scotland is beautiful, especially at this time of year, and you really should see more of the UK than just London.'

'Your family will be there.'

'That's okay, they don't bite. You'll be doing me a favour, actually. I think I mentioned that I don't go back often. It can be a little intense. Your presence will relax things a little.'

'You want me to come along to act as a buffer between you and your parents?'

'I said no such thing. You speak to my mother more than I do. She'll be delighted to meet you at last.'

Meet the parents. Not at all awkward. 'Isn't there someone else you'd rather take? An actual real date?'

Kit stilled. 'I don't introduce my dates to my parents.'

'Not ever?' Obviously she never had but there were mitigating circumstances in her case. Kit's mother sounded both sober and present, qualities Maddison's mother had failed to possess.

'Not since Euan died. No, not because I'm too heartbroken.' Her face must have expressed her thoughts and Maddison flushed with embarrassment. 'No. Introducing dates to parents raises hopes in bosoms on both sides and that's something I'd rather not do.'

His words on her birthday came back to her. 'You really don't want to fall in love again one day?'

'No.' His voice was uncompromising. 'I don't believe in love. It's just getting carried away by infatuation and circumstance.'

His views weren't so far away from Maddison's own but it was uncomfortable hearing them so baldly stated.

'Look, Maddison, it's a good opportunity for you to spend some time outside London. Besides, we can work on the way up. I'm quite happy to dictate and drive.'

'You're really selling it to me. A weekend of weddings and work.'

'If you really hate the idea, then of course you don't have to come. But I do know it will be much more fun if you're there.'

Fun? With her? Warmth stole through her at the casual words. Words of acceptance and liking. 'Okay.' Wow, she was easily bought, wasn't she? But Kit was right. She should get out of London and see more while she was here. It had taken her twenty-six years to get to Europe; what if it was another twenty-six before she returned?

And he thought she was fun...not competent or organized or reliable. Fun.

'Great. I hope you brought some warm clothes. Scotland can be nippy even in early summer and I get the impression the atmosphere at Eleanor's wedding will be positively frosty.'

CHAPTER SEVEN

'ARE WE THERE YET?' Kit looked over as Maddison stretched and yawned, noting that she looked more cat-like than ever as she did so. Her hair was a little mussed up from sleeping in the car, her face make-up free. She looked younger, freer. His stomach tightened. If only they were on their way to somewhere where *he* could feel free. Instead every mile closer to the border the air closed in just a little bit more. Duty, responsibility, expectation all waiting to descend on him like an unwanted coronation mantle.

He turned the radio down a little. 'Not even close, I'm afraid. It would help if this section of the motorway wasn't all roadworks—it feels like we're permanently stuck at fifty miles per hour.' It might have made more sense to fly or to get the train but Kit needed to know that he had an escape plan ready and active at all times—and that meant his own transport.

'I don't understand. We've been on the road for hours. England just can't be that big. It's meant to be all little and quaint.' Maddison stared out of the window at the never-ending fields—and the never-ending drizzle—as if she were searching for thatched roofs and maypoles. She'd be searching for some time. The view from the M6 was many things but quaint wasn't one of them.

Besides, there was something she needed to be put right on. '*England* is nearly four hundred miles long and we're driving about three quarters of the length of it, but, as you need to remember before you are thrown out of the country for disrespect, we're not going to be in England, we're going to Scotland. A whole different country.' Despite himself, despite everything, Kit could hear the pride in his voice, feel the slight swell in his chest. Eleanor used to tease him that the further north they got the broader his accent got. Of course, now she rolled her *r*'s as if her home counties upbringing and Oxbridge education belonged to someone else, more Scottish than Edinburgh rock.

'A whole different country,' Maddison repeated. 'Like Canada?'

'But without border patrols and with the same currency.'

'Got it.' She slid him a sidelong glance. 'Are you okay?'

'Fine, why?'

'It can't be easy, watching your ex get married.'

If only she knew the half of it. 'I've had plenty of practice. This is her second wedding and she's still in her twenties. I fully expect to watch Eleanor get married several more times before she's through.'

'It's just…' she hesitated '…Eleanor's mother seemed concerned, as if she thinks you're still in love with the bride.'

'She hopes I'm still in love with the bride,' Kit said drily. 'I bet right now she's instructing the vicar to leave a good long pause after the true impediment part so that I can stand up and claim Eleanor for my own.'

'Leaving me weeping in the aisles?' There was an appreciative gurgle in Maddison's voice as she outlined the scenario. 'If only I had a hat, one with a little veil. Oh! And gloves.'

'There's no need to sound like you want it to happen.'

'I'm just saying if it were to happen I'd want to be appropriately dressed. What's the groom like?'

'Loaded, huge estate in Argyll, another one much further up in the Highlands—rich folk pay a fortune for the hunting and fishing. Plus various concerns in the city, a town house in Edinburgh. He's a catch…'

'I can tell there's an *if* or a *but* coming up.'

To hell with it, he needed to be honest with someone. '*If* you like your life partner to be the other side of forty-five, red-faced, balding and a pontificating know-it-all.'

'He sounds gorgeous.' She hesitated. 'So why?'

'Hmm?'

'I kind of got the impression that Eleanor's parents were all about the money and the image. Aren't they glad she's marrying someone who can keep her in style? An estate sounds pretty grand.'

'The Forsyths all about the money? Whatever gave you that idea?'

'So don't take this the wrong way, you're a nice guy when you want to be and easy enough on the eye, but why does socially ambitious mama want her darling daughter to run off with you? Especially as she already jilted you once?'

'She didn't jilt me. We were never engaged.' Thank goodness.

'You know what I mean. It doesn't make any sense. Unless she's thinking about her grandkids and the gene pool. No male-pattern baldness in your family.' She looked at his hair as if assessing the thickness.

Kit suppressed a sigh; this persistence was useful in his assistant, completely necessary if she was road-testing a treasure hunt. It was a little less comfortable when she was probing into his past. His hands gripped the steering wheel tight, his eyes fixed on the grey lines of the motorway as he eased his way past a lorry. 'As the youngest son I *wasn't* much of a catch. I was a student with his own eccentric business. I didn't plan on going into the City or doing any of the respectable money-making jobs a suitable partner for the Forsyths' beautiful only daughter would do.'

'A girl's gotta eat.' There was something oddly constrained in her voice despite the light words.

'She does. The right food at the right tables in the right households.' Kit hesitated. He liked that as far as Maddison was concerned he was her boss, nothing less, nothing more. But she was going to find out exactly what the future held for him in approximately four hours' time anyway and he would rather she heard it from him. Warts, title and all. Kit took a long drink of water, handing the bottle back to Maddison and focusing on the road ahead as he chose his words carefully. 'Euan was the eldest son and that made him a much better prospect than me. The Buchanans aren't as rich, not nearly as rich, as Angus Campbell, the lucky groom. But our name is older, we have a title, an ancient one, not an honorary one, and the castle has been in our family for generations. For new money like the Forsyths, that's worth more than a second estate. Now Euan's gone...'

He could hear Maddison's breath quicken. What was it with the predatory urge that overtook formerly sane women at the mention of a title and a castle? Kit didn't want to turn and look at her, to see if her eyes were gleaming covetously.

She shifted. 'You're no longer the second son. What does that mean?'

'Mean? It means that I'm the heir. To the title, the estate and the family name.' He laughed but there was no humour in the sound, just the bitter twist of fate. 'Turns out Eleanor bet on the wrong brother all those years ago and she's been kicking herself about it ever since we buried Euan.' Kit was trying to sound matter-of-fact but there was a rawness he couldn't cover. It was a long, long time since Eleanor had had the ability to hurt him. It turned out Kit was completely capable of destroying his own life—and the lives of everyone around him—without her help.

But she'd duped Euan and he would never forgive her for that.

'You don't know that,' Maddison argued. 'She might have really fallen in love with your brother. Hard on you, sure, but just because he was the eldest, just because he was going to inherit stuff, it doesn't mean she used you.'

He swallowed, his mouth dry despite the water he'd just consumed. 'Ah, but you see she told me. A month after we buried Euan. A month after she stood weeping by his grave and shooting me sympathetic glances as I had to come to terms with the knowledge that my brother had died…' The guilt that never really left him pressed down, heavier than ever. Such a stupid death. Such an unnecessary death. And he was to blame… 'She came to me and said she'd made a terrible mistake all those years ago. That she had never stopped loving me. That she knew it was too soon but maybe one day…'

Maddison was staring at him open-mouthed. 'She said all that?'

'Of course, I had just sold that quirky little start-up for a few million quid and a nice, well-paid and respectable job. Add the title and the castle to that and suddenly her old lover was looking all shiny and new. She still had her sights on being the Lady of Kilcanon.'

'I'll bet. What did you say?'

'I said not on her life. And then I got very, very drunk.' His hands tightened on the wheel. All those years of bitterness, the loss of his brother, all because of some *princess* who thought she was entitled to have it all—and damn anyone who got in her way.

But in the end he couldn't blame Eleanor for Euan's death. No. The only person to blame was Kit. And he could never, ever atone. God knew he had tried.

Maddison watched the scenery flash by but if someone quizzed her about what she had seen she would have definitely flunked the test. It was starting to add up: Kit's lack of interest in anything but the most perfunctory of relationships, his reluctance to go back to Scotland. He must have loved Eleanor very much once. Until she betrayed him.

Betrayal was such a strong word. After all, what had Eleanor done, exactly? Married strategically? Could Maddison blame her for that? After all, wasn't that her goal?

But she wasn't prepared to trample over sibling relationships and break hearts to do it. Her case was totally different. Wasn't it?

But the moral high ground didn't feel all that high.

'This must all come as a shock to you.'

She started. 'Sorry? The castle? Yeah, that's unexpected. Is there a moat and dungeons? A talking candlestick? A butler?'

'No to all the above and no, I didn't mean the castle. I meant the unhappily ever after. You believe in love at first sight, don't you?'

She almost laughed. As if. Nothing could be further from the truth; she wasn't even sure she believed in love.

Lust, sure, although she tried to ignore it. It could take a girl horribly off track. Affection, definitely. Compatibility. They were the foundations of a good, solid relationship. Shared goals another. But true love? That was for fairy tales. If Maddison had sat in her trailer waiting to be rescued she'd still be sitting there now. 'What makes you say that?'

'Mr Grow Old on a Porch Swing. What happened when you first saw him? Cupid's arrow straight to your heart?'

'Not exactly.' The mocking tone in his voice hit her harder than any arrow could.

'So what was it? What attracted you to him? How did you know he was the one if you weren't instantly smitten?'

Maddison thought back to the party where she and Bart had first met. It had been thrown by one of her college friends who had just bought, with family money, a fabulous loft apartment on the Upper East Side. Bart had been lounging against one of the carefully distressed brick walls, deep in conversation with a couple of friends. He had just looked so *solid*: tall, broad, blonde, clean-cut with that indefinable privileged air that Maddison worked so hard to cultivate but feared she never could. He wasn't handsome, not exactly, but he was nice to look at—and she could instantly see a future with him. A safe future. She had had no idea who he was at the time—her ambitions were high but not *that* high. But she could tell by his clothes, his stance, his air that he had the background she looked for, the future she needed. He had obviously felt her staring because he had broken off the conversation to look over at her—and then he had smiled and she had been lost in a world of infinite possibilities. A world where she was safe. For a time at least.

'I...' She stopped, unable to go on, and twisted her fingers in her lap, trying to find the right words. But what words were right? She didn't want to lie to him—she who lied to everyone—but there was no truth palatable enough to be served up.

Kit winced. 'I'm sorry, Maddison, it's not been that long, has it? I'm forgetting that not everyone weeps crocodile tears. For what it's worth, anyone who needs a break from you is an absolute idiot. He's not going to meet anyone better.'

No? He might meet someone genuine, someone who wanted Bart for his conversation and body, for his passions and interests, not for their vision of a perfect future. Could she really have done it? Married someone for convenience? Oh, she hadn't used that word before, had she? But that was what it came down to. She had deceived Bart—and she had deceived herself. 'He should. He deserves to. He's a really nice guy. Maybe he was right to call a halt to things.'

'Oh?' He raised an enquiring eyebrow.

Maddison hadn't told anyone the truth for so long there were times she wasn't sure exactly what the truth *was* any more. Not the teachers at school when they had asked about her mom, not her friends, not herself. Especially not herself. And Kit would judge her, he more than most. Maybe that was what she deserved.

Before she could weigh up the consequences of carrying on she spoke, the words almost tumbling out in the rush to unburden herself at long last. 'Bart's full name is Bartholomew J Van De Grierson III.'

But of course that meant nothing to him. 'Poor guy. I thought Christopher Alexander Campbell Buchanan was bad enough.'

She ignored him. 'His family have lived in New York

going back to colonial times. They're as close as we have
to aristocracy, or to royalty. Bart works in the family
business, and by business I mean global, multimillion,
fingers in pies you've never heard of and plenty that you
will have. He owns this incredible brownstone and the
family have an estate in the Hamptons, right by the sea.
It's as big as a small village.'

'Right. You found out all the important things, then?'

She had—and they had terrified her and seduced her
in equal measure. She'd been in well over her head but
how could she turn her back on the possibility of a future
so glittering it obliterated her more modest dreams? She
stared at her hands. 'Have you ever been hungry, Kit?
Have you ever woken up to find out that the electricity
was turned off and there's no hot water for a shower?
Have you ever had to work out which clothes were the
least dirty and turn up for school in them?'

He shot her a quick look but she wouldn't, couldn't
meet his eye. 'I wasn't prom queen and I didn't have a
credit card on Daddy's account. I didn't *have* a daddy.
And my mom wasn't around much.' She took a deep
breath. 'I want a family of my own, Kit. I want security. I want to know that I'm not just a pay cheque away
from eviction, that there is always, always money in the
bank. I want kids.'

'Four of them. I remember.'

She swallowed. How had he remembered that? 'Four
children who will have the safest, happiest, most perfect childhood ever. And I know that people say money
doesn't buy happiness—but I bet you anything those people have never gone to bed hungry. Or been really, really cold. So cold they can't sleep and their bones ache.'

'No, they probably haven't. So Bart wanted four kids
too? He was happy to be your secure happy ever after?'

She laughed. 'People like Bart don't marry people like me, Kit. You must know that. Money calls to money. Sure, he might date a girl like me, walk on the wrong side of the tracks for a little bit, but he wouldn't bring her home to meet the parents, wouldn't take her away with his friends. Wouldn't marry her. I grew up in a small town by the ocean and I saw it all the time—the wealthy summer visitors only mixed with people like them. And I knew that if I wanted to be one of them then I had to transform.' She couldn't stop now she'd started, the words spilling out. It was cathartic; this must be what confession was like, handing over your sins for someone else to absolve or punish.

'Transform?'

'Into one of them. Normal, a little spoiled, entitled. I got to college and created a whole new identity—a prom-queen, cheerleading, hayride, ice-carnival princess identity. Not too detailed, not too fancy, not privileged enough to raise alarm bells but privileged enough for the right groups to let me in. The college I went to was full of prep-school graduates with the right kind of background. It was almost too easy in the end to infiltrate them. By the time I graduated and moved to New York I knew the right kind of people with the right kind of connections to take me to the Upper East Side and from there...'

'You hooked him.'

'I couldn't believe it,' she half whispered. 'I wanted someone from a solid, wealthy background but Bart was beyond my wildest dreams. I worked really hard to turn myself into the right kind of wife for him—made sure I found out about the things he liked, got on with his friends, stuck to the rules. I wasn't clingy or needy or argumentative or sulky. I dressed the way he liked, wore my hair the way he liked, cooked the right food, hiked or swam or played tennis, whatever he was in the mood for. I read the right books…' She gulped in air, shocked by the bitter tint to her voice. 'But in the end I still wasn't good enough. He walked away anyway. It serves me right for aiming too high.' Brought down like Icarus, her punishment for flying too close to the sun.

Kit didn't answer for a long moment and Maddison couldn't look at him to see his reaction. Disgust, probably, maybe dislike. Hatred. After all, she was everything he abhorred. Fake, money-grabbing, conniving…

'Maybe you didn't know him as well as you thought.'

That wasn't what she'd expected him to say. 'What do you mean?'

'Have you been pretending the last few weeks? With me?'

'No, I mean, you're my boss, not…'

'Not a suitable future husband?'

She nodded, mortified heat flooding her. 'I mean, you have a good job and all, and I didn't know about the castle.' Maddison winced. Honesty was probably not the best policy here; she wasn't helping herself sound any better. 'It wouldn't have made any difference anyway. I want the life I missed out on, you know, the prom-queen and hayride life, summers at the shore and clambakes, Fourth of July parties and huge family Thanksgivings life. It's all I've ever wanted. Much as I could come to love London, that life doesn't exist here.'

'All I'm saying is that maybe Bart fell in love with the girl I've come to know. She's witty and clever and annoyingly organized, if a bit too partial to long operas. Maybe he wanted that Maddison, not the Stepford wife you turned yourself into. Just a thought.'

His words sank in slowly, each one dropping perilously close to her heart. 'I thought you'd hate me.'

Kit's face was completely impassive, a muscle beating in his cheek a lone sign her confession affected him at all. 'We've all done things in the past we need to atone for. I'm the last person to judge anyone. But if I were you I'd stop trying so hard. Just be yourself. Do you really think money will bring you happiness?'

Maddison winced. It sounded so cold put like that. 'I know security will…'

'Then make your own. You're a clever woman with a great career ahead of her. I'd advise you to concentrate on that. Marriage to the wealthiest man in the world can't bring you security, Maddison. Just look at Eleanor. She thought she had it made and it all disappeared, leaving her to start again. Bachelor Number Two may be wealthier but he's a bitterer pill to swallow.'

Make her own security? She'd spent so long focusing on just one possible path it hadn't even occurred to her that there could be more than one way to her goal. Maybe she could buy her own apartment in the city, have her own summer house at the shore. Maybe if she relaxed then she'd meet someone who wanted a family as much as she did, who didn't need luring into commitment.

Maybe there was a happy ever after waiting out there for her after all. She stole a glance at Kit, his face still completely unreadable. One thing she knew for sure was that her future didn't include messy brown hair, blue eyes and a lilting accent. Kit Buchanan's idea of long-term was next-day dinner reservations. And that was fine. The ache in her chest wasn't some inexplicable sense of loss. Not at all. She might be considering moving the goalposts but she hadn't changed as much as that. Had she?

CHAPTER EIGHT

'IS THIS IT? Are we in Kilcanon?' Maddison craned her head. 'I can't see a castle. When you said castle did you mean small cottage because, I have to tell you, they're not the same thing where I come from.'

'No, this is Loch Lomond. I need to stretch my legs. Fancy a walk?'

'A walk?'

'It's when people move at a slow pace putting one foot in front of the other in order to get across ground.'

'I know what a walk is. I just…I mean…I wasn't sure whether you wanted company.'

'I could leave you in the car but that seems a little inhospitable.'

But he knew what she meant. She was trying to sound him out, to see if he still wanted her company after her revelations just a couple of hours earlier. Maddison had lapsed into silence after her sudden and startling confession, leaving Kit to sort through a myriad conflicting thoughts and feelings: sorrow, sympathy, disgust. Admiration.

She hadn't said much about her childhood but he could fill in the bleak gaps; her need to be in control at all times, her fear of the dark, it all made sense. As did her overwhelming desire for security.

Her targeting of a rich man to be that security was a little harder to stomach, a little too close to home, and his first instinct had been to drive her to the airport at Glasgow and send her back to London on the next plane. The last thing he needed to do was take another gold-digger back to meet the family.

But she was no Eleanor and he was a lot older and a lot wiser. At least Maddison was honest about who she was and what she wanted. And could he blame her for trying to re-create the mythologized childhood of her dreams?

No. He didn't blame her or dislike her or even pity her. Truth be told he kind of admired her. Life had thrown every disadvantage at her and she had risen above it, made something of herself. So she had made some mistakes along the way? It was better than hiding away, bitter and resentful, or being too afraid to try.

Like you? He pushed the thought away. He wasn't bitter or afraid, he was undeserving. Undeserving of happiness or of love.

Maddison, on the other hand, deserved a lifetime of both.

She joined him at the path, a light Puffa slung on over her jumper and jeans. 'This is a real loch? Is there a monster in it?'

'Several. Don't walk too close to the edge or they might pull you in, kelpies and boobries and…'

'Stop. You know what I mean. A *real* monster.'

'You need to be a lot further north for Nessie, I'm afraid. But if you're lucky you might see a selkie when we get to Kilcanon—watch the seals closely, they're usually the larger ones.'

'I'll do that.' She hesitated. 'Kit, about earlier?'

'It's fine. I'm glad you told me but you don't owe me

any explanation, Maddison. We're colleagues, that's all.'
But the words sounded hollow even to his own ears.

'Good. I've never...I mean, I don't talk about myself
very often. Thank you. For listening and not hating me.'

'I could never hate you.' In a different time, if he were
a different man, he might be in danger of exactly the opposite. But his heart was frozen somewhere back in time
and he had no intention of allowing it to be melted, not
even by this fiery American survivor.

It was a bright, warmish day and Maddison was soon
far too hot in the thick jacket she had layered over her
sweater. 'You told me it would be cold and raining.'

'It could well be when we get to Kilcanon. It's a mi-
croclimate. All of Scotland is.'

'Is it as pretty as here?' She stopped and turned, admiring once again the blue waters lapping gently against
the loch shore and the hills rising steeply on every side,
greens and purples and shadowy greys. She had thought
that they would head down to the loch but instead Kit
had chosen a path that led away, a steep path winding
up into the hills. Turned out even regular running didn't
prepare you for hill-climbing. Maddison could already
feel a pull on her calves and her lungs were beginning
to make themselves felt.

'Pretty? There's nothing pretty about Kilcanon. It's
magnificent... Here, watch out. This is a bit slippy.' Kit
extended a hand and pulled Maddison up the slick, steep
rock. His grip was firm and she had a sudden urge to lean
on him, to allow him to guide her up the narrow, slip-
pery path, but she quelled it firmly, brushing past him
instead to take the lead.

'Come on, Buchanan,' she called over her shoulder
as she set off at a pace, shocked at how her lungs burnt

as she pulled herself up. She had really got out of condition recently; this would do her good. Besides, giving her body a good workout might cure it of some treacherous urges—such as wanting to stare into Kit's eyes, keep hold of his hands or lean into that solid strength.

Oh, no, she was getting sappy. Maddison increased her pace, enjoying the ache in her calf muscles, the fiercer pull in her thighs, the heave in her chest. The distance she was putting between him and her.

'It's not a race, Carter. Slow down and smell the roses—or at least enjoy the view.'

'Slowing down is for losers. You'd be eaten alive in Manhattan,' she threw back as she concentrated on one foot in front of the other, using her hands and upper body to pull her up a particularly vertiginous twist in the path. All she was aware of was the steep rise of the way ahead, the rocks that needed to be navigated, the small treacherous pebbles that could cause a foot to slip, the slicks of mud and the...

'No! Darn it!'

And the deceptively deep puddles. This one calf deep and full of thick mud, cold as it sucked at her foot and leg.

'Ugh. I'm trapped in a swamp! Kit! Stop laughing...'

He came up beside her, slow and easy, folding his arms and eyes dancing with amusement as he took her in. 'Pride comes before a fall.'

'I haven't fallen.' Maddison tried to summon some shred of dignity, hard as it was to do when one foot was caught fast in a miniswamp, the other scrabbling for a firm foothold. Any minute now she was going to tumble and she'd be damned if she was going to fall in front of this man. Any man.

'Yet,' Kit pointed out helpfully.

'You could help me.'

'I could.' The laughter underpinned his words and she glared at him.

'Do you want me to beg?'

'Well…' He leaned in close and her breath hitched. His face was barely centimetres from hers, his shoulder close enough to grab, to hold on to, to bury herself in and let herself be saved.

She didn't need saving, did she? Just a helping hand.

'You could say *please.*'

Their eyes caught, held. His were alive with laughter, a teasing warmth curving his mouth, but behind the amusement was something hotter, something deeper, something straining to break through. And Maddison knew, with utter certainty, that all she needed to do was ask.

She hadn't asked for anything since she was six.

She glared, watching his amusement increase until a reluctant smile curved her lips. 'Please.'

'There, that wasn't so hard, was it?' Kit grasped her hand and pulled. Maddison steadied herself against him, allowing him to take her weight as she heaved her foot free. It took a couple of tugs until, with a nasty squelch, the mud gave up and she stumbled forward, letting out a small yelp of alarm as she toppled, trying to get her balance.

'Easy, Maddison, I got you.'

He had. His arms were around her, steadying her, holding her up, and she allowed herself to be held, to be steadied. Just for a second. What harm could it do? What harm one moment of resting on someone else? One moment of needing someone else? Just a moment and then she would pull back, make some quip and carry on, ignoring the discomfort of her cold, damp boot and the sodden jeans because that was what Maddison Carter did, right? She carried on.

'Thanks.' Her breath was short and she inhaled, taking in the soap-fresh, wool scent of him, allowing her hands to remain on his waist as she pulled back, searching for the right kind of cheery smile that would put this moment behind them, behind her.

It was a lot to ask from a smile. And as she looked into his eyes any urge to laugh the moment off fell away as surely as the path plunged down towards the water, the sounds around drowned out by the blood rushing around her body, pulsing in her ears. All the amusement had drained out of his face, out of those blue eyes, now impossibly molten like sapphire forged in some great furnace. Instead she looked into the sharp planes of his face and saw want. She saw need. She saw desire.

For her.

'Kit?'

He didn't speak, his breathing ragged, his grip tightening on her shoulders. She should walk away; she needed to walk away because this, this wasn't planned. She had never let desire override her common sense before, and yet here she stood, making no move to reassert herself, passive in his grip.

The blood pounded faster, her stomach falling away, an almost unbearable ache pulsing in her breasts, beating insistently deep down in her very core. Maddison had always controlled every step of every seduction, when, how far, what, but now she had no power, no choice at all. Her body was taking over, need flaring up, overtaking sense, overtaking thought, overtaking everything.

She swayed towards him and his eyes flashed as they fixed on her mouth, hunger burning in their blue depths. Hunger for her.

For her. All of her.

Not just her body. She had laid herself bare before

him, let him in to see all the nasty little corners she hid from everyone—and still he hungered. Maddison swayed closer still. His gaze was intoxicating and she could drink it in forever, bathe in the heat, helpless before his acceptance.

Kit released his grip on her shoulders, his hands moving slowly down her arms, each centimetre of her flesh blazing into life where his hands touched before burning with thwarted desire as his hands moved away. She was desperately trying to gulp in air, her chest tight with need.

Walk away, a small, sane part of her urged. *Walk away*.

But she had spent ten years being sane, ten years putting sense first, desire second. Didn't she deserve just a little time out? She was going to re-evaluate her plan anyway; she needed to explore all options, didn't she?

That was all this was. Exploring options. Because Kit didn't do love either. He was safe.

Maddison jumped as he reached out to cup her face, one finger tracing the curve of her mouth, a muscle beating insistently in his cheek. It took everything she had to hold his gaze, to stand there while his fingers explored the curve of her jaw, one tantalizing digit running slowly over her mouth, blazing a trail of fiery need. It was hard to breathe, hard to think, hard to stand still, hard not to step forward and grab him and make him fulfil that lazy promise. Her knees weakened as she watched the lines of his mouth, his eyes soften as they focused on her.

She looked up at him and allowed her mask to slip, just for a while. Allowed the desire and want and hope and need to shine through and as their eyes met she saw any resistance fall away.

She thought he would pull her close, go straight in for the kiss, but instead Kit moved back a little, one hand moving from her waist to the small of her back, leaving a trail of electric tingles as it oh-so slowly brushed over her body. Before today Maddison would have said that it would be impossible for anyone to feel anything under the thickness of her jacket but, like the princess lying on her tower of mattresses, every movement marked her. Claimed her.

'This crosses a line.' The words were so unexpected that Maddison didn't compute them at first. 'I should step away.' But he didn't.

'I think we already crossed that line.' Confidences, opening up emotionally, secret glances of shared amusement—to Maddison they were all far more intimate than mere sex. She suspected the same rang true for Kit. If there was a line to be crossed then they had walked blithely over it that day in the graveyard. Maybe even before then, when he had invited her out for a birthday drink. Maybe they had been heading here since then.

He closed his eyes briefly. 'Maybe you're right.' Then, only then did he step closer. Maddison hadn't appreciated quite how tall he was, how broad he was, how much coiled strength was hidden behind the quietly amused exterior until she was enfolded by him, in him. She had never allowed herself to feel fragile, delicate before, but the look in his eyes, the light, almost reverential touch, made her feel as if she were made of glass, infinitely precious. She shivered, heat and need running through her.

She slid her hands up his arms, allowing herself the time to appreciate the hard muscle under the thick material, until her hands met at the nape of his neck.

She stepped in, just that one bit closer so that leg was pressed against leg, her stomach against his taut abdomen, her breasts crushed against his chest. Desire rippled through her as the heat from his body penetrated her; she could barely raise her eyes to look at him, suddenly and unexpectedly shy. She was laying it all out there for him. What if she wasn't enough?

But the look in his eyes when she finally raised hers to meet his said it all and, emboldened, she pressed close and lifted her mouth to his. Softly at first, hesitant, and then as the kiss deepened she lost all reticence, holding him tighter, pulling him closer, revelling in the all-male taste of him, smell of him, feel of him. His hands hadn't moved, still just holding her close, burning where they touched her until she was almost writhing with the need for them to move, to have every inch lit up with that same sweet, intoxicating flame.

Maddison wound her hands through the soft hair at the nape of his neck, pulling him even closer, but it wasn't enough. The barriers of clothing, of skin too much. Impatient she slid her hands back down his torso, thrilling at the play of muscles under her hands, needing flesh on flesh.

'Maddison.' He broke away and she was instantly cold, even as he captured her hands in his, his thumbs caressing her palms. 'Slow down, lass. We shouldn't…'

'I…I…' She stumbled back, cheeks hot even as the rest of her shivered with an icy chill. 'You're right, we shouldn't…'

'Stay here,' he finished. 'We're a little exposed here on the public footpath.'

'Oh.' She smiled at him a little foolishly, blinking as she twisted in his embrace, aware for the first time in several long minutes of their surroundings. 'Yes.'

'We could get a hotel room, here. If you wanted, that is. We'd still be back in time for the wedding. Only if you want to, though…'

Maddison put a finger on his mouth. 'I want to.'

'Good.' His voice was hoarse, ragged with need. 'I was very much hoping you would say that.'

The early-evening sun slanted in through the window, turning the red-gold of Maddison's hair flame-coloured. Kit pulled a strand of it through his fingers, the silky texture as smooth as her skin. He liked her hair like this, dishevelled, down, free, just as he liked her like this: soft, warm and drowsy.

What on earth had happened? One moment he was stomping up a steep hill, almost blind to the beauty all around him, taking little notice of the fresh air filling his lungs, trying not to mull over their conversation in the car, and the next moment... It hadn't just been the feel of her, soft and pliant in his arms as he'd pulled her free, it hadn't been the way she had looked, so different from her usual neat and tidy self in her jeans and jacket, hair falling out of its elegant twist, face rosy with the exercise. It had been more. Maybe they had been headed here all along.

Maybe it was the feelings she had roused in him in the car. Anger—not at her, *for* her. The abandoned child, the lonely girl, the jilted lover. She deserved more. But not just anger. She made him feel compassion, a need to possess her, protect her.

His mouth curled. As if he could protect anybody. And yet he wanted to, wanted to pull out a sword and challenge all comers, shield her from hurt.

'What are you thinking?' Maddison rolled over, the sheet pulled high, shielding her lithe body from his gaze. It was the body of someone with fierce amounts of control—slim, toned and smooth. It had been lots of fun helping her lose that control. Twice.

'That I hadn't expected to find myself here when we

left London this morning.' That was an honest reply even if it wasn't all he was thinking.

She looked around and Kit followed her gaze, taking in, for the first time, the pink flowery walls, the heavy velvet curtains fringed with tassels, the huge variety of cushions and the shiny pine wardrobe. She smiled at him. 'No, I can imagine not. It's probably a little pink for your tastes.'

'We could have waited and found somewhere a little more boutiquey.' He didn't want to say romantic. This, whatever it was, wasn't about romance.

'No.' She slid a hand over his chest, a smug smile tilting the corners of her mouth as he inhaled sharply. 'This is perfect. Besides, I didn't want to wait.'

'No? Me neither.'

'Do you think the landlady bought it? The impromptu walking-weekend story?'

Kit allowed himself to twist another strand of that sunlit hair around a finger. 'Sure she did. I'm sure she's completely used to couples hammering at her door, throwing cash at her and disappearing upstairs.' The modest B & B had been the first place they had passed with a vacancies sign. It might not boast Egyptian cotton sheets, designer paint or expensive antiques, but it was clean and, most importantly, available. Neither of them had been prepared to wait for something more luxurious.

'I had a valid reason. I was covered with mud. I needed a bathroom.'

Kit whipped the sheet off, ignoring Maddison's squeals as she made a grab for it, and took a long, appraising look down at her legs. 'You still are.' He reluctantly let the sheet drop back down in response to her indignant tug and sank back down beside her. He could have feasted his eyes on her forever. 'You need a good wash. Want me to help?'

She pulled herself up on her forearm and looked down at him. 'Maybe. How good are you with a sponge?'

'Immensely talented,' he assured her and watched her eyes glaze over. 'Want to find out just how good I am?'

'Soon,' she promised him, slumping down onto him, her body hot against his skin. Kit shifted so that he was curled around her, his arm holding her tight, the heavy weight of her breast just under his hand. It had been so long since he had just lain with a woman, caught in that languorous twilight time between sex and the real world. The promise of pleasure still hanging, musky in the air, and yet sated enough to let the promise stand. For now. Maybe. He allowed his finger to circle around the tip of her breast, a light caress, a small possession as he burrowed his face into the sweet spot at the nape of her neck, tasting her skin one more time.

'Mmm…' Her sigh was all the encouragement he needed and he deepened the caress, his other hand sliding along her hip, across the flat plane of her belly, as he nibbled his way along her shoulder. 'Do we have to go to this wedding? Can't we stay here forever?'

Kit found the delicate spot at the top of her shoulder and tasted it, his tongue dipping into the hollow, following the line down towards the top of her other breast. Maddison shifted, allowing him access to her body, submissive under his gentle onslaught.

'I would much rather stay here.' He was taking his time, enjoying the quickening of her breath, her hands fisted in his hair. 'I am suddenly very fond of pink curtains.' But as he kissed his way down her body, sampling her slick, salty, satin skin, revelling in the knowledge that he was responsible for each moan, each cry, each movement, he knew that it was just a pipe dream. Duty called him home. But tonight? Tonight was all about pleasure and Kit intended to make the most of every single second.

CHAPTER NINE

THE MORNING AFTER the night before. It wasn't usually a problem. After all, he always made his position completely clear before anything compromising began—no commitment, no emotional attachment, no expectations. Just two people hanging out, enjoying the moment. And if, in the end, the other person wanted more, well, his conscience was clear. He wasn't the one changing his mind.

But there had been no laying out of the rules this time. No clarity. Just an overwhelming need overriding sense, overriding thought. He could have taken her there and then on the hillside, mud and hikers forgotten. At least he'd had enough sense to call a temporary halt.

But not enough sense to halt it altogether.

Kit gripped the steering wheel until his knuckles whitened. Need meant weakness. Need meant attachment. He didn't do either. He only dated women he was in no danger of falling for. That was the rule.

Maddison Carter broke every rule.

But it wasn't as if she were after anything more serious either. Maddison had her heart set on her perfect marriage to the perfect guy who would give her the perfect family. And he was far from perfect.

Surely she knew that this, whatever it was, was just

an interlude. She wouldn't want it to be anything more any more than he did.

Which in many ways made her the perfect woman.

Although following up a night of mind-blowing passion with a trip to the family home wasn't the best idea in the world. Even the most clear-headed of women would be forgiven for finding the signals confusing.

Maybe not just the women.

Kit turned his attention to the road ahead. Most people headed north from Loch Lomond, past Fort William, up into the deeper Highlands, but to get to Kilcanon Kit took an early turn away from the loch, dropping back down on to the long peninsula that would take them down, past the sea lochs to the coast. The road twisted and turned, climbing up into thickly forested heights where eagles soared before dropping back down to the loch side. Glasgow, just an hour and a half away, felt as remote as London or New York; a bustling city had nothing in common with this wild and natural beauty.

And Kilcanon was possibly the wildest and most beautiful part of all. The Buchanans' ancestral lands were at the very tip of the peninsula where land met sea. The road ahead was achingly familiar; here it was, the first glimpse of home. Every time it hit him anew, a sharp punch to his heart.

'There it is, Castle Kilcanon.' They were the first words either of them had spoken in the last hour and he slowed the car down so Maddison could look out at the sweep of water below, at the round grey castle dominating the landscape like a sentinel.

'That's your home?' She sat up straighter and peered down at the dark, rotund keep. 'Where's the flags on the turrets and the knights galloping over the drawbridge?'

'We don't keep the knights on a full retainer.' The

village spread out across the bay, the harbour home to several small boats bobbing on the sea, the castle on the other side of the bay. The weather had lifted a little and even though the grey of the sea met the grey of the sky on the horizon, the two blending into one, he could still see the craggy, green islands, some impossibly close, others mist-shielded ghosts.

'There's a lookout point. Can we stop?'

Kit didn't reply but he pulled over and sat there for a moment while she got out of the car and walked over to the railings, leaning over them while she took in the spectacular view. Once he'd have been hurrying her, eager to cover the last fifteen minutes' travel as the road wound down and round to the village, but not any more. Now he was glad of the opportunity to delay their arrival by even a few minutes.

In London he could push the memories away with work and play until all they could do was beat at his dreams, but as soon as he set foot in Kilcanon they would surround him, whispering ghosts reminding him that he was to blame. His eternal shame. His eternal punishment.

Maddison's hair was whipping around in the breeze, the red-gold a vibrant contrast to the greens and blues surrounding her. He got out of the car and walked to the rail, leaning next to her. 'It's beautiful, isn't it?'

'Like nowhere else.'

'I'm sorry for yesterday.'

She slid a green-eyed glance over at him, the corners of her mouth curving into a playful smile, which caught him and held him. 'Why? I'm not.'

'It shouldn't have happened. I'm your boss and you were at a low point. I took advantage of you.'

'No, you cheered me right up. Made me feel desirable and wanted when I couldn't even look at myself without disgust.' She turned to face him, laying one slender hand over his. 'Look, Kit, it's all right. I'm not Camilla. I don't expect you to suddenly fall to one knee after one night together, no matter how amazing that night was. I know that's not what you are looking for and I...' She hesitated, lacing her fingers through his, her hand warm against the ice of his. 'I don't know what I want, not any more. It was all so clear-cut a few weeks ago. Even a few days ago.'

'Four children and a rich husband?'

She leaned into him with a playful shove. 'Yes. Well, marriage, a family, security. That is really important, although maybe I need to re-evaluate how I get there. But whatever happens I think I need to start living a little, not plan so much. So you are off the hook, nobody took advantage of anybody. It doesn't have to happen again, although,' she added, her fingers caressing his, 'I'm not saying that I'd mind if it did.'

'Remind me of that later,' he said softly and felt her quiver beside him.

He stared out at the sea—still today, tranquil. 'We used to take boats out over to the island, race them. Sails only, no motors allowed. Go fishing off the pier, kayak across the harbour. Everything was a competition, everything. Even love.'

'You miss him.' It wasn't a question.

'You have no idea how much. I don't feel it so much in London. He never visited me there—the city air was bad for his asthma—but here, by the sea, he was fine. Every time I come back it hits me again, that he's not here. And this evening I have to watch his wife marry someone else, as if Euan never existed.'

'It was three years ago, Kit. She's allowed to move on.'

'Maybe you're right.' He freed his hand from hers and

moved to stand behind her, his arms around her waist holding on tight, allowing her to anchor him to the here and now. 'One of us should move on. We can't both hold an eternal vigil.'

'You are allowed to as well. It's what he would have wanted.'

If only she knew. He didn't think he would ever break free of the chains binding him to his guilt and grief— and even if he could, would he want to? Did he deserve to? Euan was dead and he was alive and nothing would ever change that.

'Come on.' He dropped a light kiss on her hair, breathing in the floral scent, glad that she was here in all her vibrancy and warmth, chasing away the shadows that dogged his every step. 'We have a family to meet and a wedding to attend. Ready?'

'Absolutely. Parents are my speciality. Lead the way.'

Kit took in a deep breath. There was no retreating now. But at least, this time, he wouldn't be alone.

Maddison wasn't quite as confident as the car swept up the long, gravelled drive to the castle. The gravel was grey like the thick stone blocks of the turrets. Grey like the sky above them, the sea behind them, and despite all her good intentions she shivered. 'Is that where you slept?' She tilted her head to look at the top of the keep, the windows narrow slits in the stone. It must be dark in there, dank. Her spine tingled as she imagined a small child, a mop of dark hair and huge blue eyes, sitting forlornly in a round, cheerless room.

'Oh, no, I was down in the dungeons. Kids are always better off behind bars. That's the family motto.' Kit was gripping the steering wheel a little tightly but his tone was teasing and the wink he gave her knowing.

'Of course you were, on a pallet of straw, a bucket in the corner.'

To Maddison's surprise the drive didn't end in front of the imposing entrance, but swept around the castle, finishing in a semicircle in front of an eye-wateringly large house situated on a slanting hill two hundred yards behind the castle. The house was built from the same grey stone as the keep but it seemed softer somehow, maybe because of the wisteria clambering over the front and upwards to the roof, maybe because of the elegant, tall towers flanking both sides, or maybe it was the three tiers of tall windows promising a light, airy interior, the stone in between them decorated with delicate ornamental stonework. Either way, despite its size, it made a more believable—and more comfortable—home than the ancient, thick-walled castle.

Kit braked the car and pointed up to the top floor. 'The nursery floor was up there. Euan, Bridget and I all had rooms up there, along with the playroom.'

She barely took in his words, her mouth open in utter shock. 'It's…it's huge!' Somehow the grand old house was more imposing than any castle could be. Twisting around in her seat, Maddison could see how the ground had been cleverly landscaped so that the keep hid the house from prying eyes and yet the house itself had an uninterrupted view, over smooth green lawns, right down to the sea. Behind the house lawns rose in wide, flower-covered terraces up into the hillside, hints of arbours, patios and summer houses hidden just out of view. She turned back to Kit and eyed him accusingly. 'I can't believe you let me think that you still lived in there.'

He grinned. 'It's a common misconception but the keep's been empty for years. By all accounts it was always cold and uncomfortable and our eighteenth-century ancestors were too nesh to keep shivering in there. With the Jacobite rebellion over they didn't need such thick walls and so they built the big house, as it's still known. Only the old castle gets the courtesy of being Castle Kilcanon, the ancestral home of the Clan Buchanan.' He deepened his voice as he said the last words, sounding more like a documentary maker than a son returning home.

'The big house?' Maddison had never quite got the British art of understatement. The house in front of her made the estates of her college friends seem small—and tacky—even though she had visited homes covering many more acres. She instinctively knew there would be no cinema rooms or bowling alleys here, no infinity pools or gyms. This was real class, real old money. She had no idea how to fake this kind of lifestyle. How to fit in.

For the first time in many years doubt clouded her mind. She shivered again as a raven landed on top of the keep, a foreboding omen.

'Kit!' Maddison had no more time to panic as the huge front door was flung open and a pretty girl in her early twenties ran down the imposing front steps. She was casually dressed in an old sweater and jeans, her dark red hair scooped back and not a hint of make-up on the creamy face, liberally strewn with becoming freckles. Maddison pulled her cashmere jumper down, smoothing it with shaking hands, doubting her outfit. Was it too put together? Artificial?

'Kit! You're home! I can't believe you left it till now. Mum has been spitting feathers. She was convinced you'd let her down and find an excuse not to come. Not that I blame you. If it wasn't a three-line whip I would be far away from here. It sounds utterly dreary.'

'Hey, Bridge.' Kit was out of the car before the girl got to them and reached down, scooping her up and swinging her round. Maddison's chest squeezed. She would give anything to have someone greet her with such uninhibited joy. 'I have plenty of time. The wedding doesn't start until five.'

'I know.' The younger girl pulled a face. 'Evening candlelit ceremony and black tie. So tacky. I blame Angus.'

'I doubt Angus had much of a say,' Kit said drily.

Maddison got out of the car, her legs stiff and awkward as she walked around to meet them, her throat dry and chest tight. She had thought she didn't care what Kit's family made of her, but she wanted this warmfaced girl who so obviously adored Kit to like her. To think her worthy.

Worthy of what? she reminded herself. *One night does not make a future. And you don't want that, remember?*

But it was hard to remember just what she did want as Kit put a steadying arm around her and led her forward. 'Maddison, this is my little sister, Bridget. Bridge, this is Maddison.'

'It's nice to meet you at last.' Bridget held out her hand. 'We've spoken on the phone so often I feel that I know you already but it's much nicer face-to-face. We'll have to have a real gossip straight away and you can tell me all about what a tyrant Kit is and fill me in on all his secrets.' She threw a speaking glance at her brother. 'There's tea and scones waiting in the drawing room. And no, you can't escape. Behave.'

'We should have dawdled more on the way.' Kit squeezed Maddison's shoulder. 'Ready? Some trials involve dragons and daring rescues, others golden apples and races. My mother conducts trial by small talk. It's deadly, it's terrifying but it's possible to survive.'

Bridget elbowed him. 'Don't scare her, idiot. It's not that bad,' she added to Maddison. 'At least the scones are good.'

When Maddison visited her college friends' homes, finding a valid reason to be free from her fictional family over Christmas or Thanksgiving, she rarely saw their parents. She'd arrive at some spacious, interior-decorated-to-within-an-inch-of-its-life mansion, be whisked off to an en-suite room bigger than any apartment she'd ever lived in and then spend the next few days in the kind of pampered bubble the set she chose to run with considered normal. Food was pulled without consideration from cavernous fridges, or prepared by smiling, silent maids. Parents rushed in with platitudes and compliments before rushing back out again to the club, to work, to a party or a personal-training session. Maddison knew how to smile, compliment prettily and make the right kind of impression to be invited back.

But scones and a small-talk-stroke-interrogation in a house older than an entire state was another thing entirely. She leaned a little more heavily against Kit as they approached the front door. The big house might lack a moat but stepping over the threshold felt as final as watching the drawbridge close up behind her.

Bridget led them into a huge hallway dominated by closed, heavy wooden doors interspersed with portraits of stern-looking men in kilts surveying the landscape and even sterner-looking ladies in a variety of intricate hairstyles. Nearly every portrait featured some kind of massive dog and a gloomy-looking sea. A wide staircase started halfway down the hall, sweeping imperiously up towards the next floor with a dramatic curve, the carved wooden bannister shining like a freshly foraged chestnut. She swallowed as her eyes passed over tarnished gilt mirrors and ancient-looking vases.

'This is all very formal.' Kit squeezed Maddison's shoulder. 'Bridge must be trying to make an impression on you. Usually we come in through the back.'

'I didn't think Maddison would want to pick her way through thirty pairs of mismatched wellies, twenty broken fishing rods, enough waterproofs to clothe an army and the dogs' toys,' Bridget said. She flashed a shy smile at Maddison. 'But Kit's right, the front door is usually just for guests. It takes far too long to open it, for one thing, and there's nowhere to dump your coat, for another.'

Maddison couldn't imagine wanting to dump her coat. The air was as chilly as a top New York law firm's offices, only this wasn't status-boosting air conditioning, it was all too natural. 'It's lovely,' she said. 'Very…' She looked up at the nearest portrait for inspiration. The sitter was scowling, his grey, pigtailed wig low on his brow, his sword angled menacingly. 'Very old.'

'The bannister is good for sliding on,' Kit said. 'And when the parents went out we used to practise curling on these tiles. There's no heating at all in the hallway so in winter they get pretty icy.'

Maddison had no clue what he was talking about so she just smiled. But she knew one thing for sure. She couldn't get carried away here, couldn't change her game plan, couldn't hope that whatever had sparked into life yesterday was real. She would never belong in a place like this; there were limits to even her self-deception. So she might as well relax and enjoy it for what it was. A fun interlude before she went home to New York and decided what she was going to do with the rest of her life.

The problem was that her original prize wasn't looking quite as golden as it used to. It wasn't that she didn't want security; she did. She still needed it just as she needed air and water. She still wanted children who teased each other the way Kit and Bridget were, children who were raised with the kind of love that Kit seemed to take for granted and with the same opportunities. She just wanted a little bit more.

She wanted the full package. Security, love and respect. And by raising the stakes she might have just doomed her entire quest to failure.

CHAPTER TEN

THERE WAS SOMETHING incredibly seductive about watching a woman getting dressed for a big occasion. The concentration on her face as she twisted her hair up just so, the way she slid the small point of an earring into her lobe, the purse of her mouth as she painted it an even deeper red.

The way she rolled on her underwear, a subtle mixture of practicality and romance, a little like its wearer. The black silky bra designed to show off her shoulders in the thinly strapped dress, the wispy knickers Kit had to drag his eyes away from because they really, really didn't have time. Yet.

Maddison was wearing the same dress she had worn to the opera, a simple knee-length black dress with a white strip around her waist, echoed by a wider band at the bottom of the dress. The invitation had specified Black Tie and Kit knew that the other female guests would be going all out. Maddison, with her knot of red-gold hair and the pearls in her ears, would probably be the simplest-dressed woman in the room—and the most beautiful, he realized with a twist of his stomach.

His mother had put them in one of the suites, two bedrooms and a shared bathroom, a sign she was unsure of their romantic status. Kit shared her uncertainty—common sense told him to walk away quickly while it was still possible to extricate himself with grace, but his body told him something very different.

Right now his body was winning.

Which had the advantage of both distracting him from the forthcoming wedding and lessening the pain of Euan's absence. So he would let his body win—for now.

'You're looking thoughtful.' Maddison moved towards him, her gait slower, sexier in her high heels, and laid a reassuring hand on his shoulder. 'Let me get that for you.' And with practised ease she adjusted his bow tie. 'Very dapper. Are you worrying about tonight?'

'Not really. I was just admiring how you managed my mother earlier. It was like watching two fencers spar.' His mother's patented brand of tea and interrogation usually either froze her opponents into stunned silence or cracked them open until they had spilled every secret. Not many managed to parry and block with the same deft touch Maddison had shown.

'I had quite a lot of fun. She's a formidable opponent. I had no idea what to call her, though—Mrs Buchanan? The housekeeper says My Lady but I'm not sure I could say that and keep a straight face. I'd feel like a house-maid in Downton.'

'I'm sorry, I should have warned you how absurdly formal it can be here. My father is the Viscount of Kilcanon and my mother is Lady of Kilcanon but in speech you say Lord and Lady Buchanan. Locally, though, they are mostly known as the Laird and Lady. I know,' he said apologetically as her forehead creased in puzzlement. 'It's all a little feudal.'

'Aren't Laird and Lord the same thing?'

'No, not really. Angus, the lucky groom...' Kit cast a look at the clock on the wall, relieved to see they still had an hour before they had to leave '…he's the local laird in Kameskill because he's the biggest landowner, but it's an honorary title. If he sold the estate the title would pass with it. If we sold this estate then Dad still stays a viscount.'

'So wait, do you have a cool title? Do I get to call you Sir?'

Kit sighed. He hated this part. 'Both Bridge and I are Honourables, but neither of us use it,' he admitted. 'And now Euan's gone I'm Master of Kilcanon.'

'Master? How very dominant of you.'

He matched her grin. 'Remind me to show you later…'

'Chicken…' she said softly and his blood began to pound at the challenge.

'Unfortunately we have been summoned to a pre-wedding drink with my family, but wait until we return and I'll show you who is master.'

'I can hardly wait…' She sashayed before him but stepped aside as she reached the door so that Kit could go first.

He touched her shoulder. 'Worried about the dogs? I can get Morag to lock them away.' One of the family pets had wandered into the drawing room when they were having tea and Maddison had paled significantly and made no move towards it, retreating a little when it had stalked nearer her.

'No.' But she didn't sound at all convincing. 'Honestly, I'm fine. It's just they are really *big*.'

'Another thing I should have warned you about. I forget not everyone has grown up with dogs the size of small ponies.'

'Small ponies? Are you kidding? I think they would outrank a medium pony and maybe even a large one.' She was smiling but there was a look of trepidation in her eyes and he decided he'd better keep the dogs away from her. They were very sweet tempered but fifty kilograms of dog could be intimidating to even the most ardent of dog lovers. 'Still,' she said, with that same game smile on her face, 'I guess a smaller dog would get lost in a house this size.'

'There's still a corgi or two somewhere in the west wing and a dachshund stuck in the tower,' he agreed straight-faced and was rewarded with a moment of puzzlement before she glared at him and stalked out of the room.

As was customary, drinks were in the library and, sure enough, when Kit ushered Maddison into the book-lined room two of the family's prized deerhounds were flaked out on a tattered old red rug in front of the fire. One of them raised a lazy head in their direction and Maddison tensed, her arm rigid under his hand, before the dog flopped back down, too tired from its day to properly investigate the newcomer.

Maddison swallowed. 'I feel even more Downton than ever,' she said, and Kit tried to see the familiar room through her eyes: the oak panels, the huge leaded windows, the tall bookcases, which needed a ladder to reach the top shelves, the leather chesterfield and the old walnut bureau where his father conducted his business just as his grandfather had before him and so on back into the mists of time.

'It's all too dusty to be truly Downton,' Kit whispered. 'No butler either, just Morag, and she never bobs a curtsey and is always gone by six.'

'Kit.' His attention was called away by his father's curt tones. Lord Buchanan was standing by the fireplace, a glass of single malt in one hand. Looking at him was like looking into a portrait in the attic, Kit in thirty years' time. Not that Kit often looked straight at his father. How could he when he was responsible for so much loss? For the lines creasing his father's forehead and the shadows in his mother's eyes?

He ushered Maddison forward. She, he noted, was still keeping a wary eye on the dogs. 'Dad, good to see you. This is Maddison Carter, my very able assistant, who very kindly agreed to accompany me this weekend. Maddison, my father.'

His father nodded briefly at Maddison but didn't speak and Kit was grateful when Bridget pulled her over to the sofa she was sitting on, thrusting a glass of champagne into his hand as she did so. Conversations with his father were rarely comfortable and he'd rather not have a witness.

This was the problem with bringing anyone home. They saw too much.

Lord Buchanan stiffened as he glanced at the champagne Kit was holding, swirling his own whisky as if in challenge. 'It's good to see you still know the way home, son.'

It was going to be like that, was it? He wasn't going to rise, he wasn't… 'Luckily there's always satnav.' Okay, he was going to rise a little.

His father didn't respond to the jibe. 'Whatever it takes.'

Kit looked over at Maddison. She seemed comfortable enough sitting between Bridget and his mother. As he'd expected his mother was dressed traditionally in a long blue dress, a sash of the family tartan over her shoulder fastened with a sapphire brooch. Bridget was less traditional and tartan free, but still in a floor-length dress in a sparkly material. Maddison didn't seem bothered though;

she had that same self-possessed look on her face that she usually wore in the office.

Maddison looked up and caught his eye and for one all-too-brief moment they were the only people in the room. Kit's heart hitched, missing a beat. What would it be like under different circumstances, bringing a girl like Maddison home to meet the family?

His father followed his gaze over and looked at Maddison speculatively before transferring his gaze to his son. His lip curled. 'What are you wearing? A kilt not good enough for you any more?'

Kit tore his eyes away from Maddison and looked down at his neatly tailored tuxedo, shrugging. The last time he'd worn his kilt had been at Euan's funeral; he'd managed to avoid any formal occasion in Scotland since then, wearing a black tuxedo when necessary in London.

'I wore the kilt to Eleanor's last wedding.' He saw his mother look up at that and remorse stabbed him at his bitter words. 'I just couldn't,' he added in a more conciliatory tone.

But it wasn't enough. His father shook his head. 'You get more Londonified by the day. You're needed here. It's time you shouldered your responsibilities and...'

And so it started, just as it did every time he spoke to his father. Every conversation they had had since the funeral. The same words, the same tone, the same message. He was needed here. He was responsible for this mess and he damn well better clean it up.

Didn't he know it? And that was why he couldn't be the son his father wanted. How could he come here and just take Euan's place as if he deserved it? Step into his dead brother's shoes?

'I have shouldered them. I can just as easily watch you ignore every suggestion I make from London.'

His father fixed him with a glare from eyes so familiar it was like looking in a mirror. 'You'll be responsible for this place one day and God knows I'll make sure you know how to run it.'

Admit it, you wish I had died instead. Kit took a deep breath, swallowing the bitter words back. 'Did you look at diversifying the cloth making and selling directly to the public like I suggested? How about setting up our own distillery? Doing up the holiday cottages?' His father remained silent and Kit threw his hands in the air. 'I did business plans for all those projects, found the right people. If you're not interested...'

His father interrupted, red in the face. 'You just want to change things. You have no interest in the traditions of the place.'

Kit was suddenly tired. 'I do. And that's why I want to make sure Kilcanon can remain sustainable.'

'Sustainable...' His father gesticulated and as he did so he let go of his glass. It fell in horrifying slow motion, whisky flying from it in a sweet-smelling amber shower, until the one-hundred-year-old crystal bounced off the sharp edge of the marble hearth, shattering into hundreds of tiny, razor-like shards. Everyone shouted out, the women jumping to their feet, Kit and his father taking an instinctive step back and both dogs bounding up from their fireside bed in a panicked tangle of howls and whines.

'Iain!'

'Damn fool, look what you made me do.'

'I'll get a cloth and a dustpan...' Bridge, of course, sidling out of the room as fast as she could; unusually for a Buchanan, she hated confrontation.

'Dad, have you cut yourself?'

'Oh, Iain, really. The car will be here in twenty min-

utes. Come with me. I'll fix you up. I told you to control
your temper. No wonder Kit never comes home and I'm
sure Maddison will never want to come here again. What
must she be thinking?' His mother's voice faded away as
she steered his father out of the room and up the stairs.

Kit turned to Maddison, an apology ready on his lips,
but it remained unuttered. She wasn't looking at him; all
her attention was on one of the dogs, still whimpering by
the fire. He touched her arm to reassure her but it wasn't
fear he saw on her face, it was concern.

'The dog…' she half whispered. 'I think it's hurt.'

Sure enough, although Heather had retreated to the
doorway, her tail and ears down but otherwise unhurt,
Thistle had barely moved from the old red rug that had
been the dogs' library bed for as long as Kit could remember.

'Thistle?' Heedless of the glass still scattered everywhere, Kit dropped to his knees beside the dog, still sitting whining by the fire, one paw held at a drooping
angle. Thistle's ears trembled and his tail gave a pathetic
thump, his huge dark eyes staring pleadingly at Kit. 'Are
you hurt, old boy?' He extended a gentle hand towards
the paw but Thistle moved it back, his ears flattening as
he let out a low growl. 'Come on,' Kit said coaxingly but
the next growl was a little louder.

Heather, still at the door, began to pace, her tail still
drooping. Kit glanced up at Maddison. This must be her
worst nightmare. She was wary enough of the huge dogs
as it was—one doing a lion impression and the other
growling like a bear was unlikely to reassure her. 'Now
I understand the point of corgis. A little easier to wrestle
into submission! I don't want to hurt him further but I do
need to see that paw.'

She was pale, her lips almost colourless, and there was

a faint tremor in her fingers, but she made an attempt at a smile and crouched beside him. 'I think one of us needs to reassure him while the other examines his paw.'

'So which end do you fancy, claws or teeth?' Kit wasn't being serious, he was intending to send her to get some water and some help, but to his amazement she laid a gentle hand on Thistle's head, slowly rubbing the sweet spot behind his ears and crooning to him in a low voice.

'Who's a brave bear? I know. I know it hurts but you need to let us look at it.' Her voice and the slow caress of her hand were almost hypnotic and Thistle gave a deep sigh, slumping down, his massive head on her knee. Maddison continued to talk to him, gentle words of comfort and love, one hand still rubbing his ear, the other sliding along the dog's shoulder until she was supporting the dog's paw. Thistle gave a quick jerk in pain and then lay still again.

With a quick glance at Maddison to make sure she was all right, Kit slowly and carefully turned the great paw over. The three dark pads, usually velvety soft, were damp, the fur between matted with blood. 'I think he's got glass in there,' Kit said as quietly as he could. 'Are you okay down there while I get some tweezers, water and some antibacterial cream?'

He rose to his feet as she nodded, and backed towards the door, one hand reassuring Heather, who had stopped pacing to sit staring anxiously at her litter mate still half lying in Maddison's lap.

And Maddison... Kit's breath caught in his throat. The fire lit her up, turning the strawberry-blonde hair gold, casting a warm glow over her pale skin. She was unmoving, her face set, partly through concentration, partly to hide the fear he knew she felt. With the blood from Thistle's paw on her hands and soaking into the white hem of her dress, she looked like Artemis straight from the hunt. Fiery, blood-stained warrior queen.

His heart gave a painful lurch, as if the ice encasing it were cracking. But that was okay. It was thick enough to handle a few cracks. He was in no danger of melting anytime soon.

'I can't wear this.' Maddison plucked at the long skirt and stared at Kit's mother anxiously. 'Really my, I mean, Lady Buchanan.' She hated that she'd stumbled over the words but what the fricking heck? She'd never thought she'd need to know the right way to address a viscountess before.

If Kit's mother *was* a viscountess. Was that even a thing?

'Don't be silly,' Lady Buchanan said briskly. 'Your own dress is covered in blood.' Her mouth twisted in an unexpectedly vulnerable movement. 'Attending my son's widow's marriage is hard enough. We'll be the victims of more than enough vulgar gossip without bringing the bride of Dracula with us.'

'That's a good point. I promise I'll try not to spill on this.' Maddison eyed her reflection nervously. There was an awful amount of fabric to keep clean and away from candles, especially in the floating skirt and the long, see-through chiffon sleeves. Apart from the neckline. There wasn't nearly enough material there; she swore she could see her navel if she looked hard enough.

'It's just so nice to see it being worn again.' Lady Buchanan's eyes were wistful as she rearranged the beading that encircled the low, low neckline and looped higher up Maddison's chest like a necklace. 'Bridget won't touch any of my clothes and dear Eleanor, well, it wasn't really her style. I wore this the first time I met Iain, at Hogmanay right here in this house. I wore a cape over it so my father didn't make me get changed. It was a little risqué back in the seventies.'

It was still risqué as far as Maddison was concerned. But the mint green suited her colouring and besides… 'It's vintage Halston,' she breathed reverentially. 'A design classic. It's an honour to wear it.' Even if it wasn't standard wedding attire, Maddison suspected she'd have got less attention in the blood-stained dress.

'It's the least I can do. You were so quick-thinking and brave, helping poor Thistle like that. Kit thinks he has all the glass out but Morag is going to stay late and wait in for the vet just in case. I'd have stayed myself but it's important we attend this wedding with our heads high. Never let it be said that the Buchanans retreat from a challenge although…' Her voice broke off, her eyes so sad that Maddison wished she could give her a hug.

But could she hug a viscountess without permission or was that some kind of treason? And besides, she wasn't confident that she could lean forward in this dress *and* stay in it.

'It was nothing. Thistle was very brave.'

'It's not just Thistle you're helping though. Kit seems different, less brittle. Happier. To see my boy smile I'd hand over one hundred dresses.'

Maddison tried not to squirm as the sincere words washed over her. It couldn't be denied that she was making Kit happy, but not in the way Lady Buchanan meant. Kit's mother was talking about his heart, not his body. One she was happily familiar with, the other she suspected had been locked away several years ago.

And she was pretty sure he had no intention of handing over the key. Even if he did, was she the right person to unlock it? What did she know of families and castles and long-standing traditions? She didn't belong in a place like this; she never would. Coming here was a reality check she badly needed. She could enjoy Kit's company, share his bed—but she would never be the right person to share his life. Cinderella might have made the move from the fireside to the castle, but the trailer was a step too far down. And pretend as she might, she would never shed her past completely.

CHAPTER ELEVEN

'HAVE I TOLD you that you look…?'

'Inappropriately dressed?' Maddison supplied, resisting the temptation to hoick the sides of her dress together back across her chest. She'd give anything for a pin right now.

'I was going to say hot. Definitely hotter than the bride.'

'That's always my goal at weddings.' Maddison stepped even further into the shadows at the back of the hall. 'At least it's so gloomy in here I'm hoping no one knows this is actual skin on show and assumes there's some kind of nude-coloured top going on.'

'When Eleanor decided on candlelight I don't think she took into consideration just how much light these old banqueting halls need. It feels more like Halloween than a wedding.'

'She looked beautiful though. Eleanor.' Maddison hadn't expected the surge of jealousy when the bride, a mere thirty-five minutes late, had glided ethereally down the aisle. She hadn't known what to expect from Kit's first and only love but it hadn't been the dark-eyed, dark-haired, diminutive beauty who had floated along in a confection of lace. No wonder both brothers had fallen for her, chosen her over their sibling bond.

Even her voice was beautiful, chiming out her vows in

clear bell-like tones. Maddison, hidden in a back corner, shrank into herself, uneasily aware of just how gaudy her own brilliant colouring could look, how brash her own decisive tones.

'She always looks beautiful.' But Kit didn't sound admiring or wistful. Just dismissive. 'It's all she has, really. She's good at turning those big eyes on you and making you think she matters, but when I look back at our year together I can't remember much that she said of any substance. Still, Angus wants someone to look good when he's hosting parties and to pop out an heir or two so they'll both be happy.'

Maddison winced as his words sliced into her. That was her plan, wasn't it? Find someone who wanted a compatible partner to keep the home fires burning, be a corporate wife and raise the kids. That was her goal. Planned for, prepared for, ready for... Maddison looked from Kit, slightly dishevelled yet absurdly sexy in his tux, to Angus, sweaty, balding, one arm proprietorially round his bride, and swallowed, a lump in her throat. It didn't seem such a laudable goal any more.

Kit followed her gaze and huffed out a short laugh. 'Good Lord, Angus is already half-cut. Some wedding night this is going to be.' As he spoke Eleanor looked round and caught sight of Kit. Was that regret in those huge eyes? Regret for turning him down the first time? Or regret for not hooking him in the second?

'I don't think I can stand much more of this. We've definitely done our duty,' Kit whispered into her ear, his breath heating the sensitive skin, sending tingling, hopeful messages straight to the pit of her stomach, to her knees, so she wanted to melt into his voice, his strength, his touch. 'Fancy finding a real party?'

Normally Maddison would be in her element in a gathering like this. Kit had pointed out several titles, a brace of millionaires and a group of heirs and a wedding was the ideal place to start up a conversation with any eligible man. Even though she wasn't looking for a UK-based guy, a picture of Maddison and the heir to an oil fortune posted somewhere Bart would see should be very satisfying. But somehow in the last couple of weeks she had lost any interest in impressing Bart.

Kit was right. Maybe he had been interested in her the way she was originally and her attempt to be his perfect woman had bored him. And if he hadn't been, then would she really want to build a whole life on a pretence? 'Sure. Only…' Maddison gestured at her dress. 'Where on earth can I go dressed like this? Studio 54?'

'You'll be fine where we're going. No one will raise an eyebrow.' He stopped to consider, his gaze travelling slowly down the deep vee in her neckline. Neckline? Navel line. 'Okay. They might raise *an* eyebrow, both eyebrows. But if we're lucky you might score us free drinks all night and they'll crown you harbour queen.'

'Harbour queen? Is that a thing?'

'It definitely should be. What do you say?'

Maddison cast a quick look around the high-ceilinged, grey stone room. It had been decorated to within an inch of its five-hundred-year-old life, the walls draped in a deep red fabric, the floor covered in matching carpeting, huge vases of red and white flowers dotted in every alcove, on every table. A violin quartet were playing traditional music high up in the minstrels' gallery and food and drink circulated freely. But even with the opulent decor, with the candles glittering from the candelabra on the wall and the gigantic chandelier, the gloom penetrated and, she shivered, the temperature remained chilly.

'It seems kind of rude to just go.'

'You're right. Besides, the ceilidh will start soon and in that dress you're going to be every man here's partner of choice. Think your neckline will stay intact after a round of Gay Gordons?'

Maddison had no idea what a Gay Gordon or a ceilidh was but the suggestive glint in Kit's eye warned she might be better off not finding out. 'As I was saying, it seems kind of rude to just leave but there's so many people here I guess no one will miss us.'

His smile was pure wickedness. 'I think you've made the right choice.'

It took a while before they actually left. Kit wanted to make sure he had fulfilled his role as Master of Kilcanon and switched on the professional facade so familiar from the office as he circulated the room, shaking hands, kissing cheeks and making easy small talk as if he had been born to it.

Which of course he had.

The whirlwind charm offensive finished at the bridal party with kisses for the bride, her mother and bridesmaids and a hearty, back-slapping conversation with the bemused-looking groom before they finally slipped out of the room.

'No one will be able to accuse me of not giving the wedding my full blessing,' Kit said as they collected their coats, heading out of a small side door into the cool, dark evening rather than making their way back along the long formal hallway to the gigantic front door.

'I think you scared the groom. He looked like he thought you were going to kiss him at one point.' Eleanor had kept that same cool half-smile on her lips, Maddison had noticed, but there had been a hint of hurt in her eyes. What had she been expecting? Pistols at dawn?

They made their way around the rectangular building, their way lit by small hidden lights on the path, the sounds of merriment floating out of the opened windows into the evening air. Angus's house wasn't as old as Castle Kilcanon or as elegant as the big house but it made up in size and ostentation what it lacked in authenticity. Surely it didn't need quite so many towers?

Looking up, Maddison saw the darkest sky she'd laid eyes on since she had first moved to New York four years ago, a deep, velvety blackness studded with stunningly bright flickers of light. Normally this level of darkness would panic her but Kit had tight hold of her hand, as if he knew that she might react.

Maddison's pulse began to throb. Nobody had anticipated her needs, her moods in such a long time. She squeezed his hand thankfully and breathed in deep. The air was so pure, so fresh it almost hurt her city lungs, better than any perfume or room spray.

The path brought them out onto the long, sweeping driveway and their taxi waited at the end, beyond the imposing wrought-iron gates, the modern equivalent of a drawbridge. Maddison gave a heartfelt sigh of relief when she saw the headlights; her shoes were pinching, her toes were cold and her bones so chilled she wasn't sure she'd ever feel warm again.

It was the same driver who had taken them to the wedding. Maddison suspected he was probably the only taxi driver in Kilcanon, which gave her little comfort as he set off at a white-knuckled fast pace down the dark and twisting road. Kit settled back in his seat, silent as the car flashed through the night, covering the three miles in what surely must be record time but, as the car raced to the top of the hill and the first lights in the village could be seen in the dip below, Kit reached out and took her hand again, lacing his fingers through hers with a strong, steady pressure.

There was an intimacy about holding hands in the dark that went beyond the kisses, the caresses, the passion they had shared yesterday. Maddison swallowed, a lump burning in her throat. She shouldn't get used to this. He didn't do love, remember? Neither did she.

Only she wasn't quite as sure about that any more. She wasn't sure she would swap this taxi for the fanciest of limos, the man next to her for a Kennedy, last night for a lifetime of security. Maddison stared out the window at the darkness. In that case what did she want—and was she in danger of trading all she'd ever dreamed of for heartbreak?

Maddison had expected that they would head either to a private house or to the whitewashed grand hotel that dominated the corner where the main road hit the harbour, but the taxi drove straight on, bypassing the hotel, bypassing the grand Victorian villas looking out to sea, bypassing the small and friendly pub she'd noticed earlier. The moon was high and full, laying out a silvery path along the dark sea, and Maddison had an urge to follow it and see what strange land it took her to.

Finally, once they had swept right around the harbour road and reached a small row of cottages, the taxi pulled up. Maddison opened her door, gratefully gulping in some air, her stomach unsettled by the fast and twisting journey. She looked around, confused. In front of her a door stood open but the inner door was closed and the windows tightly shuttered, although she could hear music coming from within.

'Where are we?'

Kit had walked around to join her. He extended a hand

to help her out of the car and gestured towards the door. 'This is where the locals come to play. Ready?'

Maddison cast a long, covetous look back along the harbour wall towards the hotel, shining beacon-like, a promise of hospitality, warmth and civilization. 'Sure.'

'Good.' And Kit opened the shut inner door and ushered her inside.

The first thing that hit her was the noise. Or the lack of it. Just like any good western, the room came to an abrupt silence as she was propelled through the door to stand gaping on the threshold. The second thing to strike her was the simplicity: whitewashed walls, wooden tables and stools, a dartboard and pool table visible in the adjoining room. The third thing she noticed was the heat, the glorious, roaring heat that came from a generous log fire.

The fourth and final thing Maddison realized was that, if she had been inappropriately dressed for a wedding, here, in a room full of jeans, plaid shirts and sweaters, she looked like a bordello girl amidst the cowboys. Only more underdressed.

'Kit!' The man behind the bar broke the stunned silence and slowly, like dominoes falling into each other, the room came back to life. Conversations restarted, darts were thrown and through the alcove Maddison could hear the unmistakable clink of pool balls being lined up. She hadn't played for years. Nice girls didn't hang around pool tables. Another thing she missed.

'All right, Paul.'

Maddison was barely listening as the two men launched into a series of 'how are you?'s and 'what have you been up to?'s. The accents in the little bar were stronger than any she had come across before and it was easier to let the voices wash over her than try and make sense of the conversation, which, from what she could glean, revolved around fishing anyway. A pint of something amber was handed to her and she took it. Beer. She didn't drink beer, not any more, not since high school, an illicit keg on the beach wearing her boyfriend's varsity jacket even though she wasn't cold. Because it marked her. Marked her as an insider.

She sniffed the beer cautiously, breathing in the nostalgia of the tangy, slightly metallic aroma, then took a sip. It was delicious. She took another.

'There's a seat by the fire.' Kit had finished his conversation and turned to her. 'Fancy it?'

'For now.' She smiled slowly, licking the slight froth from her lip as she did so, and watched Kit's eyes darken to navy blue. 'But later I want to play pool.'

Was this what a relationship was? Discovering new parts of someone, being surprised by them, delighted by them, in new ways every day. Eleanor had always been the same—cool, collected, affectionate but in a way that made it clear she was in control. He saw it now for what it was: a way to keep him in line, wanting more. And he'd never allowed anyone else close enough to find out what one facet of their personality was like, let alone several.

But here he was. And here Maddison was. The hardworking assistant, smooth and reliable. The clue solver, her quick brain jumping ahead, unabashedly delighted when she was first with an answer. The opera lover, enthralled by the music, lost in a world he couldn't touch. The warrior, conquering her fear to help a creature in pain. The lover, tender, demanding, exciting, yielding.

And now—the pool shark. It wasn't just the dress distracting him; she had borrowed a T-shirt from Paul, the barman, to even up the odds somewhat—there wasn't a man in here who could have played her in that dress and survived. It wasn't the adorable way she bit her lip as she focused on the cue ball or the way she caressed the tip of the cue while sizing up her shot, although both of those gave her a definite advantage. No, the truth was she was very, very good. Or lucky. He hadn't decided which.

She was also more than a little drunk, having moved on to whisky. She had unwittingly committed sacrilege and asked for a blended whiskey but Kit had jumped in to change her order to the local single malt, although he had allowed it to be poured on ice. Her face at the first sip had had the entire bar in stitches but she had persevered a little too well—was that her second glass or her third?

'Another round?'

Was she talking about whisky or the pool? Kit wasn't sure he could take either. 'I wouldn't mind some air first,' he suggested.

Maddison narrowed her eyes at him, reminding Kit irresistibly of a cat in her unwavering focus. 'Scared?'

'Terrified. My reputation may never recover.' Truth was some of his shots had gone awry because she was so damn adorable when she was competitive, but he wasn't going to admit that. It would just make her win all the more complete.

'Okay. Air and then I whip your ass again. Deal?'

'Deal.'

He steered her out of the door, realizing as he hit the street that she wasn't the only one feeling the effects of the whisky. Kit was mellower, calmer than he had felt in a long time. The cool night air was a welcome relief from the heat of the bar, the sound of the waves soothing after the laughter, loud talk and music pumping through the two small rooms. Kit reached for Maddison's hand, breathing in a sigh of relief as the peace hit him.

Only for the peace to retreat as the past roared in to engulf him once again. A past he would never be free of, not here, no matter whose hand he held, how much whisky he sank. No matter how much he tried.

'Hey, are you okay?'

Kit loosened his grip on Maddison's hand with a muttered apology. 'I thought this time was different, this time I could handle it.'

He crossed the road and leaned on the railings, the only barrier between land and sea, staring out at the moon path.

She joined him at the railing. 'They all seem to like you in there.'

'I haven't been back there in years. Not since...' He didn't finish the sentence.

'They treated you like a regular.'

'I was once. Place like that, once you're a regular you're always a regular.'

'Sounds nice.' There was a longing in her voice.

'It was. The hotel and the pub belong to the tourists, to the incomers, to people like my parents. Even though I lived at the big house I never ran with the set. The bar belongs to the villagers. When I was home I was in the lifeboat crew. I helped build the jetty.' He nodded over at the wooden structure bobbing about in the gentle waves. 'Euan was with me but there was a difference—no matter how much he rolled up his sleeves and pitched in, he was still the Master, the future Laird. Half those folk in there live in tied cottages. They'd be paying rent to him one day. Now I guess they'll be paying their rent to me.' The prospect was bleak. He didn't want the inevitable separation his title would bring.

'Your father wants you home.' It wasn't a question.

Kit nodded. 'He does and he doesn't. He thinks I

should be here learning about the estate but he worries that I'll want to change things. He wants the finance I can bring if I sell my house and bring my investments to the estate but not the power that will give me. He wants a Master of Kilcanon but not me.'

'What happened, Kit? How did Euan die?'

The question was inevitable; they had been approaching this conversation all day. He took a deep, shuddering breath, allowing himself to really confront the past, confront his role in it, for the first time in three long years. 'We were ridiculously competitive. Mum says we would fight over anything and everything. I had to prove I was as good as him despite being younger—despite not being the future Laird. He had to prove his asthma didn't stop him.' Kit gazed out at the bay. He could still see them: two boys night fishing from a dinghy, kayaking over to the nearest island, still visible in the dusky night.

'Anything I could do he had to do better and vice versa, but we were really close even so.' His lips compressed into a hard line. 'We sailed, fished, camped, built dens. It was ridiculously idyllic, looking back. Just look at it, Maddison. Some people hate growing up in a place like this but we thrived. Like some *Boy's Own* adventure. Only it was real life.'

'Sounds amazing.'

'I knew I had no future here and I resented that, I guess. The estate wouldn't support me as well—second sons are useful spares but they can get in the way. So I headed to Cambridge at eighteen, started to build a life away from Kilcanon although I always yearned to come home. We would pick up right where we left off in the holidays, trying to get the better of each other. I just didn't realize that nothing was off limits.'

'Some things should have been.'

Maybe. It was odd now, looking back. Remembering how hurt he had been. The sense of betrayal when Euan had just continued the game that had started before Kit could walk, carried it on to the ultimate conclusion. 'I refused to show Euan how much he had hurt me. I had my pride, after all. I wished he and Eleanor well and I walked away as if I didn't give a damn. I agreed to be best man at their wedding. But it wasn't enough. He wanted my blessing, for me to tell him it was all okay. We were okay.'

'So what did you do?' Maddison placed her soft hand on his; the gleam of victory mixed with whisky gone from her eyes, her pointed chin no longer lifted in triumph, rather her whole body leaned into him in wordless sympathy.

'Do? I refused to give him the satisfaction. I stayed in London, built up my publishing business, dated, came home for holidays and did everything I could to prove that I was better. I was insufferable. Had to coppice the most trees, catch the most fish, build the longest bit of fence, bring home a different girl each time, be the most popular brother with the locals. I was the life and soul of every party. He couldn't compete but it didn't stop him from trying.'

It was easy to look back now and see how angry he had been. Maybe they should have had a good fight and got it out of their systems with some well-aimed punches rather than letting the anger fester for four long years.

'One Christmas we got into a pointless row. We'd often raced across the harbour—row boats, sailing boats, motor boats and, being the insufferable brats we were, kept a running tally. I thought I was ahead, he thought he was and I wouldn't back down. In the end he told me, in the most condescending high-handed way, that if I needed it that much then, okay, we would say it was me.' Kit took another long look at the sea: boyhood playground, beautiful, endless, merciless. 'Of course, I wasn't having that. I insisted we sort the matter out immediately. One last race, winner takes all. He told me not to be stupid and I pushed and pushed until...by then we were both determined to win no matter what the cost. I didn't know how high the cost could be.'

He swallowed, memories washing over him, the spray of salt water on his face, the burning in his arms and legs, the sweet, sweet moment of victory turning sour as he realized something was very wrong.

'His asthma?'

Kit nodded. 'An attack right out there and of course the silly sod had forgotten his inhaler. I went back for him, God, I don't think I've ever rowed as fast in my life, but I wasn't fast enough. I got him to shore, called an ambulance but...I was too late. Too late to save him, too late to forgive him.'

He paused for a long moment. 'This was always the place I longed to be. I was so jealous of Euan, that this was his while I lived in exile.'

'So why haven't you moved back now your parents want you here?'

'How can I? I killed my brother as surely as if I had pushed him off the cliff. I knew his chest was bad that Christmas but I couldn't see beyond my own hurt pride. I forced him to race me and he died. How can I live here? How can I ever be happy when he's in the ground, knowing I put him there?'

'Oh, Kit.' Her arms were around him, holding him tight, her lips on his cheek, on his jaw, his neck. Her fingers tangled in his hair, her voice enfolding him with whispered comfort. 'You do belong here, Kit, but it's not Euan you have to forgive, it's you. Let it go, Kit.

Forgive yourself. Isn't that what Euan would want? Let it go. Live.'

Kit stared out to sea, Maddison's heat, her fire slowly warming him, bringing him painfully back to life. *Isn't that what Euan would want?* Was it? He had no idea.

He put his hands on her shoulders, standing back so he was at arm's length, so that he could see her face, her eyes, her truth. 'Why would you think that?'

'Think what? Think that three years of self-imposed exile, three years of guilt, of estrangement is enough? Because it is, Kit. You didn't kill your brother. He knew the rules, he was an active player, sometimes the instigator, always the main competitor. What happened to him is beyond sadness, beyond grief, but it isn't your fault.'

Kit desperately wished he believed that, but his mind flashed back to that bleak December day. To the pain and anger in his father's eyes, the anguish enfolding his mother, Bridget's sobs and Eleanor's stony-faced grief. The identical looks on their faces when he'd walked wearily into the hospital waiting room. The looks that had told him quite clearly that they knew exactly where the blame lay.

And he had agreed. Had willingly shouldered the toxic burden and let it infect his whole life. He deserved it.

Maddison cupped his cheek, her hand branding him with its gentleness. 'What did Euan want that whole time he was married to Eleanor? For *you* to forgive *him*. He wanted his brother back. What would he say now, if he was here?'

To get over myself. But it wasn't that easy. 'It's not just you that you're hurting.' Her voice was gentle but her words inexorable, beating away at his carefully erected shields. 'Your parents, your sister. They miss you. The way things are they've lost two brothers, two sons. You can't bring Euan back, Kit, but you can give them back you. You can become part of the family again. And sure, it'll hurt. You'll miss him every time you have to make a decision he should have made, perform a task that was his, visit a place he loved, but that way you'll preserve his memory too. Because right now? You're denying him that.'

Kit stared down at her. Was she right? Was his decision to stay away, to keep apart from his family, to carry the burden of Euan's death alone selfish? An excuse to wallow in his grief? Coming home, being part of the family again, moving on would hurt, not with the dull, constant ache he'd carried for the last three years but with sharp, painful clarity, but maybe, just maybe, it was the right thing to do. The right way to honour and remember his brother.

CHAPTER TWELVE

HE HADN'T SLEPT a wink. Kit stared at the window, the first rosy tints of dawn peeking through the flimsy curtains—sunrise came early this time of year. As boys he and Euan would often be up and out, determined to wring every second of adventure out of the long summer days.

Maddison was soft, warm, curled into him like a satisfied kitten, and he shifted, careful not to wake her. She murmured and turned, the sheet slipping to expose the creamy point of her shoulder, red-gold hair tumbling over it like spun sugar. He could nudge her awake, kiss her awake…

Kit slid out of bed and grabbed his clothes. If he woke her then he would make love to her and that, that would be amazing on many levels, especially as it would stop him thinking, stop his brain turning her words over and over and over. But it was time he faced his situation head-on—and he wouldn't be able to do it with a naked Maddison so temptingly within reach.

Everything she had said made sense. He thought that he was truly, fittingly punishing himself by staying away, but all he was doing was running from his troubles. He needed to come home, part of the time at least. He needed to shoulder the responsibilities that were his to bear now that he was Master of Kilcanon. He needed to do more than suggest business ideas to his father; he needed to provide the capital, the manpower and the know-how he could so easily manage. He needed to celebrate his brother's legacy by being part of it, not tarnish it by hiding from it.

Maddison shifted again and the sheet slid a little lower. Kit stopped and stared, his mouth dry as he drank her in. Funny to think he had known her just a few weeks, and that for the beginning of that time he had barely noticed her at all. She looked so different asleep: softer, sweeter, more vulnerable.

But she *was* vulnerable, wasn't she? The realization hit him like a freezing spring wave. That efficient exterior was nothing but a carefully honed act; at heart Maddison Carter was a lost little girl searching for a happily ever after. What had she said she wanted? *Hayrides and clambakes and a huge family Thanksgiving?* He wasn't entirely sure what a clambake was—but he was pretty sure that he wasn't planning to find out.

Kit grimaced, reality stabbing through him along with the dawn sun's rays. *What was he doing?* She worked with him, worked *for* him and he was no Prince Charming. He could offer her a few weeks of fun but he couldn't give her the porch swing, the four children, the clambakes and fireworks. He had his own life to sort out—he didn't know where he would be living, what he would be doing in three *months* let alone three years, thirty years. He didn't think he could promise three months. He didn't know how to.

And Maddison needed security like most people needed air.

Maybe she didn't want security from him. Maybe she was happy with things the way they were but he couldn't risk it. Couldn't risk her getting hurt. Or, a little voice whispered, himself; he couldn't get too used to having her around. She would be heading away, back to the future she needed, she craved. This thing, whatever it was, had got too deep, too intense far, far too quickly. He curled his hands into fists. There were many difficult decisions he needed to face today but this one was easy. He needed time and space away from Maddison Carter—it was the best thing he could do for her.

Maddison came to with a jolt, aching all over, a sweet, luxurious ache that almost begged her to push harder, again and again. She rolled over, unsure for one moment where she was, why she felt this way: sore, sated, satisfied. The windows were barely covered, the sun shining through the thin filmy curtains. She slumped back onto the soft pillows, the memories running through her mind like a shot-by-shot replay. Sex had never been like that before. Never been so intense, so all-encompassing. She had never been so lost in someone else, so lost to pleasure.

She sat up, her heart thumping.

What had she been thinking? To be so dependent on another person with no guarantees at all that the words, the touches, the intimacy meant anything, would lead anywhere. She had taken her entire rule book and just ripped it up. Maddison curled her hands into tight fists as reality set in, the cold and harsh light of day displacing her sleepy, sated dreams.

Okay, reality check. Last night had been about emotion-driven sex—that was all. That was why it had been so very intense. So all consuming. So very, very good… She was still riding high on adrenaline after her own bout of confessional honesty. It hurt, that opening up, allowing someone in. It hurt to face her own flaws. Sex was some kind of all-purpose plaster, helping make everything feel better, mind, body and soul. And then Kit had trumped her, tearing open his own secrets, facing his own demons.

No wonder their lovemaking had been so hot, both of them trying to lose themselves, forget themselves, seek absolution in the other's touch. But that was all it was. All it could be.

Maddison stretched out an arm and brushed the other side of the bed. It was cold; Kit must have left her some time ago. She pulled her phone off the nightstand. It was still early, not yet seven. He must have left her before dawn. She looked around. No note, no sign of him at all.

A chill brushed her chest and the ache in her limbs intensified, a little less sweet, a little less luxurious. Now the ache just made her wince, a physical reminder of her own vulnerability.

What if he regretted it all? Not just the sex but the emotional honesty? What if he decided their closeness had all been a mistake? There was no way she was going to hand all the power over to him; no way was she going to allow herself to be made vulnerable. She needed to re-erect her barriers and fast.

Maddison showered and dressed quickly, mechanically, building up her armour layer by layer with each brush of her hair, each sweep of the mascara wand, each blotting of her lipstick. Armour was preventative, protective. It kept you strong, kept you alive to fight another day. And the very fact that she felt that she might need it told her everything: she had let Kit in too deeply, too quickly, too intensely. And she didn't trust him not to hurt her.

She didn't trust herself not to let him.

She sank into the easy chair by the bedroom window and stared out at the stunning view, all blues and silvers and greens. It was a living picture, one she could never get tired of as the sky shifted and the sea moved restlessly. In the distance a gannet dropped, a reckless, speedy plunge into the water below, and her stomach dropped with it. She had been that reckless. She had plunged into intimacy with no thought of tomorrow. Would she, like the gannet, resurface with nothing to show for her dive?

She knew better. How many times had her mother told her that *this is the one*? The man who was going to rescue them. The man who was going to give them a home, make them into a real family. Every time Tanya Carter fell all the way in straight away, offering herself up like a sacrifice only to wonder why every time she was left with her heart ripped out, alone and defenceless. Maddison had learned early that you kept your heart locked away, you didn't let anyone into your soul—and you made sure you came out on top, always.

Only where had that knowledge got her? She hadn't allowed Bart into her heart and he had still left her—only for her to crash headlong into an ill-thought-out flirtation. She'd known Kit was dangerous early on but hubristically had thought she was invincible, that she could handle him. And what had happened? She had allowed Kit perilously close. But not all the way in. She wasn't that stupid. Thank goodness.

The ache in her chest intensified. She was so tired of being lonely, that was all. She was ready for her safe, secure happy ever after. No more deviations.

But was she really ready? Maddison sighed, staring blindly out at the sea. These last few weeks had thrown her badly off balance, all her plans, her dreams now up in the air. Did she want to try and get Bart back? She tried to picture the future she had dreamed of but the vision was blurry. No, she wanted more than a loveless marriage of convenience. Did she want to put all her efforts into her career? At least that was going right—but what if she missed out on meeting the right guy? Ended up fifty, alone and childfree?

She wanted it all. Kit's face floated into her mind, that amused smile on his mouth, laughter in the blue eyes. Maddison's mouth twisted. Had she learned nothing? He wasn't even here. Her heart began to beat painfully, each thud reminding her that she was alone once again.

Maybe she needed to look backwards before she looked forwards. Maybe it was time she faced just who she was, who she had been. Maybe that way she would find the answers she needed.

She checked the time again. Seven-thirty. She could do with coffee, juice, something to push away the ache in her head and her chest. What was the etiquette with breakfasting in castles anyway? She doubted that a maid would come in with a breakfast tray. She should find her way to the kitchen and sort out a coffee and a plan. A plan always made everything better.

Resolutely Maddison got to her feet but before she moved a step the door swung open to reveal Kit, fully dressed, shadows emphasizing his eyes, his stubble darker than usual. He looked as if he hadn't slept a wink. Maddison's heart began to beat faster, adrenaline mixing with anticipation and dread. His mouth was set in a grim line, his eyes unsmiling.

'I brought you a coffee.' He held out a huge mug and she took it gratefully, cradling it between her hands, drawing courage from the warmth.

'Thanks, I was about to venture out in search of the kitchen but I didn't have a ball of string long enough to guide me back.' She kept her voice deliberately light and carefree and saw some of the tension leave him. 'It's a beautiful day. Which is a shame because I'd really like to explore the area, I've hardly had a chance to do more than glimpse it, but I really need to be getting back.'

He must know that was a lie. He knew she knew hardly anyone else in London, knew that all her time was spent either working for him, testing out routes with him or on her own with a takeaway. But he didn't challenge her. She hadn't been expecting him to but disappointment stabbed through her anyway. 'I was thinking of staying here a few more days.'

I, not *we*. Not unexpected. 'That's a good idea.'

'I went fishing with my father this morning. There's a lot we need to discuss. About the future of this place. My role in it.'

'Kit,' she said as gently as she could. 'You don't need to explain, not to me.'

He carried on as if she hadn't spoken. 'I feel bad that you have to make your own way back, though. There's a taxi booked to take you all the way to Glasgow and I've bought you a first-class ticket back to London. As a thank you for coming with me.'

'You didn't have to do that.'

'I did.' His mouth tilted. 'You gave up your weekend again. It was very kind of you.'

'Well, thank you.' She took a sip of the scaldingly hot coffee, the pain almost welcome in this falsely polite exchange. 'I meant what I said yesterday, Kit. I'm not Camilla. We didn't make any promises and I'm not the kind of girl who reads wedding bells into every kiss.'

'Not unless you planned it that way.' There was a hint of warmth in his eyes and she wanted to hold on to it, blow it into life, but she held back, wrapping her dignity around her like a protective cloak.

'You know me, always with the plan.' And that, Maddison realized, was the part that was so hard to say good-bye to. He did know her. Almost better than she knew herself. More than anyone else in the whole wide world. And that wasn't enough for him. She wasn't enough.

She'd done good work here. She'd helped him break down some of his guilt, helped ease some of his burden, shown him that he was a man worth knowing. Maybe she'd paved the way for someone with more confidence, someone who didn't care about rejection, someone who knew what they were worth to come in and finish the job. And obviously that thought hurt because she was a little raw right now, but that was a good thing, right? She cared about him; he was her friend and he deserved happiness.

And he had done the same for her. The last couple of weeks she had been *happy*. He'd given her the tools to set her free; she just needed to use them. She was a work in progress, not set in stone after all. The future was hers if she had the courage to embrace it.

'What time is the taxi coming?'

'Soon. It's a couple of hours to Glasgow and a long train ride. I thought you would want to salvage some of your weekend.'

'I'd better pack, then.' She glanced over at the Halston dress hanging forlornly on the wardrobe door. Last night it had been fantastically, recklessly glamorous. Today it looked limp and a little worse for wear. Like its wearer. 'Don't feel that you have to keep me company, Kit. I have a few things to do and I'd like to make sure I say a proper thank you to your mother before I go. Honestly. I'm fine.'

He paused then nodded, dropping one light kiss onto the top of her head before turning away. It wasn't until Maddison watched Kilcanon disappear behind her that she realized that he hadn't even said goodbye.

* * *

Kit swivelled his office chair round and stared unseeingly out across the London skyline. A view that denoted success, status. Just as his expensive chair, his vintage desk, his penthouse office did.

It was cold comfort. In fact there was precious little comfort anywhere. Not here, in this gleaming, glass-clad, supersized office. Not at night in a house far too big for one person, especially a person who barely spent any time there. He'd never noticed before just how bland his house was, like a luxurious and tasteful hotel, not a home. Had he chosen a single one of the varying shades of cream, olive, steel or grey, positioned any one of the statement pieces in the large empty rooms? No, it looked almost exactly the same as it had when the expensive interior decorator had walked away. Like a show home: all facade and no heart.

A bit like his life.

Kit's mouth pressed into a hard line. He knew better than most how hard Maddison's life had been, how she was searching for a place of her own, for security. And what had he done? Made her feel so unwanted that her only option was to leave. Leave a job she loved, a fantastic opportunity she had been headhunted for, in order to avoid him. The irony was that his own notice was in and he would be moving on himself in a couple of months. She should have stayed; he could have moved her to another department if she really wanted to avoid him.

He'd been relieved, that morning in Scotland, at her apparent lack of emotion. Alarm bells should have been screeching. He should have looked deeper but he'd seen what he'd wanted to see. What it was easier for him to see. Again.

He'd told himself that he was doing the right thing,

that giving her some space was exactly what they had both needed. But when he'd got back to London she had gone. Family emergency, apparently. Which was interesting because he knew full well that she didn't have any family, not that she was in touch with anyway.

So, it wasn't hard to deduce that she had disappeared in order to avoid seeing him. He should be glad. It made a difficult situation a lot more tenable. No tears and constant phone calls from Maddison; she had more class than that. His mouth thinned. He couldn't just let her vanish into thin air; he should make sure she was okay, that she had somewhere to go. He owed her that. Otherwise he was no better than that idiot on the porch swing.

After all, Bart had obviously had no idea of Maddison's worth, but Kit didn't have that excuse. He knew exactly what she was, *who* she was; he knew just how brightly she shone. Had pushed her away, afraid of being burnt by her flame. The whole time he had been in Scotland he had wished that she were there, had wanted to discuss the compromise he'd made with his father with her. Wanted to hear her thoughts on his plan—a plan that involved spending half the year in Scotland and branching out as a freelancer again. Using his entrepreneurial skills to help shore up and revitalize the Kilcanon economy.

He'd told himself that pushing her away was for her own good, that she deserved someone better than him but, he realized with scalding shame, he'd been lying to himself all along. He who prided himself on his unflinching honesty. He'd pushed her away because he was scared, because she made him *feel*. She'd made him feel hope. And how had he repaid her? He needed to make sure she was okay. He needed to say sorry. He needed to tell her exactly how brightly she shone.

A call to New York established that Maddison hadn't returned there and that Hope hadn't heard from her. Kit racked his brains. She had never said where she was from. All he knew was that it was a coastal town in New England. That narrowed it down to thousands of miles of coastline, then.

Kit turned back to his desk and, with a few quick taps, brought Maddison's personnel file up on his screen. He stared at the small yellow envelope. As her line manager he had every right to look in there, more than a right; he had a duty to record appraisals, chart her performance. But, no matter what he told himself, he knew he wasn't looking as a line manager.

He wasn't even looking as a concerned friend.

He missed her. He was pretty damn sure he needed her. Terrifyingly sure that actually he was desperately and irrevocably in love with her.

Love. Was that what this was? This emptiness? This need? This willingness to fall on his sword a thousand times?

He clicked on the icon.

There they were—her application documents, anonymous forms, filled in, filed and forgotten. Until now. He opened her résumé and began reading. She had graduated summa cum laude from Martha George, a small liberal arts college in New York State, and, while there, had spent her summers working as an intern for various PR agencies before joining a new agency soon after graduating. Two years later she was applying for a job at DL Media.

He scanned further down. Graduated class valedictorian from Bayside High on Cape Cod…Bayside High… *got her.*

But he needed more. He couldn't just turn up in a

strange town armed with a photo of her and track her down, could he? He closed the document, opening up her employee details instead. Name, address, Social Security number…there it was. Next of Kin. Only it was blank. She had cut her mother completely out of her life.

What must that be like? His own parents were still hurting, still recovering from Euan's death, from Kit's own emotional and physical distance, but they were there, always there. What must it be like having nobody at all to rely on?

Kit opened another couple of documents at random: appraisals, the move from PR to editorial, her references. It was all in order and yet it told him nothing. Finally he clicked on the last document, her college reference. It was a breakdown of her entire time there, classes taken, grades achieved—and her scholarship recommendation.

He read through the recommendation, words jumping out.

Despite her difficult background…
Three jobs…
Tenacious and hardworking…
Ambitious…
Legal emancipation…
Needs a chance…
No parental support, emotionally or financially…

Seeing her past written there so baldly hit him in a way her confession hadn't. No wonder she pushed everyone away. No wonder she always had to be in control, couldn't show that she needed anyone.

She had never been able to rely on anyone.

Well, hard luck. He was going to be there for her whether she wanted him to be or not. And when he knew she was okay, then he would walk away. If that was what she truly wanted. Only if that was what she truly wanted.

He'd thought that keeping the rest of the world at bay was what he'd deserved, that he owed Euan a lifetime of remorse and loneliness. Wouldn't it be better to honour his brother's legacy by living? By feeling? The good *and* the bad.

Kit walked back to his desk and read the reference again, noting down the address.

He was going to find out exactly what made Maddison Carter tick, and when he had done so he was going to fix her. He was going to make everything better for someone else for once in his life, no matter what it cost him.

CHAPTER THIRTEEN

MADDISON'S HANDS GREW clammy and she gripped the steering wheel so tight the plastic bit into her palms. Ahead of her the road segued smoothly onto the bridge that separated Cape Cod from the mainland.

The bridge that would take her home.

It was eight years since she had bid it farewell in her rear-view mirror. Waved and sworn never to return. Up until today she had kept that vow.

But it was time to face her demons, confront her past—then maybe she could move forward. Maybe she too would finally deserve some kind of happiness. Her stomach twisted and she gulped in air against the rising panic. Would she be able to find happiness without Kit?

No. This wasn't about Kit. This was about her, Maddison, finally taking stock of who she was and where she had come from. This was about moving on. This was about learning to be happy. If she could…

The bridge soared over the narrow strip of water separating the Cape from the mainland. Mouth set, eyes straight ahead, Maddison maintained a steady speed over the bridge and onto the highway, which ran the full length of the Cape all the way up to Provincetown on the very tip. She wound down her window and the smell hit instantly: salt and gorse. Despite everything she breathed in deeply, letting the familiar air fill her lungs. Despite everything it whispered to her that she was home.

Her turn-off was thirty miles up the Cape, at the spot where the land narrowed and twisted, like an arm raised in victory. She turned instinctively, driving on autopilot, until she found herself entering the small town of Bayside.

Bayside always looked at its best in early summer, when everything was spruced up ready for the seasonal influx that quadrupled the town's population. The freshly painted shopfronts gleamed in the morning sun, the town had an air of suppressed anticipation just as it did every May, a stark contrast to the weary fade of September.

But some things had changed; several cycle-hire stores had sprung up offering helmets, kiddie trailers and tandems as well as a bewildering assortment of road and trail bikes. Maddison's mouth twisted as she remembered how she had been teased for riding her rusty bike around the town, not driving like her classmates. She guessed she had just been ahead of the curve. The cycle shops weren't the only new stores; driving slowly, Maddison noticed an assortment of new delis, coffee shops, organic cafes and bakeries, many of which wouldn't have been out of place in the Upper East Side or on Stoke Newington Church Street. It was a long way away from the ice-cream parlours and burger joints of her youth.

Bayside had always been a town divided, not once, but two or three times. Locals versus visitors. Summer-home owners versus two-week vacationers. Vacationers versus day trippers. And at the bottom of the heap, divided from everyone, were the town's poor, dotted here and there in trailers or falling-down cottages, on scrubland worth millions less than the prime real estate on the ocean edge. That had been Maddison's world.

Her stomach tightened as she drove out of town, past the small, dusty road that led to Bill's Bar, a small, shabby establishment frequented only by locals—her mother's second home. If she took that road and pulled in would she see the all-too-familiar sight of her mother, propping up the bar, another drink in front of her? She accelerated past, heading for the Bayside Inn where she had reserved a room. Once she'd asked them for a job and been turned away. Now her money was as good as anyone's.

Two hours later, showered and refuelled by some excellent coffee, Maddison was back in the car, continuing on the road out of town following the shore. The town was situated by a huge natural bay and the beaches were sheltered, the water warm and safe; in low tide it was possible to walk out for what seemed like miles and still only be waist deep. The beautiful sand-dune beaches on the other side of town plunged swimmers straight into the icy swell of the ocean, where seals frolicked within swimming distance—and where the seals swam the great whites weren't far behind. Property overlooking the ocean on both sides was at a premium and Maddison drove past tall electronic gates prohibiting access to the vast, sprawling houses within, their views worth more than their opulent interiors.

Maddison pulled into the ungated driveway of one of the oldest and more modest houses: a two-storey white-shingled house. True, anywhere else the five-bedroomed dwelling with its beautiful wraparound porch, outside pool and beach views from every room would be pretty impressive, but it lacked the helipad and pool houses of some of its more vulgar neighbours. On one side stood a separate double garage, and Maddison looked up at the apartment overhead, that sense of coming home intensifying. This was the first place where she had ever had the luxury of security.

She rang the bell and waited, wiping her hands on her skirt, trying not to jiggle impatiently. No answer. Maddison looked around, hope draining away. Why hadn't she called ahead? The house might have changed hands, or the owners be away. This whole impetuous road trip was probably a waste of time, a self-indulgent wallow in memory lane. She took a step back, poised to turn away, but the movement was arrested by the sound of a key turning. Maddison turned, hope hammering in her chest, the relief almost too much when the door opened to reveal a familiar face. Mrs Stanmeyer. A little older, but her blonde hair was still swept back in an elegant coil, she was still as regally straight-backed, exquisitely dressed in linen trousers and a white silk shirt.

'Hello, can I help…?' The voice trailed off. 'Maddison? Maddison Carter? Oh, my dear girl.'

As Mrs Stanmeyer's face relaxed into a welcoming smile and she stepped forward, arms outstretched to pull Maddison into a hug, the pain in Maddison's chest, the load she had carried since she was eighteen, the load that had seemed unbearable since she left Scotland, lessened just a little. Enough to make it manageable.

'Maddison, oh, my dear, come on in. I am so very glad to see you.'

Maddison found herself ushered into the wide, spacious hallway. Little had changed, she was relieved to see, the house still a tasteful blend of creams and blues, beautiful but practical in a home where children ran straight in from the beach and most of the day was spent outside. Mrs Stanmeyer led her through the living/dining/family room that made up most of the first floor and out onto the deck where a trio of cosy wooden love seats were pulled up invitingly.

'It's so lovely to see you,' Mrs Stanmeyer said as they settled themselves onto the seats, iced water flavoured with fresh lemons on the table before them. 'I have often wondered how you were.'

For the first time in eight years guilt hit Maddison. How could she have cut everyone off so completely when some people had done nothing but offer her help and support?

'This is the first time I've come back,' she admitted, her eyes fixed on the sand dunes and the gleam of blue sea beyond. 'I'm sorry. Sorry I didn't call or email you, sorry I didn't try. I just wanted to wipe it all out. Start again.'

'And how has that gone for you?'

'I thought it was going perfectly. I thought I had re-invented myself, that I was untouchable.' She grimaced. 'But I guess I never stopped judging myself. In the end I was the one still looking down on me, never believing I was worthy of anything, deserved anything. Maybe that's why I spent the last few years chasing after all the wrong things.' She swallowed hard, the lump in her throat making words almost impossible. 'And now it's too late. I'm worried that it's too late.' Her mouth quivered and she covered it with one hand.

'Oh, Maddison. It's never too late. The girl I knew, the girl with three jobs when she was just fourteen? The girl who supported herself at sixteen and still graduated as class valedictorian, she knew that.'

Maddison looked up at that. Was that how Mrs Stanmeyer saw her? Not as a monumental mess but as a survivor? 'Supported myself and graduated thanks to you. If you hadn't given me a job when no one else would, offered me the maid's room, sorted out the scholarship to Martha George, I don't know where I would have ended up.'

The older woman reached out and laid a hand on Maddison's arm. 'I didn't do anything, Maddison. If anything I felt guilty for not doing more—a child of your age here all winter on her own, cleaning for me! But you were so determined and so proud, I knew you wouldn't take charity. As for the scholarship, all I did was recommend you. You did the rest yourself.'

For the first time in maybe forever a glow of achievement warmed her. She *had* worked hard, saved hard, studied hard. Hadn't allowed her beginnings to define her end. But she knew that without the home, the money, the trust Mrs Stanmeyer had shown her it would have been a far harder journey.

'I wondered...' Maddison twisted her hands together, trying to find the right words. 'I wondered why you helped me, if maybe it was...if I was...' She glanced through the open glass doors to the large sideboard, at the collection of family portraits gathered there. She had dusted each of them time and time again, searching for some kind of resemblance between herself and the two blonde, elegant daughters and the boyish, handsome son. There were more photos now, babies and small, round children playing in the sand. 'Did you help me because your son... Is he my father?'

The smile faded from Mrs Stanmeyer's face, replaced by a weary sadness. 'Oh, Maddison. If you were my granddaughter I hope I'd have done better than employing you as my maid and housing you in a room over the garage. I don't think Frank even knew your mother. He was away interning the summer you were conceived.'

Warring emotions hit her, intense disappointment that she could never be part of this family mingled with relief that she wasn't the guilty secret hidden away in the maid's room after all. 'Do you know who it was? Who my father is?'

Mrs Stanmeyer shook her head. 'No, but I knew your mother. You look very much like her, you know, the same hair, the same eyes—and the same ambition. I'd known your grandmother a very long time but I really got to know Tanya the summer before you were born. She was hoping for a scholarship to Martha George too, and I was already on the admissions board.'

Maddison stared. Her mother had applied to the elite liberal arts college? She didn't remember her even opening a book, let alone studying. At least she certainly hadn't after Grandma died.

'My mom?' Her voice squeaked despite herself and she stopped, silent. She wasn't supposed to care.

Mrs Stanmeyer nodded. 'It was a scandal when she fell pregnant with you. Everyone said it was such a waste of potential. I think some thought it a judgement—she was just so alive, so free, so sure she could do it all. She told me she didn't care what they said, that she was excited about the future, that she would raise you and study at night. Like you she was very independent. She moved out of your grandmother's house into the trailer when you were still a baby, determined not to ask for help. I think they clashed a lot.'

'They did, but they loved each other too,' Maddison admitted. 'She was devastated when Grandma died.' She took a sip of the ice-cold water, trying to reconcile this picture of a vibrant, ambitious teen mom with the bitter reality. 'What happened? Because the woman I knew? She had no ambition beyond the next drink, the next boyfriend.'

Mrs Stanmeyer shook her head. 'I wish I knew. I saw a

little of her when you were a baby and a toddler and everything seemed fine. I was a friend of your grandmother's, you see, since we were girls ourselves, and I always took an interest in your mother. I knew she found it hard, making enough money, keeping up her studies and raising you, but she was very optimistic. Your grandmother's illness hit her hard but at that time my own girls were growing up, had their own teen worries and troubles and I didn't see your mother—or you—for several years. I heard gossip, of course, but I discounted it as mutterings of scandal-loving old cats. Maybe I shouldn't have been so quick to judge them. When I next saw her it was as if something had broken inside her. She seemed to have given up. I tried to help but she pushed me away, many times.'

Maddison's eyes burned and the pressure in her chest swelled to almost unbearable degrees. It had been so long since she had thought of her mother without scorn and anger but she could all too vividly imagine the struggling young woman, breaking down under the burden of poverty and hardship. And sitting here contemplating a bleak future of her own making, a future without Kit, she understood, a little, the intoxicating appeal of just checking out of life.

Maybe her bleakness showed on her face because Mrs Stanmeyer's voice was very gentle, very kind. 'What's brought you home, Maddison, after all this time?'

She blinked, trying in vain to hold back the tears that had been building but not allowed to fall since the moment she had driven away from Kilcanon, each one scalding her as it escaped. 'I thought I had it all planned out but I'm lost. And I have no idea how to find my way.'

'Do you have any plans for today, dear?' Mrs Stanmeyer—Lydia, as she had instructed Maddison to call her—put a plate of pancakes, bacon and maple syrup in front of Maddison as she spoke. 'Eat up. You are far too thin.'

In some ways the last twenty-four hours had been like stepping into a much-loved and cherished daydream. Mrs Stanmeyer had insisted she cancel her room at the inn and stay with her, putting Maddison in the whitewashed corner room with views out over the ocean on two sides. When Maddison had been the live-in maid she had always pretended that the room was hers. It wasn't the largest or the fanciest, but the views were superb and the sloping ceiling gave it a quaint, old-fashioned air.

'Thank you.' Maddison picked up her fork, not needing much more encouragement to get stuck in. Maybe it was the sea air, maybe the best night's sleep she had had in years, but she had woken with a hearty appetite. 'This looks amazing but you really shouldn't have gone to so much trouble.' Maybe not, but seeing as she *had*… Maddison speared a piece of bacon and pancake, dousing them liberally in the amber syrup, before allowing herself to savour the taste. 'I need to get in touch with the office and take some leave officially. I just kind of left…'

Did she even have a job anymore? After all, she was technically absent without leave; she doubted she could claim compassionate leave for an imaginary family crisis. How could she, organized, always-planning-ahead Maddison, have just walked out on her job—would there even be a place for her in New York? Maddison shivered, cold despite the sun on her shoulders. She had thrown everything away in her impetuous flight.

The doorbell rang and Maddison pushed her chair back, automatically readying herself to answer it. 'Don't be silly, dear. You eat.' Lydia gave her a gentle push back into her seat as she walked past her and into the hallway.

Maddison scooped some more food onto her fork but didn't move it off her plate, her mind whirring. She would do what she had to here and then what? Sort out her job situation. Contact Kit.

Should she have left Kit without telling him how she felt?

How could she have told him when she'd barely admitted it to herself?

'Maddison.' She looked up as Lydia called her. There was a curious tone in her voice, curiosity mixed with satisfaction. 'It's for you.'

For her? Who on earth could be visiting her? Maybe someone at the inn had mentioned seeing her, maybe an old school friend had heard that she was back—but no, she hadn't been much of one for friends. Her high-school boyfriend had married in his early twenties, but even if he hadn't she couldn't imagine he'd cared enough about her to hotfoot it over the second she sailed back into town.

Her stomach shifted and she clasped one hand to it. Surely not her mother…

Maddison got to her feet, reaching out to the table for support, and moved slowly into the hallway and blinked, trying to focus on the tall, dishevelled man standing there. 'Kit?' She wasn't sure if she thought it, breathed it or shouted his name aloud. 'What are you doing here? You look tired,' she added as he came into focus. His skin was almost grey, his eyes bloodshot and his chin darker than usual with extra stubble.

'Isn't that the point of a red eye? I left London yesterday afternoon, spent several hours in Toronto and landed in Boston…' he checked his watch, swaying a little as he did so '…about three hours ago.'

He sounded so matter-of-fact. As if his turning up here were completely normal. She blinked. 'But why?'

'If I were you, Maddison, I would take poor Mr Buchanan into the kitchen and feed him coffee and pancakes before you interrogate him any further. I am heading out for the day so please both make yourselves at home. There are spare bathing suits and towels in the drying room if you want to go to the beach. Help yourself to anything you need.'

Before Maddison could say anything Lydia had whisked out of the door, leaving them quite alone. She stood still, staring at Kit. She wanted to touch him, check she wasn't imagining things, but she didn't quite dare.

'Was that coffee I heard mentioned?' Kit asked hopefully. 'I drank at least a gallon in Boston before collecting the hire car but I think it wore off somewhere around Plymouth.'

'Coffee? Yes, come on in.' It *must* be a dream, Maddison decided as she led him through into the kitchen. In which case she was going with it; she hadn't had a dream this comforting in, well, in forever.

There was still a stack of pancakes in the warmer and some bacon in the pan and she ladled a substantial helping of both onto a plate, handing them and a large mug of coffee to Kit.

He received them rapturously, almost inhaling the first cup of coffee and half the plate of food before leaning back with a satisfied stretch. 'These are good. I couldn't get a first-class flight or a direct flight so I have suffered more hours than I care to admit of limited leg room and plastic food. But for these pancakes I would fly all the way to Australia.'

'But you didn't fly all this way for pancakes.' Maddison pushed her plate away; even Kit's hearty enjoyment of his breakfast hadn't rekindled her appetite.

'No.'

'How did you find me?'

'It's a good thing I like treasure hunts. You've covered your tracks pretty well. Actually,' he confessed, pouring a second large cup of coffee, 'I didn't. Expect to find you here, that is. This address was my first—and only—clue.'

Maddison cast around for the words that would some-how make it all right. The words that would make her worthy of a man who had flown across the world to find her with nothing but an old address to spark the hunt. She didn't have them.

'Why?'

'I wanted to make sure you're all right.'

She stared at him incredulously. 'You wanted to make sure I was all right? So you flew to Toronto and then to Boston and then drove here just to check up on me?'

'That about sums it up,' he agreed. 'I was worried about you. I didn't handle Scotland very well.' His eyes gleamed with warmth and something deeper, something she hadn't seen in them before and yet recognized in-stantly.

Maddison was suddenly, unaccountably shy. She didn't know if she could handle whatever he'd come here to say, not yet. Not until she'd done what she'd come here to do. 'How tired are you?'

'I don't know. Part of me is so wired on caffeine and sunshine I could run a marathon, the other part exhausted enough to sleep for the proverbial hundred years. Why?'

'I wondered if you wanted to go on a treasure hunt. With me.'

Kit smiled then, a slow, sweet smile that wiped the weariness off his face, and Maddison's heart leapt as she watched his eyes spark back to life. 'A treasure hunt? What's the prize?'

She wanted to answer *me* but how could she presume

he wanted her, would think her any kind of prize? Sure, he had flown here but he hadn't told her why, had made no move towards her, uttered no words of love. It might have been pique or anger that had set him off to hunt her down.

'I'm not sure,' she said instead. 'But we'll know it when we find it.'

CHAPTER FOURTEEN

SHE LOOKED VULNERABLE: too thin, too pale, all the vitality leached out of her, and all Kit wanted to do was hold her close and tell her that it didn't matter, none of it mattered. But he couldn't, not yet. Because to her it did. And that meant it mattered to him too. Whatever Maddison had returned home to do, he would support her with, help her with.

Maddison drove, pointing out that he hadn't slept in goodness knew how many hours and was liable to find himself on the wrong side of the road even if he didn't doze off, and Kit didn't argue, happy to sit relaxed in the passenger seat, enjoying the view. Maddison's home town was picture-perfect, all blue skies, beaches and quirky, local shops all located in painted, wood-shingled buildings. It was like a film set.

'So, what are we looking for?' he asked at last as she turned into a small housing development. Cheerful detached houses sat on hilly lots, each garden flowing into the next, trees all around them. He could imagine children biking up the driveways, playing ball by the hoops fastened in many of the garage roofs.

She didn't answer for a long moment, pulling up outside a corner house. It was a pretty blue wooden house, a covered porch on one side. Maddison stared at it, her heart in her eyes. 'Me,' she said finally. 'We're looking for me. I want to see where it all went wrong, where I went wrong.'

He wanted to contradict her, tell her that she didn't have a wrong bone in her body, but he sensed this wasn't what she needed, not today, and instead just nodded. He'd guessed as much. 'Okay. Is this where we start?'

'This was my grandma's house.' She killed the engine and shifted to face him, her eyes very green in her pale face. 'My mom was very young when she had me and I didn't know my dad. When I was little she worked a lot so I came here. My grandma told me that she wished I could live there forever and I wished it too, that I could spend every night in my little yellow bedroom with the rocking horse. But my mom wanted to prove she could do it on her own and so most evenings she'd pick me up and take me home. Then, when I was seven, I got my wish. We moved in. Only my grandma was really sick.' Her mouth quivered.

Kit wanted to pull her in tight and tell her everything was okay. But it wasn't, not yet. Not until she had told him, whatever she needed to. 'Then what happened?'

Maddison stared at the house, her eyes unfocused as if she could see her younger self playing in the wooded yard. 'Then she died. My mom was supposed to inherit the house, only there were medical bills and she had to sell it. I think that's when it all got too much for her.'

'How about you? How did it affect you?'

She didn't answer for a long moment, her hands twisting in her lap, then turned back to the wheel and re-started the engine. It wasn't until she was backing out of the driveway that she answered, her voice hoarse with repressed tears. 'Like I'd lost my world. I guess I had.'

It took nearly a quarter of an hour to reach her next

destination. Maddison headed out of town before taking an abrupt turn down an untreated road, the woods encroaching on both sides of the rough track. At various intervals the trees were hacked back and small cottages or trailers built in the scrubby wastelands. Kit held on as the car bumped over stones and potholes. 'I hope you got a good insurance deal,' he said through gritted teeth.

Maddison didn't answer, her focus on the road ahead. Finally, just when Kit was sure his insides had been turned into a cocktail definitely shaken not stirred, she pulled into a rough clearing. At the back, on breeze blocks, stood a trailer, the windows boarded up and the door swinging off its hinges. Surely not...

Kit stared at the trailer, unable to disguise his revulsion. 'Please tell me this is where you lost your virginity or went all Blair Witch,' he said. 'Please don't tell me you lived here.' But she was afraid of the dark. She'd mentioned being hungry and cold. He'd known it was bad. He just had hoped it wasn't this bad.

'It was only meant to be temporary. Till Mom got some money and a proper job.' Her voice cracked. 'We had a fund, the Maddison and Mom fund, and we were going to use it to travel, to get a proper house, to go to Disneyland. But it was hard to save even before Grandma died and afterwards...I'd get ill or needed new shoes or there were bills and so the fund kept getting depleted even though Mom worked all the time.'

'Who looked after you while she worked?' But he already knew the answer. 'You were a child. Alone, out here?'

'She said I was never to tell. That if they knew they'd take me away.'

Kit thought back to his own wild childhood. Roaming free, swimming, sailing, hiking, utterly secure in his parents' love. He'd never realized just how lucky he had been. How lucky he still was in many ways. How much he had taken for granted, how much he had pushed away.

Maddison carried on, her voice expressionless, as if she were reading from a script. 'She got more and more tired and then she was just angry all the time. One night she picked up the phone to call for pizza and the phone had been cut off. She was so mad, swearing and screaming and kicking things—and then she left. Picked up her car keys and walked away. I thought she'd gone for pizza but she didn't come back and when I woke in the morning she was passed out on the sofa. She'd never really drunk before that but I think she just needed to stop thinking—and the drink helped her forget for a time at least.'

It didn't take too much detective work to guess the rest. 'And she carried on drinking?'

Maddison nodded. 'Soon I became that child, you know, the one no one wants to sit next to in case they catch something. It's hard to keep clean when the hot water is cut off and you don't have a washing machine. It's hard to look smart when all your clothes are second-hand.' Her voice dripped with bitterness and Kit's heart ached to hear it. Ached for the lonely, neglected child.

'And no one did anything? Your teachers? Social workers?'

'A few tried to talk to me but I said I was fine. I didn't want to be taken away. This might not look like much but it was all I knew. Mom made just enough of an effort when she had to come in to school, at least she did back then. I'm glad she's not still here,' she said, her voice shaking. 'I'm glad she got out.'

The trailer looked like no one had lived there for a very long time and Kit was relieved when Maddison reversed and pulled away. He wasn't sure he could have looked inside the trailer and not cracked. 'Do you know where she is?'

'Mrs Stanmeyer said she got clean the year I left. Apparently she finally got her degree and got a job as a teacher, can you believe it? Married three years ago and moved to Chatham. She has a little girl, she's about two. My sister.'

'Are you going to go and see her?'

Maddison's mouth trembled. 'I haven't decided.'

'I'll come with you, if you want me to.'

'Thank you. Not today. I'm not ready. But maybe tomorrow.'

She was talking about tomorrow. With him. Kit waited for panic to hit him but it was gone as if it had never been. Tomorrow was just a word.

'Okay, in that case, where next?'

'Next?' Her mouth curved into an unexpected smile. 'Clue Three. The reinvention of Maddison Carter.'

She took them back into town, driving straight through the centre and turning into a large car park situated beside playing fields and an official-looking building that proclaimed itself 'Bayside High, Home of the Sea Hawks.'

'Sea Hawks, huh?' Kit tried to lighten the mood. 'Were you a cheerleader? I bet you looked amazing in one of those skirts.'

'No, girls like me didn't get to be cheerleaders. Although you're right, I would have looked pretty darn good in that skirt.'

'So which were you? The jock, the princess. The geek? Ally Sheedy?'

He was relieved to hear her choke out a laugh. 'Which do you think? I was Ally Sheedy both before and after the makeover. Only mine was better. A real reinvention.'

'I'm glad to hear it.'

'In junior high I began working. I was too young for a proper job so I hustled for work: babysitting, car washing, grocery shopping, anything I could do to get money so I could dress better, get a bike, try and fit in. By the time I reached high school I knew I needed more. I needed to take control of my life so I took on as much work as I could get, studied like mad and started to plan my exit route. I moved out the day I turned sixteen and became a live-in maid at Mrs Stanmeyer's.'

'At sixteen? Was that even legal?'

Maddison nodded. 'She hated that I insisted on working. She would have let me have a room for free, helped me out with money for much less work, but I refused any sign of charity—I'd been the town's trash for long enough. I wanted to earn every cent, make sure everyone knew I wasn't like my mother. I loved living there. I had the room over the garage. It was the first time I'd felt safe in a really long time.' There was a wealth of untold detail in that last statement and Kit curled his hands into fists, hating how it was too late to make any of it all right.

'I just wanted to fit in,' she almost whispered. 'I wanted to be one of the cool kids, the ones who were so secure they knew exactly who they were and what they deserved.'

'That's understandable.'

'It was no use trying with the girls, my social status was too low. So I targeted the boys. Targeted one boy. It was almost too easy. I could afford to dress better, get my hair cut and I knew boys liked to look at me. The next step was finding out what else he liked and making sure I liked it too, that we met at the same movies, in the same comic-book store, that we always had something to talk about. No one could believe it, Jim Squires, captain of the football team, and Maddison Carter. But when he held my hand in the hallway or I wore his varsity jacket I knew I belonged. At last. I was safe.

'That's when I knew what I wanted. I wanted to leave this Maddison behind and become someone else, the kind of girl who expected to walk down a hallway holding the hottest boy in school's hand, the kind of girl that took dates and friends and proms and an allowance for granted. The kind of girl who had never worked one job, let alone three, who had never set foot inside a trailer. And so when I left here I made it up, invented the life I wished I had. I think at times I even believed my own lies, I've been living them so long. I'm pathetic.'

'Pathetic?' Kit stared at her, incredulous. Was that really what she thought? What she believed? 'You had nothing and you didn't let it stop you. You worked your socks off to achieve your dream. I admire you, Maddison. You're the strongest, bravest person I know. You are absolutely incredible.'

The words reverberated round and round her head, his eyes shining with sincerity and truth. Maddison wanted to believe him but she couldn't, not yet. She pulled away, driving away from the school, away from her memories, away from his words.

Maddison didn't stop until she reached the car park by her favourite beach. She parked haphazardly and jumped out, the sun's warmth a shock after the air-conditioned car. Kit stepped warily out of the car but she didn't acknowledge him, instead turning and walking across the car park, along the boardwalk and past the clam shack until she reached the beach. The smell of fried clams hit her, mingled with the salt in the sea air. The scent of a dozen beach parties.

Despite the heat of the day it was quiet, just a few preschool families about—the schools not due to break up for another couple of weeks. Maddison pulled her shoes off and walked, barefoot, through the foot of the dunes, wincing as her feet struck the heated sand. Kit matched her step for step, not saying a word, allowing her to set the pace.

'I had this fantasy that my dad was one of the summer-home owners. That his parents hadn't let him acknowledge me but that one day he would stride into school and scoop me up and take me away to live that gilded life. They'd come to town, the summer kids, with their platinum credit cards and their boats and their country-club memberships, and I wanted to be one of them so much it actually hurt, right here.' She tapped her chest.

'Once I got to high school I knew that my daddy wasn't coming for me, that he probably didn't even know I existed. But I still wanted that life. When I moved to New York it was with one goal: to find the right man who could give me the right kind of life and marry him.'

Kit nodded. 'All you wanted was a family. You told me that almost straight away. Four children who would have the most perfect childhood ever. I don't think that's such a terrible crime, Maddison. If you wanted to marry for status or jewels or a platinum credit card of your own, then that would be understandable, considering what you've been through, but you didn't. You wanted a family. A family you could keep safe.'

'And then I started to spend time with you.' She stopped and swallowed, trying to find the right words. 'It had all gone wrong. I thought I knew exactly what I was doing, had found the right guy, but Bart derailed all my plans and knocked my confidence. I arrived in the UK knowing I had to start all over again. When you suggested I spend my weekends doing the treasure trails with you I agreed mainly because I thought it might make Bart jealous, but soon it was more. A lot more. I liked your company. I liked you. And I thought, why not? I was only in the UK for a short while, why not have some fun? Deviate from the grand plan just for a while. I didn't expect to fall in love with you.'

Her words hung there as she kept walking, afraid that if she stopped or turned back then he would walk away. Would leave her. 'But I did. I did fall in love with you. Me, Maddison Carter with my plans and my dreams and my whole *love is for losers* mindset. Guess I wasn't as good at the game as I thought, huh? The ironic thing was that if you had been anyone else it would have been fine, but how could I tell you the truth when you were so adamant that love wasn't for you? How could I open up when you have the kind of background I've been searching for? What could I say? "Please, Kit, I used to want to marry someone rich and important but that's not why I've fallen for you." I wish you weren't. I wish you didn't have any of it. I don't want you to think I played you. Because when I was with you I wasn't playing at all.'

She hadn't planned on telling him any of this, but once the words had spilled out she realized that she was free. Free of her past, her secrets, her schemes, her plans. She had no idea what happened next but that was okay. And if Kit turned, left and she never saw him again, then that was okay as well because she had given it her best shot. A real shot, not a fake, perfectly thought-out, planned response.

She'd given him her heart.

Maddison turned, drinking him in. The faint sea breeze ruffled his hair as he stood at the foot of the sand dunes, his eyes fixed on the endless ocean. 'Why did you come here, Kit?'

'To find you,' he said simply. 'I left Scotland full of plans and the one person I wanted to share them with wasn't there, had just disappeared. I didn't think you were a quitter, Maddison, in fact I knew you weren't, so for you to just up and disappear? Whatever was going on it seemed to me you needed my help. I wanted to help.'

He passed a hand through his hair, rumpling it into an even more disordered state. 'I was a mess that morning in Scotland. Everything had changed in twenty-four hours. Thanks to you I could confront my feelings about Euan, admit it wasn't just guilt I felt but anger—anger at him for dying, for competing, for not fighting hard enough that night. Anger at myself for pushing him. For holding on to my bitterness when I had long since fallen out of love with Eleanor. Thanks to you I really spoke to my dad, about that night, about the future.'

'Sounds intense.'

'Oh, it was quite the fishing session. And then there was you. In my bed. Making me feel things I still wasn't ready to face—that I had been in no way the kind of man that deserved a girl like you. It seemed easier to just let you go but as soon as you were gone I realized I wanted to fix everything, fix me, make myself worthy of you.'

He stepped close and took her hand. 'I missed you, Maddison. I missed you planning every little detail, I missed you searching out every clue, I missed you finishing my crossword, I even missed that damn list. I missed the way you challenge me.' His eyes dropped to her mouth. 'You only spent two nights in my bed but I haven't slept right since. My dreams are full of you, Maddison Carter.'

'I had to come back here,' Maddison said, needing him to understand. 'I needed to face who I was, who I am now. But all I see is that if you're not with me then my life is empty, even with all the security in the world. You flew across the world for me.' Her mouth wobbled. 'I don't deserve that.'

Kit raised one of her hands to his lips and her heart leapt at the old-fashioned gesture. 'You do. You deserve it all. All the security your heart desires.' He smiled down at her. 'Four children, the house, anything you need.'

'Your family needs you, Kit. Your father needs you even if he won't say so.'

'I know and I have obligations in Kilcanon that I've ignored for long enough. I hope you would be happy to spend some of the year there, but we wouldn't have to live in Scotland all the time. We could have a place in London or a house here on the Cape, whatever you wanted.' His mouth twisted into a smile. 'Fourth of July, clambakes, hayrides, Thanksgiving—I'm willing to give it all a try.'

The last clamp finally loosened from her heart. 'I think as long as we're together I have everything I need.'

'So you're saying yes?'

'To what?' But she knew; it was in the blazing blue of his eyes, the curve of his mouth, the heat in his hands.

'To me, to us, to forever.'

Maddison finally allowed herself to reach up, to pull his head down to hers, to press her mouth to his. It was like coming home at long, long last. 'Yes,' she breathed against the warmth of his lips. 'I'm saying yes. To forever.'

EPILOGUE

One year later

KIT SHIFTED FROM foot to foot, anxiously scanning the rows of chairs, looking beyond the seated people to the sun-filled horizon beyond. *Where is she?* He took a deep breath. He should be calmer; after all, they *were* actually already married. Maddison had been very keen to marry him in his kilt but had reluctantly conceded that the Cape Cod beach in summer wasn't the most appropriate place for thickly woven wool and a formal tux—and Kit hadn't wanted to wait a full year before claiming his bride. The answer was a happy compromise—two weddings. A small, private spring service in Kilcanon church and now, two months later, a blessing and party on the Cape.

He scanned the rows of people, all decked out in their summer best: his parents and Bridget were in the front row, looking relaxed and happy after a couple of weeks of sun and playing tourist. His father seemed years younger—handing some of the business responsibilities over to Kit had obviously relieved him of a great burden. They still clashed—they wouldn't be Buchanans if they didn't—but his father grudgingly admitted that some of Kit's ideas weren't too crazy and had thrown himself into setting up the new distillery with enthusiasm. Bridget had finished university this month and had asked Kit if there was a place for her on the family estate, an offer he had accepted straight away. Bridget's presence would make it easier for Maddison and him to spend the summers and long vacations here on the Cape, just as he had promised her they would.

Next to the Buchanans sat a beaming Mrs Stanmeyer clutching a hanky just in case—she had cried throughout the first wedding and had declared her intention to do exactly the same this time round. Further back Kit noticed Hope, his old assistant, clutching the hand of a handsome dark-haired man, a soft smile on her face.

In the back row a beautiful woman in her early forties sat tensely on the aisle seat, her hands locked, her face set. Maddison still didn't have an easy relationship with her mother, their interactions were very formal and stilted, but they were both trying. But he knew that Maddison adored being a big sister, having blood kin of her own. And, stilted or not, Maddison had hosted Thanksgiving in the house they had bought on the Cape with her family, old and new, around her.

And at that moment the aria she loved so much began to swell out all around them, the guests got to their feet and Kit turned, met a pair of sparkling green eyes and was lost once again.

Maddison hadn't wanted to be given away—after all, she didn't have anyone to ask—so instead of leaning on someone else's arm she was clasping a small hand. It might not be customary for the bride and her flower girl to walk down the aisle hand in hand but Savannah wasn't just a flower girl, she was her little sister. She was hope. Testament that people could change, that the future was unwritten.

The small hand tugged at hers and Maddison bent down.

'Kit looks really handsome,' her small sister whispered and Maddison dropped a kiss on the fair curls, careful not to disturb the carefully arranged flowers. 'I know,' she whispered back.

He didn't look as formally handsome as he had in Kilcanon, clad in the black and green family tartan, but she liked the soft grey linen suit almost as much, just as she loved this flowing, simple lace dress she was wearing as much as the corseted, fuller wedding gown she had worn in Scotland. No veil this time, just fresh flowers in her hair, her feet bare as she walked through the sand towards the sea, towards her groom, towards her future.

She couldn't believe that it was all real. That this was her life now. The sand squished beneath her bare toes, the sea rippled just a few metres away and the sun beat steadily down, but it all felt like a dream. A perfect dream. It wasn't the future she'd thought she'd wanted but it was a million times better.

Maddison had kept her job at DL Media for the first few months of their engagement while Kit juggled freelance editing with revitalizing the Buchanan estate, but he had asked her advice so often she had ended up taking a formal role in Scotland, overseeing all the marketing of the estate and its various subsidiaries. It meant spending the bulk of the year in Scotland but Kit had promised they would always return to the beachside cottage here in Bayside for the summers, for Thanksgiving and any other time she wanted to see her sister, and Maddison loved the dramatic Scottish coastline. It felt like home.

The music died down as she reached the end of the

aisle and she let go of Savannah's hand, offering hers to
Kit instead. How could she feel so shy? Almost unable
to look him in the eye. They were already married, after
all! But here she was, standing here, in front of the community she had hidden from, run from and returned to,
promising once again to worship Kit body and soul and
listening to his steady voice promise her the same.

The official closed her book and smiled. 'I now pro-
nounce you husband and wife. You may now kiss the
bride.'

Kit's eyes darkened with intent and Maddison's pulse
began to race. Their friends and family were all on their
feet, clapping, but the sound died away as the blood
pounded in her ears and the world narrowed until all
she could see was Kit. 'My favourite part,' he murmured
as he stepped closer. Maddison quivered as his hands
lightly caressed her bare shoulders and he leaned in to
brush her mouth with his. She closed her eyes and fell
into the deepening kiss, pulling him closer, not wanting
the moment to end.

She'd never thought that girls like her would get a happily ever after but today, in this moment, she was more
than happy for Kit to prove her wrong—and to keep proving her wrong. Forever.

* * * * *

HER HOT
HIGHLAND DOC

BY
ANNIE O'NEIL

Annie O'Neil spent most of her childhood with her leg draped over the family rocking chair and a book in her hand. Novels, baking and writing too much teenage angst poetry ate up most of her youth. Now Annie splits her time between corralling her husband into helping her with their cows, baking, reading, barrel racing (not really!) and spending some very happy hours at her computer, writing.

This book goes out to—and I'm stealing her phrase here—the best friend I never met: the marvellous Nettybean. She's always there for me and I am ever grateful. Thanks, Netts—hope you don't mind having to go to an inclement Scottish island for a big slice of gratitude pie!

Annie O' xx

CHAPTER ONE

No amount of torrential rain unforgivingly lashing his face would equal the storm brewing inside of Brodie McClellan. Not today. Not tomorrow. A month of Sundays wouldn't come close.

And yet he had to laugh…even though everything he was feeling was about as far off the spectrum of "funny ha-ha" as laughter could get. He'd seen death on a near daily basis for the months he'd been away, but this one…? This one had him soul-searching in the one place he'd longed to leave behind. *Blindsided* didn't even come close to what he was feeling.

"Hey, Dad."

He crouched low to the ground, unable to resist leveling out a small hillock of soft soil soaked through with the winter rains. The earth appeared months away from growing even a smattering of grass to cover his father's grave. It was no surprise that his brother hadn't come good on his promise to lay down some turf. It was difficult enough to drag him down from the mountains, let alone—

Enough. Callum had a good heart, and he had to be hurting, too.

Brodie dragged his fingers through the bare earth again. Time would change it. Eventually. It would become like his mother's—the grave just to the left. The one he still couldn't bear to look at. He moved his fingers behind him, feeling long-established grass. A shocking contrast to the bare earth in front of him.

Yes, time would change it. Just as it had all the graves, each one protected with a thick quilt of green. Time he didn't have nor wanted to give to Dunregan. Not after all it had taken from him.

He scanned the parameters of the graveyard with a growing sense of familiarity. Brodie had spent more time here in the past fortnight than he had in a lifetime of growing up on the island. Asking, too late, for answers to all the questions he should have asked before he'd left Dunregan in his wake.

Gray. It was all he could see. Gray headstones. Gray skies. Gray stones making up the gray walls. A color washout.

He ran a hand across the top of his father's headstone. "We'll get this place fixed up for you, Father. All right? Put in some flowers or something."

A memory pinged into his head of Callum and himself, digging up snowdrop bulbs when he'd been just a young boy. His father counting out a few pence for each cluster. He swiped his face to clear off the rain, surprised to discover he was smiling at the memory of his paltry pocket money. The small towers of copper pennies had seemed like riches at the time.

"I'll get you some snowdrops, eh, Dad? Those'll be nice. And some bluebells later on? For you and Mum. She always loved bluebell season."

He shook his head when he realized he was waiting for an answer.

"It's a bit of a nightmare at the clinic. I've had to call in a locum. It'll buy me time until I figure out how to explain to folk that it's okay. *I'm* okay."

He looked up to the skies again, unsurprised to find his mood was still as turbulent as the weather. Wind was blowing every which where. Rain was coming in thick bursts. Cold. It was so ruddy *cold* up here on Dunregan.

He pressed his hands to his thighs, stood up and cursed softly. Mud. All over his trousers.

For the few minutes it took to drive home Brodie tried his best to plumb a good mood from somewhere in the depths of his heart. He wasn't this guy. This growling, frowning man whose image he kept catching in the rear-view mirror. He was a loving son. Older sibling to a free-spirited younger brother. Cousin, nephew, friend. And yet he felt like a newcomer. A stranger amidst a sea of familiarity. A man bearing more emotional weight on his shoulders than he'd ever carried before.

He pulled the car into the graveled drive in front of the family home, only to jam the brakes on.

"What the—?"

Wood. A huge stack of timber filling the entire driveway. He'd barely spoken to anyone since he'd returned to Dunregan, let alone ordered a pile of wood!

Brodie jumped out of his four-by-four and searched for a delivery note. He found it tucked under a stack of quarter-inch plywood. His eyes scanned the paper. The list of cuts and types of wood all began to slot into place, take on form…build one very particular item.

The boat.

The boat he and his father had always promised they would build.

The one he'd never been able to think about after that day when he'd come home from sailing without his mother.

Another sharp sting of emotion hit and stuck in his throat.

Today.

All he had to do was get through today. And then tomorrow he'd do it all over again, and then one more time until the pain began to ebb, like the tides surrounding the island he'd once called home.

Kali's grip tightened on her handlebars.

The elements vs the cyclist.

Game on.

She lifted her head, only to receive a blast of wind straight in the face. Her eyes streamed. Her nose was threatening to run. Her hair…? That pixie cut she'd been considering might've been a good idea. So much for windswept and interesting. Windswept and bedraggled was more like it—but she couldn't keep the grin off her face.

Starting over—*again*—was always going to be an uphill struggle, but she hadn't thought this particular life reboot would be so *physical*!

Only one hundred more meters between Mother Nature's finest blasts of Arctic wind and a hot cup of tea. Who would win? Fledgling GP? Or the frigid forces of Scotland's northernmost islands?

Another briny onslaught of wind and sea spray sent Kali perilously close to the ditch. A ditch full of…*ugh*. One glimpse of the ice-skinned murk convinced her to swing a leg off her vintage-style bicycle and walk. A blast of icy water shot up from her feet along her legs, giving her whole body a wiggle of chills. She looked down at the puddle her ballerina flats–clad feet had landed in.

Splatterville. A shopping trip for boots and a proper jacket might be in order. So much for the romantic idea of tootling along Dunregan's coast road and showing up to her first day of work with rosy-cheeked panache. There were tulips blooming all over the place in London! How long was it going to take the Isle of Dunregan to catch up?

"Dr. O'Shea?"

A cheery fifty-something woman rode up alongside

her, kitted out in a thick waterproof jacket, boots, woolen mittens, hat…everything Kali should've been wearing but wasn't. Her green eyes crackled with mischief…or was that just the weather?

"Yes." Kali smiled, then grimaced as the wind took a hold of her facial features. She must look like some sort of rubber-lipped cartoon character by now!

"Ailsa Dunregan." She hopped off her bike and walked alongside Kali, and laughed when Kali's eyes widened. "Yes. I know, it's mad, isn't it? Same name as the island. Suffice it to say, my family—or at least my husband's family—has been here a long time. *My* family's only been here a few hundred years."

Hundred?

"How'd you know it was me?"

Ailsa threw back her head and laughed. The sound was instantly yanked away by the wind. "Only someone not from Dunregan would—"

Kali struggled to make out what she was saying, her own thoughts fighting with the wind and making nothing comprehensible.

"Sorry?" Kali tried to push her bike a bit closer and keep up the brisk pace the woman was setting.

"I'm the practice nurse!" Ailsa shouted against the elements. "I get all the gossip, same as the publican, and not too many people come to the island this time of year."

Kali nodded, only just managing to keep her bike upright with the approach of another gust.

"It has its merits!" Kali shouted back when she'd regained her footing.

"You think?" Ailsa hooted another laugh into the stratosphere. "If you're after a barren, desolate landscape…" she groaned as her own cycle was nearly whipped out of her hands "…you've come to the right place!"

As if by mutual agreement they both put their heads down, inching their cycles along the verge. Kali smiled into the cozy confines of her woolen scarf—her one practical nod to the subzero temperature. Compared to the other obstacles she'd faced, this one was easy-peasy. Just a healthy handful of meters between her and her new life.

No more hiding. No more looking over her shoulder. Okay, so she still had a different name, thanks to the heaven-sent Forced Marriage Protection Unit, and there were a boatload of other issues to deal with one day—but right here, right now, with the wind blowing more than the cobwebs away, she felt she really was Kali O'Shea. Correction! *Dr.* Kali O'Shea. Safe and sound on the uppermost Scottish Isle of Dunregan.

As if it had actual fingers, the frigid tempest abruptly yanked her bicycle out of her hands, sending her into a swan dive onto the rough pavement and the bicycle skidding into the ditch. The *deep* ditch. The one she'd have to clamber into and probably shred her tights.

She looked down at her knees as she pressed herself up from the pavement. Nope! That job was done already. *Nice one, Kali.* So much for renaming herself after the goddess of empowerment. The goddess of grace might've been a better choice.

"Oh, no! Are you all right, darlin'?" Ailsa was by her side in a minute.

Kali fought the prick of tears, pressing her hands to her scraped knees to regroup. *C'mon, Kali. You're a grown woman now.*

If only...

No. Focus on the positives. She didn't do "if onlys" anymore.

"What's going on here?"

A pair of sturdy leather boots appeared in Kali's

eyeline. They must go with the rich Scottish brogue she was hearing.

"You pulling patients in off the streets now, Ailsa?"

Kali's eyes zipped up the long legs, skidded across the thick wax jacket and landed soundly on… Ooh… She'd never let herself think she had a type, but this walking, talking advert for a Scandi-Scottish fisherman type with… ooh, again!…the most beautiful cornflower-blue eyes…

She swallowed.

He might be it. There was something about him that said…*safe*.

Thirtyish? With a straw-blond thatch of hair and a strong jawline covered in facial hair a few days past designer stubble to match. She'd never thought she was one to go for a beardy guy, but with this weather suddenly it made sense. She wondered how it would feel against her cheek. Reassuringly scratchy or unexpectedly soft?

She blinked away the thought and refocused.

He was no city mouse. That was for sure. It wouldn't be much of a step to picture him on a classic motorbike, lone wolfing it along the isolated coastline. And he was tall. *Well*… Everyone was tall compared to her, but he had a nice, strong, mountain-climber thing going on. You didn't see too many men like that in London. Perhaps they were all hiding out here, in Scotland's subarctic islands, waiting to rescue city slickers taken out by the elements.

"All right, darlin'?" He put a hand on her shoulder, his eyes making a quick visual assessment, gave a satisfied nod and headed for the steep embankment. "Here, I'll just grab your bicycle for you."

Chivalrous to boot!

Strange how she didn't even know him and yet her shoulder seemed to almost miss his touch when he turned toward the ditch.

Kali's hormones all but took over her brain, quickly re-dressing her Knight in Shining Gore-tex in Viking clothes. Then a kilt. And then a slick London suit, just to round off the selection. Yes. They all fit. Every bit as much as his hardy all-weather gear was complementing him now. Maybe he'd just come from an outdoor-clothing catalog shoot.

"Brodie?" Ailsa called to him as he affected a surfing-style skid down the embankment toward the ditch. "She's no patient! This is Kali O'Shea. The new GP."

"Ah."

Brodie came to a standstill, hands shifting up to his hips. His bright blue eyes ricocheted up to Kali, to Ailsa and then back to Kali before he took a decisive step back up the bank.

Kali's eyes widened.

Was he taking back his generous offer?

Abruptly he knelt, grabbed the bike by a single handle and tugged it out of the ditch.

"Here you are, then."

In two long-legged strides he was back atop the embankment, handing over the bike as if it were made out of pond scum…which, now, it kind of was. In two more he was slamming the door to his seen-better-days four-by-four, which he'd parked unceremoniously in the middle of the road.

Brake lights on. Brake lights off.

And with a crunch of gravel and tarmac…away he went.

"Oh, now…" Ailsa sent Kali a mortified look. "That was no way…" She shook her head. "I've never seen him behaving…"

The poor woman didn't seem to be able to form a full sentence. Kali shook her head, to tell her that it didn't matter, nearly choking on a laugh as she did. Her Viking-Fisherman-Calendar Boy's behavior was certainly one

way to make an impression! A bit young to be so eccentric, but…welcome to Dunregan!

She shook her head again and grinned. This whole pala-
ver would be a great story to tell when— Well… She was
bound to make friends at some juncture. This was her new
beginning, and if Mr. Cranky Pants' sole remit was to be
eye candy…so be it.

She waved off Ailsa's offer to help, took a hold of the
muddy handlebars, and smiled through the spray of mud
and scum coming off the spokes as she walked. She was
already going to have to change clothes—might as well
complete the Ugly Duckling thing she had going on.

"I am *so* sorry. Brodie's not normally so rude," Ailsa
apologized.

"Who is he?"

"Don't you know?" Ailsa's eyes widened in dismay.

A nervous jag shot through Kali's belly as she shook her
head. Then the full wattage of realization hit.

"If I were to guess we were going to see him again at
the clinic, would I be right?"

"You'd be right if you guessed you would see his name
beside the clinic door, inside the waiting room and on the
main examination room."

"*He's* Dr. McClellan?"

*Terrific! In a really awkward how-on-earth-is-this-going-
to-work? sort of way.*

Kali tried her best to keep her face neutral.

"You'll hear a lot of folk refer to him as *Young* Dr. Mc-
Clellan. The practice was originally his father's, but sadly
he passed on just recently." Her lips tightened fractionally.
She looked at the expanse of road, as if searching for a
bit more of an explanation, then returned her gaze to Kali
with an apologetic smile. "I'm afraid Brodie's not exactly
the roll-out-the-red-carpet type."

Kali couldn't help but smile at the massive understatement.

"More the practical type, eh? Well, that's no bad thing." Kali was set on finding "the bright side." Just like the counselor at the shelter had advised her.

She could hear the woman's words as clearly as if she'd heard them a moment ago. "It will be difficult, living without any contact with your family. But, on the bright side, your life can be whatever you'd like it to be now."

The words had pinged up in neon in her mental cinema. It was a near replica of the final words her mother had said to her before she'd fled the family home in the middle of the night, five long years ago. Taking a positive perspective had always got her through her darkest days and today would be no different.

"There's only a wee bit to go." Ailsa tipped her head in the direction of an emerging roofline. "Let's get you inside and see if we can't find some dry clothes for you and a hot cup of tea."

Tea!

Bright side.

Brodie had half a mind to drive straight past the clinic and up into the mountains to try to hunt down his brother. Burn off some energy Callum-style on a mountain bike. He was overdue a catch-up since he'd returned. And it wasn't as if he'd be seeing any patients today anyway.

She would.

The new girl.

He tipped his head back and forth. Better get his facts straight.

The new *woman*.

From the looks of Dr. O'Shea, she was no born-and-bred Scottish lassie, that was for sure. Ebony black hair. Long.

Really long. His fingers involuntarily twitched at the teasing notion of running them through the long, silken swathe. He curled them into a fist and shot his fingers out wide, as if to flick off the pleasurable sensation.

There was more than a hint of South Asia about her. Maybe… Her eyes were a startling light green, and with a surname like O'Shea it was unlikely both of her parents had been Indian born and bred. He snorted. Here he was, angry at the world for making assumptions about him, and he was doing the same thing for poor ol' Kali O'Shea.

When he'd received the email stating a Dr. O'Shea was on her way up he had fully been expecting a red-headed, freckle-faced upstart. Instead she was strikingly beautiful, if not a little wind tousled, like a porcelain doll. With the first light-up-a-room smile he'd seen since he didn't know how long. Not to mention kitted out in entirely inappropriate clothing, riding a ridiculous bicycle on the rough lane and about to begin to do a job he could ruddy well do on his own, thank you very much.

He slowed the car and tugged the steering wheel around in an arc. He'd park behind the building. Leave Kali and Ailsa guessing for a minute. Or ten, given the strength of the gusts they were battling. Why did people insist on riding bicycles in this sort of weather? Ridiculous.

He took his bad mood out on the gear lever, yanking the vehicle into Park and climbing out of the high cab all in one movement.

When his feet landed solidly on the ground it was all too easy to hear his father's voice sounding through his conscience.

You just left her? You left the poor wee thing there on the side of the road, splattered in mud, bicycle covered in muck, and didn't lend a hand? Oh, son… That's not what we islanders are about.

We islanders... Ha! That'd be about right.

And of course his father, the most stalwart of moral compasses, was right. It *wasn't* what Dunreganers were about.

He scrubbed at his hair—a shocker of a reminder that he was long due for a trip to the barber's. He tipped his head up to the stormy skies and barked out a laugh. At least he was free to run his hand through his hair now. And scrub the sleep out of his eyes. Rest his fingers on his lips when in thought...

Not that he'd done much of that lately. A moment's reflection churned up too many images. Things he could never un-see. So it was little wonder his hair was too long, his house was a mess and his life was a shambles ever since he'd returned from Africa. The only thing he was sure of was his status on the island. He'd shot straight up to number one scourge faster than a granny would offer her little 'uns some shortbread.

He slammed his car door shut and dug into his pocket for the practice keys, a fresh wash of rain announcing itself to the already-blustery morning. The one Ailsa and Dr. O'Shea were still battling against.

Fine. All right. He'd been a class-A jerk.

To put it mildly.

He'd put the kettle on. A peace offering to his replacement. *Temporary* replacement, if he could ever convince the islanders that he wasn't contagious. Never had been.

Trust the people who'd known him from the first day he'd taken a breath on this bleak pile of rocks and earth not to believe in the medical clearance he'd received. A clearance he'd received just in time to be at his father's bedside, where they'd been able to make their peace. That was where the first hit of reality had been drilled home. And then there had been the funeral. It was hard to shake off those memories just a fortnight on.

His brother—the stayer—had received the true warmth of the village. Deep embraces. Claps to the shoulder and shared laughter over a fond memory. Only a very few people had shaken hands with him. Everyone else…? Curt nods and a swift exit.

He blamed it on his time in Africa, but his heart told him different. No amount of time would bring back his mother from that sailing trip he'd insisted on taking. No amount of penance would give the island back its brightest rose.

He had thought of giving a talk in the village hall—about Africa, the medicine he'd practiced, the safety precautions he'd taken—but couldn't bear the thought of standing there on his own, waiting for no one to show up, feeling more of an outsider than he had growing up here.

He shoved the old-fashioned key into the clinic's thick wooden door and pushed the bottom right-hand corner with his foot, where it always stuck when the weather was more wet than cold.

The familiarity of it parted his lips in a grudging smile. He knew this building like the back of his hand. Had all but grown up in it. He'd listened to his first heartbeat here, under the watchful eye of his father. Just as he had done most of his firsts on the island. Beneath his father's ever benevolent and watchful eye.

And now, like his father and his father before him, he was taking over the village practice in a place he knew well. *Too* well. He grimaced as the wind helped give the door a final nudge toward opening.

Without looking behind him he tried to shut it and met resistance. He pushed harder. The door pushed back.

"You're certainly choosing an interesting way to welcome our new GP, Brodie."

Ailsa was behind him, trying to keep the door open

for herself and—yes, there she was…just behind Ailsa's shoulder—Dr. Shea.

Dr. *O*'Shea?

Whatever. With the mood he was battling, he was afraid she'd need the luck of the Irish and all of…whatever other heritage it was that he was gleaning.

"Hi, there. I'm Kali." She stepped out from behind Ailsa and put out a scraped hand.

He looked at it and frowned. Another reminder that he should've stuck around to help.

She retracted her hand and wiped it on her mud-stained coat.

"Sorry," she apologized in a soft English accent. One with a lilt. Ireland? It wasn't posh London. "I'm not really looking my best this morning."

"No. Well…"

Brodie gave himself an eye roll. Was it too late to club himself in the forehead and just be done with it?

"Ach, Brodie McClellan! Will you let the poor girl inside so we can get something dry onto her and something hot inside of her?" Ailsa scolded. "Mrs. Glenn dropped some homemade biscuits in yesterday afternoon, when she was out with her dogs. See if you can dig those up while I try and find Dr. O'Shea a towel for all that lovely long hair of hers. And have a scrounge round for some dry clothes, will you?"

"Anything else I can do for you?" he called after the re-treating figure, then remembered there was still another woman waiting. One not brave enough to shove past him as Ailsa had. "C'mon, then. Let's get you out of this weather."

Kali eyed Brodie warily as he stepped to the side with an actual smile, his arm sweeping along the hallway in the manner of a charming butler. Hey, presto! And…the White

Knight was back in the room. Sort of. His blue eyes were still trained on the car park behind her, as if the trick had really been to make her disappear.

Kali quirked a curious eyebrow as she passed him. Not exactly Prince Charming, was he? *But, my goodness me, he smells delicious.* All sea-peaty and freshly baked bread. With butter. A bit of earthiness was in there, too. An islander. And she was on his turf.

She hid a smile as she envisioned herself helming a Viking invasion ship, a thick fur stole shifting across her shoulders as she pointed out to her crew that she saw land. A raven-haired Vikingess!

Unable to stop the vision, she mouthed, *Land-ho!* with a grin.

Oops! Her eyes flicked to Brodie's. His gaze was still trained elsewhere. Probably just as well.

She looked down the long corridor. A raft of closed doors and not much of a clue as to what was behind them.

"Um…where should I be heading?"

"Down the hall and to your left. First door on your right once you turn. You'll find Ailsa there in the supplies cupboard."

Brodie closed the outside door and rubbed his hands together briskly, his body taut with energy, as if someone had just changed his batteries.

He had a lovely voice. All rich and rolling *r*'s and broguey. If he weren't so cantankerous… She tilted her head to take another look. Solid jawline, arrestingly blue eyes bright with drive, thick hair a girl could be tempted to run her fingers through.

Yup! Brodie McClellan ticked a lot of boxes. He might be a grump, but he didn't strike her as someone cruel. In fact he seemed rather genuine behind the abruptness.

She envied him that. A man who, in a split second, came

across as true to himself. Honest. Even if that honesty *was* as scratchy as sandpaper. Her eyes slid down his arms to his hands. Long, capable fingers, none of which sported a ring. *Huh*... A lone wolf with no designs on joining a pack.

She shook her head, suddenly aware that the lone wolf was speaking to her, though his eyes were trained on his watch.

"So...you'll want to get a move on. I'll just put the kettle on and see you in a couple of minutes so I can talk you through everything, all right? Doors open soon."

He turned into a nearby doorway without further ado. Seconds later Kali could hear a tap running and the familiar sound of a kettle being filled.

Note to self, she thought as her lips twitched into yet another smile, *civilities are a bit different up here.*

None of the normal *How do you do? I'm Dr. fill-in-the-blank, welcome to our clinic. Here's the tea, here's the kettle, put your name on your lunch if you're brave enough to use the staff refrigerator, and we hope you enjoy your time with us, blah-de-blah-de-blah.*

Dr. Brodie McClellan's greeting was the sort of brusque behavior she'd expect in an over-taxed big-city hospital. But here in itsy-bitsy Dunregan, when the clinic wasn't even set to open for another...she glanced at her waterlogged watch...half hour or so... Perhaps he *wasn't* too young to be eccentric. She was going to go with her original assessment. Too honest a human to bother with bog standard social niceties. Even though social niceties were...*nice.*

A clatter of mugs on a countertop broke the silence, followed by some baritone mutterings she couldn't make out.

Well, so what if her new colleague wasn't tuning up the marching band to trill her merrily into her first shift? She'd faced higher hurdles than winning over someone who had obviously flunked out of Charm Academy.

Kali leaned against the wall for a minute. Just to breathe. Realign her emotional bearings. She closed her eyes to see if she could picture the letter inviting her to come to Dunregan. She'd been so ridiculously happy when it had arrived. With so much time "at sea" it had been a moment of pure, unadulterated elation. When the image of the letter refused to come, she pulled her phone out of her pocket so she could pull it up from her emails.

The screen was cracked. Shattered, more like it.

Of course it is! shouted the voice in her head. *It's the least you deserve after what you've done. The trouble you've caused your mother. Your little sister.*

She pressed her hands to her ears, as if that would help silence the voice she fought and fought to suppress on a daily basis.

She huffed a sigh across her lips and looked up to the ceiling. Way up, past the beams, the tiled roofing and the abundance of storm clouds was a beautiful blue sky. And this…? This rocky, discombobulated start was one of those things-could-only-get-better moments. It *had* to be. This was her shot at a completely fresh start. As far away from her father's incandescent rage as she could be.

"Kali, are you—" Ailsa burst into the corridor. "Darlin', did Brodie just leave you standing here in your wet clothes? For heaven's sake. You would've thought the man had been raised by wolves!"

An eruption of colorful language burst forth from the kitchen as Kali eyed the long-sleeved T-shirt from a three-years-old charity run. That and a pair of men's faded track pants were all Ailsa had managed to rustle up.

"Brodie's," Ailsa had informed her.

Her first instinct had been to refuse, but needs must and all that…

Kali stopped for a moment as the soft cotton slid past her nose and she inhaled a hint of washing powder and peat. A web of mixed feelings swept through her as the T-shirt slipped into place boyfriend-style. Over-sized and offering a hint of sexy and secure all at once. She shook her head at her dreamy-eyed reflection in the small driftwood-framed mirror.

It's a shirt! Get over it.

"When are we going to get this blasted kettle fixed?"

Blimey. Had the walls just vibrated?

"Cool your jets, Brodie. For heaven's sake, it's not rocket science. You *do* know how to make a cup of tea, don't you?"

Ailsa's voice whooshed past the bathroom as she went on her way to the kitchen, her tone soothing as the clink and clatter of mugs and spoons filled out the rest of the mental image Kali was building.

"Stop your fussing, will you?" Brodie grumbled through the stone walls.

"Let *me* have a look," Ailsa chided, much to Kali's amusement. Then, after a moment, "I'll need to get some dressing on that, Dr. McClellan."

"Oh, it's Dr. McClellan now I'm injured, is it?"

"Brodie. Dr. McClellan. You're still the wee boy whose nappies I changed afore you jumped up on my knee, begging me to read you stories about faeries and cowboys over and over, so hush!"

Kali's smile widened as the bickering continued.

Local Doctor Defied by Feisty Kettle:
Nurse Forced to Mollify GP with Bedtime Stories.

Was that the type of story the local newspaper would run? The population on Dunregan wasn't much bigger than some two thousand or so people, and if memory served she was pretty sure that number accounted for the population surge over the summer months. The *hospitable* months.

"For heaven's sake, Ailsa! Stop your mithering. I don't need a bandage! It's not really even a burn!"

"Well, that's a fine way to treat your head nurse, who has twenty years experience on *you*, Brodie McClellan!"

Kali chalked one up to Ailsa.

"But it's a perfectly normal way to treat my auntie who won't leave well enough alone!"

Brodie's grumpy riposte vibrated through the wall. Kali was relieved to hear Ailsa laugh at her nephew's words, then jumped not a moment later when a door slammed farther along the corridor. *Crikey.* It was like being in a Scottish soap opera. And it was great! No-holds-barred bickering, banter and underneath it all a wealth of love. The stuff of dreams.

Her family had never had that sort of banter— *Stop-stop-stop-stop-stop.* Kali deftly trained her hair into a thick plait as she reminded herself she had no family. No one to bicker with, let alone rely on. Not anymore.

Turn it into a positive, Kali.

The other voice in her head—the kind one, the one that had brought her out of her darkest moments—came through like the pure notes of a flute.

There's always *a bright side.*

Good. Focus on that. Turn it into a positive... Not having a family means I'm free! Unencumbered! Not a soul in the world to care about me!

The familiar gaping chasm of fear began to tickle at Kali's every confidence.

Okay. Maybe a positive mantra was going to be elusive. For today. But she *could* do it. Eventually. And realistically there was only one mantra she really needed to focus on:

K.I.C.K.A.S.S. Keep It Compassionate, Kind and Supremely Simple.

It had kept her sane for the past five years and would continue to be her theme song.

She tightened the drawstring on the baggy pants and gave her shoulders a fortifying shake. Who knew? Maybe she could get someone with bagpipes to rustle up a tune!

The piper's "K.I.C.K.A.S.S. Anthem."

Hmm. It needed work.

Regardless, the rhythm of the words sang to her in their own way. They were her link to sanity.

She jumped as a door slammed again. Hearing no footsteps, she thought she might as well suck it up and see what was going on out there. No point hiding out in the toilet! In less than thirty minutes she'd be seeing a patient, and it would probably be a good idea to get the lie of the land.

Kali cracked the door open and stuck her head out—only to pull it right back in when Brodie unexpectedly stormed past. If he'd had a riding cloak and a doublet on he would have looked just like the handsome hero from a classic romance.

Handsome?

She was really going to have to stop seeing him in that way. Rude and curt was more like it. And maybe just a little bit sexy Viking.

He abruptly turned and screeched to a halt, one hand holding the other as if in prayer, his index fingers resting upon his lips. His awfully nice lips.

Stop it! You are not to get all mushy about your new boss. Your new, very grumpy boss. You've been down that road and had to leave everything behind. Never again.

She stood stock-still as Brodie's eyes scanned her from top to toe. A little shudder shivered its way along her spine. His gaze felt surprisingly…intimate.

"That's one hell of a look, Dr. O'Shea."

As Brodie's blue eyes worked their way along her scrappy ensemble for a second time Kali all but withered with embarrassment. Snappy comebacks weren't her forte. Not by a long shot.

"Once I get a lab coat on it should be all right."

Nice one, Kali.

"Sure." Brodie turned and resumed his journey to the front of the clinic. "I'll just get the patient list."

Kali did a skip-run-walk thing to catch up with his long-legged strides.

"Would you like me to take a look?"

"That's generally the idea with a patient list."

Kali blew out a slow breath, her eyes on Brodie's retreating back as she continued race-walking to keep up with him. Touchy, touchy! She was next to certain he wasn't angry with *her*, but there was a bagpipe sized chip on that shoulder of his.

"I meant your hand."

Brodie stopped short and whirled around. Kali only just skidded to a halt in time not to run into his chest. Which, given how nice he smelled, wouldn't have been too bad a thing, but—

"I'd have thought you'd be too afraid."

"Wh-what?" Kali instinctively pulled back at Brodie's aggressive response. She'd been afraid before. Terrified, actually. For her life. And she'd survived.

She pressed her heels into the ground. If she could make a last-minute exit out of an arranged marriage under the threat of death she could deal with a grumpy thirty-something doctor with a self-induced kettle burn.

"I've dealt with difficult patients before," she continued levelly, her eyes on his hand. Meeting his gaze would only increase the heated atmosphere. "I'm sure we'll come out all right in the end."

"Difficult patients with Ebola?"

Brodie thrust his hand forward and with every pore of strength she could muster Kali held her ground. She had no idea what he was talking about, but she was not—absolutely, positively *not*—going to start out her new life fearfully.

"Aren't you going to touch it?"

He thrust his hand straight into her eyeline—millimeters from her face. What *was* this? Some sort of hardcore newcomer test? Whatever it was, she was not going to be frightened by Brodie McClellan or anyone—ever again.

Brodie watched, amazed, as Kali stood stock-still, seemingly unfazed by his ridiculously aggressive behavior. She took his hand in hers, one of her delicate fingers holding open his own as they instinctively tried to curl round the injury. It was the first time he'd been touched by someone outside of a medical exam in weeks, if not months. The power of it struck him deeply.

Kali's delicate touch nearly released the soft moan building in his chest. He couldn't—*mustn't*—let her see how much this single moment meant to him. He looked at her eyes as they moved across his hand. Diligent, studied. Their extraordinary bright green making them almost feline. More tigress than tabby, he thought.

Moments later, as he exhaled, he realized he'd been holding his breath while Kali was examining him with clinical indifference—examining the burn mark he'd all but shoved directly in her face. It wasn't a bad burn. His pride had been hurt more than his hand. Her touch had been more healing than any medicine. Not that he'd ever tell her. She'd be off soon. Like all the good things that came into his life. Just passing through.

Her long lashes flicked up over those green eyes of hers meeting his inquisitive gaze head-on. Could she see how strange this was for him? Being treated as if he *weren't* a walking, talking contagious disease? No. It ran deeper than that. She was treating him compassionately. Without the stains of his past woven through her understanding of who he actually was.

"That's all you've got?"

"I'm sorry?" Brodie near enough choked at her about-face, bring-it-on attitude.

"Ebola?" She scoffed. "That's your best shot?"

Now it was Brodie's turn to be confused. Was she trying to double bluff him?

"I get a bit of hazing, Dr. McClellan. The less than warm welcome, the mocking about this ridiculous outfit. But seriously…?" She snorted a *get real* snort, took a step back, her hand still holding his, and gave him a smile wreathed in skepticism. "That's your best shot at getting me to hightail it back to the mainland, is it? Ebola?"

CHAPTER TWO

BRODIE PULLED HIS hand out of Kali's and received an indignant stare in response.

"What? Now I'm not fit to see to a first-degree burn? I am a qualified GP, I'll have you know."

This time there was fire behind her words. *She was no pushover.* He liked that. Decorum ruled all here on Dunregan and it had never been a good fit for him. It was what had forced him to head out into the world to explore who he could be without That Day branded onto his every move.

Enough with the bitterness, McClellan. You're not a teenager anymore.

"No, that's not it at all." Brodie waved away her presumption, opting to get over himself and just be honest. "I think the booking agency might not have been entirely forthright with you."

"What are you talking about? Four weeks—with the possibility of an extension. What's there to know beyond that?" Her forehead crinkled ever so slightly.

"I…" Brodie hesitated, then plunged forward. No point in beating round the bush. "I've recently finished my twenty-one-day clearance after three months working in an Ebola hospital. In Africa," he added, as if it weren't ruddy obvious where the hospital had been.

Three countries. Thousands dead. He'd wanted to make

a difference. Needed to make a difference somewhere—
anywhere—before coming back here. And he had done.
Small-scale. But he'd been there. A pair of hazmat boots
on the ground in a place where "risky" meant that sharing
the same air as the person next to you might mean death.
Only to come back and face a sea of incriminating looks.

*Is this what you had in mind, Dad? Making me promise
to work on the island for a year after you'd gone so I could
be reminded how much of an outsider I am?*

He shook off the thought. His father had been neither
bitter nor vengeful. It had been his fathomless kindness
and understanding that had driven the stakes of guilt deep
into Brodie's heart.

"Hmm…"

Kali's green-eyed gaze remained steady apart from a
blink or two. Could she see the inner turmoil he was fighting? Filial loyalty over a need to cut loose? To forge his
own path.

Kali's voice, when she finally spoke, was completely
neutral. "Guess they *did* leave that bit out." She considered
him for a moment longer. "I am presuming you wouldn't
be here if you hadn't had the all clear so…it does beg the
question: what am I doing here if you're good to go?"

"Ah, the mysteries of life in Dunregan begin to reveal themselves." This was the part that rankled. The part
where Brodie found himself slamming doors, spilling boiling water and leaving unsuspecting GPs with their muck-
covered bicycles by the side of the road on a stormy day.

"Some of—*most* of the patients are *concerned*…about
being seen by me." Total honesty? *All* of them. Fear of
catching Ebola from Ol' Dr. McClellan's son had gripped
the island.

Or…the thought struck him…maybe they had simply

preferred his father and were using the Ebola scare as an excuse to refuse his treatment. Now, *that* hurt.

He cleared his throat. One step at a time.

"Even though you've had the all clear?" Kali's voice remained impartial. She was fact gathering.

"Right. Apparently most folk round here don't put much faith in the Public Health Office's green light." He snorted derisively. "And to think of all the viral infections I've treated here. Rich, isn't it?"

He stopped himself. He was going to have to check the bitter tone in his voice. Yeah, he was angry. But he was hurting much more than he was spitting flames. And to add on moments like these—moments that reminded him why he wanted more than anything to live somewhere else. Oh, to be anonymous!

"I'm going to presume, as someone who has also taken the Hippocratic oath, that you wouldn't have returned to your practice until you felt well and truly able to."

Despite himself, he shot her a look. One that said, *Obviously not. Otherwise I wouldn't be so blinking frustrated.*

"Don't shoot the messenger, Dr. McClellan! I wouldn't be doing my job if I didn't check with you."

"Fair enough."

And it was. It just felt…*invasive*…being questioned again. And by someone who hadn't been through the post-Ebola wringer as he had.

Kali might be a fully qualified GP, but her face was unlined by personal history. With skin that smooth, no dark circles under her eyes, excited to be working in *Dunregan*… She had to be green around the ears.

"What are you? Two…three days out of med school?"

She looked at him as if he'd sprouted horns. The rod of steel reasserted itself.

"Old enough. Apart from which, I don't really think that's any business of yours."

"No." Might as well be honest. "You just look—"

"Yeah, yeah. I know." She all but spat the words out, crossing her arms defensively across her chest. "Baby-faced."

"Not exactly what I was going to say," Brodie countered. *Arrestingly beautiful* would've been more accurate. Her smooth skin was entirely unweathered by life, but now that he was paying more attention the wary look in her eyes spoke of wisdom beyond her years.

"Well…" She adopted a tone one might use for toddlers. "I'm a fully fledged grown-up, just like you, so you can rest easy, Dr. McClellan."

"Brodie," he countered with a smile.

He was warming to Kali. The more they spoke the more it seemed they might be two of a kind. Quick to smart when someone hit the right buttons. Slow to trust. A well-earned friendship if you ever got that far.

"Well, guess you're just lucky. Good genes from your parents, eh?"

She stiffened.

More sensitive territory, from the looks of things. Maybe her relationship with *her* family was as terrific as the one he had with his. One wayward brother, a meddling auntie and a godsend of a niece who'd stepped in at the reception desk when his "loyal" long-term sidekick had flown the coop. Okay…so they weren't that bad. But right now he was feeling a bit more me-against-the-world than he liked.

"So…you were working in Africa…?"

Score one to Kali for deftly changing the topic!

"Right, sorry." Brodie regrouped with a shake of his head. "Okay—long story short: I did the work through Doctors Without Borders who—as I'm sure you will appreciate—

have some pretty rigorous safety systems in place for this sort of thing. I was lucky enough to be working in one of the newly built facilities. Upon my return to the UK…" he glanced at the date on his phone "…which was about five weeks ago, I went to a pre-identified debriefing under the watchful eye of Public Health England."

"PHE? I know it." Kali nodded for him to continue before noticing Ailsa coming down the corridor, her arms laden with patient files.

"Oh, Dr. O'Shea! Glad to see you in some dry clothes. If you'd just like to hang yours on the radiator in the tea room at the back there—where we came in—they should be dry in no time. I'll see about finding you a white coat as well, but folk don't stand too much on formality here. What you have on now will do just fine."

Ailsa squeezed between the pair of them on her way to her office, giving Brodie a bit of a glare as she did. He gave her a toothy grin in return. He knew he was a pain in the bum, but that was what number one nephews were for!

Ailsa Dunregan was a brilliant nurse. And a vigilant auntie. It meant more than he could say that she hadn't fled the coop like the rest of his staff. Well, the receptionist. Best not get too hysterical.

He returned his focus to Kali. All gamine and sexy looking in his castoffs. Who knew a scrubby T-shirt and joggers could look so…rip-offable?

He gave his head a quick shake. Kali was showing professionalism. Now it was his turn.

"Okay, the clinic is going to be opening soon so—in a nutshell—there's a twenty-one-day incubation period. I stayed near a PHE-approved facility and did the following: I took my temperature twice a day, called my 'fever parole officer,' did a full course of malaria prophylaxis, because malaria symptoms can mimic Ebola symptoms. Any hint of a fever and I was meant to isolate myself and call the paramedics—like that doctor in New York. Who also got the all clear, by the way," he added hastily.

"Where did you do all this?" Kali asked.

"I stayed in London so that I was near an appropriate treatment center should any of the symptoms have arisen, and I spoke regularly with hospital staff just to triple-check everything I was experiencing was normal."

She quirked an eyebrow.

"It makes you paranoid. Hemorrhagic fever ain't pretty." He checked his tone. Kali hadn't said a word of judgment. She wasn't the enemy. Just a GP doing her job. *His* job. Whatever.

He started over. "Three months in protective gear, vigilant disinfections and then nothing. I'd never realized how often people sneeze on public transport before." He tried for a nonchalant chortle and ended up coughing. *Sexy.* Not that he was trying to appeal to Kali on any level other than as a doctor or anything.

"Right." Kali took back the conversation's reins before his thoughts went in too wayward a direction. "I take it you've spoken with everyone? The islanders?" she clarified.

He swallowed. *Not in so many words...*

Kali watched Brodie's Adam's apple dip and surge, her eyes flicking up to his in time to see his gaze shift up to the right. So *that* was his tell.

She was hoping he hadn't felt her fingers shaking earlier when she had held his palm in hers. Countless self-defense courses hadn't knocked the infinitesimal tremor out of her hands. But when Brodie had thrown the Ebola grenade into her lap years of medical training and logic had dictated that she'd be fine. Instinctually she knew that she had a jacked-up instinct for survival. It had never come to that, but if she needed to fight for her life she had the skills to give it her all.

"Depends upon what you mean, exactly...by 'spoken with.'" Brodie's gaze returned to hers, his fingers dropping some air quotes into the space between them. As their eyes met—his such a clear blue—she wondered that anyone could doubt him. They were the most honest pair of eyes she had ever seen. She felt an unexpected hit of disappointment that she wouldn't be here in Dunregan longer than a few weeks.

She shook her head, reminding herself they were in the middle of a pretty important conversation.

"So, you've not held a town hall meeting or anything like that?"

Just the look on his face was enough to tell her he hadn't.

"Maybe you've had an article in the...what's the local paper?"

"The *Dunregan Chronicle*."

"I'm asking, not telling," she reminded him when his tone lurched from informational to confrontational. "Have you had anything published? An article? An interview?"

"No, I've been a bit busy burying my father, amongst other things," Brodie snapped, instantly regretting it.

Quit shooting the messenger, idiot!

He gave Kali an apologetic glance. "I thought the ever-reliable gossip circuit on the island would cover all of my bases. Which it did. Just not in the way I'd thought."

"Look. If it's all right, I'm going to stop you there," Kali jumped in apologetically. "I'm really sorry to hear about your father. Now—not that the nuts and bolts of how this island works aren't interesting—I really need to get a handle on how things work right here." Kali flicked her thumb toward the front of the clinic. "If you're happy to meet me after the clinic's shut I'd love to hear all about it. Your work in Africa," she qualified quickly. "It sounds fascinating."

"It was an unbelievable experience. I'll never forget it."

Wow! The first person who'd actually seemed interested!

"So…" She gave her shoulders a wriggle, as if to re-group.

A wriggle inside *his* shirt, with more than a hint of shoulder slipping in and then out of the stretched neck-line. A tug of attraction sent his thoughts careening off to a whole other part of his—er—brain? Another time, another place?

Focus, man! The poor woman's trying to speak with you.

"If I was in your shoes I wouldn't want me here either. It's *your* practice! But I'm here to help, not hinder."

He nodded. Wise beyond her years. Those green eyes of her held untold stories. He'd been wrong to think otherwise.

"Can we shake on it?" She thrust her hand forward, chin jutted upwards. Not in defiance, more in anticipation of a problem.

He put his hand forward—the one he hadn't burned—for a sound one-two shake.

"Are we good?"

"Yes, ma'am?" He affected an American accent and gave her a jaunty salute.

Her eyes narrowed a bit.

Okay, fine. He blew that one.

"We're good. I'll steer clear of tea duty."

She furrowed her brow at him in response.

Quit being such a jerk. Like she said, she's here to help!

She shifted past him in the corridor, leaving the slight-est hint of jasmine in her wake. "I should probably go in-troduce myself up front."

"Yes—yeah. On you go. Caitlyn's my niece and is about as much of a newcomer to the clinic as you are."

"Excellent." Kali gave him a polite smile. "She and I can forge into unknown territory together, then. And don't worry about the tea. I'm more of a coffee girl."

Her tone was bright, non-confrontational.

"We've not given you much of a welcome, have we?"

Kali rocked back on her heels with a squelch, not looking entirely sure how to respond until she saw the edges of Brodie's lips tweak up into a slow but generous grin.

"Ailsa's great!" Kali shot back with her own cheeky grin. Adding, "I've yet to make a decision on the boss man..."

"He's a real piece of work." Brodie was laughing now. "But he's good at his job."

"I don't doubt that for a minute."

And he could see she meant it. He *was* a good doctor. A little shy on bedside manner, but—

"Oh, and as for that hand of yours—you probably don't need a bandage, but it might be a good idea to put some topical sulfonamide antibacterial cream on there. Although, as you probably know, some new studies suggest it might actually lengthen the healing time."

Brodie gave a grin as Kali shrugged off her own advice before tacking on, "I'm sure you know what's best, Old Timer..." as she pushed through the swinging door into the front of the clinic.

Kali gave as good as she got. Just as well, given his zig-zagging moods.

Brodie put his hand to the door to talk Caitlyn and Kali through their intro but stopped at his aunt's less than subtle clearing of her throat.

"And what can I help you with on this fine day, my dear Auntie?"

"You're not thinking of going in there and looming over Caitlyn, are you?"

"No."

Yes.

"Give the girl a chance. She's only just out of school and she doesn't need her uncle hovering over her every step of the way."

"What? Do you think I might accidentally breathe too much in the reception area and frighten away even more patients?"

"Brodie McClellan." Ailsa wagged a finger at him. "You'd best think twice about pushing so hard against the support system you have. Caitlyn's here until she starts university in September—but after that… Only a few months for you to make your peace with everyone. Including…" she steeled her gaze at him "…Dr. O'Shea. She's here to *help*, might I remind you?"

"Help for something that's not actually a problem?"

"You know what I mean, Brodie. C'mon." She gave his shoulder a consoling rub. "You can't blame folk for being nervous. And besides, you're only fresh back. It'll give you time to settle back in. Mend a couple of fences while you're at it."

She gave him her oft-used Auntie Knows Best stare.

He could do as she suggested. Of course he could. Or he could go back home and pack his bag and head back on another Doctors Without Borders assignment until Kali was gone.

A hit of protectiveness for his father's surgery took hold.

Unexpected.

Or was it curiosity about Kali?

Interesting.

He leaned against the wall and gave his aunt his best I'll-give-it-a-try face.

"So, after all the miraculous recoveries of the bumper-to-bumper patients we normally have over the past couple of weeks, do you think they'll come flooding back now that we have Kali here?"

"Most likely."

His aunt had never been one to mince words.

"So what am *I* meant to do? Just twiddle my thumbs whilst Kali sees to folk?"

"I suspect she'll need some help. You would be showing her the *good* side of yourself if you were to talk her through a patient's history. Give her backup support if she needed it. Prove to her you're the lovable thirty-two-year-old I've had the pleasure of knowing all my life instead of that fusty old curmudgeon you showed her this morning. I'll tell you, Brodie—I didn't much like seeing that side of you. It's not very fetching."

"Fine." He pressed back from the wall with a foot. "Maybe it'd be best if I just leave well enough alone. Let you two run the show and I'll—I don't know—I'll build that boat I always had a mind to craft."

The words were out before he could stem them.

"You mean the one your father always wanted to build with you?" Ailsa nodded at the memory, completely unfazed by his burst of temper. "That's one promise you could make good on. Or you could put all of that energy you've got winging around inside of you helping out the new doctor who's come all the way up here to get you out of a right sorry old pickle. Then make good on the *other* promise you made to your father."

They both knew what she meant.

"I'm here, aren't I?"

"That's not what I meant, nor your father and you know it, Broderick Andrew McClellan."

Brodie had to hand it to her. Whipping out all three of his names—that was fighting talk for Ailsa.

She pursed her lips at him for added measure, clearly

refusing to rise—or lower herself—to his level of self-pity. And frankly he was bored with it himself. He'd never been one for sulky self-indulgence. Or standing around idly doing nothing.

He had twiddling his thumbs down to a fine art now. Not to mention a wind farm's worth of energy to burn. He gave the wall a good thump with the sole of his boot.

Ailsa turned away, tsking as she went back into her office to prepare for the day. Which would most likely be busy now that Kali was here.

"It's not like I was away having the time of my life or anything!" he called after her.

She stuck her head out into the corridor again, but said nothing.

"People were dying in droves!"

"Yes, you were an incredibly compassionate, brave man to go and do what you did—and it's a shame folk here haven't quite caught up with that. But with you looking like you've got the weight of the world on your shoulders it's little wonder you've become so unapproachable."

"Unapproachable! *Me?*" He all but bellowed it, just as Kali walked into the hallway—only to do an immediate about-face back into the reception area.

Ailsa gave him an I-told-you-so look. Brodie took a deep breath in to launch into a well-rehearsed list of the things wrong with Dunregan and her residents, and just as quickly felt the puff go out of him. It would take an hour to rattle off the list of things wrong with *himself* this morning, let alone address the big picture.

For starters he'd been rude to Kali. Unprofessional. Then had thrown a blinkin' tantrum over a burn that had happened solely because he'd been slamming around a kettle of boiling water in a huff because he had to tell yet *another* person why he was toxic.

The word roiled round his gut.

He wasn't *toxic*! He was fit as a fiddle set to play for an all-hours fiddle fest! But he knew more than most it ran deeper than that. How to shrug off the mantle of the tortured laddie who'd sailed out on a handmade skiff with his mum, only to be washed ashore two hours later when the weather had turned horribly, horribly fierce?

He knew it was a miracle he'd survived. But he would've swapped miracles any day of the week if only his mother could have been spared.

"You know, Ailsa…"

His aunt gave him a semi-hopeful look when she heard the change in his tone.

"A second pair of hands round this place would be helpful longer term, wouldn't it? Female hands. You're wonderful—obviously—but Dad always spoke of having a female GP around. Someone not from Dunregan to give the islanders a bit more choice when they need to talk about sensitive issues."

As he spoke the idea set off a series of fireworks in his brain. New possibilities. With Kali on board as a full-time GP he wouldn't have to kill himself with office hours, out-of-hours emergency calls, home visits and the mountain rescues that cropped up more often than not during the summer season.

Not that he minded the work. Hell, he'd work every hour of the day if he could. But working here was much more than ferrying patients in and out for their allotted ten minutes. And if he was going to make good on his deathbed promise to his father to work in the surgery for at least a year he wasn't so sure doing it alone would get the intended results…

His grandfather and his father had prided themselves on being genuine, good-as-their-word *family* doctors. Their time and patience had gone beyond patching up wounds, scribbling out prescriptions and seeing to annual checkups. Here on Dunregan it was personal. Everything was. It was why his father's premature death from cancer had knocked the wind out of the whole population. Everyone knew everyone else and everything about them.

Sharing the load with Kali might be the way he'd get through the year emotionally intact. Maybe even restore some of his tattered reputation. Everyone who'd ever met his father thought the world of him. John McClellan: treasured island GP.

The same could not be said of himself.

Ailsa eyed him warily. "You're not just saying this to get out of the promise to your father, are you?"

"No." He struggled to keep the emotion out of his voice. A bedside promise to a dying father… It didn't get more Shakespearean than that.

"Well, my dear nephew, if you're wanting Dr. O'Shea to stick around you best check she's not already legged it out the front of the clinic. You need to show her the other side of Brodie McClellan. The one we all like."

She gave his cheek a good pinch. Half loving, half scolding.

He laughed and pulled her into her arms for a hug.

"What would I do without you and your wise old ways, Auntie Ailsa? I've been a right old pill this morning, haven't I?"

"I'm hardly old, and there are quite a few ways I could describe your behavior, Brodie—but your way is the most polite." Ailsa's muffled voice came from his chest. "Now…" She pushed back and looked him square in the eye. "Let me get on with my day, will you?"

As she disappeared into her office so, too, did the smile playing across his lips. Here he was, blaming the islanders for the situation he was in, when truthfully all his frustration came from the fact that he loved his father and his work and right now the two were at odds. Not one part of him was looking forward to the year ahead.

Truthfully? He needed Kali O'Shea more than he cared to admit. If he could convince her to stay she might be the answer to all his prayers. A comrade in arms to help him get through the thicket of weeds he was all but drowning in.

He jogged his shoulders up and down.

Right. Good.

Time for what his father had called a "Starty-Overy, I've Done A Whoopsy." His behavior this morning had been childish. He might as well give it the childish name. Then start acting his age and focus on winning over the mysteriously enigmatic Dr. Kali O'Shea.

Kali tapped at her computer keyboard a second time. Then pressed Refresh. And again.

Weird.

There didn't seem to be anyone next in the queue. She stuck her head round the corner into the office where Brodie had been lurking… Okay, not exactly lurking. He'd been "on hand" in case she needed any information. But it had felt like lurking.

"Hey, does the computer system get jammed sometimes?"

"All the time is more like it," he answered with a smile.

Her stomach grumbled. Kali's hand flew to cover it, as if it would erase the fact it had happened.

"Er…"

"Hungry after only seeing three patients?" Brodie teased.

"Something like that. I was too excited for my first day at work to eat breakfast."

"Only fifteen more patients to go before lunch!"

"Or…" She drew out the word and thought she might as well push her luck. "I do seem to recall an offer of a cup of tea and a biscuit."

He blinked, dragging a tooth across one of those full lips of his. Distracting. *Very* distracting.

"Would you like it if I put on a pinny and pushed a wee cart along to your office for delivery, Dr. O'Shea?"

A flush of embarrassment crept up her cheeks. He was an experienced doctor. Her superior. Had she pushed that envelope too far?

"Ach, take that nervous expression off your face, Dr. O'Shea. I'm just joshing you." He stood up from his desk and gave her shoulder a squeeze. "A nice cup of tea is the least I can do an hour after I promised it."

He dropped her a wink and her tummy did a flip. The sexy kind.

Oh, no. Not good. Not good at all.

"Right, well… I guess I better check with Caitlyn who's next." She gave the door frame a rap, as if that was the signal for action. Then didn't move.

"Anything good this morning?"

"Depends upon your definition of 'good,'" she replied with a smile. She liked this guy. He was a whole load nicer than Dr. McCrabby from this morning. "A prenatal check, a suspected case of the flu—which thankfully wasn't more than a really bad cold—and a check on a set of stitches along a feisty four-year-old's hairline. Rosie Bell, I think her name was."

"That's her mother. The daughter is Julia."

"Right—that's right. I mean, of *course* you know it's right—you know everyone." She stopped herself. She was blathering. "The stitches were just fine. She had them put in on the mainland, at the hospital, there…so…that was a quickie. Everyone has been incredibly welcoming…"

So much for no more blathering.

A shadow darkened Brodie's eyes for a moment. He abruptly slipped through the doorway and headed down the hall. "Best go get my pinny on and leave you to it, then, Dr. O'Shea."

"Thank you," she said to his retreating back, wishing the ground had swallowed her up before she'd opened her big mouth.

But it was the truth. Everyone *had* been really welcoming and it felt amazing! Never in her adult life had she been part of a community, and this place seemed to just… *speak* to her.

Her tummy grumbled again.

Dinner.

She would ask Brodie to join her for dinner and then maybe she would stop saying the wrong thing all the time. Fingers crossed and all that.

"Who's next, please, Caitlyn?" Kali stuck her head into the receptionist's room, willing herself onto solid terrain. Seeing patients was the one thing in the world that grounded her. Gave her the drive to find some place where she could settle down and play a positive role in her patients' lives.

"Sorry, Dr. O'Shea… I've been trying to send it through on your computer screen. I've not yet got the hang of the system with all of these patients showing up like this."

Kali peeked beyond Caitlyn and out into the busy waiting room.

"It's not normally like this?"

"Well…" Caitlyn used her feet to wheel herself and her chair over to Kali, lowering her voice to a confidential tone. "Since I started last week it's all been mostly people here to see Auntie Ail—I mean, Sister Dunregan. But most of the people who canceled appointments when Unc—Dr.

McClellan came back seem to have all magically turned up now they've heard you arrived…"

"I only got in last night."

"Aye, but you were on the public ferry, weren't you?"

Kali nodded. It was the only way onto the island unless you owned a private helicopter. Which she most assuredly did not.

"Word travels fast round here."

Kali laughed appreciatively as the outside door opened and another person tried to wedge her way onto the long window seat bench after giving Caitlyn a little wave in lieu of checking in.

"Hello, Mrs. Brown. We'll see what we can do, all right? You might have a wee wait," Caitlyn called.

"That's fine, dear. I've brought my knitting."

"So people are just coming along and trying their luck?" Kali's eyes widened.

"Something like that." Caitlyn nodded. "No harm in trying, is there? Hey!" Her eyes lit up with a new idea. "I bet you'll get in the paper!"

Kali felt a chill jag along her spine and forced herself to smile. "Well, I doubt me being here is *that* big a deal."

"On *this* island? You'd be surprised what turns up in the paper. There was a notice put in when my hamster Reggie died."

She pulled her chair back up to the window that faced the reception area and started tapping at the computer keyboard to pull up the next patient's information.

Kali crossed her fingers behind her back, hoping that her arrival on Dunregan didn't warrant more attention than a full waiting room. *That* she could deal with. Public notice? No. That would never do. So much for unpacking her bags and staying awhile.

"Oh! Dr. O'Shea—I'm such an airhead. Sorry. Would

you mind seeing Mr. Alexander Logan first? He's just come in and says it's an emergency. He didn't look all that well..."

"Absolutely." Kali nodded.

Medicine. And keeping her head down. Those were her two points of focus. Time to get on with medicine.

CHAPTER THREE

"ALEXANDER LOGAN?" Kali swung open the door leading into the waiting room.

"Aye, that's me." A gentleman with a thick shock of gray hair tried to press himself up from the bench seat, flat cap in one hand, cane in the other. "And you are...?"

"Dr. O'Shea. I'm the new—the locum doctor."

"With a name like O'Shea and those green eyes of yours I'm guessing you must be Irish." He grinned at her, eyes shining.

Kali hoped he didn't see the wince of pain his question had elicited. He wasn't to know that her mother—her *ballast*—with her distant Irish connection was the only reason she was alive.

"My wife was Irish. Feisty."

Just like her mother.

"She sounds like a great woman," she replied with a smile, grateful to dodge the question about herself. "You all right there, Mr. Logan? Would you like a hand standing up?"

"Oh, no—well, a bit." He looked up at her with a widening smile. "Yes, those eyes of yours remind me of Tilly, all right."

Kali hooked her arm through his, relieved to feel him

put a bit of his body weight on her arm. "Shall we try and work our way to the exam room?"

"Oh, sure. Not as quick on my—" He lifted his hand to his mouth, as if he were waiting for a sneeze to arrive. When the sneeze came, he stumbled forward, losing his grip on his cane as he fell, then let out a howl of pain.

Half the people in the waiting room lurched forward to lend a hand as Kali tightened her grip on his elbow and shifted an arm round his waist.

She heard the swinging door open behind her.

"Sandy?" It was Brodie.

"I'm all right…just me hip."

He was clearly the opposite of all right, but as Brodie stepped forward to help support Mr. Logan Kali could feel the older man press closer to her.

"No, no…" Mr. Logan gave a little wave of his hand. "It's all right, Brodie. I've got Dr. O'Shea here, seeing to me."

Kali was surprised to see fear in the man's eyes. No one in that waiting room looked healthier than Brodie McClellan. The man was a veritable poster boy for the ruggedly fit.

"I was just—" Brodie began, then gave up. "Caitlyn, can you call Ailsa and have her help Mr. Logan into the exam room? I'm guessing your hip is giving you gyp again, Sandy?"

"Aye, well…"

That was all the older man would allow. Kali couldn't figure out if that was a standard Scottish response or if he was trying to breathe less now that Brodie was in the room. Out of the corner of her eye she saw one of the other patients bring a tissue to her lips. The sea of helping hands had been withdrawn entirely.

She was surprised to realize she was feeling indignant. On Brodie's behalf. She'd known within minutes of meeting him that he wouldn't compromise someone's health…

well, maybe in *quite a few* minutes… Even so, the man meant no harm. Quite the opposite, in fact.

"If you two have a history, I'm happy for you to see Dr. McClellan, if you prefer," Kali offered. Might as well try to build bridges out here in the public eye.

"Oh, no dear." Mr. Logan put more of his weight on Kali. "You understand, Brodie—don't you? I wouldn't want to seem rude to Dr. O'Shea, when she's gone to all this trouble to come up here to Dunregan." His eyes flicked between the two doctors. "Would I, Dr. McClellan?"

It was an apology. Not a question.

"Of course not, Mr. Logan." Brodie dropped the informal abbreviation he'd used earlier and grabbed a couple of antiseptic wipes from the counter before bending over to pick up the man's cane. He gave it a visible scrub along the arch as he did.

Kali's eyes flicked to Ailsa as she entered the room, watching her assess the situation before taking the cane from Brodie with a bright smile. He disappeared into the back of the clinic before Kali could catch his eye. Get a reading on how much the incident had hurt. She would've felt it if it had happened to her, and she didn't even know these people.

"Oh, dearie me, Mr. Logan," chirped Ailsa. "It looks like your new hip isn't quite playing ball, is it?"

"It's been fine, but Bess and I were walking along Ben Regan—"

"Away up on the cliffs?"

"Aye, well… Going up was all right, but the going down part… Well, it's just not felt quite right since then."

"Are you up to the journey down the corridor, Sandy? Any sciatic pain before you went on your walk?"

"No, no. I did that flexing test thing Brodie showed me

the last time." He shot a guilty look at the space Brodie had vacated.

"Did you feel the hip come out of the socket?" Kali asked.

"Just now? Aye, that I did."

Ailsa shot Kali a look which she interpreted as, *Are you up to doing a hip relocation?* Kali nodded, her lips pressed grimly together. Mr. Logan wasn't exactly light.

"With the two of you lassies helping me, I should be fine to get to the room." Mr. Logan gave them each a grateful smile.

Not two or three steps into the corridor he sneezed again and all but crumpled to the floor.

"Well, all right, then, Mr. Logan." Kali nodded at Ailsa as she spoke. "I guess we'll get to it right here, if that's okay."

"Anything…" he huffed out. "Anything to stop the pain."

Kali straightened both of the gentleman's legs out onto the corridor floor—one was visibly shorter than the other—taking a glimpse up to his face as the left knee refused to unbend. The color was fading from Mr. Logan's cheeks and his breath was coming in short, sharp pants.

"Mr. Logan? It looks like you've got a posterior dislocation here. I'm just going to take your leg—"

"Do whatever you need to do quickly, lassie!" Mr. Logan panted.

"Ailsa—Mrs. Dunregan—Nurse—" Kali stumbled over the words—she still wasn't up to name etiquette in this place where everyone knew everyone. "Would you mind holding Mr.—Sandy's head steady?"

"I'd probably be best holding down his pelvic bones for you when you do the reduction," Ailsa corrected gently.

"Mr. Logan and I aren't going anywhere. You go on and get whatever medication you need."

"Right." She shot a look over her shoulder, as if some medication would magically appear, then whispered, "I've only ever done this procedure with a patient under general anesthetic in surgery."

"But you've done it?" Ailsa's voice was low.

"Yes, but…"

"We don't have a hospital on Dunregan, dear. Mr. Logan's had a hip replacement, so he's got an artificial ball joint. You'll need to perform a reduction of the dislocated hip prosthesis, okay? Sooner rather than later. You'll be fine," she added with a reassuring smile.

Kali rose and jogged to the exam room she'd been using to find Brodie, hands sheathed in protective gloves, filling a syringe with something.

"Morphine." Brodie pinched the syringe between two fingers, handing it to her with the needle still capped. "And you will probably also want to give him this."

"Which is…?" Kali hoped the panic she was feeling wasn't as obvious as it felt.

"Midazolam. For sedation." He handed her the syringe with a gloved hand. "Are you sure you're good with this?"

"Yes, of course," she answered—too swiftly.

"So you've done a hip relocation in these circumstances?"

Not in the strictest sense of the words.

She looked up at Brodie's face. Was he doubting her or offering reassurance? There was kindness in his eyes. He gave her a *go on* nod.

"I've got it. I'm good." She gave a firm nod in return, convincing herself as much as Brodie. This was just another one of those moments when life wasn't giving her much of a choice. Her patient had specifically requested her as his doctor, and it seemed Brodie was in her corner.

"Any special tips for Mr. Logan's hip?" She hoped the question wasn't a giveaway that her brain was short-circuiting.

"Nope."

Brodie turned back to the sink to peel off his gloves and wash his hands. Or to ignore her.

Both?

So much for being in her corner! She stared at his back, tempted, just for a moment, to stick out her tongue at him. She wasn't *that* long out of med school and, whilst she *had* done a reduction before, she certainly hadn't done one under these circumstances.

Well, tough. That was what she had and she would just have to cope.

"Are you going to do the reduction or do you need help?" Brodie didn't turn around, his question rising only slightly above the sound of running water. It was difficult to tell if his tone was kind or frustrated.

"It's not as if there's anyone else we can ring, is there?" Kali asked rhetorically, instantly wishing she hadn't when his shoulders stiffened.

Open mouth…insert foot. The poor man's father wasn't long gone and he was having just about the worst period of mourning a son could go through. He had her compassion.

"I'm good. I've got it." She spoke to his back again, shook herself into action and took a careful look at each of the syringes she held. Brodie had labeled them.

A tray appeared in her eyeline, preset with alcohol prep pads, tape and a blunt-end needle already attached to a high-flow extension tube with a four-way stopcock. Her eyes flicked up and she gave Brodie a grateful smile. His neutral expression gave nothing away—but his actions were clear. The man was meticulous. And his patient's welfare was paramount. Otherwise he wouldn't be here—hovering, checking she was up to snuff. Which she'd better get busy proving she was.

"Thanks for doing the syringes. And the tray. Everything."

She didn't catch his mumbled reply as she picked up her pace to get back to her patient.

"You'll need these as well."

Kali turned as Brodie reappeared in the corridor with a box of gloves, a roll of hygiene paper and a paper blanket.

Ailsa took them from him, then asked Brodie to let Caitlyn know what was happening so she would stop sending people through for a moment.

Kali tugged on a pair of gloves, taking the time to focus.

Mr. Logan's breaths were deeply labored and his face was contorted with pain.

"All right, Mr. Logan, we're going to have to give you a couple of injections—"

"Just get on with it, already," he gasped. "I can't bear it much longer and Bess is in the car."

"Your dog will be just fine, Mr. Logan. We can always get Caitlyn to check on her." Ailsa took charge again. "Just lay still for a moment, Sandy, so we can get some of this painkiller into you. You've not got any allergies, have you?"

"What? No, no. I'm fine."

Ailsa took an antiseptic swab off the tray Brodie had prepared and rubbed it along Mr. Logan's left arm. Deftly she inserted the needle, holding the extension tubing out for Kali to put the syringe on. They watched as the morphine left the tubing and went to work, combatting Mr. Logan's acute pain. Kali carefully injected both the morphine and the midazolam, trying to think of something to chat with him about to monitor the effects of the painkiller.

"And how is Bess these days, Sandy?" asked Ailsa, coming to her rescue.

"She's getting on, like me." Sandy chuckled, a slight wince creasing his forehead as he did so.

"And are you still spoiling her rotten?"

"I don't know what you're talking about," he replied with a soft smile. "No point in going daft over a dog, is there?"

"Course not, Sandy. Even such a loyal one like Bess." Ailsa slipped her fingers to Sandy's wrist before whispering across to Kali, "There's a monitor in the exam room there—the one Brodie's in. Would you mind—?"

"Absolutely. No problem." Kali glanced at her watch as she rose. She could tell by the gentle slurring in Sandy's voice that the painkiller was kicking in...they would just need to wait a few more moments.

Brodie met her at the doorway, portable monitor in freshly gloved hands.

"You're not just standing there earwigging, are you?" Kali quipped.

"Hardly." Brodie's brows tucked closer together, his eyes lighting with a flash of barely contained anger.

Frustration. That was all it was. She'd feel the same.

Kali took the monitor with a smile of thanks.

After Mr. Logan's voice had become incredibly sleepy in response to her questions about how he was feeling, followed by a soft snore, she felt confident to go ahead with the maneuver.

"We're going to have to take your trousers off, Mr. Logan."

Another snore and a soft grunt was her response.

"I think you're all right to proceed, dear." Ailsa smiled.

One look at his face was proof that Sandy Logan didn't care if they dressed him up to look like the Easter bunny as long as his hip was fixed in the process. He wore a goofy grin and was definitely seeing the brighter side of life as the painkillers did their work.

Kali straddled Mr. Logan and raised his hips as Ailsa swiftly tugged off his trousers, offering soothing words of consolation as she did so. Mr. Logan's smile remained intact, his eyes firmly shut.

"Posterior or anterior?" Ailsa asked Kali.

Just one look at the inward pointing knee and foot indicated posterior. For good measure Kali examined the hip, trying to keep her touch as light as possible. The ball joint was very obviously protruding to the rear.

"Posterior." Her years of training took over. "The lower limb will need to be flexed, adducted and internally rotated."

"That's right," Ailsa said, as if her memory had needed jogging as well. If she hadn't been such a great nurse, Kali would've recommended she take up a career in acting.

Kali bent Sandy's knee, tucked her arm in the crook and, with a nod of her head, indicated that Ailsa should begin applying pressure to the hip as she pressed her heels into the floor and, with a fluid tug and a moan from the semiconscious Mr. Logan, the hip shifted back into place.

Her eyes met Ailsa's and they both laughed with delight.

"I did it!"

"Well done, Dr. O'Shea."

"Nice work."

Kali started at the sound of Brodie's voice. He'd been watching?

"Well…" She shrugged off the compliment. Being in the spotlight had always made her feel uncomfortable.

"Shall we get him onto a backboard and let him have a rest in one of the overnight rooms?" Ailsa asked—the question aimed more at Brodie than Kali.

"Good idea. I'll go get the gear."

"You've got overnight rooms?"

Not a nine-to-five surgery, then. Good. The more all-consuming things were here, the less time she'd have to think about the past. The family she'd left behind. The arranged marriage she'd narrowly avoided.

"A couple." Ailsa nodded. "They're always a good idea, with the weather up here changing at the drop of a hat and…" she nodded at their patient "…for situations like this."

"Thank you."

"For what?" Ailsa looked up at her in surprise.

"You know—for all the help with this. It's all a bit…" As she sought the right word Brodie came back into the corridor with a backboard.

Ailsa gave Kali's arm a squeeze before clearing away the tray of medical supplies, detaching the monitor pads and making room for Brodie to slip the backboard under Mr. Logan at Kali's count.

"Right…" Brodie looked down at the soft smile on Mr. Logan's face. "Glad to see another happy patient. Shall we get him moved before he wakes up and sees I've had anything to do with this?"

"Thank you." Kali looked straight into his eyes. She needed him to know she meant it. "For everything."

"Not a problem. Lift on three?"

He counted at her nod and as they walked Mr. Logan down the corridor she heard Brodie softly laugh to himself.

"What's so funny?"

"I forgot to make your tea."

Three o'clock in the afternoon and still not one patient. Plenty for Kali—but not one had come to see him.

Brodie was about as close to tearing his hair out as he'd ever been. He'd finally managed to remember to make cups of tea, only to find Caitlyn had just done a round for everyone. Terrific. He couldn't even get that right!

Brodie was beginning to get a good understanding of how innocent people on the run must feel.

Criminal.

Here he was, healthy as a professional athlete—he knew that because the doctor monitoring him had expressed envy at his level of fitness—and all for what? To lurk around his own surgery in the desperate hope of picking up a few medical crumbs?

At least Kali was getting a good feel for how the surgery worked. She had a smile on her face every time he saw her. Which would be good if he wasn't so desperate for something to do! There was only so much surfing the internet a man could do. He hardly thought this was what his father had meant when he'd made his final request: *Just one year, son. Just give it one year.*

If—and this was a big if—people were just giving him grieving time, didn't they know he'd be far better off grieving by making good on his promise to his father to run the surgery for a year?

Or maybe… No. *Would* he? Would his father have told folk to do this? Give him wide berth?

No. He shook his head resolutely. His father had always championed him. There were few things he was certain of, but his father's undivided loyalty was one of them.

A message pinged through on his office computer. He looked at the screen hopefully, despite his best efforts to remain neutral.

Mr. Donaldson—urgent.

A patient?

It was almost silly how happy he felt. A *patient*! He was

out of his chair and on his way to Reception before Mr. Donaldson—a long-time patient of both himself and his father—had a chance to change his mind.

When he opened the door his heart sank.

"Dad, are you absolutely sure?" Mr. Donaldson's daughter, Anne, had her back to Brodie and hadn't seen him come in.

"Of course I'm sure. He's my doctor," Mr. Donaldson insisted.

"But…" Anne looked across at Caitlyn—presumably to get some backup—only to find the receptionist was busy on the phone.

Shame, thought Brodie. He would've been curious to see how she reacted to this. He checked himself. The fact Caitlyn had taken the job showed her support. Never mind that she was family and could do with the money. She didn't let fear override her common sense. Or, he conceded, her nan's say-so.

"Now, Mr. Donaldson. What can I do for you today?"

Anne all but recoiled at the sound of his voice, her arm moving swiftly up to cover her mouth.

"You're all right, Anne." Brodie forced himself to stay calm. "I've been cleared. I'm not contagious."

"Oh, I know, Brodie—Dr. McClellan. It's just—" She stopped speaking, her eyes widening in horror—or embarrassment. She widened the gap between the fingers covering her mouth. "It's just that poor nurse who went where you did in Africa is back in hospital…"

Ah…he'd seen the headlines on the internet. Must've hit the broadsheets as well. That explained the hands and arms covering people's mouths. Fresh media scares about recurrences and isolation units and that poor, poor woman. Her courage and generosity was going heavily unrewarded.

"I saw that." Brodie shook his head. "And I was very

sorry to hear it. But I can absolutely assure you that is not the case with me."

"Brodie, I would get up to greet you, but..." the elderly gentlemen interjected, pointing at his foot.

Brodie's eyes widened at the sight. A blood-soaked rag was wrapped around the middle of his foot.

"Is that just a wool sock you're wearing there, Mr. Donaldson?"

"Sure is. My foot would've had a boot on as well, but my daughter, here, said you were likely to cut it off and I wasn't going to let that happen. I only just bought them five years ago. Still got miles to go in them yet."

"Dad!" Anne jumped in, forgetting to shield her mouth. "The boot's got a gaping great hole in it now your turf spade's gone through it. It couldn't have done your foot one bit of good to be yanked out of your boot after you pulled the spade out of it."

"You put a turf spade through your boot and into your foot?"

Brodie couldn't help but be impressed. Wielding a spade with that sort of strength would have taken tremendous power. Then again, at eighty-five years of age Mr. Donaldson showed few signs of succumbing to the frailty of the elderly. *Vital* was just about the best description Brodie could conjure.

"Aye, that I did, son—no need to broadcast it round the village."

"I'd take it as a compliment, Mr. Donaldson. Let's get you into my exam room, shall we?" He moved to help him up just as Kali entered the waiting room with a patient's chart.

"Are you coming, Anne?" Mr. Donaldson turned to see if his daughter was behind them.

Brodie saw Kali catch the look of horror on Anne's face at the suggestion.

"Can I help?" Kali stepped forward without waiting for an answer, offering another arm for Mr. Donaldson to lean on. Brodie gave her a grateful smile.

This was tough. He'd had a few other doctors warning him something like this might happen, but he'd just blown it off. Dunregan was his *home*! He hadn't expected a victory parade—but having people frightened of being treated by him…? It seared deeper than he'd ever have anticipated.

"Thank you, dear." Mr. Donaldson's fingers wrapped round Kali's forearm. "I'm sure you're busy, but you wouldn't mind, would you?" He raised his voice as they were leaving the waiting room. "Explaining to my daughter that John McClellan's son is *not* going to give me or anyone else who sets foot on Dunregan the plague."

Brodie's eyebrows shot up. An unlikely champion! He had known Mr. Donaldson his whole life, but they certainly weren't close. Then again…he didn't know how many hours of chess had passed between Mr. Donaldson and his father down at the Eagle and Ram. Thousands. Most likely more.

"I'd be delighted to," Kali replied. "Public health is one of my areas of interest."

"As well it should be." Mr. Donaldson nodded approvingly. "Now, you do know, dear," Mr. Donaldson continued, putting his paper-skinned hand atop hers as they inched their way along the corridor, "that Brodie, here, is one of the island's most eligible bachelors?"

"Well, that *is* news!" Kali's eyebrows shot up and…was that a fake smile or real one?

"Yes, it's absolutely true. Isn't that so, Brodie? Most of the suitable girls have already been married off, and we know he will need someone who's a bit of a brainbox to keep him interested. So…"

He didn't wait for an answer. Brodie was too gob-smacked to intervene. Since when had Mr. Donaldson been made the Matchmaker of Dunregan?

"You cannae go far wrong if you marry a Scot, Dr. O'Shea. They're loyal, truehearted…and, of course, if you're into strapping laddies our Brodie here looks very nice when he's all kitted out in his kilt."

"I—I will take you at your word on that," Kali replied, her expression making it very clear she wasn't interested.

"Mr. Donaldson—" Brodie was goldfishing, trying to search for the best way to cut this conversation short. His romantic escapades—and that was about as far as he'd ever taken any of his relationships—were things he'd always kept very close to his chest. Talking about it so openly made him feel about twelve!

"Brodie, why don't you invite Dr. O'Shea, here, along to one of our Polar Bear outings? They're great fun and a wonderful way to really get to know one another. I've seen more than a few Polar Bear weddings!" He hooted at the memory, then chided Brodie, "And it's been some time since we've seen you down at the beach."

Something in the neighborhood of ten years!

"We should just be taking a left here, Mr. Donaldson." Brodie tried to steer his patient and the conversation firmly off the topic of marriage. He had more than enough on his plate without worrying about getting a fiancée as well.

Not that Kali would be a bad choice, but—

His eyes caught hers. Her expression gave little away. If not the slightest hint of *Uh-uh…you can keep your Scottish yenta.*

"So, Dr. O'Shea," Mr. Donaldson continued, clearly enjoying himself, "you'll do me the favor, please, of going back out there and informing my daughter and the rest of that mob that I've not set to with a fever or anything, won't you?"

"I'll do my best, Mr.—"

"Donaldson. And my daughter is Anne. Now, which way am I going, son?"

"To the left, Mr. Donaldson," Brodie repeated with a shake of his head and a smile. Life on a small island, eh?

Kali looked perfectly bemused, and who could blame her? Not on the island twenty-four hours and already she was being set up by the locals. He sniggered, thinking of how animals always tried to widen the gene pool when their numbers dwindled. Maybe Mr. Donaldson was trying to increase the population of Dunregan. *Ha!*

Kali shot him a look. Whoops. Had that been an outside laugh?

"Later..." he stage-whispered. "I will explain everything later."

If she was going to carry the lance for him regarding the Ebola virus he owed her. As for the whole eligible bachelor thing... Well... At least Mr. Donaldson didn't think he was going to catch the plague.

"Where do you want me?"

"Just over here, Mr. Donaldson. Kali, would you mind helping me get our most loyal and truehearted patient up onto the examination table?"

"Oh, son. Don't go about trying to set *me* up with this young lassie because I've embarrassed you. That's what old people *do*. It's our specialty. My courting days are over. Mrs. Donaldson was more than enough woman for me," Mr. Donaldson scolded as he eased himself up onto the table. "Let's look at this foot, if you don't mind. What a silly old codger! I was away with the faeries when I was cutting the peat and there was a two-hour wait to see Dr. O'Shea. All this silliness going on over you and the Ebola nonsense..."

He shook his head at the madness of it all. "As if someone could contract Ebola on an island this cold!"

He looked at the pair of them for agreement that his hypothesis was a good one.

"Well, it doesn't really work like that…" Brodie began reluctantly.

"Ach, away! I know perfectly well how it works, Brodie McClellan. I was trying to make a joke. Your face is more somber than most folk look at a funeral! Yours, too, dear."

He gave a little cackle and patted Kali's hand as she helped him shift his legs up onto the examination table.

"You go on out there, dear, and please explain—very loudly—to my daughter that no one is catching Ebola on this island if Dr. McClellan says so. John McClellan's son would do no such thing."

Brodie looked away, surprised at the hard sting of emotion hitting him.

Even after he'd passed his father was still looking after him.

He cleared his throat and refocused his attention when he felt Kali shift her gaze from Mr. Donaldson's twinkling eyes up to him. There was something almost anxious in her expression. Something he couldn't put his finger on. And just as quickly it was gone, replaced by a warm, generous smile.

"It would be my very distinct pleasure to answer any of your daughter's questions, Mr. Donaldson."

"Thank you very much. All right, then, dear. Leave us men folk to inspect my idiocy. I'd like to get it bandaged up so I can get the rest of the peat in without the whole of Dunregan knowing I rent my foot in half."

Kali left the room, throwing a final smile over her shoulder at the pair of them. A smile that awoke an entirely new set of sensations in Brodie. He'd done little to nothing to deserve the understanding she'd shown him today.

"Aye, she's a right fine lassie. Isn't she, Dr. McClellan?"

"What?" Brodie turned his attention back to Mr. Donaldson.

"You're not suggesting I'm losing my eyesight as well, are you, son?"

"Absolutely not, but—"

"But nothing. When someone like that arrives on the island, you take notice."

They both turned to look at the closed door, as if it would offer some further insight, but no. It was just a door, covered in various and sundry health notices and how-to sheets. No lessons in romance, or changing terrible first impressions.

Brodie closed down that thought process. Kali wasn't here to be wooed. Or won. And he had a patient!

"Right, Mr. Donaldson…when was the last time you had a tetanus booster?"

CHAPTER FOUR

"IT'S NOTHING FANCY, but the pub does good, honest food."
Brodie loaded Kali's bike onto the rack atop his four-by-four
in a well-practiced move. She put her arms up in a show of
helping, but he'd clearly done this before.

"I'd rather that than a bad meal of fripperies!"

Brodie laughed as he tugged the security straps tight.
"I'm not entirely sure if fripperies are a food group, but I
can assure you, you won't get any up here." He opened the
car door for her with a slight bow. "Madam?"

Kali felt herself flush, instantly thanking the short days
for the absence of light. She climbed in and busied herself
with the seat belt buckle to try and shake off an overwhelming urge to flirt. Her gut and her brain were busy doing bat-
tle. She *never* wanted to flirt with people…and now she was
getting all coquettish with Mr. Disagreeable. Ridiculous!

Probably just her empathy on overdrive. The man had
had a tough day. It was natural to want to comfort someone who was hurting, right?

An image of Brodie laying her across a swathe of sheep-
skin rugs in front of a roaring fire all but blinded her. She
clenched her eyes tight, only to find Brodie hiding behind
her eyelids—peeling his woolen jumper off in one fluid
move, his lean torso lit only by the golden flicker of flames.

Was this what *choice* was? The freedom to choose who you loved?

Loved?

Pah! Arranged marriage was how things worked in the world she'd grown up in. Love was…a frippery. Icing on the cake if your father's choice for your intended turned out to be a good match. Unlike hers. She shuddered at the thought.

Love.

The island air must be giving her brain freeze or something.

She yelped when the driver's door was yanked open. Brodie jumped in and banged his door shut with a reverberating clang.

"The catch on the door is a bit funny," Brodie explained with an apologetic grin. "Suffice it to say Ginny's seen better days."

"Ginny?"

"This grotty old beast."

"Ah…" she managed, still trying to scrub the mental image of her dark past and a half-naked Brodie out of her mind's eye.

Perhaps Mr. Donaldson had put one too many subconscious ideas into motion. This sort of thing had never happened to her in Dublin. Then again…she tipped her head against the cool window as Brodie fired up the engine…in Dublin she'd never felt entirely safe. Up here…

"Now, I should warn you…" Brodie began cautiously.

What? That you've got three girlfriends on the go and the idea of another is repellent?

"Yes?" Kali asked in her very best neutral voice.

"I haven't exactly been to the pub since this whole stramash kicked off."

"Stramash?"

"Sorry. It's Scots for a rammie."

"Still not following you." Her smile broadened. She could listen to Brodie talk forever. All those rolling *r*'s and elongated vowels with a pair of *the most* beautifully shaped lips forming each and every— Oops! Tune in!

"A bit of bother. Or in this case a *big* bit of bother."

"We could always go somewhere else."

Brodie threw back his head and laughed. It was a rich, warm sound. Kali liked the little crinkles that appeared alongside his blue eyes.

Another time, another place…

Another lifetime was more like it. Not with the steamer trunks full of baggage she was hauling around.

"Darlin', this time of year there really *isn't* anywhere else. It's the Eagle and Ram or a fish and chips takeaway from Old Jock's. That's yer choices." He tacked on a cheesy grin for added salesmanship.

"I'm happy with whatever you choose."

"Well…" He gave her a duplicitous wink. "Shall we risk the pub and see if the Ebola public-awareness campaign you kicked off with Anne Donaldson has had any effect beyond the reaches of our humble clinic? It's a bit warmer than a picnic table outside Old Jock's."

Kali nodded, grinning at his choice of words.

Our clinic.

It had a nice ring to it. Chances were slim he'd meant anything by it, but the words warmed her. Not just because her hormones had decided to kick into action and turn her tummy into a butterfly hothouse, but because she'd never had a chance to be a part of anything in that way before. Put down roots.

Dunregan was the first place she'd been that had absolutely no connection to her past. It was why she'd applied for the so-called hardship post. Safe place was more like it.

There was no way her father could find her here, up in the outer reaches of Scotland's less populated islands.

"Right." Brodie pulled the four-by-four in front of a low-slung stone building. "Here goes nothing!"

Moments later Brodie was pulling open a thick wooden door to reveal a picture-postcard pub. The Eagle and Ram was duck-your-head-under-the-beams old. Being short was an advantage here—unfortunately for Brodie. Kali took in stone walls as deep as her arm. A clientele who looked as though they'd known the place since the rafters were green. A landlady robust enough to turf out anyone who wasn't playing by the rules.

She turned her head at the sound of male voices coming in from the back door. Nope. Scratch the chaps-only presumption. There was a varied clientele. A group of young men kitted out in all-weather gear were clustered round the bar, greeting the landlady familiarly, jokes and banter flying between them and the chaps with flat caps already at the bar. And a couple of ruddy-cheeked women elbowing past the rowdy crew to order drinks.

And then…a complete hush as all eyes lit upon Brodie.

"All right, lads?" Brodie stepped into the room with a broad smile. His physical demeanor looked relaxed, although Kali thought she could hear a tightness in his voice.

Her eyes flicked to a nearby table where a newspaper's headline screamed out the poor nurse's recurrence of Ebola.

A few of the men nodded and a couple of muttered "all rights" slid onto the floor and pooled around their ankles, as if weighing everyone down with the lack of truth in them. The atmosphere was tense. Quite the opposite of all right.

"I've brought the new GP along—Dr. O'Shea—to meet you. Thought I'd give her an Eagle and Ram welcome."

Kali was half-hidden behind Brodie, and felt like hiding herself entirely behind his broad back. She hated the limelight. But something told her she needed to step up and be seen—no matter how much it frightened her. This moment wasn't about *her*.

"Right you are, Brodie." The fifty-something woman came out from behind the bar and stood between them and the ten or so men around the bar. "You're looking well."

"Thank you, Moira. I am feeling fit as a fiddle."

"So I hear. It's the *English* Health Authority, is it? Cleared you to come away back up to Dunregan?"

"That's right."

"The Scottish Health Council no good for you, then?" Her face was serious but her tone carried a teasing lilt.

Brodie nodded, clearly appreciative of what was going on. An impromptu public forum. With pints of beer.

"What do the Scots know about getting sick? Healthy as oxen—the lot of you." His eyes scanned the crowd, then returned to Moira. "Excepting the odd run-in with a peat spade. I take it you've spoken with Anne, then?"

Ding! A lightbulb went on in Kali's head. Moira bore an uncanny resemblance to Anne Donaldson.

"Oh, aye. She rang after she brought Dad back from the clinic. We heard all about it. And about Dr. O'Shea answering all of Anne's questions." The landlady's words were loaded with meaning.

Brodie raised his eyebrows. "Well, good. Your father'll heal up in no time. And there'll be no mention of him coming to the clinic." He tapped his finger on the side of his nose with a *got it* gesture. "That peat came in without incident, right?"

Moira nodded and grinned. "Understood. Good to see you looking so chipper…and healthy. Especially with all you've been through after your father passing and everything—right, boys?"

There was a fresh wave of murmurs and nods—and focus was realigned on what really mattered. To Brodie, at the very least.

"Now, what do you say you two go over by the snug and I'll bring you some nibbles? The fire's on."

Kali followed Brodie's gaze. The snug was way across the other end of the pub and could be closed off with a very thick door.

"I suspect you two'll be talking business, and you won't want us butting our noses in while you get to know each other a bit better," Moira clarified.

Kali got a whiff of matchmaking about the suggestion rather than using the snug as an isolation room. What *was* it with these people and pairing her off?

"That'd be grand, Moira. After you, Kali." Brodie stepped to the side and put out his hand for Kali to lead the way.

She felt her cheeks go crimson, with all pairs of eyes trained on her. *Just smile!* She forced her lips to tip upwards and met one or two sets of eyes. She received nods and a couple of hellos as she passed.

How could walking across a room take an eternity? Her eyes shifted to the floor. The thick wooden planks were covered every now and again with old tin signs. A brand of beer here. A vegetable vendor there. It felt like walking over history while making history. She had no doubt this moment would be talked about.

A headline popped into her head:

Ebola Doc Enters Pub for First Time with Blushing Bride...

Locum! *Locum.* She'd meant to say locum. In her head. Where she was busy lecturing herself in turbo speed.

She felt the color in her cheeks deepen as she scuttled to enter the snug ahead of Brodie. Being in the public eye wasn't ideal when very inappropriate thoughts were charging through her head.

"Oh, look," Brodie stage-whispered. "How romantic! We get it all to ourselves!"

It wasn't until she whirled around to face him, a positively goofy smile of expectation lighting up her features, that she realized he was aiming the comment to the crowd of earwiggers over at the bar.

Now officially mortified, she sank into a cushioned bench seat across from the huge inglenook fireplace, feigning total absorption by the flickering flames. Looking into those crystal clear blue eyes of his just might tip her over the edge.

A bit prickly? Definitely. But his edginess had a depth to it. Like an errant knight slaying dragons only he could see.

"What can I get you to drink?"

Kali nearly jumped in her seat. "You're going to go back out there?" Her fingers flew to her lips. She hadn't meant to say that out loud.

"Absolutely." Brodie gave a wide grin, as if energized by the thought of going back into the lion's den. "Moira's laid the groundwork for my reentry into society here at the pub. And I owe a debt of thanks to you for your handiwork at the clinic today, so no point in turning this into an 'us and them' situation, eh?"

She nodded. Absolutely right. The less acrimony, the better.

See? Errant knight. She gave a satisfied sniff of approval.

"Besides…" He dropped a duplicitous wink. "Now that you've seen all there is to see of the bright lights of Dunregan, I'm guessing the sooner you get back to civilization the better. Am I right?"

Hmm...okay. So he could do with a few tweaks.

"I'm sure I could bear to stay for the duration." She had to force a bit of bravura to her tone. The thought of losing her job before she'd barely begun brought home just how many eggs she'd unwittingly put into the Dunregan basket.

All of them.

Brodie tilted his head, taking a none-too-subtle inspection of the impact of his words. "Easy there, tiger. I'm not doubting your staying power." He laughed. "This is nothing to do with your GP skills. You've proved, beyond a doubt, you can hold your own at the clinic. I just can't imagine why anyone would want to stay up here if they didn't have to."

She pasted on a smile.

It's the first time I've felt safe in years.

"Hey..."

Brodie reached across the table, covering her hand with his. The warmth of his hand worked its way through hers, sending out rays of comfort.

"Honestly, Kali. It was just a joke. If you think I can go in there, order a couple of drinks and change the minds of all those knuckleheads in one night, you're in for a surprise. Apart from being emotional Neanderthals, these folk are stubborn. They put mules to shame."

She managed an appreciative snort. "Sounds like the voice of experience."

"Who knows?" He withdrew his hand and shrugged. "They might take so much of a shine to the new GP you'll be stuck here forever."

Kali chewed on her lip, preventing too broad a smile from breaking out. "Would a wine spritzer be all right?"

"A few shots of whiskey would be more understandable

after the day you've had," Brodie intoned, his eyebrows doing an accompanying up and down jig.

"What? You mean sorting out the irascible Young Dr. McClellan? Child's play." She arched an eyebrow expectantly.

"Got it in one!" Brodie laughed appreciatively.

What was going on with her? She didn't flirt. Or behave like a sassy minx. And yet...

Suffice it to say her tummy was alight with little ribbony twirls of approval.

"Hold that thought. I'll just get the drinks. Wish me luck?"

He dropped another one of those slow-motion, *gorgeous* winks, sending the ribbony twirls into overdrive.

"Thank you."

Oh, gross. Did you just coo?

Brodie quirked an eyebrow. "Not a problem."

When he had safely disappeared out of the snug, Kali buried her head in her hands with a low groan. What was going *on* with her? She'd have to have a little mind-over-matter discussion with herself later on. All by herself in the dinky stone cottage she'd rented. The one that didn't strictly have any heat. Or much in the way of windows. But there was a nice sofa!

Hey, she reminded herself, it's home. For this month, at least, it's home.

"So..." A wine spritzer slid across the table into her eye-line a few moments later. "Let's hear it, then."

She sat up, pleased to see Brodie looking unscathed by his trip to the bar.

"Hear what?" Kali took a sip of her spritzer.

"Your life story."

She tried her best not to splutter, and if he'd noticed, Brodie gave nothing away.

"Oh, nothing much to tell." She trotted out the practiced line whilst feeling an unfamiliar tug to tell him the truth.

"I doubt that," Brodie retorted amiably.

"Nothing out of the ordinary," she lied. "Childhood, medical school and now a locum position up here."

It was staggering how much had happened in between each of those things. Her father's vow to avenge the family's honor when she'd backed out of the match he'd made for her. The terrifying flight for her life with a fistful of cash. So much…*too* much…for a young woman to carry on her shoulders. If it hadn't been for the government's ability to give her a new identity—

Enough.

Those were her stories to keep safely hidden away.

"Is that a bit of an Irish accent I detect?" Brodie wasn't giving up.

"Yes." She nodded. "I did my medical degree in Dublin." That much was true.

"But you grew up in England?"

She nodded, taking a deep drink of her spritzer.

"No matter what I do, or what corner of the world I find myself in, I can't seem to shake my accent." Brodie shook his head as he spoke.

Why would he want to? Brodie's accent was completely and totally gorgeous. Which she wasn't going to tell him, so best change the subject.

"So…you've traveled a lot?"

"Some." He nodded. "Lots, actually. Unlike everyone else who was born and raised here, I couldn't wait to get off the island."

"Why?"

"Is it so hard to believe?"

"Yes!" Kali nodded her head rigorously. "I think Dunregan's great."

"Aye, well…" His eyes shot off to that faraway place she couldn't access. "You don't have history here."

Fair enough. She had her own history, and no one was going to pry that from her.

"Where have you traveled?" she asked.

"Everywhere I could at first."

"At first?"

"My father always hoped I'd take over the clinic after medical school, but I…" He paused for a moment searching for the right words. "I struggled to *settle* here."

There was a reason behind that. That much was clear. One only he would decide when to reveal.

Kali was about to say something, but clamped her lips tight when Brodie continued without prompting.

"I'd do stints here, to help relieve my father. The job is bigger than one man's best. Especially during tourist season. But over the winter I kept finding myself volunteering abroad. Orphanages, refugee camps needing an extra pair of hands, villages without access to hospitals." He laughed suddenly, his eyes lighting up. "I used up the paltry first aid kit the agency gave us in my first couple of weeks away! Got my dad to send more supplies along whenever I changed country…"

His eyes shifted to the fire, his brow crinkling as something darker replaced the bright acuity of the happy memory.

Kali pulled him back to the present with a question about his work in Africa. Then another. And before she knew it their conversation had lifted into something effortless and taken flight.

Time slipped away with stories shared and anecdotes compared as their mutual passion for medicine carried them away from whatever had encumbered them during the day into the undefinable giddy excitement that came from meeting a—*a soulmate*.

Kali froze at the thought, her gaze slipping to Brodie's hands. His fingers loosely circled his pint, one index finger shifting along the dewy sheen of condensation as he told her about his grandfather and the crew of men he'd corralled into helping him build the stone clinic in exchange for some of his wife's shortbread. It was how folk did things up here, Brodie was saying. Together. Always together.

And she'd spent her entire adult life alone.

Was a soulmate something she even deserved after leaving her mother and sister behind with her father?

"…and then, when he retired up to the mountains, the key was passed on to my father," Brodie concluded with an affectionate smile. "I don't know if I've told anyone the whole story in one go before. You must've bewitched me with your beguiling ways!"

Kali laughed shyly, her eyes flicking up to meet Brodie's. When their gazes caught and meshed she felt her body temperature soar as the magnetic pull of attraction multiplied again and again, until she forced herself to look away and pretend it hadn't happened.

"So, you coming back here to run the clinic is kismet, really, isn't it?"

She saw him blink away something. A memory, perhaps. Or a responsibility he had neither asked for nor wanted.

She tried again. "Or was it more preordained?"

"Something like that." He took another drink of his pint, eyebrows furrowing. "Look, Kali…while I'm on a bit of a very uncharacteristic 'tell all' roll, I think you should know something—something about *me*. Because you'll no doubt hear it at some point while you're here and I'd rather you heard it from me."

Her heart lurched to her throat as her chin skidded off

her hand. Had he felt it, too? The click of connection that made her feel as if she could find sanctuary in telling him who she really was?

She sat as still as she could, her fingers woven together in front of her on the wooden table as he began.

"When I was about ten I went out on a sailboat with my mother. Begged her, actually. She and I hadn't been out since my kid brother had been born." He cleared his throat roughly. "Long story short: the weather turned nasty. Our boat got overturned. I made it back. My mother didn't."

Kali's fingers had clenched so tightly as he spoke her flesh had turned white with tension.

"Oh, Brodie. I am *so* sorry."

He shook his head. "No, I didn't tell you for your pity. I just want you to understand why sticking around this place isn't top of my list."

"Then why are you here? If there are so many bad memories?"

"A promise." He circled his fingers round his pint, weaving them together on the far side and moving them back again. "To my dad. He loved it here so much and wants— *wanted*—the same for me. So he asked me to stay for a whole year. No trips, no inner-city assignments, a year solid on the island. And I think he wanted someone—family— to be here to look after Callum. My brother," he added.

"And after the year is up—was he expecting you to close the clinic or hand it on to someone else?"

Was this where she came in?

"Ha! No." Brodie smiled at her as if she were an innocent to the world of hard knocks, then his expression softened. "I suppose it was his not very subtle way of hoping I'd fall back in love with the place."

"How's that working out for you?" Kali chanced in a jokey tone.

"Absolutely brilliantly, Dr. O'Shea! Nothing like winning over the people you've kept at arm's length all your life with a nice little Ebola scare." He raised his glass and finished his pint in one long draught.

"You know…" Kali said after they'd sat for a minute in silence. "What's happening here…with you, the islanders… it's really quite exciting."

Brodie couldn't help but laugh. "You've always got a positive spin on things, don't you, Kali? Is this excitement you speak of manifesting itself in the way nary a soul would step foot in the clinic until you arrived, or in the way they've stuck us in this room where no one hardly ever goes except to read the paper in a bit of peace?"

"See—that's where you've got it all wrong."

Her green eyes shone with excitement, as if she had a huge secret she was about to share. If anyone else had told him he'd got it wrong he would've bridled. But coming from Kali…?

It seemed completely bonkers, but he felt closer to her after just a handful of hours than he had near enough anyone outside of his family.

Beguiled or bedeviled?

He didn't know what it was, but he was spilling private thoughts like it was going out of style. And a part of him felt…*relief.* As if with the telling of his story he'd somehow lessened the levels of internal pain it caused.

"I don't mean it in a bad way, Brodie. It's just—you're taking the reaction of the villagers incredibly personally. Which, obviously, it would be hard not to. *But*," she continued quickly, before he could jump in to protest, "it seems to me people are using the Ebola thing as an excuse."

He grunted a go-on-I'm-listening noise.

"Now that I know why you don't want to be here, I get it.

That's a lot of weight to carry on your shoulders for something you surely realize wasn't your fault."

She held up her hand again, making it clear he was going to have to hear her out—gutsy beguiler that she was.

"Perhaps—and this is just a *perhaps*—everyone here thinks you've turned your back on *them*. Your job is to help people. Help them at a time when they're feeling weak, or frightened or downright awful. And if you add a bit of fear into the mix…fear that you won't be around when they've entrusted you with their private concerns…"

"It makes for a pretty poisonous pill," he finished, seeing his plight from an entirely new angle. "I see where you're going with this," Brodie admitted with a nod.

He was so intent on ticking days off the calendar to get through the year he was blinded to everything else. But he wanted to fulfill his promise honorably—so until he took full control of the clinic he couldn't mark a single day off the calendar. He scrubbed at his hair and jiggled his empty pint glass back and forth. Maybe that was why everyone was refusing to see him. So he could never turn over the hourglass and begin the countdown.

He gave her an impressed sidelong look. "You sure you didn't specialize in psychology?"

"Positive."

Kali flushed as their eyes met. A sweet splash of red along the porcelain lines of her cheekbones. She was a beautiful woman. And smart.

Frustration and anger had eaten away at his ability to be compassionate. Show the people he'd known his entire life the same care and attention he'd given each and every patient he'd treated abroad. The same care and attention they'd shown him when first he'd lost his mother and then again when his father had passed. Even if they weren't all huggy-kissy about it.

Anonymous plates of scones had been delivered. Stews heated up. Distance kept…

"You're quite the insightful one, Dr. O'Shea."

"Well…" She drew a finger round the base of her wine glass. "We've all had hurdles to jump. I know how frustrating it can be when it seems like no one is on your side. You against the world, sort of thing. But it's not exactly as if you're powerless to change things, is it?"

Something told Brodie she was talking about something a world away from what *he* was experiencing. An instinct told him not to push. His were the only beans getting spilled tonight.

"I get the feeling you have an idea or two about how I can win the hearts and minds of my fellow islanders." Brodie leaned forward, rubbing his hands together in a show of anticipation.

"I do!" she chirped, enthusiasm gripping her entire body. "GPs are at the forefront of the medical world as far as a community like this is concerned, right? They're authority figures, really."

Brodie nodded. He'd always pictured his father as the authority, but now he supposed that baton had been well and truly handed over.

"And what do you see me doing with all of this authority?"

"Well…it sounds like you've had some amazing experiences overseas. You combine that with your local knowledge and you've got an amazing opportunity for public outreach. To teach people firsthand what's going on in the world beyond the sensationalist headlines." She picked up a discarded copy of the nation's favorite rag and held it in front of him like a red cape to a bull. "Make them wise, not reactionary. From Ebola to…to Zika virus."

"What? Quell their fears about Ebola, only to get everyone up in arms about every mosquito arriving on their hallowed shores being laden with the Zika virus? Now *there's* an idea?"

Kali swatted at the space in between them, taking his words as he'd meant them. In jest. With a healthy splash of affection.

The strangest feeling overtook him as he watched her speak. He was no spooky-spooky sort, but meeting Kali felt meant to be. Their long talk, which had all but emptied the pub, seemed like a homecoming of sorts—as if they'd been cinching the loose strings of a relationship they'd let fade and were now eager to rekindle.

Her own voice came to him in the perfect way to describe the sensation.

Kismet.

And then he realized she was still talking about public awareness.

"You know what I mean. The only reason people are being funny about you is because they don't understand. About Ebola. Why you don't like it here. And, frankly, I'm a little on their side with that one. You're keeping them at arm's length. It makes you scarier."

"Loveable, approachable me?" Brodie put on his best teddy bear face. "I come across as *scary*?"

"Yes! Exactly!" She grinned, her smile lighting up those green eyes of hers from within.

Funny how a guy could take an insult when it came from a woman with such a genuine smile.

"Luckily I've already learned your bark is worse than your bite," Kali replied regally.

She was obviously enjoying herself. The young medical disciple offering words of wisdom to the block-headed Scottish doctor.

"So…how do you suggest I open my arms to people who don't even want to breathe the same air as me?"

"Get a gas mask," she replied with a straight face.

He stared at her, waiting to see if she'd break.

She didn't.

"A gas mask? That's your big idea."

Kali burst into gales of laughter, tears of delight filling the rims of eyes now flecked with golden reflections of the fire.

"Sorry, sorry…" She swallowed away the remains of her giggles, pressing her lips together in an attempt to regroup. "Look. You don't have to do it alone. I'm happy to go to bat for you."

"So soon?" He feigned astonishment, though in truth he was genuinely touched.

"Oh, it's more for me than you," she replied with mock gravitas. "I don't know if you noticed, but there's an awful backlog of patients to see. Time is of the essence, Dr. Mc-Clellan."

Brodie grinned. Couldn't help it. Probably his first genuine smile since he'd lost his father. "Anyone told you your enthusiasm is infectious, Miss O'Shea?"

"That's *Dr.* O'Shea to you," she riposted with a shy smile.

He tipped his head to the side and looked at her with fresh eyes.

Strikingly pretty. Petite, but not fragile. Thick mane of black hair framing the soft outlines of her heart-shaped face. And those eyes…

He'd better watch it. This whole two-peas-in-a-pod thing had *wrong time, wrong place* written all over it.

"So, what do you say?" He rubbed his hands together briskly. "We take on the islanders one by one, or gather them all up in a stadium and do it warlord-style?"

"I was thinking more softly, softly—kitten-style."

"You think I'm up to being a *kitten*?" Brodie snorted as Kali feigned imagining him as a kitten.

"Maybe more of an alley cat. With an eye patch and a broken tail."

"Ah—so we'll have a cat fight at the end?"

"*Purrr*haps," she purred, completely capturing his full attention.

Her lips were parted, chin tilted up toward his, eyelids lowered, half cloaking that mystical green-eyed gaze of hers as a thick lock of hair fell along her cheek. He was itching to shift it away, feel the peachy softness of her skin.

Brodie readjusted as his body responded.

Kali had just shape-shifted from beautiful to downright sexy.

And an instant later…the shutters closed.

Kali's gaze had gone from inviting to *stay away* in an actual blink of the eye.

He chalked up another reminder about barriers as she tugged on her coat, pulling the zip right up to her chin.

She wasn't here to stay. Nor was he.

Kali threw her coat on top of the duvet, shivered, then grabbed her suitcase and shook the whole pile of clothes along the bed in a line stretching the length of her body.

Her fire-making skills, as it turned out, were not great. Thank goodness she'd convinced Brodie to let her ride her bicycle home in lieu of a lift, otherwise she'd have no body heat at all! Not that he hadn't put up a fight.

He'd insisted. She'd insisted more firmly. Said it was all part of the rugged island adventure she'd been banking on when she took up the post. She tugged on a pair of tights and zipped a fleece over her layers of T-shirts and jumpers, acutely aware that an online shopping spree was growing increasingly essential.

Her eyes flicked over to the bedroom door. Firmly shut. Front door? Dead-bolted. Checked twice. She'd never let anyone walk, drive or cycle home with her in the past five years. The fewer people who knew where she lived the better. And yet...

How many times had she been tempted to blurt out her life story tonight?

Too many.

How many times had she let herself wonder...*what if*?

Each time she'd caught herself staring at Brodie's lips was how many.

Too many.

This was a working relationship. Not an island romance.

Apart from which, Brodie wanted nothing to do with Dunregan and she...she wanted *everything* to do with it. Just one day here was as appealing as one day with her "intended" had been repellent.

She huffed out a sigh of exasperation, eyes widening as she did.

Was that her *breath*?

She pulled up the covers, trying to keep the pile of clothes balanced on top of her, and snuggled into the fetal position. Shivering created body warmth.

She giggled. Now she was just being silly. But it felt good. She hadn't been plain old silly in...*years*. Perhaps it was the cold, or the delicious lamb stew she'd virtually in-haled at the Eagle and Ram. She felt warm from the inside. A cozy glow keeping the usual fears at bay.

She was safe here in Dunregan. And, for tonight at least, she couldn't wipe the smile off her lips if she tried.

CHAPTER FIVE

TOO LATE, BRODIE saw the beginning of the end. It was a miracle the wood had stayed atop his four-by-four this far.

"Noooooooooo!"

The planks of wood were crashing and slithering all over the place. Smack-dab in front of the clinic.

He glanced at his watch.

Kali would be there soon. No doubt expressing her despair at yet another way he'd made her time at the clinic less than straightforward.

Three days in and she seemed a more regular part of the place than he ever had. Correction. Than he had ever *felt*.

Big difference.

He nudged a bit of wood with his foot and shook his head.

Woodworking was a class he really should have taken when he'd had the chance. He'd scoffed at his brother's choice at the time. Now he was beginning to see the advantages of having learned some practical skills. Or having stuck around so he could've built the blasted thing with his father, a man as at home with a hammer as a stethoscope.

He heard a throat clearing on the far side of his car.

Kali.

Kali trying desperately not to laugh.

She'd been keeping him at a courteous arm's length after

their strangely intimate night at the pub, so it was nice to see that smile of hers.

"New project?" she asked, barely able to contain her mirth.

"Aye. I'm sure you will have noticed just sitting round the clinic waiting for patients to magically appear hasn't worked quite the treat I'd hoped."

She made a noncommittal noise, turning her head this way and that, obviously trying to divine what the pile of wood in front of her—*his*—clinic was meant to be.

"It's a boat."

"Ohhhh…" She nodded. "I can see that now."

"Ha-ha. Very funny."

"No, I mean it." She sidled up beside him, crossed her arms and gave the hodgepodge pile of wood a considered look before pointing to one of the shorter cuts. "That's the pram, right?"

"The prow," he corrected, the language of boats coming back to him as if it were genetically embedded.

"And you're building this here because…?" Kali tactfully changed the subject.

"I was rehashing our talk the other night—about public awareness and all that—and I thought, how can I get through to everyone island-style?"

"And this is what you came up with?" Kali gave him a dubious look.

"I told you—it's a boat." He frowned at the pile of wood. "Or it will be once word gets out I'm trying to make one. The folk here can't resist giving advice when it comes to building a boat."

"And that means you're staying?"

A jag of discord shot through him at the wary note of hope in her voice. He'd heard it often enough in his father's voice each time he'd returned. The thought of disappointing Kali bothered him, but he wasn't there yet. In that place where settling down—setting down *here*—felt right. Might not ever be. That was why he'd decided to get out of the clinic, where they had been warily circling each other after that night of so much connection. No bets taken as to why he was building the boat right next door to the clinic, though.

It was Kali. One hundred percent Kali.

He scrubbed his jaw and tried to look like a model citizen.

"I was thinking more along the lines of the public health campaign first."

She gave him a sidelong glance. One he couldn't read. One that made him wonder if she could see straight through his bluster.

"This is your master plan to convince people you don't have Ebola?"

"Who could resist such a rugged, healthy-looking soul?" Brodie looked off into the middle distance supermodel-style. Sure, he was showing off, but the reward was worth it.

A shy grin.

Each of Kali's smiles was like a little jewel—well worth earning.

He struck a bodybuilder pose to see if he could win another.

Bull's-eye.

A fizz of warmth exploded in Kali's belly. Then another. *Would he just stop doing that?*

"Well? What do you think? Irresistible or repugnant?"

Brodie's blue eyes hit hers and another detonation of attraction hit Kali in the knees. What *was* she? Twelve? *Regroup, girl. This man has danger written all over him.*

"Well…you're not exactly repugnant…"

Brodie threw back his head and laughed. "Touché."

He dropped her a wink. Another knee wobbler.

"Serves me right for floating my own boat." Brodie's eyes scanned the higgledy-piggledy pile of wood. "Or not, as the case might be."

Kali gave him a quick wave and hightailed it around the back of the building and into the clinic.

Despite her best efforts to keep her nose to the proverbial grindstone…to see patients and race her bicycle back home to her icy cold house…she knew she was falling for Brodie. Fast.

It scared her. But as unsettling as it felt it also felt good. A little *too* good.

He wasn't hanging around. It was easy enough to see the boat was a project with a timeline and once that was done… *Poof.*

Goodbye, Romeo.

Or, more accurately, goodbye, Kali. Brodie would win the hearts of Dunregan back in no time and then there'd be no need for her here. Before she knew it, it would be time for her to begin again.

"Kali?" Ailsa called to her from the tea room as the back door shut with its satisfying click and clunk. "I've just put the kettle on. Milk and no sugar, isn't it?"

"Got it in one!" She grinned despite the storm of unwelcome thoughts.

"Are we going to be blessed with my nephew's presence today?" Ailsa popped her head round the corner and gave Kali an exasperated smile.

"He's out front," Kali answered. "Building a boat."

Ailsa's eyebrows shot up. "Aye?"

Kali nodded, keeping her own expression neutral.

"Well…"

It was a loaded word. Suspicious. Loving. Expectant. Curious.

Kali couldn't help but smile. She might not have much

time here, but at the very least she was becoming much more fluent in Scots!

"Kali! First patient's come early!" Caitlyn called from the front office. "Will you be all right to take a look?"

"It would be my pleasure," she replied, accepting the hot cup of tea Ailsa had just handed her. "Let's get this show on the road."

"Someone's up with the lark."

A woman in her early thirties spun round at the sound of the bell ringing above the door, her face lighting up with a smile when she saw it was Kali.

"The usual?"

Kali grinned. This was the third morning running she'd relished the warmth and sugary sweet air of the Dunregan Bakehouse. This first "thawing station" on her bicycle ride into work. It had nothing to do with the fact they also made the fluffiest scones she'd ever tasted. And with lashings of the fruitiest, raspberriest jam in the world. She'd bought treats for everyone at the clinic each day since she'd discovered the place.

"I'm Helen, by the way."

"Nice to meet you. I'm Kali—"

"O'Shea," finished Helen with a laugh. "If you haven't found out already, word travels fast in Dunregan. By my count, you've been here about a week now."

"Only three more to go!"

The words were double-edged. She didn't want to leave. Little bits of her heart were already plastered about the small harbor town. Once she got a chance to explore some more she was sure the rest of it would follow suit.

"I guess you'll know my being here is actually a bit pointless. With Brodie having the all clear." It was hardly subtle, but they'd passed that point.

"I thought he'd given up doctoring to build that boat of his?"

Kali pulled a face. To say Brodie was making a success of turning the pile of planks into a boat would be...very kind. He'd eventually brought all the wood over and laid it out in a completely indecipherable series of piles in the open shed next to the clinic. Some nails had gone in. Some nails had been pulled out. The piles remained.

"I'm no expert on boat building myself, but I get the feeling medicine is more of his forte," she said as tactfully as she could. "But it keeps him busy while he waits for his patients to feel more comfortable about coming back to see him."

Helen laughed conspiratorially, but Kali saw a generous dose of compassion in her brown eyes.

"I don't think I ever saw him near the woodworking classes at school. Complete and total brainbox." Distractedly she added a couple more scones to the box she was filling. "You know, I have an idea of someone who could lend a hand. In the meantime..." She flicked the lid shut, putting a Dunregan Bakehouse sticker in place to seal it as she did so. "I've got something special for you to try."

She put up her finger to indicate that she'd be back in a second and disappeared into the back.

"Me?" Kali whispered to the empty room, a giddy twirl of anticipation giving an extra lift to her smile. She knew it was silly, but the gesture made her feel—*better* than welcome. As if she were part of something. A community.

"Right. Give this a taste." A piece of toast appeared in her eyeline. Thick cut, oozing with butter and a generous smear of soft cheese. "You're all right with goat's cheese?"

"Absolutely. I love it." Kali took the bread and was three bites in before she remembered Helen was expectantly waiting for a response. "This is the most delicious thing *ever*," she said through another mouthful. "Ever!"

"Really?" Helen's eyes glowed with happiness. "It's a new bread I've been working on. Hazelnuts and a mix of grains for all the island's health nuts. I'm still debating about raisins. But it's locally produced cheese so I thought I might put it on the board as a lunch offering. What with you being an outsider, I thought you'd give an honest response."

"It's completely yummy."

And thanks for the reminder that I don't belong here. Surprising how much it stung.

"Thanks, Dr. O'Shea."

"Kali," she corrected firmly. They were around the same age. And on the off-chance that she were to stay...

Don't go there. As long as your father is alive, you'll always live a life on the run.

"Thanks, Kali. It means a lot. And don't worry about Brodie's boat. We'll get him sorted out—island-style."

Mysterious. But positive! Kali left the bakery with a wave, feeling a bit unsettled. Could a place do that to someone? Or, she thought, as an image of Brodie flickered through her overactive brain, was it a person that was unsettling her?

"Look who made it all the way up the hill today!" Brodie applauded as Kali dismounted from her bicycle with a flourish. "A mere week on the island and you're a changed woman!"

Kali flushed with pleasure, glad her cheeks were already glowing with exertion.

"It has helped that the wind isn't quite so—"

"Hostile?" offered Brodie.

"Exactly."

Kali smiled at his choice of word, but now she officially needed to get indoors as soon as possible. No heat again in her house meant riding her bicycle and the pit stop at the bakery were the only ways she got warm in the morning. It was absolutely freezing! Which did beg the question...

"How many layers are you wearing?"

"You like?"

Brodie did a little catwalk strut for her. Man, he had a nice bum. A nice *everything*. Even if it *was* covered in a million layers of down and fleece.

"You'll do."

Understatement of the universe!

"So how is Operation Public Awareness going?"

"Well, in terms of gathering in the crowds, you can see how well *that's* going." He swept his arm along the length of the empty street.

"Mmm...could be the weather?"

"Or could be they just prefer you," Brodie replied, his tone lighter than a week ago, when even mentioning the cotton bud delivery had been enough to set him off. Keeping her distance had been easier when he was all grumbly.

This Brodie... All rugged and tool wielding... *Yummy.*

"What's in the magic basket today?"

Brodie leaned toward the wicker basket he had helped Kali attach to the front of her bike with a whole pack of zip ties. Suffice it to say his stitches were better than his DIY skills.

"Wouldn't you like to know?" She protectively covered the box with her hand, eyes sparkling with excitement.

For a split second Brodie envied her the purity of emotion. Every joy he experienced seemed to come with conditions. Obligation after obligation, intent on dragging him down.

Although lately...

"Don't open it yet." He nodded at the box. "I bet I can

sniff it out. I've got a nose that knows…" He tapped the side of it with a sage nod.

Kali laughed, dimpling with the simple pleasure of silly banter.

"It's definitely not bridies hiding in there."

She shook her head, lips pushed forward in a lovely little *guess again* moue.

"Too early for hot cross buns…"

"Correct again." She nodded. "That you're wrong, that is."

"Scones." He took a step back. "That's my final answer."

"Is it, now?"

The *guess again* moue did a little back and forth wiggle. *Suggestive. Very, very suggestive.*

She unpeeled the sticker to reveal a pile of fluffy scones. Then snapped the lid shut again before he could get his hand in there to steal one.

"Uh-uh." She wagged a finger at him. "These are for later. For *everyone.*"

"You know, you've got to stop spoiling us like this."

"Why?" She looked at him like he was nuts.

"We just might get used to it."

"We?" she countered, with a flirty shift of the hips.

"Me," he admitted, not wanting to put words to the feeling of emptiness he knew was inevitable once she left.

"Go on, now." He shooed her off. "Run off to your lovely warm clinic whilst I freeze to death out here with my pile of wood."

"Take your time," Kali teased. "Gives me more time to steal all of your patients!"

Her grin disappeared instantly at the sight of Brodie's defenses flying into place, blue eyes snapping with anger.

"I'm perfectly happy to come in and see patients. It is, after all, *my* name on the clinic."

The words flew at her like sharp arrows and just as rapidly her own walls of protection slammed down.

Too soon.

She'd let herself believe in the fairy tale too soon.

"I'm perfectly aware it's a temporary posting, all right? I just—" She looked away for a minute, trying to ward off the sting of tears.

She'd been too keen. Too enthusiastic about settling in. Brodie's sharp reaction served her right. She'd fallen hook, line and sinker for the friendly island welcome. The frisson she'd thought existed with Brodie. Her heart had opened up to give too much faith too soon. Trusting people was always a mistake—how could she not know that by now? After everything she'd been through?

Fathers were meant to look after their daughters. Care for them. Protect them. It had never occurred to her that he would choose a man with a history of violence to be her husband. Perhaps her father had fallen for the smooth public demeanor her "intended" had down to a fine art. The one that hid the fact he saw nothing wrong with hitting her to get what he wanted. Her hand flew to her cheek as if the slap had happened yesterday.

She stamped her feet with frustration and forced herself to look Brodie in the eye. It was what people who were in control of their lives did. Met things head-on.

They stood there like two cowboys, each weighing up whether or not it was safe to holster their weapons.

From the looks of Brodie's expression—a virtual mirror of her own—Kali was fairly certain they were both wishing they could swallow back their words.

Had she been this touchy when she went to the Forced Marriage Protection Unit and pleaded for a new identity? She'd been so consumed with fear and a near-primal need to survive she didn't really have a clue *what* sort of impression she'd given. If Brodie was feeling half the trauma she'd experienced, it was little wonder his temperament was whizzing all over the place.

"I didn't mean to stake some sort of claim on your clinic."

"And I didn't mean to sound like such an ass."

She watched as Brodie raked his long fingers through his thatch of wayward blond hair.

He met her questioning gaze head-on. "Start again… *again*?"

There it was. That melt-her-heart-into-a-puddle smile.

"Sounds good," she managed, without too much of a waver in her voice.

"Shall I make you a cup of tea?"

Kali couldn't help it. She burst out laughing. "The solution to everything? No, thanks, you're all right. I don't want to stand in the way of a man who's got a boat to build!"

Brodie shook off her refusal and commandeered her bicycle, hooking his free arm through hers as he did so, turning them both toward the clinic door. A small step in the right direction to start afresh.

"Now, then, Dr. O'Shea, if I can't make you a fresh cup of tea, I'm not going to be much good at building a boat, am I?"

"I suppose not." Kali giggled. "But how long is this going to take? It did take you about five hours to make me one on my first day."

"Well, lassie…" He increased his brogue, rolling his *r*'s to great effect, mimicking his auntie Ailsa. "Can you afford me a second chance to make you a nice cuppa tea within the hour, accompanied by a wee bit of Mrs. Glenn's delicious shortbread?"

"That would be lovely." Kali smiled up at him, eyes bright, cheeks flushed with the cold and the cycle ride.

* * *

Brodie found himself fighting an urge to bend down and kiss her. But getting attached to Kali when he had no idea what his own future held… *Bad idea.*

He unhooked his arm from hers, focusing on getting her bicycle into the stand at the back door. Wooing the locum was probably *not* what his father had had in mind when he'd hoped his son would fall in love with the island.

Besides, Kali wasn't here for an island fling—she was here to do a job. *His* job! And it rankled. Perhaps he wouldn't go inside with her after all.

"Right, then, here you are, Dr. O'Shea. Enjoy your day in the clinic. I've got a boat to build!" He gave her a silly salute he didn't quite feel just as Ailsa poked her head through the door.

"Oh, there you both are. I've been wondering if it was just me who was going to run this place today. Kali, you look like you've just been pried out of an iceberg!"

Brodie took a closer look. "Are you shivering?"

"No. Not really." Kali's lips widened into a wince, only succeeding in making her shivering more obvious.

"Oh, for heaven's sake!" cried Ailsa. "Come in out of the cold, would you? I've just put the kettle on. I'll make us all a nice cuppa tea. And perhaps some of Mrs. Glenn's delicious shortbread."

Kali and Brodie shared a glance, bursting into simultaneous laughter.

Ailsa waved them off as if they'd each lost their wits. "Ach, away with the pair of you. Now, hurry up so I don't heat up the outdoors more than the clinic."

Kali gathered together the day's files, tapped them on the top and sides so they all aligned, then picked them up to give them a final satisfying *thunk* on the desk.

There.

She'd done it.

Another full day of seeing patients—and, she thought with a grin, it had all gone rather swimmingly.

Brodie had been in and out of the tea room, reading various instruction manuals for an ever-growing array of tools. She'd chanced a glance out into the large shed when he'd come in for a cuppa and had smiled at the untouched pile of wood. But she wouldn't have a clue how to build a boat, so she would be the last one to cast aspersions.

Her phone rang through from the reception line.

"Hello, Caitlyn, are you all ready to close up shop for the day?"

"I am, but I was wondering if you wouldn't mind seeing one last patient. Mr. Fairways has popped in. Says his hearing aid is acting up."

"Wouldn't he be—" Kali was going to ask if he'd be better off seeing a hearing specialist, but remembered there was no hospital. "Absolutely." It wasn't as if she had anything else to do. "I'll come out and get him."

She pushed through the door into the waiting room, where a wiry gentleman—an indeterminate fiftysomething, wearing a wax jacket and moleskin trousers—was leaning on the counter, speaking with Caitlyn. He looked familiar to her, but that was hardly likely seeing as she'd only been on the island for a week.

"Mr. Fairways?"

He continued to regale Caitlyn with a blow-by-blow account of the weather. Was that feedback she was hearing? She walked toward him. Yes. There was definitely feedback coming from one of his hearing aids.

"Mr. Fairways?" She touched his shoulder.

"Ah, hello there." He turned to reveal a pair of deep brown eyes and the most wonderful mustache Kali had ever seen outside of a nineteenth-century photo. Or…had she seen him before? There was something familiar about him she couldn't put a finger on.

"So you're the mad spirit who's come up to join us on our fair isle?"

Kali smiled. "Something like that. I understand you're having a problem with your hearing aid?"

A screech of feedback filled the small waiting room.

"What was that, dear?"

Caitlyn stifled a giggle. Kali shot her a horrified look. She couldn't *laugh* at the patients!

"I said, I understand you're here about your hearing aid?"

"I can't quite understand your accent, dear. I'm here about my hearing aid." He glanced at the window facing the street. "I see Young Dr. McClellan is taking a hand to building that boat."

"That's what he says." Kali smiled, then hid her flinch at another piercing hit of feedback.

"What volume do you have your hearing aid on, Mr. Fairways?"

"Eh?"

"The volume?" Kali turned an invisible volume control near her ear.

"Oh, it's up as high as it'll go! It was getting harder to hear so I ramped it right on up."

"That might be your problem."

"Eh?"

Caitlyn out-and-out laughed. Kali hushed her, but not in time for Mr. Fairways not to take notice.

"Oh, you'll want to watch it, lassie." He teasingly waggled a finger in front of the receptionist's eyes. "You might be bonny now, but soon enough you'll be all old and wrinkly like me—eyes not working so well, ears packed up and wondering what on earth people are talking about."

"Ach, away." Caitlyn waved off his comment with a youthful grin. "You're hardly an old codger, Mr. Fairways. My great-gran's about twice your age. You're obviously doing something funny to those hearing aids of yours, though, with the amount of bother they're giving you."

"Since the day I was born, lassie. Since the day I was born."

"So you've *always* had hearing aids?" Kali asked.

"Aye, well…"

Kali smiled. She was getting used to the Scots' all-purpose response. Never giving more information than absolutely necessary. She was hardly one to quibble with the tactic.

"Why don't you come down to my office and we'll take a look?"

A few minutes later Kali had eased down the volume on her patient's hearing aids, syringed his ears and clipped away the long hairs that had accrued outside his ear canal. Once he had the hearing aids safely back in place Kali spoke at a normal volume.

"There doesn't seem to be anything wrong with the hearing aids so far as I can tell, Mr. Fairways, but it's a good idea to keep your ears as clear of hair and wax as you can."

"I know, dearie, but with no one to keep myself dapper for I sometimes forget."

"Well, you're always welcome to come along and see me." As the words came out of her mouth she realized they weren't true. This was temporary. Just like so much in her life had been. Temporarily safe. Temporarily happy. Temporarily a normal woman doing her dream job with a hot Viking building…something or other just outside.

"Aye, well…" Mr. Fairways's brow crinkled with concern. "Let's make you an appointment with the audiologists next time they're on the island. Unless you usually go to the mainland for this sort of thing?"

"Oh, no. I stay here. I'm the honorary mayor of Dunregan, and it wouldn't do for me to be leaving willy-nilly. I'm happy here. On the island," he qualified, as if that weren't obvious.

"Right, then, so I'll check with Dr. McClellan about the audiologists and we'll get in touch."

"Fine." Mr. Fairways gave a satisfied nod, but made no move to leave.

"Is there anything else you want to talk about?"

"No, no…not really—it's just that…"

"Mmm…?" Kali nodded that he should feel free to speak.

"I just noticed Brodie doesnae have a proper base set up for his A-frames. He won't be getting the right sort of balance on the skiff if he's doing it that way."

Kali's grin widened. "Mr. Fairways, I am afraid everything you just said flew straight over my head. I'm about as landlubbery as a girl can get!"

"Well, if you could let Brodie know—"

Kali put up a hand. "I'm afraid I'm going to have to stop you there. I am quite certain anything you tell me would be lost in translation. How about you tell him yourself on your way out?"

She watched him consider the idea. Neutral territory… A way to tease away the groundless fears…

"Oh, I wouldnae want to get in his way or anything."

"You wouldn't be," she assured him. "I think he'd quite like it. Especially since you'd be doing him a double favor."

"How's that, then?"

"Well…" She leaned forward conspiratorially. "So many people don't seem to understand he's been given the all clear as far as his health and his time in Africa are concerned."

"Oh?" Mr. Fairways' fingers twiddled with the end of his handlebar mustache. "Is that right?"

"Absolutely." She crossed her heart and held up two fingers. "Girl Scouts' honor."

"Aye…there was some talk about it at the Eagle and Ram."

Kali checked a broad grin. *That* was where she'd seen him before. The pub!

"Given that you're the mayor of the island—"

"Oh…" Mr. Fairways tutted, a modest smile on his lips. "Only *honorary*, dear. We don't go for too much pomp and ceremony up here."

"Well, even so, it seems to me you have the islanders' respect, so if you were to be seen speaking with Brodie… you know, just giving him a few pointers…it might put a lot of people's minds at ease." She paused while he took in the information. "I've seen Brodie's medical paperwork myself. If you like, I can show you."

"No, dear, no. That won't be necessary. I saw him at his father's funeral. Didn't want to interfere, is all." He pushed himself up to stand. "I think I might head on out and have a word with Brodie now. No need to take up any more of your time."

"It was my pleasure, Mr. Fairways."

He gave her a nod and a smile as he tugged on his overcoat. "You'll do well here, lassie—with a smile like that. And sensible, too. Who knows? We might make an islander of you yet?"

From your lips, Mr. Fairways…

"You take care of yourself, then, Mr. Fairways." Brodie gave a wave as the sprightly fellow headed off down the road toward the pub for his evening pint, flat cap firmly in place.

Would wonders never cease?

Mr. Fairways…standing right out there in the middle of the street…chatting with him about boat mechanics. He'd been the first one to cancel his appointment when Brodie had returned to Dunregan. It had felt like being struck by a battering ram. Only to be hit again and again as one by one his patients had dropped off the appointment list like flies.

Had it been the Ebola or had it been an unofficial mourning period?

It had been easier to blame the nonexistent contagion rather than face up to years of pushing people away. With his father gone, he might have finally succeeded in pushing near enough everyone away.

Except his auntie. Stoic Ailsa. Unflappable at the worst of times. She was the only one who could tease Callum out of the mountains. Something *he* needed to put a bit more energy into, with all this unexpected free time.

"Did you get your advice, then?"

"Kali!" Brodie turned abruptly. "Sorry, I was miles away. What was that?"

"Mr. Fairways was saying something about props or frames—"

"Kali O'Shea…" He took a step toward her. "You didn't have anything to do with Mr. Fairways suddenly turning into a chatterbox, did you?"

"Oh, no. Nothing like that. He was just interested in your project, and I didn't have a clue what he was talking about, so I thought—"

"Kali," Brodie interrupted with a knowing smile, "you are about as transparent as a glass of water."

She grinned, the smile lighting up her eyes. Was that a dimple on her cheek?

"Well, whatever you did or didn't say…thank you." He pulled a tarp over the pile of wood and began to organize his tools into some newly purchased boxes. "I'm not going to hold my breath for everyone to come back tomorrow demanding an appointment with me, though."

"Well, isn't that the mad thing about life? You just never know." She raised her eyebrows and tacked on, "Do you?" for added emphasis.

"I suppose."

If he could get back to work at the clinic then the ticker would start on his promise to his father, he could wipe his hands clean of his past, move on with the future and…and Kali would be gone.

He wasn't quite ready to give her up just yet.

"Don't you worry, Kali. Things work at a glacial pace up here. Besides, what would you do if I were hogging all the patients? Your contract is for a month, and if you weren't busy at the clinic—"

"I'm sure I could think of a load of things to keep me occupied."

"In Dunregan? You must be joking!" Then again…he could think of a number of things to do with Kali to keep her occupied.

Uh…where did that come from?

"Of course Dunregan," Kali replied emphatically, blissfully unaware of his internal monologue.

What would she want with someone who hauled around baggage as oversized as his anyway?

"There's this Polar Bear Club I still have to find out about," Kali continued enthusiastically, "and I've discovered there's no need to go to the tourist office. The patients have told me about so much more. There's the cake-baking club, hiking up in the mountains, fell running—"

"You're a runner?"

Kali nodded, his question jolting her back to another time and place. She'd never give up running. It was her escape.

"Good call." Brodie interrupted her silent musings. "Running is one thing I missed about being here. The mountain tracks are out of this world. Just the views alone are worth the burn."

"Finally!" She forced on a cheery smile. "Something you like about the island."

"Ach…" He waved away her playful gibe. "There's plenty I like about the old lump of rock. Doesn't mean I have to stay here till my bones are creaking, does it?" He gave her a sly grin. "So…given that we've established neither of us are going to be here forever…maybe you and I could go for a run sometime before you go back?"

"That'd be great!" Her smile faltered a bit.

"Or not. If you prefer running alone."

"No, no. A run together would be great."

There was something in her response Brodie couldn't put a finger on. She wanted to stay? She didn't like running with other people? She didn't like being with him? None of the puzzle pieces fit quite right.

She leaned her bicycle on her hip and rubbed her hands together, blowing on them even though they were kitted out in a new pair of mittens.

"I see you've been to the shops for a bit of warm-weather gear."

"Yes!" She nodded with a self-effacing laugh. "I think I must've spent my entire month's salary on a Dunregan wardrobe, but I'll finally be warm tonight."

"You're joking, right?"

She shook her head.

"Doesn't the heating work where you are?"

"Um…not really. But it's fine. Although my fire-making skills could do with a bit of improvement."

"I could show you. I'm all wrapped up here." Brodie gave the shed a final scan and flicked off the overhead lighting. "Where is it you're staying again?"

"Oh, it's fine. Honestly. It's just a small cottage, and I've got loads of warm clothes now. As long as I wear all of them I'm cozy as a teapot."

"Kali. Which cottage?" he pressed.

"It's fine—honestly."

He wagged a finger at her. "I think you've been in Dunregan long enough to know it doesn't take a man long to figure out every single thing there is to know about a person if he sets his mind to it. I can have a word with your landlord, if you like. Who is it you're renting your cottage from?"

"Seriously…" Her voice went up a notch. "I'm absolutely fine!"

Kali looked anything but fine. There was near panic in her voice, and even through the descending murk of the early evening it was more than apparent that any happiness had drained away from her eyes. A need to protect her overrode his instinct to back away.

"Hey, you're all right," he said gently.

He checked an impulse to pull her in for a hug when her body language all but shouted, *Back off!*

"I'm not trying to pry, Kali. I'm just trying to help you. Make sure you don't freeze to death while you're busy covering my back."

"So which is it, then? I'm covering your back or taking over?"

"Easy there, tiger! What's going on? This isn't just about dodgy heating, is it?"

"Sorry, sorry. It's just been…" Her voice trailed off.

"A long day. I know. A long week. And you've done

well." Again he fought an impulse to tug her in for a protective hug.

She grabbed the handlebars of her bicycle. "I'll see you tomorrow, then."

"No, sorry… Kali, I can't let you go back to a house with no heating. Let's get your bike atop the four-by-four, then I'll get you home and we'll build you a fire."

Kali eyed him warily, then shook her head. "Sorry, I don't mean to make such a fuss." She held her bike out for him to put on top of the four-by-four.

"Too many boyfriends chasing you round London?"

"Something like that."

Even in the dark he saw her lips tighten. There *had* been something. He was sure of that now. Something that made her wary of letting people know where she lived. Letting a *man* know where she lived?

Whatever it was, he wasn't going to pry it out of her tonight. He'd build her a fire and leave her to it. He, of all people, should understand a person's desire to keep things close to their chest.

CHAPTER SIX

"SO IT'S NOT just me, is it?" Kali was almost pleased to see Brodie struggling as much as she had with getting the fire to light.

No. *Pleased* wasn't the right word. *Relieved* was more like it. Proof she wasn't useless at looking after herself.

Not that it covered over all the fuss she'd made about him knowing where she lived. Behaving like she had only drawn attention to the fact she had something to hide. And the whole point of coming up here had been because it had seemed safe. A place where she could finally stop the relentless need to check over her shoulder.

Years of medical school in Ireland had felt safer...but her mother had an Irish connection. One she had always been terrified her father would investigate. Perhaps the passage of time had softened his anger.

"It appears not, Dr. O'Shea," Brodie replied, leaning back on the heels of his work boots. "I've got a guess as to why it isn't working, though."

"Why's that?"

"This is a summer cottage."

"Why would that mean the fireplace wouldn't work? It's not like summer is tropical up here."

He raised an eyebrow.

"Well, it isn't."

Brodie turned his focus back to the fire. "It could be loads of reasons, but my guess is the top cap was knocked off the chimney and your flue has been stuffed with leaves, or a birds' nest, so you've no longer got a draw. Easy enough to fix, but only with the right tools. We can get Jimmy Crieff to take a look tomorrow, but tonight…" Brodie's tone changed from informational to nonnegotiable. "You're coming home with me."

"I'm *sorry*?" she protested, but just as suddenly realized there was a part of her that felt relief. Someone to look after her. And not just anyone. Someone who made her feel safe.

"I'm not going to let you stay here in the freezing cold, am I? What sort of man would I be, leaving you here all alone to catch pneumonia?" He put on a jaunty grin. "Then we'd have to get another locum in to cover for the locum, who is covering for the doctor, who would have to learn how to make chicken soup."

Kali felt herself relaxing. "So would it be a good idea for me to offer to make dinner tonight in thanks?"

"Throw a few things in a bag," Brodie ordered before she could rescind. "I'll get the car warmed up while you get your things together."

She went to her bedroom, a bit astonished at how easy it was to go along with the plan. As if her trust in Brodie was innate. The first person in—years, really. *Years.*

Her mother had been right. *"Have faith,"* she had whispered, pressing some money into Kali's hand before hugging her one last time. "One day you will find a man you love and trust, and your lives together will be *good.*"

Kali pressed her eyes shut tight, too late to prevent a couple of tears from popping out. Maybe that was what linked her to Brodie. Two pseudo-orphans, hoping for a safe harbor from all that had passed before.

* * *

"You grew up *here*?" Kali could hardly believe her eyes.

Even in the darkness it was easy to see the McClellan family house had a substantial footprint. When Brodie flicked on the lights as they entered what she saw took her breath away.

The design was a stunning combination of modern with a healthy nod of respect to the traditional stone buildings speckled across the island. The house was almost Scandinavian in design, with an equal division of glass, wood and stone. Thick oak beams soared up to the roof, supporting vast floor-to-ceiling windows. The central wall of thick stone gave the house a solid grounding.

While the view wasn't visible now, Kali imagined being in the house, particularly in the summer, would feel like being part of the environment that surrounded it. Wild. Protective. Free.

She was so caught up in absorbing all the details of the house she barely heard Brodie when he answered her.

"I was born in one of the cottages you might've seen on the seafront, near the ferry docks, but when my parents found out my brother was coming along a few years later— he was a surprise—they put an unexpected inheritance toward building this place."

"Tell me about your brother."

The subject brought a light to her eyes that it had never brought to his own.

"The wayward McClellan! Never met a mountain he didn't like." He tried to affect a comic voice to cover up how he really felt. His kid brother—Callum. The brother constantly disappearing off, only to be returned hours later by a friend or a neighbor, twigs in his hair, moss on his jumper, an unapologetic grin on his face. The brother he could have looked out for a whole lot better than he had.

"He sounds interesting."

"He is that," Brodie agreed. And he meant it. "He's on the mountain rescue squad…does test rides for off-road cycle companies all over Europe. First-class nutter."

"He sounds like fun."

That was one way to put it.

"He doesn't live here with you?"

"No. Well…sort of. He comes down when he needs things. A twenty-seven-year-old man trapped in the habits of a teenager. But mostly he stays in his but 'n' ben up in the mountains."

"His *what*?"

"A cottage. It's basically two rooms. One for sleeping in and one for all the rest. Kind of like the one you're staying in, but with a working fireplace and all his mountain bikes. He comes down every now and again to stay. And steal." He jiggled his eyebrows up and down.

Brodie's show of brotherly consternation couldn't mask the obvious love he had for Callum. What Kali wouldn't give for just one day with her sister. To make sure she was safe. Ensure her father's fury hadn't shifted to her when Kali had fled.

She forced herself to focus on the house. Wood. Stone. Glass. Deep-cushioned sofas inviting a person to come in and stay awhile. A huge hide on the flagstones in front of a large open fireplace. Highland cow? It was certainly hairy enough.

"It's so different from all of the other houses here." She lowered her voice, speaking in the hushed tones one used in a church. "It's absolutely beautiful."

"Aye, well…"

Kali giggled. Spell broken. She could see in Brodie's eyes there was an untold story nestling there amongst the throwaway line. "Is that something all of you Scots say—or just the islanders?"

"I think you'll find it's most Scots. Our rich and varied dialect hard at work! Now, then…" Brodie rubbed his hands together. "Let's get you a room, shall we? And then we'll see about getting something rustled up for tea."

Brodie took Kali on a high-speed tour of the rest of the house. An expansive kitchen, a pantry the size of her flat in Ireland, a cozy snug with a television, and, toward the rear, a more formal sitting room and a huge swirl of a staircase leading up to the bedrooms.

He showed Kali to one of the two guestrooms his parents had had built—styled to make the guests feel like they were in a tree house—and brushed off Kali's compliments, muttering something about seeing her down in the kitchen after she'd had a chance to settle in.

As he walked back down to the kitchen Brodie tried to see the house though Kali's eyes. Time had dulled the memory of just how amazing they'd all thought it was as they'd seen it coming together, stone by beam, by slate. There was no question about its appeal. But it was weighted with just about every single reason he found it hard to stay in Dunregan.

Putting down roots. Family. Commitment. All things he was quite happy to put on hold. Indefinitely. And yet showing Kali around had tapped a pretty deep well of pride… and affection. She had a way of bringing out the positive… and it felt good. Healing.

Kali swooped into the kitchen, layers of clothes peeled off to reveal a simple flowery button-up blouse and a swishy little skirt, her delight still wholly undisguised.

"It's so warm in here!"

"My parents had the house built with under-floor heating. It keeps the place pretty cozy, even in winter."

"You mean spring, right?"

"It might be spring where *you're* from, darlin'—but Dunregan doesn't acknowledge spring for at least another month. If you're lucky."

"No matter how hard you try, you're not going to convince me to see the downside of living here, Brodie."

"An eternal optimist, aren't you?"

It would've been so natural to reach out and tug her in close to him. Snuggle into the nook between her neck and the silky swoosh of hair cascading over her shoulder.

"Something like that." Kali's green eyes flicked away for a second, then back to his. "Did your parents design this place?"

"My mother. She was an architect and this was her third child. Her words, not mine," he added hastily. He might have issues to spare, but no one had begrudged her the passion she'd had for their family home.

"It's really gorgeous."

Brodie stuck his head into the refrigerator, making a show of rifling through the cluster of packets to see what would go together. He could hardly bear to think of all the buildings his mother would have designed if she'd lived.

"Guess I forget to stop and appreciate it," he mumbled from the refrigerator, not believing his own words for a second.

He missed her every single day. Had never understood why his father and brother hadn't turned on him after her death. Logic dictated that squalls were tempestuous things. Sometimes one side of the island would see the crueler side of Mother Nature whilst the other side carried on none the wiser. But he knew she wouldn't have been out there at all if it hadn't been for him.

Being here, living in this house, was a penance of sorts. One he'd be doing for the rest of his days, no matter where he was. Being on Dunregan in the family home minus the family just made it more…acute.

He pulled a couple of things out of the refrigerator and followed Kali's gaze.

"She did all this herself?"

"Not entirely. It is the interwoven dreamchild of my architect mother and the beautiful craftsmanship of my never-met-a-tool-I-didn't-like father."

"Did the skill base skip a generation?" Kali teased gently.

"Just a child. Callum got the handy genes," Brodie conceded, a smile playing on his lips as he looked at the house afresh.

Having Kali here gave him an unexpected bolstering of strength. The ability to see his family from a loving perspective rather than one tainted with the guilt and sorrow he'd hauled around all these years. It also brought back the unexpected intimacy he'd felt on That Night at the pub. As if he'd opened another door to himself he would normally have kept locked tight.

What was it he'd felt?

Kismet.

Just as his parents' relationship had been. Predestined. Two like-minded souls bucking staid ways and setting new trends on their beloved Dunregan.

At least his mother had seen the house finished. Lived in it three years with her "flock of boys," as she'd called them all.

And his father! The iron rod of strength in that man was unparalleled. Only heaven knew how he'd done it, but his father had treasured that house, *and* his sons, every hour he'd lived. A testament to his love for his wife and family.

"Right!" Brodie clapped his hands together and surveyed the pile of food on the kitchen counter for a moment.

Enough memory lane. Time to focus on the present. "How do you feel about chicken stroganoff?"

"Never heard of it," Kali replied, accepting the bundle of vegetables Brodie was handing her.

"That's because…we are going to invent it." He flashed her a smile. "If it's really good we could always call it Chicken *à la* O'McClellan?"

What a difference an hour made! Between the music blaring away on the stereo, the food sizzling on the stove-top and the quips they were slinging at each other, Kali felt as if she'd entered an alternative universe. Or maybe the house was enchanted. Being here with Brodie felt like…*home*.

She tried to squelch the thought instantly, for fear of jinxing it.

"Turn it up!" Brodie called from across the broad flagstone kitchen.

"I just did!" she shouted above the already-blaring pop tune.

"Even more! I *love* this song!" he called, hands either side of his mouth, his voice barely audible above the volume. *"Let's dance!"*

He jumped and twisted his way into the middle of the room and let loose. Arms flying in the air, hair taking flight with his accelerated movements, his face a picture of pure abandon.

Kali didn't need to be asked twice. How often had she let herself just…*be*.

She started slowly at first. Hips taking on the beat of the music, eyes closing as she let her practical self float away while her body tuned in to the rhythm. She began to lose track of time and place. It was an old pop song. One that had been popular when she was a teenager, living at home with her mum, dad and sister. When trust had been a given and fear something other people felt. It said nothing but *happy* to her.

She raised her hands above her head and began to twirl as her arms took on a life of their own—obeying nothing but the rhythm of the song as it filled her, from head to toe, with joy.

When she opened her eyes she felt Brodie's eyes on her in an instant. There was a look in them she hadn't seen before and she let herself be drawn in by the magnetism of the bright blue. They danced and whooped and by some sort of silent agreement their movements became more synchronized. The sway of their hips matched each other's, their breath was coming in deep, energized huffs.

And then without either of them seeming to notice the music changed. Their movements changed with it. Slow, sensual, instinctive. Brodie was close now. Incredibly close. She looked up into his face, felt their shoulders still gently swaying back and forth, back and forth, in a cadence that almost demanded intimacy.

He slipped his broad hands onto her hips and tugged her in, closer to him. "May I have this dance?"

His eyes were a bright blue, lit up by an accelerated heart rate and—she was sure of it now—a mutual attraction.

A shower of untethered electricity lit up parts of Kali she hadn't known existed. Her breasts were hyperaware of the satin and lace of her bra. The soft swoosh of skin just below her belly button could feel where the lace lining of her panties shifted and smoothed against her skin—almost as if Brodie was tracing his finger just out of reach of her most sensitive areas.

She felt one of his hands slide up her back as the other sought to weave his fingers through hers, then held her close enough to his chest that she could feel his heart beat.

Everything about the moment felt forbidden. And inevitable. She could feel her hair shifting back and forth along her shoulders as Brodie's hand swept down her back to her waist. The shift of his fingers over the curves between her breasts and hip elicited hypersensitive tingles, as if she were being lit up from within.

If she had thought she knew what being touched by a man was like before, she knew for certain she had had no idea until now. Each infinitesimal movement of Brodie's fingertips, hips, even his breath spoke to her very essence.

He untangled their fingers and tipped her chin up as he lowered his lips to meet hers. Tentative at first. A near-chaste kiss. Then another. Longer, more inquisitive. His short beard was unbelievably soft. Kali's fingers crept up to trace along his jawline as his hands cupped hers. Her lips parted, wanting more than anything to taste and explore his full lips.

A soft moan passed between the pair of them—she had no idea where it had started or how it had finished—she was only capable of surrendering to the onslaught of sensations: on her skin, inside her belly, shifting and warming, further, deeper than she'd ever experienced. She felt delicate and protected in his arms. And utterly free to abandon herself to the erotic washes of heat and desire coursing through to her very core.

Already her lips were feeling swollen. In one swift move she felt Brodie tuck his hands under her buttocks, pull her up to his waist and swing her round to the countertop. She couldn't help it. She tipped her head back and out came a throaty, rich laugh she hardly recognized as her own.

Brodie nuzzled into her exposed neck, kissing the length of it with the periodic flicker and tease of a nibble or lick. Kali felt empowered to give herself up to nothing other than feeling and responding, touching and being touched.

Brodie's fingers teased at the hem of her jumper, shifting past her singlet and touching bare skin. Never before had she understood the power of a single caress.

As his hands slipped along her waist and on to her back she wove her fingers through his thick blond hair, tiny whimpers of pleasure escaping her throat as his thumbs skidded along the sides of her breasts.

"Are you okay with this?" Brodie's voice was hoarse with emotion.

"Very," she managed. And she meant it. This was entirely mutual.

He cupped her chin in one of his hands and drew a long, searching kiss from her.

"Want to see the room I grew up in?"

She managed a nod, her brain all but short-circuiting with desire.

Brodie took her hand as she jumped off the countertop and, laughing, she reached out to turn off the stove with the other. Dinner could wait.

Dinner would have to wait.

Giggling like a couple of teenagers, they ran up the stairs. The music shifted as they took the steps in twos, this time to a gentle male voice lazily singing along to the simple melody of a guitar.

"You're sure you're sure?" Brodie looked over his shoulder as they hit the landing. "It won't be weird for you or anything? Working together?"

"If we'd listed all the things that are weird about this we probably wouldn't have kissed in the first place," Kali replied, more for her own reassurance than Brodie's.

"That, my lovely, is a very good point." He pulled her in close to him for another long, deeply intentioned kiss.

My lovely.

The words trilled down her spine. She couldn't remember a single time when she'd been called lovely before. She'd had the odd med school romance, but nothing had stuck. No one had brought her to life in the way Brodie had. And for the next few hours at least she was his—all his. Gladly. Willingly. *By choice.*

And it felt amazing.

Kissing and touching and exploring, and with a frantic dispensing of winter clothes, they eventually made their way to a doorway flung open with grand finesse by Brodie, before he hooked a hand onto her thigh and tugged her legs up and around his waist again.

"Mind your head," he cautioned—unnecessarily, as she'd lowered her lips to taste his yet again.

There was only a deep purple singlet and a lace-edged bra between them. Brodie's shirt had disappeared somewhere between the bottom of the stairs and the top, and his body heat was beginning to transmit directly to Kali, stoking her hunger for more.

"What if I were to throw you on the bed and have my wicked way with you?" Brodie pulled back, eyes crackling with anticipation.

"Go on, then," she dared him, hardly believing the words were coming out of her own mouth as she spoke. "Finish what you started."

More tigress than tabby was right.

The sexual tension igniting between the pair of them was the most intense thing Brodie had ever felt with a woman. He loved holding Kali's petite body, feeling the weight of her thick hair on his hands as he spread his fingers across her back. If he'd ever thought her timorous, he was being set straight now. This was alpha with alpha. Each using their personal advantages to bring the other pleasure.

He took one hand and shifted it lower, to cup one of her buttocks, and then half threw, half laid her upon his bed.

Seeing her stretching to her full length as she hit the deep blue of his duvet, he felt another surge of desire.

"Protection?" she asked softly, pulling her ebony hair into one hand and twisting it into a spiral.

He stood, mesmerized, like a man who was seeing a goddess for the very first time. She looked up at him, eyes heavy lidded and sexier than ever. *Definitely more tigress than tabby.* With a fluid whoosh of her hands she fanned her hair out across her shoulders.

"On it." He turned to check his chest of drawers, then whipped around. "Don't move… I want you to stay exactly as you are."

Kali blinked once, as if processing the thought, and then again, as though she'd made her decision. "What are you waiting for?"

Socks flew everywhere as Brodie searched the top drawer for the little foil packets he vaguely remembered putting in there after he'd cut yet another relationship short. All he could think of right now was Kali, and giving her the most pleasure a woman could have. His fingers struck gold and he turned round with a flourish.

Her beauty near enough sucker punched him. He was the moth and she was the flame. Her fingers were teasing at the spaghetti straps of her singlet.

"Stay still," he whispered, easing himself onto the bed beside her.

He wanted to be the one to slip the fabric up and over her head. To tease the hooks away from her bra, freeing her breasts to his touch, his kisses. He wanted to give her a night of undiluted pleasure.

Kali obliterated his moment's hesitation as she wriggled close to him, rucking up the soft fabric of her top as she moved. Skin against skin. Lips exploring. The tip of her tongue slowly circling the dark circle of his nipple. Her fingers and his fought with his belt buckle and won. Each move, each discovery, only increased Brodie's desire to be with her. Tenderly. Passionately.

He rolled on top after yanking his trousers off, his forearms holding part of his weight above her soft-as-silk body as he sought her eyes for permission to continue. There was no question now of how much he wanted her. She must feel it, too, as she pressed and shifted against the length of his erection.

A nod and a smile were all he needed. And exactly what he received.

Slowly. He would take his time. This was a woman worth taking his time over, and he wasn't going to risk missing a single square inch of Kali O'Shea.

CHAPTER SEVEN

CONTENT DIDN'T EVEN begin to cover how Kali felt. This was the sixth…no, the seventh day she and Brodie had decided her place was too cold to stay in and she had accidentally on purpose ended up in his bed. Sure, they were both being a little coy about it during "office hours"—but here in bed? *Mmm*... A whole new world of trust and intimacy had woven its invisible threads, linking them in a way she hadn't imagined possible.

She stretched like a cat, reveling in the contrast of her skin against Brodie's body. She felt soft and pliable whilst he… *Whoo!* He was all muscle and strength. A spray of fireworks went off in her belly when she remembered their night together. If she had a trophy, she'd hand it to Brodie for his skills in the art of lovemaking. She had never, ever, in her limited romantic history, felt as amazing as she had with the man who had protectively held her in his arms all night long.

"Is that you up?" Brodie murmured.

She pushed herself up on her elbows and gave his cheek a kiss.

"Yup! Rise and shine—we've got another big day of work ahead of us!"

"Already?" Brodie put his arm around her shoulder and tugged her back in to nestle alongside him.

Sweet monarch of the glen, that man smells good!

"Guess we'd better get you fed and watered, then," he murmured after a few minutes.

"What? Like a horse?" She whinnied and asked for coffee in her best horse voice.

"Is that how you win everyone over?" he intoned.

"Something like that. You should hear my duck voice."

"Go on, then."

She asked for toast with butter in her duck voice. She'd used it countless times to entertain her little sister when she'd been in the toddler indefatigable *"Again!"* phase.

Kali fought with the sobering fact that her sister would be a young woman now. Completely changed.

The shard of reality all but shattered the undiluted joy she'd been feeling over the past week. Nights of old-fashioned fun and frisson with just about the most gorgeous man she'd ever laid eyes on.

Okay, fine. *The* most gorgeous man she'd ever laid eyes on.

"Impressive." Brodie pulled himself up to sit, making sure a pillow was tucked beneath her head as he did so. "I'll give you a pound for every patient you see using only that voice." His light tone showed he was oblivious to her shift of mood.

Live in the moment, Kali. It's the only thing you have in your power.

"I think I'll use my Dr. O'Shea voice and save all my other voices for you."

"Well, that's very generous." He popped a kiss on her forehead. "So many hidden talents, Kali! I wonder what other hidden treasures I'll uncover over the next two weeks."

"Two?" she squeaked. *Was that it?*

"Just under, actually." He frowned. "Not so long now, my little whip-poor-will."

Kali bit into the inside of her cheek. There it was again. The reminder that she wasn't staying. She turned away from Brodie, snuggling into the warmth of his embrace so he couldn't see the complex emotional maze she was navigating. It seemed absolutely mad...but a mere fortnight here on Dunregan with Brodie and she felt the safest and happiest she had since she'd left the family home all those years ago.

It was the first time she'd felt whole. As if Kali O'Shea was a real person and not a name she'd had to invent so she could never be found by her father and the man he'd arranged for her to marry.

Brodie made a contented *mmm*...noise and tugged her in closer. It was almost ridiculous how good she felt with him. A crazy thought entered her head. She knew that if in some mad turn of events Brodie were to ask her to stay, she would say yes.

Her gut, heart, the *tips of her toes* were telling her that this feeling she was experiencing right now—this deep, instinctive peace she was feeling—was the elusive "it" she'd heard so much about when people spoke of love.

Which, of course, was utter madness.

Particularly given the fact they'd all but been living in a self-contained lust cocoon, all safe and cozy, tucked away from the world and all its problems. Problems just waiting to be dealt with...

She heaved a silent sigh, turned around to face Brodie. His eyes opened just enough to give her a flash of their cornflower-blue brightness before shutting with heavy-lidded contentment. She traced a finger along his cheekbone and bounced it to his lips. Eyes still closed, he gave her fingertip a kiss. A kiss she transferred to her own lips with a smile. He rolled over to face the window and she cuddled into him for a cozy spooning. His body and her body matching with a made-in-heaven perfection.

It was probably just as well she only had a couple of weeks left on Dunregan. Getting too attached would only mean lying to this gorgeous man beside her. There was no way she was going to burden him with the complexities of her past. The family she'd been forced to leave behind. The father who had irrevocably betrayed her trust.

Brodie abruptly flung the duvet to the side, as if cued by the universe to remind her how fleeting their time together was.

Only two more weeks.

He leaped out of bed and she rolled into the warm spot he'd left behind as he stood at the windows, facing the expansive sea view.

"Is that snow?"

"Oh, my gosh!" Kali scrambled out of bed, pulling on Brodie's discarded rugby jersey, and joined him, expertly stuffing the dark thoughts to the back of her mind.

Outside the window, big fat flakes were floating down from a gray sky completely unencumbered, ultimately finding purchase on a bit of slate, the deep green tines of a fir tree, or the dock she could see stretching out to the edge of the bay the house had been built on. It would take some time for a thick blanket of snow to build up—but the still beauty of the scene took her breath away.

"How beautiful…"

"Always see the bright side of things—don't you, my little Miss Sunshine?"

If only you knew!

"It's mesmerizing to watch."

"And dangerous."

"*You* always see the dark side of things, don't you, Mr. McGloomy?" Her lips twitched.

Brodie held her gaze as if daring her to break character. Soon enough her lips broadened into a wide smile.

"I suppose so. But with you here…" He tugged her close, wrapping his arms around her so that they both faced the wintry scene. "It's impossible not to see what's right with the world."

If she could preserve this moment in time she would.

Together they stood, enjoying the wintry scene, before a clock somewhere down on the ground floor bonged out the fact that it was high time for them to get ready for work.

"Back to reality?" Kali quipped—not really minding a jot. If this could be her everyday reality she would take it in an instant.

"Right, my beauty. We'd best get a move on." Brodie dropped a kiss on top of Kali's head. "All those sick people for you to see, and I've got to figure out how on earth to build a boat."

"I'm sure there's a video on the internet," Kali teased, disappearing into the bathroom.

She stopped when the reflection of a woman caught her eye in the mirror. A happy, tousle-haired woman, her lips peeled apart in a wide smile.

It was, she realized with a start, herself. The woman she never thought she'd have a chance to be. Plain ol' happy.

"That's an interesting approach."

"Johnny! I didn't see you there."

Brodie put down the sander and wiped his brow with his forearm before shaking hands with his old classmate. It might have been snowing all morning, but he was feeling the satisfying warmth that came from physical labor.

"I was just going to clamp the…uh…the sheer clamp to the front bit. The bow."

"You've not really got a clue, have you, Brodie McClellan?" Johnny asked with a friendly guffaw. "I've built nine of these skiffs since you took yourself off to get your fancy medical degree, and I can spot a man who doesn't have the first idea how to put together a boat from a mile off. Had to run up here from the docks to set you straight."

"Why'd you have to build so many? None of them watertight enough to float?" Brodie gibed back.

He'd missed this. Just being able to blether with his schoolmates. The folk who knew him best. Although Kali was coming up a very close second…

"All of them, you cheeky so and so," Johnny mocked, quickly starting the one-two, one-two fist jabs of a man ready to clock another one in the jaw.

"So, are you going to stand there waiting for a fight that's not going to help, or are you going to help me?"

Brodie handed him a clamp. Not that he knew if it would be useful, but it was to hand.

"I'm guessing they didn't teach you anything useful like shipbuilding down at your medical school, then?" Johnny teased the clamp expertly into place and put together two bits of the boat Brodie had thought would forever remain apart.

"Right before the diseases of the liver lecture," answered Brodie with a grin.

Johnny ran a practiced hand along the golden grain of the planks and started reorganizing them into a more recognizable pattern. A boat shape.

"So, it's looking like your trip to Africa didn't kill you, then," he said, after a few moments of turning Brodie's "workshop" into something that actually *looked* like a workshop.

"Nope. You're stuck with me."

Johnny looked up from the woodpile, mouth agape. "For good? You've moved back to the island?"

Brodie's gut instinct was to laugh facetiously. But the hint of hope in his friend's eyes made him check himself. Johnny was a through and through islander. And, truthfully, the idea of staying, whilst not exactly growing on him, was distinctly more appealing than it had been a few weeks ago.

"You've definitely got me here for the foreseeable future." Brodie chose his words tactically. He still had an out if he wanted one.

"That's good to hear." Johnny nodded his approval. "We always thought you'd bugger off to some exotic country for good once your dad passed."

"We?"

"Helen and I. You remember Helen from school?"

"Of course I do! Seared into my brain, the lot of you." Brodie mimed branding his brain. "Looks like she's keeping you well fed."

"Aye, that'd be about right." Johnny patted his gut appreciatively. "Her steak bridies won me over years ago. I can't get enough of them. It's what inspired her to start the bakery. She makes a mountain of them every Hogmanay, remember?"

"I don't think I've been to yours on New Year. Not since you shacked up with Helen anyway."

"Hey, that's my wife you're talking about. I made an honest woman of her."

"Well, congratulations to you both! Belated, they may be, but no less heartfelt." Brodie shook his friend's hand, genuinely happy for him.

"No one's made you bend *your* knee, then?"

"No," Brodie answered quickly. Too quickly. He'd been too busy trying to outrun his past ever to think about starting a future. A flash of Kali lying in his bed, hair fanned out on the pillow, came to him. If he were the type to settle down…

Johnny examined the wood again, giving it another once-over with hands that had known more than their share of physical labor. "We reckoned none of us were good enough for you—that's why you had to go off seeking your fortune elsewhere."

Brodie shook his head. "No, that's not even remotely true, Johnny. I'm just—" He looked up to the dark skies, still ripe with snowfall, and sought the right words. "I suppose I just wanted to see what the world had to offer."

"And now, like a wise man, you've come back to Dunregan. The home of Western civilization!"

They laughed together, their eyes taking in the tiny village hardly a stone's throw from the clinic. Butcher, baker and a newsagent/post office/coffee shop on one side. Pub, grocery and a charity shop supporting the Lifeboat Foundation on the other. And, of course, the Dunregan Bakehouse. What more did a village need?

"What's the wee girl like? The locum you've got in for all the folk who still think you've got the touch of death about you?"

"Ha! You never minced words, did you, Johnny? Kali? She's fine. Great, in fact."

In more ways than one.

Memories of their nights together were very likely the reason why he had made next to no progress on his skiff. Since when had he become a daydreamer?

"Well, I guess I'll find out in a minute."

"Everything all right?"

Johnny nodded. "Just a wellness checkup for my diabetes. It's pretty much under control now, but Helen always badgers me into coming for these annual checkups."

He gave a *women, eh* harrumph, and turned toward the clinic.

"Good to see you, Brodie. Perhaps we'll catch up at the pub one of these nights, eh? And I'll come along and lend you a hand on that boat of yours later this afternoon, if you're still here. Make sure you don't sink when you put her out to sea."

Johnny winced the moment the words were out of his mouth.

"Oh, mate, I'm *so* sorry—I didn't mean—"

For the first time in he didn't know how long, Brodie took the joke at face value. It *wasn't* a dig about his mother and the dark course their sailing trip had taken.

"Not to worry. I could do with your wise counsel. It's an excellent idea." And he meant it. "See you soon?"

"Soon." Johnny nodded affirmatively.

They shook hands again and Brodie watched him disappear into the clinic.

It was good of Johnny to stop by and have a word. He'd been so engrossed in his sanding he wouldn't have noticed if his old school pal had walked straight on by. But that wasn't the Dunregan way. You saw someone you knew— you stopped and you chatted. People looked after each other as they had done in small communities like this from the dawn of time. Tribal.

He watched his breath cloud and disperse as he huffed out a laugh. He would bet any amount of money this was the type of moment his father had been hoping he would have when he'd made him promise to stay. Clever sod. It was easy enough to stay at arm's length from the people he'd grown up with when he was thousands of miles away. But receiving offers of help on a boat he didn't have a clue how to build…? That was humbling. And it was starting to tease away at the very solid line he'd drawn between himself and those who'd chosen to stay.

He felt his phone vibrate in his pocket before the ring sounded. He tugged it out and took a look at the screen, eyes widening when he saw who it was.

"Callum?" He stepped out of the shed, moving his eyes up to the mountains as if he could see his brother. "What's going on?"

"There's been a wreck."

"What kind of wreck?" Brodie felt his heart rate surge. Was his brother all right?

"I'm fine," Callum said, as if reading his mind. "But you better get up here—with help if you can—the Taywell Pass road."

"What's happened?"

"The snow's right thick up here and a lorry towing a huge load of logs has jackknifed, taking out two oncoming cars as he went. One's flipped and the other is on the edge of a wee loch. Get the fire brigade up as well. We'll need the Jaws of Life. And make sure you've got tow ropes in your four-by-four."

"Do you have your medical kit on you?"

"Only the small bag. I was taking a new bike for a ride down the mountain in the snow."

"Have you got your four-by-four? We can put patients in it if necessary."

"No, just the bike."

Brodie heard his brother give a sharp gasp.

"Callum, are you all right?"

"Fine. Quit your fussing and get up here."

Brodie headed toward the rear entrance of the clinic.

"Right. Ten, twenty minutes max—I'll be there with reinforcements."

"Make it fast, Brodie. The truck driver's in a bad way.

Probably internal bleeding. And there's a wee laddie trapped in one of the cars as well."

"Did you ring the air ambulance?"

"Not yet. I wanted to find out your ETA."

"Give them a ring. At least as a heads up."

"Aye—just get a move on, Brodie."

He didn't need telling twice. His brother had said he was fine, but there was something off in his tone.

Brodie hung up the phone and yanked open the clinic door. In a matter of moments he'd got Caitlyn to cancel the rest of Kali's appointments, put Ailsa in charge of ringing the volunteer fire brigade and coordinating with the ferry captain in case they needed to hold the ship for patients needing hospital care.

He grabbed his own portable medical kit and loaded a couple backboards and everything else he thought would be useful in the cab of his vehicle.

"Where do you want me?"

Kali appeared at the back of the clinic, her new winter coat zipped right up to her chin.

"Passenger seat for now. We can fold down the seats in the back if we need to transport anyone."

"Is there not an ambulance?"

"You're looking at it." Brodie pulled a blue light attached to a wire out of his glove box and clamped it to the top of his four-by-four.

"Brodie?" Johnny stuck his head out through the back door of the clinic. "I hear you're wanting the fire brigade?"

"Aye." Brodie jumped into the four-by-four.

"That's me."

"What happened to Davie Henshall?"

"Retired, pal. See you up there as soon as I get a couple of the other lads together. Won't be long."

He waved them off and disappeared back into the clinic,

only to be quickly replaced by Ailsa running to Kali's side of the car.

"Here you are, dear." She handed over three flasks. "Hot water if you need it. There's tea bags and sugar and things in the glove box."

"Thanks, Ailsa." Brodie leaned across Kali whilst shifting the car into gear. "We'll give you an update when we get there."

As he hit the road, driving safely but with intent, Brodie could feel his suspicions increase. The call from his brother ran in his head on a loop, refusing to offer up any clues. He would've told him if something was wrong. Wouldn't he...?

Even to think of suffering another loss constricted his throat. That was what this island did. Take and take and take.

He swore softly under his breath.

Stop thinking like a petulant teenager. Life's not perfect anywhere and Dunregan's no different. It's the home your parents loved as much as they loved each other. And you. You're alive. Practicing medicine, which you love. There's a beautiful woman sitting right next to you who could light up your life for the rest of your days if you let her. Now, go find your brother.

Concentrating didn't begin to describe how deep in thought Brodie looked. He was navigating the snow-covered roads with the dexterity of someone who could've walked the island blindfolded. The landscape seemed a part of him. Even more so right now.

"You all right?" Kali finally broke through the deepening silence in the car.

"Fine. We'll be there in just a couple of minutes. I was just trying to work through how we'll sort everyone."

"Triage, you mean?"

"Yes."

"You must be used to this sort of thing with all of the work you've done out in the field. With Doctors Without Borders."

"Mmm-hmm."

Brodie wasn't giving anything away. She wasn't going to lower herself by getting insecure, but this Brodie was an entirely different one from the sexy man who'd pinned her against the wall in the supplies cupboard earlier that morning for a see-you-at-lunchtime snog. Maybe this was Work Brodie, and she was confusing his refusal to engage in conversation with his concentration over what was to come.

She glanced across at him. Jawline tight. Eyes trained on the road. No guesses as to what was going on in his head.

"This'll be my first accident," Kali said.

Brodie shot her a sharp look.

"Outside a clinic or a hospital, I mean," she quickly qualified.

"You'll be fine. A bit less equipment and no nurses to fetch things, but with the help of the fire crew—they've all got basic paramedic skills—you'll be fine."

He shot her another look, one exhibiting a bit more of the Brodie she knew off duty.

He gave her thigh a quick squeeze. "Sorry, Kali. My brother's up in that mess, and he said he was fine but I have a bad feeling."

"In what way?"

"He's trained in mountain rescue—basic paramedic stuff—but he didn't sound like he was doing anything. Normally he would've called while he was doing fifteen things as well as talking to me. One of those rare multitasking males." He gave a weak smile. "Hold up—I think I see them up ahead."

Kali nodded. She got it now.

Family.

The one thing you could never escape. They were woven into your cell structure.

Brodie pulled his four-by-four to an abrupt halt and scanned the scene. Not good. The opposite, in fact. He was out of the cab and crunching across ankle-deep snow toward the stationary vehicles in an instant.

"Callum?" His voice echoed against the hillsides, then was absorbed by the ever-thickening snow.

Kali appeared by his side, all but dwarfed by the large medical kit slung over her shoulder.

"Here." He took a hold of the free strap. "I'll take that. Can you grab the backboards off the roof? *Callum!*" he called again, his tension increasing.

The name reverberated from hillside to hillside, leaving only the hushed silence of snowfall.

He jogged to the logging truck, where there were huge lengths of freshly sawn trees splayed hither and yon, and climbed up to the cab. The driver was slumped over the wheel. Brodie yanked open the door and pressed his fingers to his pulse point. Thready. But he was alive.

"All right there, pal? Can you hear me?"

No answer. The driver's airbag had deployed, bloodying his nose. He could've easily knocked his head on the side window and concussed himself.

"Here's the backboard. Where do you want me?" Kali looked up at him from the roadside.

Brodie used the high step of the cab to scan the site. As his brother had described, there was a car twenty or so meters away at the edge of the loch, and one flipped onto the roadside just a few meters beyond.

He jumped down from the cab.

"Let's do a quick assessment then board up whoever needs it. Get blankets to everyone. *Callum!*"

Nothing.

They ran toward the overturned vehicle and knelt at the windows.

A woman hung, suspended by her seat belt, looking absolutely terrified.

"Madam, are you all right?"

"My boy!" she screamed, hands pressed to the roof of the car. "Can you get my boy out? Billy! Are you all right, darling? Mummy's just here."

"Hello, in there."

Brodie kept his voice calmer than he felt. The accident victims he could deal with. Not hearing from his brother… A sour tang of unease rose in his throat.

He saw the woman trying to release the catch on her seat belt. "I'm Dr. McClellan. We'll help get you and your boy out of the car, but can you keep your seat belt on, please? Don't try to undo it. You could hurt your neck. What's your name?"

"Linda. Linda Brown. Billy—can you hear Mummy?"

Kali tried to pull the rear door open on the driver's side, where a toddler was hanging from his child seat. "I can't get it open!"

"The roof must've been crushed when the car flipped." Brodie gave the door a tug as well, his foot braced against the body of the vehicle. No result. "Can you run down and check the other car while I get these two out?"

The whine of a siren filled the air. The fire department.

"Go on." Brodie waved to Kali to get to the other car while he pulled out his window punch. "Linda, can you cover your face, please? I'm just going to break Billy's window—all right?"

"What about Billy's face?" the panicked mother asked.

"I'll do my best—he should be all right, but we really need to be getting him out."

He held the tool to the window and pressed. The glass shattered but remained intact. Brodie stuck the slim tool into a corner of the window to make a small hole, then tugged as much of the glass away from the boy's face as he could. It fell away in a sheet, exactly where Brodie needed to kneel. He ran over to the backboard and tugged it into place by the window, grabbing his run bag as he did so.

He unzipped his medical kit and raked through the supplies, his fingers finding the neck braces by touch as he tried to find a pulse on the boy's neck.

Yes!

Three out of three so far.

Where the hell was his brother?

"How is he? Is he all right?" called Linda.

"I've got him. He looks good on the outside, but we'll have to wait and see if he's sustained any internal injuries."

Linda began to cry softly, a low stream of "No, no, no…" coming in an unrelenting flow.

Brodie rucked up the boy's shirt. He could see the sharp red marks from the seat belt, but no swelling that would indicate internal bleeding. He'd need tests. X-rays. Everything he didn't have here. The boy needed a proper hospital.

Had Callum called the air ambulance? Could it even fly in this weather? The snow had managed to thicken in the space of ten minutes, shrouding the surrounding mountains and hillsides in cloud.

C'mon, little brother. Throw me a sign you're okay.

"Brodie?"

Johnny appeared by his side, kitted out from head to toe in his all-weather firefighting uniform. Brodie blinked and for an instant saw the young redhead he'd used to play footie with as a youngster. That young lad had been replaced by a man who was ready for action.

"Tell us what you need."

Brodie quickly ran through instructions to get the truck driver out onto a backboard—but not before he'd had a neck brace applied. Then he'd need checks on internal bleeding, heart rate, blood pressure—the usual stats for an extraordinary situation.

"Can you help me get Billy's mother out of the car so we can get the two of them into a warm vehicle?"

"On it, mate."

Brodie looked toward the car by the loch and couldn't see anyone around it. Where had Kali disappeared to?

He forced himself to be still for a moment, to crush the growing panic. He'd dealt with thousands of people fearing for their lives in Africa. He could do this.

"Brodie?" Johnny tapped his leg. "We've got this if you want to go down to the other car."

"Thanks, pal. I'll do that. Extra blankets and things are in the back of my four-by-four."

Brodie took off at a jog, quickly ratcheting his pace up to a run when the details of the scene became clear. The front of the estate car was completely concertinaed. If anyone was alive in there it would be a miracle. He could hear barking. Dogs in the back? Had to be. There weren't any running around free.

He reached the front of the car, a seventysomething woman inside. The crash's first fatality.

The barking began again in earnest, as if the dogs sensed their owner had been killed. He made a mental note to ring the vet, see if he could come out as well.

He raced to the other side of the car. There was Kali, kneeling next to the mangled remains of a bicycle and…

Oh, no, no, no…

"Callum?"

CHAPTER EIGHT

BRODIE DROPPED TO his knees beside Kali, barely taking in the stream of information she was efficiently rattling off. Something about the car beginning to roll into the loch, Callum skidding on his bicycle in an attempt to get it behind the wheel to try and stop it, and not being able to unclip his bicycle shoes from the pedals before the car started rolling. Possible lacerations or puncture. Bones crushed.

His own observations took over as he absorbed the sight of his brother's pale face and contorted torso, only just visible outside the edge of the vehicle. Limited to zero blood flow would be going to his legs. Muscle damage. Tissue damage. Possible paralysis. He'd seen worse. So much worse. But seeing Callum like this sent shock waves of hurt through him. Pain unlike anything he'd ever experienced.

He forced himself to swallow down the emotion before he spoke. "Hey, little brother."

Callum, his head resting on a heat blanket Kali had put under him, tried to crane his neck to see Brodie better, despite the handlebars of his bicycle pinning his chest to the ground.

"Ach, no, Callum. Don't move your head. Why isn't he in a neck brace?" he snapped at Kali.

"He's not complained of any neck pain," Kali replied gently.

He knew the tone. The one he'd used with countless family members of patients. The one that said, *You're missing the big picture, so why don't you take a big breath and—*

"It's his leg, Brodie. I've not administered anything for the pain yet. Until we see what's going on under there it'll be like working in the dark," Kali stated simply. She pulled a phone out of her pocket and wiggled it in his eyeline. "Your Aunt Ailsa's rung your brother's phone here. She couldn't get through to you. An air ambulance is on its way. There is only one that can risk it in this kind of weather."

"How long?" Brodie wished he could take the bite out of his tone, but this was his *brother* they were talking about.

"Ten…maybe fifteen minutes?"

"Right." He cursed up at the sky, then checked his watch. "I suppose they didn't manage to stop the last ferry?"

"No." Kali shook her head, putting up a hand to cut off Brodie's reaction. "But Ailsa rang round and finally got hold of the captain. He's going to drop everyone and come back with a couple of ambulances. Then he'll make the trip back to the mainland."

Brodie nodded, taking in the enormity of the gesture. These were islanders pulling together to help each other. Lives woven together in good and bad. *This*, he suddenly realized, was what island life was about. Being there. Each person doing what they could to enrich and strengthen the vital community.

Brodie gave Kali's hand a quick squeeze. One that he hoped said, *I know I'm being an ass, but help me get through this.* He felt her squeeze back. It was all the sign he needed.

"All right, little brother…let's take a look, eh?"

He shifted to his hands and knees, the snow sending the cold straight through his trousers. But that was nothing compared to what his little brother must be feeling, with half his body trapped underneath that car.

The scene was impossible to break down into simple components. Just a mesh of metal, bicycle wheels, winter clothes and his brother's legs. Everything was indiscernible except the ever-increasing pain on his brother's face.

He shook his head, trying to keep his expression light as he faced his brother. "What have you done, you numpty? Why didn't you say you were in a bit of bother yourself when you rang?"

Brodie tried his best to keep his tone loving. Funny how anger and love wove together so tightly when a person was terrified.

"I wasn't when I rang. I was freewheeling down the mountainside and saw it all happen. Got down as soon as I could, checked out everyone and then saw Ethel's car going backwards toward the loch."

"Ethel?"

"The woman driving this car." He tried moving an arm to indicate the front of the vehicle, only to cry out in pain. "I—had—to—stop—it—" he panted.

"The world's first human cribbing." Brodie gave him an impressed smile. No need to point out the obvious flaws in the plan.

"I think my bike trail days might be on hold for a while. Always happens when I leave the refrigerator door open." Callum laughed before another wince of pain took over.

Brodie shot a look at Kali. His brother was talking nonsense and—as man-childish as he was—he had never been a babbler.

He gave his brother's arm a rub and felt Callum's body

beginning to be consumed by shivering. Could be the cold. Could be shock.

"Kali, have we got a couple more blankets?"

"You bet." She nodded and ran back to the car to retrieve them.

"Callum. How are you feeling, mate? You still with me?"

Callum shut his eyes, but spoke with deliberation. "There weren't any blocks out here, and I wasn't going to let the dogs go into the loch to drown on top of everything…" His voice began to lose what little strength it had.

"You saved them, pal."

He gave his brother's shoulder a gentle squeeze as his eyes traveled the length of his body to his leg, pinned beneath both his cycle and the back wheel of the estate car. Any number of things could be going wrong underneath that mess. If a spoke had jammed into his leg when the car had moved it might easily have pierced a posterior tibial or fibular artery.

"Talk me through what you feel." Brodie's eyes were on his brother.

"Done that." His brother's eyes flicked up in Kali's direction. "Little to no sensation below the knee. Clear of injury other than a strain in the back from such a kickass move!" Callum finished, with a grin that rapidly shape-shifted into a grimace.

"Okay, superhero—we know you're the coolest kid on the block. Any light-headedness?" Brodie's tone was all business.

"Yeah—but there's a blinkin' car on top of me, bro. I'm hardly going to feel great."

"Since when do you talk like one of the boys in the hood?" The words were out before he could stop them.

"Since when did *you* start caring?"

Callum shot. Callum scored.

"Blankets?"

Kali's voice broke through the silence Brodie couldn't fill. Her bustle of action—swiftly wrapping the specialized heat blankets around Callum's torso—was a welcome cover for the surge of guilt threatening to drown Brodie. He was going to get his brother out of this, and he didn't know how but he was also going to make things up to him. Some way. Somehow.

"Kali…" Brodie lowered his voice. "We need to get this car off him."

"Absolutely. But I haven't done a thorough check inside because I saw Callum first. And the car will definitely go into the loch if we pull him out right now. The car could be the only thing holding him together…" Kali countered, not unreasonably.

She was right. If Callum began to bleed out before they had proper medical supplies there, or a means to get him to an operating theater… The very thing that was threatening his life could be keeping him alive.

"Can you get the dogs?"

"What?" Brodie leaned in closer to hear his brother.

"The dogs…in the back of the car."

Callum flicked a familiar pair of blue eyes toward the rear of the vehicle. Sometimes it was like looking in a mirror.

"On it."

Brodie knew his brother would do anything to help an animal before a human. The man should've been a vet, but that would've meant he had to leave the island for five years' training. And that was never going to happen.

He wouldn't rest easy now unless he knew the dogs were sorted.

The back of the car was undamaged, so the hatch top easily rose when Brodie unlatched it. Two enormous dogs leaped out of the vehicle, one landing with a sharp yelp. A broken leg? Brodie scanned the car for their leashes and easily found them, along with a bag of treats tucked into a side compartment. It was all precious time away from his brother, but Kali was there, assessing and treating him. He trusted her.

He tried unsuccessfully to get the dogs to sit… If the Newfoundlands would just play ball…

"Brodie?"

Kali's voice stopped him in a near-successful attempt at getting the leashes onto the dogs.

"Could you bring the dogs over? Your brother wants to say hello."

"I'm not the ruddy dog whisperer in the family," he grumbled, and only just stopped his eyes from rolling. His brother was in serious trouble here. Time to quit playing the despairing older brother.

One limping, one resisting, Brodie finally managed to get the dogs over to his brother, where they immediately turned into entirely different beasts, licking Callum's face, gently placing their paws on his shoulders as if petting him. These three weren't strangers. They shared a warmer relationship than he did with his own brother, and the hit of shame was hard to shrug off.

But he had to do his best. There was an accident scene to sort. The air ambulance crew would need a situation report when and if they arrived. With the weather closing in they would be lucky. And Linda and her son would need some extra care, not to mention the truck driver. This car needed lifting and towing away from the loch, and the poor soul who was inside needed extracting.

"It's Ethel."

Kali was looking up at him. He shook his head, not understanding.

"Your brother says it's Ethel *Glenn* inside. These are *her* dogs."

His mind raced to connect the dots and in an instant he made the link. Ethel Glenn and her famous shortbread. The long-term widow had stayed up in the croft she and her husband had lived on long after his death some twenty years ago. The villagers went to her, instead of the other way round. She guarded that rickety old croft like an explorer staking a claim on an island full of treasure. Peat and stone. Impossible to make a living on. He'd never understood the draw.

"Brodie?" Johnny jogged over beside them. "We've got the chap in the lorry boarded up. He's not looking too bad."

The interruption was exactly what Brodie needed to knock him back into action. Working in an emotional daze wasn't going to help any of these people—least of all his brother.

"Anyone keeping an eye on him for cardiac fallback?"

"No, he seems fine."

"If he really got a bash from that airbag—his nose was bleeding, right?"

"Yeah, it's broken. It'll need resetting."

Brodie nodded. "He'll need some scans. If he was within ten inches of that thing when it deployed it won't present now, but we'll want to check for aortic transection, tricuspid valve injuries, cardiac contusions. There's a raft of things that could still go wrong."

"Got it. I'll get one of the lads to keep an eye out. We've got Linda and Billy in our rig, getting warm. Again, nothing obvious—but from what you've said it sounds like they'll be needing a trip to the hospital as well. What now?"

The entire scene crystallized into a series of steps they would need to take as a team. Brodie gave Johnny a grim but grateful smile, then rattled off a list of assignments for everyone, taking on communications with the air ambulances and patient checks for himself. Kali was to continue monitoring his brother, while the remaining fire lads prepared the vehicle on top of Callum for removal.

It couldn't have been more than ten minutes before they all heard the whirr and thwack of the bright yellow helicopter's rotors as it began its descent.

Kali had been running on pure adrenaline, each moment passing with the frame-by-frame clarity of a slow-motion film—Brodie the confident director, able to shift from patient to casualty to fire crew to dog handler and back again.

It was a blessing that the crash had happened on the broad stretch of valley where it had, making the helicopter landing possible. Snow, time and limited visibility were the enemies. Every person present was a hero, pushing themselves to the limit to turn a bad situation into something better.

"Where do you want me?" Kali asked when Brodie appeared on her side of the car.

"Stay where you are. The crew will work around you." He lowered his voice. "He all right?"

She nodded. Callum's eyes were closed, but he was resting rather than unconscious. It had to be tough, seeing your sibling like this. It was exactly why she'd stayed away from her family. To keep them safe from harm. The violence her father had threatened... She shuddered away from the fearful thoughts that kept her up at night. She just had to have faith. Faith that her mother and sister were all right.

"We're good," she said with a firm nod.

"You warm enough?" Brodie took a half step forward and drew a finger along her jawline. The distance she'd thought he'd put between them on the way to the crash evaporated entirely.

Times like this prioritized things. She knew that better than most.

She nodded, giving the palm of his hand a soft kiss. The move was totally unlike her, but why the hell not? From the moment she'd stepped off the ferry onto Dunregan she'd felt a change was afoot. She cared for Brodie and she was going to show it. If it backfired then so be it. She'd just have to learn to cope with a whole new level of heartbreak.

Brodie's hand cupped her chin, tipping it up toward him so she could see the gratitude in his eyes. Her heart cinched…then launched into thunderous thumps of relief.

Her instinct had been right.

The intimacy of their moment was snapped in two as the air ambulance doctors jogged toward them with their own backboards and run bags.

On Brodie's signal, the fire department volunteers began preparing the vehicle to be raised and then towed away from Callum and the loch's edge.

"I'll grab hold of the bike," Brodie called as the noise of the rescue crews increased. "We don't want it yanked away from Callum's leg. If any of the spokes have pierced through we could easily make it worse. Straight up—and only then do you pull the car forward. Got it?"

A chorus of "Aye" and "You got it" filled the air as lines were attached to the mangled front of the vehicle. All the clamps and foot pump lifts were put in place. A hush descended upon the team.

Brodie knelt down by Kali, his fingers automatically shifting to his brother's neck to check for a pulse. She didn't envy him. Not one bit. The intensity of the ache in her heart shocked her, cementing the need to shake it off and focus on Callum.

The car was lifted in seconds, and the cycle went with

it, its metal twisted into the undercarriage of the vehicle and—as Brodie had suspected—not one but two spokes had been jammed into his brother's leg. Callum's scream of pain at the release hit the sides of the mountains, pulsing back and forth as each person flew into action.

"All right, let's get him out from under here and onto the scoop stretcher," Brodie called. "Can somebody trench it into the snow so there's not too much movement for him?"

A blur of activity took over. Everyone was acting on well-practiced instinct and skill. Everyone was hiding their dismay at the wreckage that was Callum's leg.

"Compound fractures to the tibia and fibula," one of the doctors said unnecessarily.

"He's got an arterial bleed." Kali jumped forward, pinching the geyser of blood with her gloved hands. "Can I get a clamp?"

"On it," replied one of the air medics, raking through his run bag.

"We're also going to need blood, IV and morphine." She ticked off the list with her other hand.

"Not before splinting him," Brodie interjected. "If you're injecting into the muscle he will feel everything during the splinting."

"Do you have any inhalable diamorphine?" Kali asked the air medic. "He's losing consciousness, so swallowing anything is out of the question."

"Right you are." He handed Kali a clamp and set to mining another part of his bag for supplies.

"Callum? Stay with us, pal. I'm here with you." Brodie held a hand to his brother's face. "Nonresponsive," he muttered, using his other hand to give Callum a brisk sternal rub with his knuckles. "His blood type is A positive. You can give him A positive and negative and O positive and negative. Can we get a defib machine over here?"

"They're using it on the truck driver. He just coded."

Brodie cursed, giving his brother another sternal rub. "C'mon…c'mon! Show me something, here."

Kali flinched in unison with Brodie at Callum's searing scream of pain as they began the messy splinting process. It was a sorry thing to be thankful for—but at least he was alive. The leg was a mess. Months of rehab were in his future. Pins. Bolts. Who knew what other hardware he'd need?

"I'm his brother," Brodie told the crew as they each took a handle of the stretcher and walked as steadily as they could across the frozen ground toward the chopper. "If there's room, I'd like to come along."

"I'll send one of my guys with the two less urgent cases. The mother and child can go on the ferry, so there's room."

"How's the lorry driver? Did he make it through the resus?"

"Only just" was the grim response as they reached the helicopter, where the truck driver was being strapped in. "Definitely something dodgy going on with his heart. He'll need seeing to straight away."

Brodie glanced at his watch, then at Kali. "Will you be taking the ferry as well?"

"Don't you trust my guys?" the head of the aircrew said with a joshing smile.

"Nothing like that, mate. I think I'll just need to see a friendly face in a couple of hours with the way things are going."

Brodie's eyes locked with Kali's. More passed between them in that single moment than ever had before. The feelings all but tearing her heart in two were shared.

Kali was entirely speechless. What a moment to realize she was in love! Her entire body surged with energy. She felt she was capable of doing anything now that she knew how Brodie felt about her.

"We need to load up!" one of the paramedics called from the helicopter. The rotors were already beginning to swirl into action.

Brodie dug into his pocket and handed her a set of keys, his gloved hand giving hers a quick squeeze. "Go in convoy with the lads from the fire station. They'll help with the transfer to the ambulances. I will try to meet you on the other side. If not—I'll see you at the hospital. Ailsa will meet you at the docks as well, no doubt."

Kali nodded, the to-do list in her head growing, turning into vivid detail and then action.

She ran across to the fire truck, where Linda and Billy were keeping warm, just as the helicopter took its first tentative moves to lift and soon soared off, skidding across the white landscape. She stopped to watch it go, taking away the man she was giving her heart to, having no idea what would happen next.

"Doc?"

Kali whipped around to see Johnny holding the two dogs on leads.

"Are you able to drop these two by the vet's?"

"Yeah, absolutely. Um…" Two big furry faces looked up at her expectantly. They were like small yetis!

"We'll give you a hand loading them up. If you could bring your car here it would save this one's leg an unnecessary journey?"

"Yes, absolutely!" Kali jumped into action—embarrassed to have held them up. "I'll be right behind you in a second."

And right behind you, Brodie, she added silently, with a final glimpse at the helicopter before it completely disappeared from sight.

* * *

"I'll come check on you soon, all right?"

Kali waved as Linda and Billy were wheeled off on their gurneys for a full set of scans and X-rays. Bumps and bruises were a definite. She held up a set of crossed fingers that there wasn't going to be anything else.

"Can we get you anything, Dr. O'Shea? A coffee or tea? I think you might be stuck on the mainland tonight."

The charge nurse was halfway out of her station before Kali's brain kicked back into action. The long day was beginning to show.

"No, I'm good, thanks. Just directions to where I might find another one of the patients who came in on the air ambulance."

"Reggie Firle?"

"No." Kali shook her head. "He was the lorry driver. He's all right, though?"

Best not let the heady combination of lust and love cloud her priorities. Patients. They were number one right now.

"Yes, he's fine. In Recovery, where they are monitoring his heart. So it's…" She ran her finger along the patient list.

"Callum McClellan."

"Oh, yes!" The nurse's finger hit the name at the same time as she spoke. "The one with the doctor brother."

The extremely gorgeous doctor brother, whose existence is eating all of my brain particles.

"Yes."

A more politic answer, she thought, given the circumstances.

Turned out the hour-long ferry ride had given her *way* too much time to think…overthink…and then to worry. Was she thinking she was in love too soon? Reading far too much into *that look*?

She sucked in a deep breath. It was *carpe diem* time.

She nodded and smiled as the nurse gave her directions to the surgical department, where Callum was currently undergoing the first of several surgeries. Her breath caught in her throat. Poor guy. Doing his best to save the dogs, the car, dear old Ethel's remains and now—courtesy of a bicycle shoe—compromising his own future. His life.

The relief Brodie felt when he saw Kali walk into the surgery unit threatened to engulf him. Weighted to the chair he'd only just sat down in, he finally felt able to succumb to the emotions he'd been struggling to keep at bay. He was raw. More so than he'd ever been. And the thought of letting someone see him this exposed was terrifying.

One look at Kali and he knew he shouldn't have worried. The soft smile, the compassion in her eyes, the outstretched arms all said, *You won't have to go through this alone.* As she wordlessly came to him he tugged her in between his knees, his arms urgently encircling her waist when she pulled his head close to her and hit after hit of untethered emotion finally released.

"Want your coffee straight up or with a splash of artery-hardener?" Kali held the small pitcher of cream aloft, poised to pour.

"With a dram of whiskey, but that's a no-goer," Brodie replied, his eyes searching just a little hopefully round the deserted hospital canteen for a bar. Kali's ever-present optimism must be catching.

"Artery-hardener and some not very appetizing biscuits it is, then, sir!" She handed him a paper cup, with cream still whirling its way through the steaming liquid, and wiggled a packet of vending machine ginger biscuits in front of him that looked as though they could have been made in the last century.

"The middle of the night seems to have its advantages round here."

He put his arm round her shoulder, biscuits and coffee held aloft in his other hand. Being close to Kali was healing. Touching her was downright curative.

"How's that?" She smiled up at him with an *oops* shrug after losing half of her biscuit in a too-deep dunk.

"Lots of sofas to commandeer."

He steered her toward a dimly lit corner of a waiting room not too far from surgery and sank into the well-worn cushions. The stories they could tell...

"I used to dream of working in a place like this."

"Oh, yeah?"

"Well," he qualified, "not exactly like *this*. Inner city. Busy. Never-get-a-moment's-rest busy."

"I thought you preferred international work?" She toed off her thick-tread boots and tucked her feet up underneath her.

"I really love it. Doctors Without Borders does amazing work. But the idea of being part of a city I know and helping people there—being part of something..."

"Like being part of the community on Dunregan?"

"Touché!" He raised his coffee cup and took a noisy slurp, because he knew it sent a shiver down her spine. But she was right. "This sort of thing does put a lot in perspective."

"Gives you different priorities?"

She wasn't asking. She was telling.

"That sounds like the voice of experience."

Kali's green eyes flicked up to the ceiling, then did a whirl round the room. "Suffice it to say when the unexpected happens for me it all boils down to family."

"The family you never talk about?" He was feeling too worn by the day's events to mince words.

She shook off his question and put one of her small hands on his cheek. He pressed into as she said, softly but deliberately, "Today is about you and your family."

Brodie put his coffee down. Another wave of emotion was hitting him and there would be spillage. Literal and figurative.

"I—I could've done so much more..."

"What do you mean? You did everything you could today."

"Not today. His whole life!" He scrubbed both hands through his hair. "*I'm* the reason he didn't grow up with a mother, and then I couldn't even stick around to be a big brother for him. I just let him go feral. What kind of a person does that?"

Kali let the words percolate and settle before softly replying, "The kind who hasn't forgiven himself for something that isn't his fault?"

"But it *is*! Was..." He still couldn't believe she wasn't able to see why the blame lay solidly at his feet. He'd *begged* his mother to go out with him that day.

Kali pulled back and folded her hands in her lap, her index finger tapping furiously, the rest of her completely still.

"The only thing you can change," she said at last, "is the future. That is completely in your control."

"Who turned *you* into a sage little Buddha?" He nudged her knee with his own.

"Ohhhh..."

Her lips pressed together and did that little wiggle that never failed to make him smile.

"Let's just say life's had a way of regularly shoving me into the Valuable Lesson department." She tipped her head onto his shoulder.

"Oh, yeah?" He wove his fingers through hers and leaned

his head lightly on top of her silky black hair. "What's to-day's valuable lesson, then?"

"Sticking together," she said without a moment's hesitation. "Through thick and thin."

"This being the thin?"

He could feel her head nod under his.

"This being the thin."

They both stared blankly out into the room. The beeps and murmurings from the wards were more of a white noise than a frenetic addition to the chaos of the day. Callum's surgery shouldn't take too much longer. Then they'd have a much better idea of what lay ahead of him.

Brodie's thumb shifted across Kali's and he took a fortifying inhalation of her wildflower-and-honey-scented skin.

A sudden hit of clarity came to him. He stayed stock-still for risk of shaking the perfection of it away. Kali was right. He *was* in charge of his future—and she, he knew in his heart, was the missing piece of the puzzle.

"Kali? Have you got anything booked after this gig? The locum post on Dunregan?"

"Not yet."

"Would you consider staying?"

He felt her sharp intake of breath before he heard it.

"You mean at the clinic?" Her voice was higher than usual.

He kept his eyes trained on the double doors of the surgical ward, but continued.

"At the clinic, yes. I don't know how long I'm going to need to be here at the hospital, but..." This was the hard part. The part that scared him silly. "Would you stay with me? Give up your igloo of a cottage? Come stay with me? At home?"

Okay—so it was a little open-ended. It was no proposal, but...

Her fingers, so tiny in amongst his own, squeezed his tightly. But she didn't say a word.

"It's not much of an offer, is it? Stay with a messed-up guy, with a messed-up brother, on an island with a whole lot of messed-up history to untangle."

He laughed. Life had finally pinned him into a corner, forcing him to deal with everything head-on—and, oh, he wished Kali would stay here by his side. He knew he'd have to do the fighting on his own, but knowing that she'd be there waiting for him… He felt his heart skip a beat. Was this how deeply his father had felt for his mother?

"Kali," he said quickly, before she could answer, "I'm not sure what I'm offering you, but…please don't go."

He turned, pressed his lips softly to hers, words suddenly too flimsy for what he needed to communicate. She returned the kiss. Gently…silently.

They sat there for a moment, forehead to forehead, the world around them dissolving into a blur of white noise and shadows. He felt closer to her now than he had when they had made love. Those intimate moments they'd shared? Sheer beauty. But right now…? This…this was the stuff true love was made of.

"Yes," she finally whispered. "I'll be here for you as long as you need me."

CHAPTER NINE

Missing you.
Can't wait to see your beautiful eyes again.
Just dreamed of holding you in my arms.

KALI GAVE A loved-up sigh, forcing herself to put her mobile phone down. She and Brodie had been texting like moonstruck teens since she'd left the mainland three days ago. In spite of all the difficult moments they'd shared at the hospital, these messages were like little drops of heaven.

Ailsa knocked on her office door frame, mugs of tea in hand. "How many are you up to now? I heard Caitlyn put another call through a few minutes ago."

"I can't believe there hasn't been a nationwide alert!" Kali looked at her growing list of volunteers.

"You don't need an alarm system here on Dunregan. Telephones and a trip down to the Eagle for a pint do the trick fast enough." Ailsa slid a mug of tea onto Kali's desk and perched on the edge. "Here you are, dear. You'll need this."

Kali ran her finger along the list. "So…how do you think I should work it? Brodie's insisting on staying for the next few days, while Callum's still in Intensive Care."

"He's not in Recovery yet?" Ailsa's eyes widened.

"No. He's been in and out of surgery for the past two

days." She cleared her throat, trying to keep the emotional fallout at bay. "And this morning Brodie was pretty concerned about his blood pressure. Callum lost a lot of blood before they got him into hospital with the arterial bleed and they were talking about bringing him back into sur—" She choked on the word, unable to continue.

"Hey, now. Our Callum's strong as an ox. If anyone can pull through it's that lad." Ailsa pulled her up and into a warm hug. "Brodie tells me you were an absolute rock. That he couldn't have got through the past couple of days without you."

Kali pulled back, tears streaming down her face. "He said that?"

"'Course he did, love." Ailsa reached across the desk and tugged a tissue out of the ever-present box and handed it to her. "And if I were a betting woman I would guess things are running a bit deeper than that."

Kali felt red blossom on her cheeks.

Ailsa laughed. "I might be well into middle age, darlin', but do you think I haven't seen the sparks between you two?"

"It's not— Well, it's…"

Of all the times to be at a loss for words!

"It is what it is," Ailsa filled in for her. "But you be careful. This is quite a time of turmoil for Brodie, and I love my nephew to bits but I've never known him to be into much of anything for the long-term except for his work."

A fresh wave of tears threatened to spill over onto Kali's cheeks.

"Ach, away." Ailsa pulled her in tight again for a lovely maternal hug. "I'm not saying Brodie will let you down. I'm just saying mind your heart. We've all really taken to you and we'll hate to see you go."

"Brodie's actually asked me to stay on."

"As a partner in the clinic? He'd been talking about it before you came, but I didn't think he meant it." A look of happy disbelief overtook Ailsa's features. "Are you *sure* we're talking about my Brodie? The errant nephew of mine who won't commit to dinner in a couple of hours' time—that Brodie?"

"The very same. But—" Kali quickly covered herself, not wanting to get too excited. "He wasn't specific about the clinic. I presume he just meant until Callum's out of hospital and things are back to normal."

"There's no such thing as 'normal' for Brodie, Callum *or* Dunregan for that matter, love."

Kali's brain was pinging all over the place. And her heart was thudding so loudly she was surprised it wasn't boinging out through her jumper, cartoon-style.

"Are you saying it's best if I leave?"

"Oh, heavens no!" Ailsa looked horrified. "Absolutely not, Kali, love. I'm just an interfering auntie. What happens between you and Brodie is none of my business. You're about the best thing that has happened to him ever since the poor lad's mother died. I'm only saying he's never been settled here. Not in his heart. But these past few weeks I've seen you take to the community here like a duck to water." She sighed. "I suppose I'm saying make sure you know what you want. Brodie and the island don't necessarily come as a package."

Kerthunk.

Could hearts defy the most intricate internal structuring and actually plummet to the pit of your stomach?

That was what it felt like. A best day and a worst day colliding midchest and sinking like a lead weight. Taking all of the air in her chest with it.

Kali looked down at the list of names she'd compiled on

her desk, feeling genuine fatigue creeping in and replacing the positive energy that had been keeping her afloat.

Brodie had asked her to stay! Not as his wife or anything, but he'd asked her to *stay*. And here was a list of people all willing to help him as he transitioned from globe-trotter to islander. A *list*! A list in black-and-white of at least two dozen people who'd rung her up this morning, volunteering to take stints of time with Callum so Brodie could get some rest.

She pulled the papers off the desk and forced a bright smile. "I guess we'd better get cracking on putting this rota together before the patients start coming. There's a busy day ahead."

"That there is," Ailsa agreed. She knocked her knuckles against the door frame, as if chiding herself. "Don't let me get you down, Kali. I'm just an overcautious Scot. You might be pleased to hear that Johnny was looking to head over to the mainland soon, to stand in for Brodie so he can come back and get a fresh change of clothes."

Kali's eyes lit up, but she did her best to contain her smile as Ailsa disappeared out into the corridor.

Perhaps Ailsa was right. She wasn't being cautious enough. Wasn't looking after the heart she'd so hoped to set free up here on this beautiful, wild island.

She closed her eyes and there was Brodie, clear as day. All tousled hair and full lips parting in that smile that never failed to send her insides into a shimmy or seven. She guessed it was time to venture into unknown territory yet again, because closing her heart to Brodie… An impossibility.

"C'mon. Budge over. I need a bit of normal." Brodie pulled a chair up next to Kali's as she looked through the afternoon's patients, wanting to make sure she'd crossed her i's and dotted her t's...or was it the other way round? Brodie must be just as tired as she was. It had taken four days for Callum to get out of ICU. He had been lucky, his doctors had cautioned. *Very* lucky.

She pulled a folder from the top of her ever-growing pile and scanned it.

"All right, then, Doctor. How's about a 'normal' case of toe fungus?" She hung air quotes round the *normal*.

"If it's who I think it is..." Brodie flashed her a quick smile "...it's perfectly normal."

She held up the file so he could see.

"Bingo! Got it in one!" Brodie clapped his hands together happily. "That chap needs to develop a better friendship with his washer-dryer."

"Or just buy some fresh boots and start over?"

They laughed, not unkindly, while Kali made a couple of notes, then moved on to the next patient.

Together they worked through the dozen or so patient files—Brodie offering a bit of insight here, Kali making her usual meticulous notes. The atmosphere between them was perfect. Warm. Companionable. No—even better than that. *Loving.*

She could've sat there all day with him, doing her best to keep the odd hits of panic at bay. Panic that what she was feeling whenever they were together wasn't real. Panic that she didn't deserve such happiness.

Ailsa's words kept echoing in her head... *Brodie and the island don't necessarily come as a package.*

"When are you going to be done?" Brodie's sotto voce tone sent shivers down her spine as his hands spread out across her back in search of her bra strap. "I want to get you up on the exam table and do some examining of my own."

"Someone's in a good mood." Kali nudged him away

with her elbow while she tried to input some information into the computer system.

"Someone's too busy working to indulge me," he teased, tickling her side to no effect.

He sat back in his chair and assessed her.

"Someone else is ignoring very important paperwork." Kali didn't want to be under the microscope right now. Not with the zigzags of emotions she was experiencing.

"Are you putting patient care over your—?" He stopped for a moment, his eyes flicking up to the left in the telltale sign that he was searching for the right thing to say.

"My what?" Kali asked, trying her absolute, very, very best to keep her tone light.

"Boyfriend sounds stupid, doesn't it? And partner always sounds too clinical for me. Too businessy."

Brodie turned her round in her wheelie chair and tugged her closer toward him so that he could lay a deeply satisfying, sexy-as-they-come kiss on her lips.

Uh-oh! Boy, was she in trouble!

He pulled back and feigned a detached inspection, silently chewing a few words round in his mouth before sounding them out into her office.

Seafaring Lothario, main squeeze and *plus one* were rejected outright. "Man-friend?" he tried, to Kali's resolute horror.

"Or…" He pulled back even farther, eyes firmly glued on hers. "You don't look entirely happy, here. Have I jumped the gun?"

"No!" Kali all but shouted, then forced herself to turn her own volume down. "No, I think it's sweet."

"Sweet?" Brodie recoiled. "I thought you liked me because I was all silent and broody and muscly. A pensive Viking."

"Oh, definitely!" Kali was giggling now, fears laid to rest. At least for now. "You're my pensive Viking."

"You don't have a whole string of us out there, do you?" Brodie pulled her in again, dropping kiss after kiss on her lips. "A doctor in every port?"

"As if."

She returned one of his kisses with the ardor of a Viking mistress whose man had only just returned from months at sea. Shirts became untucked, fingers started exploratory journeys, backs arched, soft moans unfurled out of throats receiving naughty nips and licks as hands squeezed and caressed and—

A knock sounded.

Kali and Brodie hastily tugged everything back into place that should be in place, still giggling when Ailsa opened the door with a wary expression.

"I'm not interrupting anything here, am I?"

"No, Auntie Ailsa. What can we do for you?"

"I've got some patients."

"Already? I thought I had another twenty minutes." Kali's eyes flicked to the clock to double-check.

Ailsa stood back from the door frame and in bounded two very familiar furry beasts, one with a bright pink plaster on her leg.

"Hamish! Dougal!" Kali dropped to her knees, only to be covered in big slobbery kisses.

She'd been visiting the vet's on a daily basis, sending photos to Brodie to show to Callum to prove that Ethel's—now his—beloved dogs were being taken care of.

"Glad to see it's such a happy reunion." Ailsa smiled down at her, before squaring her gaze with Brodie's. "Now, you're sure you're all right to have these two massive bear cubs running round your house until your brother is well enough to look after them?"

"Definitely." Brodie nodded solidly whilst Ailsa's stern expression remained unchanged.

"I know Kali's willing to help, and we can rely on her, but the onus is on *you*, Master McClellan. No swanning off to Africa, or whatever exotic location takes your fancy, with these two relying on you."

Brodie looked down at the two dogs, their big eyes now locked on him. Hopeful. Gleaming. And between them, of course, was Kali. The most beautiful face in the world. Her green eyes were filled with the same glint of hopeful anticipation. One that cemented his decision.

"Yes, Aunt Ailsa." He nodded soberly. "You have my word."

"Well, then…" She gave a brisk *that's done* swipe of her hands. "That's good enough for me. Now, will you be bringing them to Ethel's funeral? I'm fairly certain Callum said she stipulated in her will that they be there."

"That's this Friday, isn't it?" Kali asked, her arms still around her new furry companions.

Ailsa nodded.

"It's a shame it's so soon. Callum would've been the best one to speak."

"Could we get him to do a video link on someone's phone or tablet?" Kali suggested.

"That's a good idea." Brodie nodded as the idea took shape. "Or maybe—as we can't do the pyre until Ethel has been cremated—we could wait until he's back. Even if he's on crutches or in a wheelchair we can wheel him down to the beach before we set the boat alight."

"I'm sorry?" Kali looked like she was choking on the image he'd painted.

"Didn't Callum tell you?"

"The last time I saw him he was so high on painkillers

he mostly talked about putting Ethel in a boat and setting it on fire, then shoving it out to sea. I thought he was just away with the faeries."

"Nope. Not in the slightest." Brodie shook his head, and his aunt nodded along with him. It was one of the island traditions he had actually always loved. A traditional Viking funeral. "It won't be completely traditional, because I think Health and Safety have something to do with it. But Ethel requested that her ashes be put out to sea Viking-style. I think she traced her lineage back to the Norse gods, or something mad, and she always was a bit of an old battle-ax…"

An idea shot through him like a jolt of electricity.

"What if I got some of the lads to help me finish my boat and we used that instead of one of those smaller model-types? It would take a couple of weeks, and that would hopefully buy Callum the time to get out of hospital."

"Oh, no—Brodie. Not that one." Ailsa shook her head disapprovingly.

"Why not?" He looked between the two astonished women as if it was perfectly obvious that he should send his handcrafted boat out in a burning pyre of flames.

"Don't worry, ladies. Leave it with me. Ethel will go out in style!"

"Mmm…this is my favorite part of the day." Kali stretched luxuriously, using Brodie as ballast for her small frame as she twisted and wiggled herself from early-morning sleepy to fresh-faced awake.

"And why's that, my sweet little raven-haired minx?" Brodie had a pretty good idea why, but he wanted to hear Kali say it anyhow.

"Calm before the storm."

"Which storm is that? The patients who can't get enough

of you? The boatbuilding brigade? The two larger-than-life dogs we've been looking after until my softie of a brother can walk again? Do you want me to keep going?" he asked when she started giggling.

"I don't see them as storms—they're just…life."

"You're *my* calm." Brodie tugged her in so he could give her a smooch on the forehead.

"Hardly!" Kali protested, accepting the kiss anyway, tiptoeing her fingers up along his stomach until they came to rest on his chest. "Does that make you the storm?"

"It's not as if I've brought much tranquility into your life."

They both laughed as Brodie began to tick off the number of things that had happened since his return to Dunregan, and Kali dismissed each of them as insignificant.

"If you'd actually *had* Ebola this would've been a very short-lived romance."

"That's true. And you'd have had to die as well, since we've been snogging ourselves silly."

"How very *Romeo and Juliet* of us!"

"Except my family doesn't hate your family because you keep them all secret and locked up in your little Kali hideaway," Brodie teased.

He felt Kali instantly stiffen beside him. Bull's-eye on the sore subject, and he hadn't even been trying!

He propped himself up on an elbow and drew a finger along her jawline, compelling her to meet his gaze. "Sweetheart… I don't know why you don't talk about your family, but if you ever need to talk about it—about them—we both know you've helped me a lot with mine…"

Kali put on an impish grin—one that didn't make it all the way to her eyes—gave him a quick peck on the lips and then skittered out from under his arms.

"We've got to get a move on. I want to get the dogs

walked before I go to the clinic." She wrapped herself up in his hugely oversized dressing gown, looking like a terrycloth princess in her ceremonial robes. "Today's the big day."

"Ethel's ceremony! And getting Callum back from hospital, of course. Do you think we should make up the downstairs bedroom for him or just let him bed down with the dogs?"

Kali smirked at him and pointed at the linen cupboard down the hallway.

"Well, we'd best crack on, love." He shooed her out of the bedroom. "Hie thee to the shower, lassie. I'll not have you entering the clinic smelling like anything less than a dewy rose."

Brodie fell back into the pile of pillows when he heard the shower go on, glad to have put a smile back on Kali's face. He'd let it slide this time. But now that he realized what an idiot he'd been to turn his back on his family he really hoped she would open up to him about hers. Good or bad, they were worth coming to terms with.

He'd thought he didn't need his family. What had never occurred to him was how much they'd needed *him*. They hadn't been trying to suffocate him. They'd just been trying to love him. And for the first time since his mum had passed he was beginning to believe he was *worthy* of their love.

Just a few days more and he would find out if he was worthy of Kali's.

He rolled over to the far side of the bed and tugged open the drawer of the bedside table, where he'd hidden the tiny green box he'd brought back from the mainland after his last trip to see Callum. He flicked open the box and smiled…one perfect solitaire. All that was left to do now was find the perfect moment.

* * *

"Are you sure you're comfortable?" Kali tucked an extra blanket over Callum's knees. Tartan, of course. Over the tartan of his kilt.

"I'm not geriatric. I'm simply...transitioning to bionic. It's a process," Callum grumbled good-naturedly, swatting her hands away. "If that brother of mine could learn to steer this thing better I might not have shouted so loud when we hit that bump."

"What's that about my driving?"

Brodie sidled up, also kilted-out to the nines, slipping a warming arm across Kali's shoulders. She loved the "everydayness" of the gesture. How protected she felt. Secure.

"Your driving is absolutely wonderful, big brother." Callum grinned.

"That's what I thought you were saying. How's the leg?"

"As I was saying to the beautiful Dr. O'Shea—"

"Hey, watch it," Brodie interrupted, his fingers protectively tucking Kali a bit more possessively under his arm. "I saw her first."

"I know... I know!" Callum held his hands up in the surrender pose. "Seriously, though. Thanks to you two and your stellar calls on my leg, I want you to know I am *feeling* bionic. Even if it will take six months to test run all the new hardware inside it. You'll get front-row seats to the inaugural run, if you can bear looking after me that long."

"Don't worry, Callum. We'll be here to watch you take the first tenuous steps all the way to your first hill run." He gave Kali's arm a little rub. "Won't we, love?"

Kali smiled and nodded, hiding as best she could the hint of anxiety this glimpse into their mutual future had unleashed. She had never planned for the future. Never been able to. The fact that she'd made it through medical school was little short of a miracle.

And her little-girl hopes of falling in love and marrying the man of her dreams one day… Her father had shown her just how much of a nightmare that sort of dream could become.

"Hey, you." Brodie nestled in to give her a peck on the cheek. "Everything all right?"

"Absolutely." She gave him a wide smile. One filled with every ounce of gratitude that she had for having him in her life at all. "I was just thinking—do we have your brother parked in the best place to give his eulogy?"

"Celebratory remembrance, Kali! Ethel would've hated the idea of a eulogy," Callum cut in. "And here was me, worried you'd put me at the end of the dock so Brodie could push me off. What do you think, Kali? You've got to know this wayward beast over the past couple of months…are his intentions honorable?"

Her eyes widened and zipped from Callum's to Brodie's. One set of cornflower-blue eyes was filled with laughter, whilst Brodie's… Was that panic she saw? Whatever it was, it sent her stomach churning.

"Relax, Kali. I'm just messing with you." Callum laughed heartily. "Wow! Take a look at the crowds. I don't think I've ever seen the beach this crowded. Do you think I'll be needing a microphone?"

"Don't worry, little brother. Your dulcet tones are plenty loud enough."

Brodie would've punched his brother's lights out if he hadn't already been laid up in a wheelchair. Trust him to near enough let the cat out of the bag before he'd even had a chance to propose. It wasn't as if Kali had professed her undying love for him or anything. Or said she wanted to stay on Dunregan forever. Something he could picture himself doing. Especially tonight.

He finally saw what his father had wanted him to see. A place where people came together to help. Yes, they knew your secrets, and whether or not your shortbread was better or worse than the woman's next door. But they were a united front in the face of adversity and—in tonight's case—the celebration of a life fully lived. People were absolutely flooding the broad arc of a beach.

Tall torches were secured in the sand every five meters or so, the flames adding a warm glow to the scene. Up above them the stars were out in force, and even though it was freezing cold he felt warmer in his heart than he had in years. Being here with the woman he loved, his brother and his extended family—virtually the entire population of Dunregan—all gathered together to send off Ethel Glenn in about the most dramatic fashion possible. It was heaven-sent.

Kali lit the first candle on Callum's say-so. The atmosphere was hushed, a mix of tears and laughter as everyone remembered Ethel in their own way after Callum gave a simple but loving speech in memory of the woman who had touched each of their lives—if not with her deep understanding of the island, then with her excellent command of shortbread.

Within minutes the sky was filled with scores of Chinese lanterns. Hamish and Dougal each raised their furry head to the skies and howled their farewells.

"Brodie?" Callum prompted, when a few moments had passed and another collective silence was upon them. "Will you do the honors?"

Brodie stepped forward, his eyes solidly on the boat he had built with the unfettered help of the community. Young and old had gathered to craft her, and for just an instant he felt remorse at the decision to set her alight. But there'd be time to build another one. And he couldn't think of a more appropriate send-off for a woman who had embodied the very essence of the place he was now proud to call home.

"This boat—*The Queen Ethel*—she's a project that's been—" He stopped, feeling the choke of emotion threatening to overwhelm him.

He looked to Kali and gathered the strength he needed from her beautiful green eyes and warm smile.

"This boat was built by many hands. The wood—grown on Dunregan, ordered by my father—has been lovingly crafted—"

"You mean put together with sticky tape?" Johnny shouted from the crowd.

A ripple of laughter lifted the mood, bringing a smile to Brodie's lips.

"Near enough, mate. That and plenty of glue. A thank-you is definitely required for Johnny's long-suffering wife, Helen, for keeping all of us chaps in bridies, scones and raspberry jam for the duration."

He patted his air-inflated stomach, to the delight of the crowd.

"But seriously—and I do mean this from the bottom of what most of you know to be my very wayward heart—this boat would not exist without all of you."

He reached out to Kali and gave her hand a squeeze, buying himself a moment to swallow another surge of emotion.

"We all know I couldn't think of enough reasons to leave this island as a teen—but, having seen the world and come back home… I can assure you all that Ethel exemplified all of the reasons to stay. Will you all charge your glasses, please, as we offer up a toast and a farewell to our dear friend, Ethel Glenn?"

Callum handed Brodie the flaming torch he'd been holding throughout his brother's speech. Brodie raised it aloft as the sound of bagpipes began. Another man untied the boat and with an almighty shove set her out to sea, with the torch Brodie flung in the very center of the craft.

Collectively everyone held their breath as a huge whoosh of flame took hold of the boat and it was transformed into an otherworldly Viking craft.

Huzzahs and shouts of delight filled the air, and for a few moments Kali stood spellbound by the sight of the boat floating out to sea. By the contrast of the billowing flames reaching up to the heavens and the foamy crash of waves against the hull of the boat.

Out of the corner of her eye she saw motion. An awful lot of motion. Her eyes shifted closer to the shore.

Was that…?

Were those…?

Had they really…?

Her fingers flew to her mouth in disbelief.

Scores of islanders were flinging off their clothes and jumping—some in old-fashioned swimsuits, others completely stark naked—into the sea! Including, she saw with complete amazement as a kilt landed in her arms, Brodie!

Kali laughed and laughed. She'd heard all sorts of people mention the Polar Bear Club, but until this very minute she'd had no idea what they were talking about. With all the white bums bobbing about in the sea, children and adults alike shrieking with delight at the frigid arctic temperatures, the scene had the undeniable feel of a party.

Ethel's boat was quite a distance out now, the fire illuminating the effervescence of the waves with a golden tinge. Completely magical.

Kali could imagine living here until the end of time. Yes, there would always be a hole in her heart where her mother and sister had lived. Maybe over time she could make it a warmer place. A sacred place where she kept them safe, preserved in a time before she'd known the cruel twists life could sometimes take.

"Here you are, love. Mind giving me a hand?" Ailsa materialized by her side with an enormous bag overflowing with huge fluffy towels.

"Wow! Did a spa go out of business or something? These look amazing!"

"We held a charity do a couple of years back, after folk kept misplacing their towels along the beach. This way the swimmers come out, they towel off, get a warm drink—see the table set up over there by the shore?—and everything goes down to the pub for washing the next day."

"The pub?"

"Aye, they've got one of those big industrial washing machines because of the rooms and the little cabins they let over the summer. That was their donation. Scrubs and suds."

Kali grinned at the wording. If it was possible for her to like Dunregan even more, it was happening.

She stopped for a second, shifting up her chin as if it would help her hear better. Just out of earshot she heard a sharp, frightened call. A woman.

"Jack!" shouted the voice. *"Jaaaack!"*

Kali knew that tone.

Fear.

Complete and utter fear.

CHAPTER TEN

FROM WHERE SHE STOOD, atop the pier, Kali quickly linked the voice with a woman, eyes frantically scanning the sea and the crowded beach, her voice growing more and more strained amidst the loud party atmosphere.

The atmosphere which had just seemed so festive turned abruptly discordant.

The sea water would be warmer than the air—which was just hovering at freezing—but Kali knew cold water like that could kill a child in seconds.

"Ailsa…" She touched her arm and whispered, "Can you go help that woman there? Search along the beach for her child. I'll look in the water."

Ailsa's eyes widened with understanding and she quickly ran down to the beach, pulling people along with her as she went, somehow mysteriously silencing the bagpipes along the way.

Kali forced herself to remain steady, her eyes systematically working along the first few meters of the shoreline.

"Take the dogs." Callum's voice cut through her concentration.

"Sorry?"

"Ethel's dogs," Callum repeated, handing her the leashes. "They're water rescue dogs."

Of course! That would explain why Ethel had been heading to the loch in the dead of winter to "play" with her dogs.

A siren sounded, bringing the whoops and chatter to a complete halt.

Kali's eyes flicked back to Callum.

"That's the lifeboat rescue siren."

"Who's in charge?"

"Johnny. He probably set the siren off. Go." Callum shooed her away. "I know you want to help."

The cove abruptly became a floodlit area, with shocked faces standing out in sharp relief against the night as they regrouped, turning from revelers into a focused search party. Boats appeared, their searchlights fanning this way and that along the broad reaches of the cove.

The beach spanned a good two or three kilometers. What had seemed a cozy and protected arc shifted into a shadowy, borderless expanse.

"Kali?"

She whirled around at the sound of Brodie's voice. A rush of emotion overwhelmed her heartbeat for an instant when he appeared—safe—towel in one hand, dry suits in the other.

"I'm going out in one of the boats." He rapidly scrubbed the sea out of his hair. "Here's a dry suit. I'd like to take one of the dogs out on the boat with me. The suit will be a bit big, but do you mind suiting up and going with Dougal along the shoreline?"

She nodded, slotting all the information into place. "Absolutely."

Seconds morphed into minutes.

The calling of the little boy's name—Jack was a mischievous four-year-old who'd slipped the protective grip of his mother's hand—rang out again and again.

Kali was hyperaware of how precious each passing moment was. If Jack had run into the water hypothermia was a threat. Children had a higher ratio of surface area to mass than adults, causing them to cool much faster. But there was a plus side. Cold water would instantly force his body to conserve oxygen—it would slow down the heart instead of stopping it and would immediately shift blood to vital parts of the body. The brain. The heart. Particularly in children.

Kali felt a surge of energy charge her as the community turned from being mourners to a mobilized search and rescue team.

"Here. Let me make sure you've got these sealed up properly."

Brodie shifted and tugged the bright orange neoprene suit she'd pulled on, sealing her into a cocoon of body heat. Something that poor little child, if he were in the sea, wouldn't have.

Brodie locked his bright eyes to hers. "Jack's wearing a sky blue puffer jacket. He has hair the color of your suit—all right?" He dropped a distracted kiss on her forehead. "See you soon. Be safe."

"You, too," she whispered to his retreating figure, extra glad for the company of the warm shaggy dog beside her.

"Right, Dougal." She gave his head a good rub. "Let's go to work."

Kali saw him at a distance, and Dougal made the same link a lightning-fast second later. She blew on her whistle as hard as she could and ran so fast her lungs burned with the exertion.

Jack was farther down the beach than she would've believed possible. Whether he'd been caught in a crosscurrent or had wandered off and then been sucked under by a wave they'd probably never know. All that mattered now was getting the tiny figure out of the water.

Dougal reached Jack, instantly grabbing a hold of the

hood of his coat. Kali swam as hard as she could. The tide was stronger than she'd anticipated, but she got there. Her toes were unable to touch the sea floor. Jack's pallor was a deathly blue white. It was impossible to check his pulse, but she knew he was hovering somewhere between life and death.

She took the life ring attached to Dougal's safety line and got it round Jack as best she could, ensuring his head was above water, blowing her whistle again and again in between choking on mouthfuls of briny seawater.

Just when her toes had managed to gain purchase on the sea floor she saw Brodie arriving, poised at the helm of a speedboat, its searchlight all but blinding her. With a Herculean effort, and a well-placed nose-nudge from Dougal, she managed to hoist the little boy out of the water and into Brodie's waiting arms.

Someone else's arms reached out to pull her in. She waved off the offer, needing to slosh through the water back to the shore. Just a few minutes alone, to walk off the shakes of adrenaline now shuddering through her.

The speedboat whizzed off to the pier, where a team of people were already on standby to receive the tiny patient.

Something in her gut told her the boy would live.

Something in her heart clicked into a place she'd long dreamed of.

She knew where she belonged.

She was irrevocably part of the island now. Sea, sand, sky—the entire package felt imbedded in her in a way she'd never believed possible. And she would do everything in her power to hold it tight.

Brodie checked the boy's pulse again, shaking his head when he felt nothing. "Can someone grab the pelican cases from my four-by-four?" he shouted, to no one in particular.

They appeared by his side moments later, along with a huge pile of dry towels, blankets and clothing. He could see feet jostling and hear the murmur of the crowd shifting and changing, but his focus remained steadfastly on his hands, clasped together, delivering the steady cadence of compressions required to bring Jack's heart back to life.

"The air ambulance is going to be at least an hour. They're just finishing another call. What do you need me to do?"

Kali dropped to her knees on the other side of Jack, the AED in her hands.

"He's not responding. Severe hypothermia. Body temperature twelve degrees below normal." He kept his voice low. The anxious keening of the boy's mother still came in waves of sound above them.

"Twenty-five Celsius? You've got a thermometer that registers temperatures that low?"

Brodie nodded. "Have to up here. Unfortunately this sort of thing isn't unusual."

It was how his mother had died. He more than most knew the importance of warming this child in the safest way possible.

"We need to get some fluids inside him. I don't want to use the defibrillator until we're inside."

"If the ambulance is going to be a while, should we get him to the clinic?"

"Yes, but he's going to need constant CPR." Brodie was panting. He'd already been administering CPR for over ten minutes, and the intensity of his focus was beginning to take a toll. "Can you help me intubate?"

"Absolutely—then let's get him on the biggest backboard we have and I'll ride it."

"I've got a surfboard right here," someone called.

"Great." Brodie nodded. "Get the board." His eyes flicked up to meet Kali's. The steady green gaze assured him that they had this—as a team.

Swiftly, efficiently, they intubated Jack and then transferred him to the board. Kali straddled the small body and took over CPR while Jack compressed the airbag providing oxygen to the little boy's lungs.

"Steady, lads," Brodie cautioned as six men lifted the board on his count. "Precious cargo."

His eyes were on Kali, whose expression was one of utter focus on the child. She was in a class of her own. He would count himself lucky to have had her in his life at all, let alone for the rest of his life. He made a silent promise to propose sooner than later.

"Fluids?" Kali threw him a questioning look.

"Nothing warm enough to put into a drip. Everything will have gone cold in the car."

"Warmer than his body?"

He nodded. It was a good point. They'd have to warm him gradually. Anything else would be too much of a shock to the small body that had already been traumatized.

"All right, lads? Slide them in as steady as you can."

The trip to the clinic passed in a blur of CPR, pulse checks, IV insertion, airway checks and temperature monitoring.

"It's not looking good, is it?" Jack's mother asked tearfully. She was leaning over the seat into the back of the car, where Kali was still carrying out CPR.

"I read about a case of a two-year-old…" Kali huffed between compressions. "Fell into an icy river—must've been in it for half an hour at least. They performed CPR for over an hour and a half. Between that, fluids and other warming methods they got him back."

"But was he all right? You know…" Jack's mother asked, not wanting to put words to everyone's concern. Irreparable brain damage.

Kali nodded. She thought so, but wasn't 100 percent. She wanted to offer hope, but knew there was a degree of caution required in all hypotheticals.

"We're here," Brodie said unnecessarily as the vehicle slowed to a careful halt.

He'd thrown the keys to one of the lads. CPR was tiring. If Kali needed to be relieved he wanted to be by her side to help.

"Kali, if you grab the IV bag I'll take over."

Again, the concentrated blur of saving someone's life had shifted everything else out of his consciousness. If they could just get…

"We've got a pulse!" Kali finally said, a few minutes after having hooked Jack up to the monitoring system. "It's weak, but we've got one."

A collective sigh of relief released the taut tension in the exam room, where Jack's family had anxiously been looking on.

"Will you be needing the ventilator?" Ailsa appeared in the doorway.

"Thanks, Ailsa. Yes. It'll make it easier for the little guy to breathe, and maybe we can get some aerosol medication in him."

Brodie curled his fingers into a loose fist and gave Jack a quick sternal rub. He felt a twitch of a response. Heard a cough, then a gag.

"Quick! Let's get him in the recovery position."

He and Kali quickly shifted Jack onto his side, a stream of seawater gushing out of the little boy's mouth as they did so, and a wail of relief from his mother filled the room.

They'd done it. They'd brought him back to life.

Kali gave Brodie a happy nod, her lips shifting in and out of her mouth as she tried to keep the emotion at bay. He felt it, too. Deep in his heart. All he wanted to do was pull Kali into his arms, but they weren't out of the woods yet.

"Right, guys. We're still fighting the hypothermia. Anyone have word on that air ambulance?"

Kali gave him a soft smile as a new flurry of activity began to whirl around them. They would do this. Together.

"Look who's on the front page!" Brodie flourished the *Dunregan Chronicle* in front of Kali.

She felt the blood drain from her face in an instant. She could hear Brodie happily chattering away, but his voice was only coming to her in the odd hit of vowels and consonants she couldn't put together. She blinked hard, forcing herself to concentrate on what he was saying.

"Craig thinks it's so good the nationals might pick it up. It's already all over the internet—so some of the international papers might run it."

Her breath came out in short, sharp huffs.

"What's wrong?" Brodie sat down beside her, laying the paper down on the round table in front of her. "I think it's an amazing shot. You should be proud."

"I am—it's not that—I just…"

She stared at the photograph in disbelief. A picture of the moment she and Dougal had hoisted the near-lifeless body of little Jack into the lifeboat was printed in full color— her face was utterly unmistakable. She was struck by the confidence, the passion she saw in herself. The complete antithesis of the fear she felt welling within her now.

"Hey, babe." Brodie slid a hand across her back in a slow circular motion. "What's wrong with being the heroine of Dunregan for a day? It's well deserved."

"Everything!" The word came out as a wail as years of

fear came to the fore. Hot tears poured down her cheeks, and the back and forth *no, no, no* shaking of her head flicked them onto the paper, instantly blurring the ink.

"Kali, you're scaring me. What's going on?"

She turned to him, knowing that this might be one of the last moments when Brodie's belief in her was absolute. The moment she'd been dreading had finally arrived. The moment when she had to explain to Brodie that the Kali he knew…was a fiction.

"Come here."

He held open his arms but she couldn't move. The weight in her heart was rendering her motionless except for her head, which persisted with its shaking. *No, no, no.*

"Right." Brodie pushed back from the table and headed toward the kitchen counter. "I'm making you a fresh cup of tea—and then, Kali O'Shea, you are going to tell me exactly what has got you so—"

"I'm not Kali O'Shea."

The words were blurted out before she could stop them and they seemed to assault Brodie physically. His blue eyes clouded, steady blinks shuttering them from her view every few seconds, and his body became absolutely rooted to the spot.

"Who are you, then?"

Ice water ran through her veins. All she could hear in Brodie's voice was the betrayal he had to be feeling. She pressed her fingers together to stop their shaking and forced herself to tell him the story.

"My birth name is Aisha Kalita."

Brodie folded his arms across his chest, as if protecting himself from what she was about to say. She didn't blame him. This was a blindsider. A trust breaker. So it was now or never if she was going to win his trust again.

"My father is originally from India. He is…very *traditional*…"

In a monotone, Kali heard herself telling Brodie about her naively happy childhood, the support her parents had given her in her quest to become a doctor.

"So what happened?"

"He arranged a marriage for me. My father."

"What?" Brodie all but shouted the word.

The dogs came scrambling in from the lounge, where they had been lolling in the morning sun, big furry heads shifting from Brodie to Kali, waiting to see who needed them most.

Kali sat rigidly as Brodie digested the news, her hand distractedly giving each of the dog's heads a rub.

"Sorry, Kali. Please. Go on."

The clinical tone of his voice sent another chill of fear through her. She swallowed and forced herself to tell the story that had been told out loud only once, five years earlier at the Forced Marriage Protection Unit.

"My father had been planning it for months, but none of us knew about it. Not my mother or sister—"

"You have a sister?"

She shook her head yes, and continued. If she didn't get it all out now…

"It was someone from my father's hometown. A man highly esteemed for his business acumen—but not for his morals. My father organized for me to marry this man and secured a visa for him in England."

She choked back a sob.

Brodie came toward her, stopping himself halfway, as if undecided about whether or not to comfort her. Her heart physically hurt. For him, for herself, for the lies she'd been forced to tell and for the life she'd thought she could have.

She put up a hand. "Please. Let me finish."

He pulled out a chair on the opposite side of the table and nodded for her to continue. It was impossible to tell what was happening behind those pure blue eyes of his. She prayed to everything she could think of that he would be empathic. Compassionate. Forgiving.

"I was completely clueless. My father brought him over to dinner one day and then later made my sister and mother leave the room with him so that it was just the two of us. He wasted no time in telling me how the marriage would work. Who would be in charge. That I would have to shelve my medical degree and do something more…something that would give me more time to look after him. When I protested and said I would only go ahead with the marriage if I were able to complete my medical studies he—"

A ragged sob escaped her very core.

"He hit me. The rest of it happened horribly fast. My father was in the room in an instant, apologizing—can you believe it?—*apologizing* to this man for my behavior. When he left I begged my father to be released from the union. He said the only way I could escape the marriage—humiliating him as I had—was death."

Brodie's hand shot across the table. He needed to touch her. Comfort her. Aisha… Kali—whatever her name was—she was the same woman she'd been ten minutes ago. If there was any way he could have taken back his initial reaction he would have.

Kali slid her own hand across the table, then retracted it.

"What happened next?" Part of him didn't want to know, but it was imperative he heard the full story.

"In the middle of the night my mother came to me with a small amount of money and an address for a distant relative in Ireland. She said I should seek her out if I absolutely must—but if it were possible to just go. Never speak of them or think of them again."

In a rush she blurted out the rest. The tremors of fear juddering through her body as she'd stuffed a handful of clothes into a small backpack. The fearful silence in the house as they'd tiptoed to the back door, terrified of waking her father. The tears she'd been unable to shed as she'd hugged her sister and mother goodbye that one last time.

"And then I just began to run."

Brodie itched to hold her. Ease away the pain. But she had to finish. He could see the determination in her eyes.

"I stayed at a cheap hostel the first night. And then—because I didn't want anyone to know where I was, especially if my father was going to go on the hunt for me—I spent my days in London's biggest hospitals. Just reminding myself why I had chosen to become a doctor. I spent my nights in the waiting room of an ER until a nurse finally figured out something was wrong and helped me contact the Forced Marriage Protection Unit. They helped me with a new identity. But with the invention of Kali O'Shea I had to let my mother and sister go."

Brodie felt his throat go dry, his body physically aching for her. He'd left his family of his own accord. A selfish decision by a teenager blinded with grief and anger after a tragic accident. But Kali…? She'd been betrayed by her own father and forced to live apart from the people who could have comforted her most.

"And you've never been back?"

"Never." Her eyes were wide with disbelief, though she was the one who'd lived with the pain, the reality of a life lived in fear. "I moved to Dublin so I could feel close to my mother's relatives. It was a weak link—but it helped, believe it or not."

"That's why you picked the name O'Shea?"

"No." Kali finally looked across at him, her beautiful green eyes shining with vitality. "It was the name of the nurse who helped me that night. Helped me to find the FMPU and make a fresh start. Become who I'd always thought I could be."

She was so much braver than he had ever imagined. Stronger.

Brodie couldn't restrain himself anymore. He was pulling her into his arms before he could stop himself, running his fingers through her hair, holding her tight to his chest so she could weep long pent-up tears of grief, fear and loss.

"My beautiful, brave Kali…Aisha," he corrected, then laughed awkwardly. "What do you want me to call you?"

"Kali," she answered without hesitation. "It's the name I chose because I thought it would give me strength. And it has. And," she added, looking at him as if she hardly believed he was still there, "I *have* become who I thought I could be. Thanks to you, to Ailsa—everyone here on Dunregan."

"But mostly me, right?" he teased gently.

"Mostly you." Her fingers pressed into his.

"You've never looked for them? Your family?" Brodie asked, leading her out to the sofa in the lounge, where they nestled into a big pile of humans, dogs and cushions.

"I was far too frightened the first couple of years. There were enough scary stories of retribution killings to keep me as far away from my father as I could. Though I worry about my mum and sister. Every day I worry that my father turned his anger on them."

She shook her head, suddenly looking overwhelmed with exhaustion.

"Are you—are you okay with this? With me?"

"Are you kidding?" Brodie shook his head in disbelief. "Obviously it's all a bit of a shock, but I love you, Kali. I don't think having a different name changes who you are and what you mean to me."

Kali blinked, her teeth biting endearingly into her lower lip as she did so. "You *love* me?"

"Of course I do. What did you think? I go parading around Dunregan with every beautiful woman who shows up here?"

"I—uh—"

"Don't answer that." Brodie laughed, scooching along the sofa so he could hold her in his arms. "I love you, Kali O'Shea, and I will do everything in my power to ensure you're never put in harm's way. You have my word."

He dropped a kiss onto the top of her head, enjoying the weight of her body as she slowly let herself relax into his embrace.

They were words he'd never said to a woman before.

I love you.

And they were words he meant from the bottom of his heart. The only thing left to do was rustle up the most romantic setting he could and propose.

"Kali?"

It was Brodie, gently knocking on the door to her office.

"You left your mobile in the staff room and it rang. I hope you don't mind, but I answered it for you."

"Who is it?"

A jag of fear ran through her. It had been twenty-four hours since the photo had gone public and she'd heard nothing so far.

"Is it a man or a woman?" she whispered, more to herself than Brodie. She would never forget the malice in her father's voice. Not as long as she lived.

"A woman," Brodie said with a smile, his blond hair

shining in the late-morning sun coming through the back door. "I think you'll want to take it. It's a Mrs. Kalita."

Tears leaped to her eyes as one set of fingers popped to her lips and the other to her chest, as if trying to hold her heart inside.

Her entire body shook with anticipation as she reached forward to accept the phone from Brodie. She had to hold it with both her hands as she took it from him, the tremor in her fingers was so strong.

Over five years. It had been over five painfully long years.

Brodie took a step back, dismay furrowing his brow. He mouthed a question. *Want me to stay?*

She shook her head, no, then quickly changed it to yes. Brodie was part of her life now. No more secrets.

She took a big breath and lifted her fingers off the phone's mouthpiece. "Hello?" Her voice was barely audible.

"Aisha?" The familiar name came down the line, the voice causing her tears to spill over. "Aisha, is this connection all right? Can you hear me?"

Kali nodded silently, only just remembering to speak the word she hadn't allowed herself to say out loud for over half a decade…

"Mummy-ji?"

CHAPTER ELEVEN

KALI SET DOWN the phone in disbelief.

She was free!

She felt herself go into autopilot—stepping away from her desk, only just remembering to give Brodie's hand a little squeeze, blindly taking the handful of steps to the small kitchen, filling the kettle, listening to it come to a boil as she had on her very first day here.

She watched, almost as if she were someone else, as her hands reached for mugs, opened the tea canister, fingers deftly, knowingly, going about making cups of tea for everyone. An extra splash of milk for Ailsa, a sugar-even-though-she-knew-she-shouldn't for Caitlyn, strong builder's tea for herself and, of course, leaving the tea bag in the longest for Brodie, and adding just a few drops of milk…one…two…three…four.

Four weeks.

Four weeks of living on the sanctuary of Dunregan. Embracing the life here every bit as much as it had embraced her. And now she could just…go…?

"Hey, you."

Brodie slipped into the tearoom behind her. Kali felt the warmth of his hands shifting along her hips and lacing loosely around her waist. The inevitable tremor of desire skittered down her spine as he nestled into the crook of her neck to give her a smattering of soft kisses along her neck.

She murmured instinctively, tipped her head toward his, loving his scent, his touch, the fact that she knew how to make his tea and which side of the bed he slept on—and the instant she turned around to clink mugs with him felt a cascade of tears begin to pour down her face.

"Oh, hey, now…" Brodie's face was wreathed in concern. "What did she say?"

He took Kali's mug of tea and set it on the counter.

"It's my parents…my family," she choked out as the wash of tears grew thicker.

"So that was her?" His voice tightened, concern woven through each word. "Your mother?"

She managed a nod.

"And…?" He tugged a hand through his hair, losing his knit cap in the process, his eyes completely locked on her. "Kali, are they—have they been hurt in any way?"

She shook her head, no, and forced herself to calm down. Happiness came in so many forms, and the flood of tears streaming freely down her cheeks were tears of pure joy.

At last.

"They're safe." She hiccuped and laughed. "Sorry, it's just…"

"Pretty overwhelming?" Brodie finished for her.

She nodded, and blew out a slow breath before beginning to explain what she'd just learned from her mother. "They're living in Ireland, near the village where her relatives are. My sister's great. She's—" Her eyes filled with tears again. "She's training to be a doctor."

"Like her big sister?" Brodie clapped his hands together.

"Yup." She felt a burst of pride taking shape in her heart, then a shot of sorrow. "My dad…" She shook her head at the enormity of putting all of these sentences together. "My dad…he—he is divorced from my mum and lives in India now. He's become a *monk*."

Her eyes widened in wonder.

"He spent one year solid looking for me, and my mother said the rage and anger all but killed him. He returned home one night and nearly hit my sister when she stood up to him—told him to leave me be. It was then that he broke down, told my mother he just couldn't live with the shame of how he'd behaved. So…now he's a monk in a religious sanctuary somewhere in India."

"So…" Brodie began tentatively. "It's all good?"

"I've just been so scared they wouldn't have been able to get on with their lives, you know? I so wanted to write to them, tell them to please carry on with everything as if I was still with them, because they were with *me*." She clasped her hands to her heart. "Every step of the way I brought them with me."

"Of course you did." Brodie laid a hand atop of hers, as if to cement what she'd said.

Brodie rubbed his hands along her arms and pulled her in for a hug—but not before she saw a hit of anxiety flash across his face.

She pressed her fingertips into his back, loving the strength of feeling and connection passing between them. Of all the people in the world she could share her news with—the most joyous news she could ever imagine—this was the one she wanted. The man she could imagine a future with.

She felt his chin shift along the top of her head, his hand brushing her hair back from her tearstained face, his fingertips tracing along her jawline before tugging her back into his chest for a tight, long-held embrace. She stood, so grateful just to breathe and listen as their hearts began to beat in synchronicity.

As their breathing shifted and changed, each of them taking on the enormity of the news, she sensed a shift in Brodie's mood. He was happy for her—she didn't doubt that. But there was… She tipped her head up to take a look at his face. There was anxiety creasing his forehead, shifting the crinkles alongside his eyes into winces of doubt and worry.

"So." Brodie abruptly pulled back from their embrace and put on a bright smile. "I guess this means you'll be leaving us."

"Well, I—" Kali scraped her nails along her scalp, as if it would help clear the jumble of thoughts. "I have to go to them."

"Of course." Brodie nodded as if he were agreeing with a patient about a need to get a second opinion on an unusual condition. "You must."

The coolness in his voice physically chilled her. She knew him well enough to know this was Brodie in protection mode, and as much as it pained her she understood completely. If she had been in his shoes she would have done the same.

"Brodie?" Callum flicked off the television. "Stop pacing, would you? She'll be back."

"It's been over a week now."

"You've texted. And called."

"I know. But everything's going great for her! She's having the time of her life."

"Aren't you happy for her?"

"Of course I am!" Brodie shouted, then checked himself. "Of course I am. It's just…"

What if I never see her again?

"I don't think Kali is the type to just leave a man hanging," Callum replied calmly, and his voice was an echo of their father's.

Since when had his kid brother become the mature one?

Brodie wheeled around. "What makes *you* so sure?"

Callum's lips twitched as he unsuccessfully held back a snigger.

"Oh, go ahead. Get a good laugh in, why don't you? Enjoy it while you can because—because…" He threw up his hands.

Helpless. He felt absolutely and utterly helpless. Maybe he should go chop wood or something. If he knew where the ax was that was exactly what he would do.

"Brodie…" Callum looked his brother straight in the eye. "You may be many things—but the last thing you are is someone who gives up."

Brodie harrumphed.

Callum laughed openly this time, giving his brother a playful jab with one of his crutches.

"Why don't you go down to the docks?"

"What on earth for?"

"There's a boat coming in." Callum checked his watch. "I have something on there I need you to get."

"So I'm your slave boy now?"

"Hardly!" Callum laughed again. "But I think you'll like this delivery." He aimed the remote at the television, feigning a renewed interest in the show neither of them had been watching. "It'll make you a lot easier to be around, that's for sure."

"What is it? Earplugs so you don't have to listen to me wallowing anymore?"

Callum pushed his lower lip out and jigged his chin back and forth. "Something along those lines. Go." He pointed toward the door. "And take the dogs while you're at it."

* * *

"What is it, Dougal?"

Brodie could barely keep a hold of the huge dog's leash as passenger after passenger walked off the boat. Deliveries always came last.

Dougal jumped up with a joyful woof and broke free of Brodie's hold. Hamish dragged Brodie along with him, across the gangplank and onto the boat, where they near enough clobbered someone to the ground. Wagging tails, whines of pleasure—this was no stranger.

"Dogs! What are you—?" Brodie shook his head in disbelief when he caught a glimpse of green eyes amidst the furry bodies. "Kali?"

Flat out on the ferry deck, being covered in dog licks, was Kali, her face wreathed in smiles. Brodie elbowed past the dogs and helped to pull her up, pulling her tightly into his arms.

"What are you doing here?"

She pulled back from the embrace and smiled shyly up at him. "I thought I would come home…"

"Are you asking or telling?" Brodie wasn't going to take any chances here.

"A bit of both, I guess." Kali wove her fingers through his and scooped up one of the dog's leashes, handing him the other. "Fancy a walk on the beach?"

A few minutes later Brodie, Kali and the dogs piled out of the four-by-four onto the beach. The ride had been largely silent. Just two people grinning at each other as if it were Christmas morning. From the deep hits of magnetic connection each of his smiles brought, Kali knew she'd made the right decision.

"So…seeing your family again…" Brodie began tentatively, unlooping the dogs' leashes from around their necks, watching them race out to the shoreline for a swim.

"It was amazing," Kali answered honestly. "My sister is incredible and my mother—strongest woman I know."

A rush of tears filled her eyes. It *had* been amazing. To be with her family. To find the inner peace she'd long sought.

"And how was it to be back in Ireland?"

It was impossible not to hear the worry in Brodie's voice. Worry she never wanted him to feel again. "It was great, because my family is there, but home…" Her lips parted into a broad, hopeful smile. "*This* is home." She scanned the beach, then laid a hand on Brodie's chest. "*You* are home."

She felt the whoosh of release from Brodie's chest.

"I'm pretty happy to hear that."

"Just 'pretty happy'?" She grinned up at him.

"Relieved—over the moon—ecstatic." He threw a few more words out into the ether for added measure until they were both laughing.

He cupped her face in his hands, tilting it up to his for a long-awaited kiss. *Passionate* didn't even begin to cover it. As their lips touched, sparks of desire burst throughout Kali's body. Her arms smoothed along his chest, up and around his neck, and her feet arched up onto tiptoe. She could feel Brodie's arms tighten around her waist, pulling her in close to him, close enough for her to feel his heart racing as fast as her own.

Minutes, hours could have passed for all she was aware. Nothing mattered—nothing existed outside of Brodie.

"I love you, Brodie McClellan." Her lips shifted and whispered across his as she spoke.

"I love you, too, my little one."

He loosened his hold on her, then held her out at arm's

length, a serious expression taking over the wash of desire they had both succumbed to.

"I have something to ask you. Something I probably should've asked before you left."

"Oh?" Kali's eyes widened. It was difficult to tell if it was going to be good or bad.

She held her breath as Brodie reached into his jacket and tugged out a small box. He held it between them, flicking the lid up with his thumb. The soft spring sunshine set the diamond alight, glinting and sparkling like the sea.

"Kali O'Shea—would you do me the honor of marrying me?"

He dropped to one knee, holding the diamond up between them.

She stared, openmouthed.

"Kali?"

"Yes!" She nodded and laughed, dropping to her knees so she could smother him with kisses. "Yes! A thousand times yes!" She kissed him again and again then abruptly pulled back. "We're staying *here*, right?"

"As long as you're happy with that."

"Are you mad? There is no place I would rather be. As long as you don't mind a nutty Indian family with bonkers Irish accents coming to visit."

"As long as they're happy having mad Scottish in-laws."

"They'll love you." Kali tackled him to the sand, stealing kiss after happy kiss. "But not quite as much as *I* love you."

"You think?" Brodie wiggled his eyebrows up and down.

"I *know*." Kali smirked back, before wrapping her arms around her future husband and giving him a soft kiss. "There isn't a soul out there who could love you more than me."

"Good." Brodie held her tight to him, the sound of the

waves swooshing back and forth only magnifying the joy he felt. He dabbed a finger on her nose. "So, which name do you want on the surgery door? O'Shea? Kalita?"

"McClellan," Kali answered solidly. "The Doctors McClellan."

* * * * *

Join Britain's BIGGEST Romance Book Club

50% OFF your first parcel

- **EXCLUSIVE offers every month**
- **FREE delivery direct to your door**
- **NEVER MISS a title**

Call Customer Services
0844 844 1358 *

or visit
millsandboon.co.uk/bookclub

CB4

MILLS & BOON®

Why shop at millsandboon.co.uk?

Each year, thousands of romance readers find their perfect read at millsandboon.co.uk. That's because we're passionate about bringing you the very best romantic fiction. Here are some of the advantages of shopping at www.millsandboon.co.uk:

* **Get new books first**—you'll be able to buy your favourite books one month before they hit the shops

* **Get exclusive discounts**—you'll also be able to buy our specially created monthly collections, with up to 50% off the RRP

* **Find your favourite authors**—latest news, interviews and new releases for all your favourite authors and series on our website, plus ideas for what to try next

* **Join in**—once you've bought your favourite books, don't forget to register with us to rate, review and join in the discussions

Visit **www.millsandboon.co.uk**
for all this and more today!